AGAINST THE LAW

MICHAEL C. EBERHARDT

AGAINST THE LAW

A DUTTON BOOK

ACKNOWLEDGMENTS

My sincerest thanks to my co-author and friend, John Tullius. Additionally, our sincerest appreciation to J. Kalani English, Bruce Raney, and Les Kuloloio for sharing their knowledge of Hawai'i and the ways of the Hawai'ian people.

To our agent, and good friend, Peter Miller, and all of his associates at PMA, especially Anthony Schneider and Jennifer Robinson, whose confidence, guidance, and help have made our endeavors so enjoyable and rewarding.

To Ed Stackler, whose editorial talents have made this book the best it can be. And to Michaela Hamilton and Elaine Koster for their belief in us and their efforts to assure our books are published with care and enthusiasm.

DUTTON
Published by the Penguin Group Penguin Books USA Inc.,
375 Hudson Street, New York, New York 10014, U. S. A.
Penguin Books Ltd, 27 Wrights Lane, London W8 5TZ, England
Penguin Books Australia Ltd, Ringwood, Victoria, Australia
Penguin Books Canada Ltd, 10 Alcorn Avenue, Toronto, Ontario, Canada M4V 3B2
Penguin Books (N. Z.) Ltd, 182–190 Wairau Road, Auckland 10, New Zealand

Penguin Books Ltd, Registered Offices:
Harmondsworth, Middlesex, England

First published by Dutton, an imprint of Dutton Signet,
a division of Penguin Books USA Inc.
Distributed in Canada by McClelland & Stewart Inc.

ISBN 0-525-93994-6

Printed in the United States of America

PUBLISHER'S NOTE
This is a work of fiction. Names, characters, places, and incidents either are the products of the author's imagination or are used fictitiously, and any resemblance to actual persons, living or dead, events, or locales is entirely coincidental.

CHAPTER
ONE

He pushed away the cold, sunset-colored drink a waiter had put before him and watched as the governor made his way to the podium that had been set up on the beach at Waikīkī. He watched as Jim Slaton, waving to his well-wishers, glad-handing this one, patting that one's back, stepped up onto the portable platform that listed in the uneven sand. While he watched, his hand fingered the sheathed pig-boning knife in his pocket.

He checked his watch. He knew the governor's routine by heart. He had rehearsed it in his mind over and over. After the rally Slaton would go up to his room for a short "nap." Of course, one of his whores would be there. Knowing Slaton, he would slap her around awhile before he got down to business. All the while he would be on the roof above waiting for the moment when he could slice open the governor's throat so his jugular shot spurts of blood to the rhythm of his dying heart.

Dan Carrier slouched back in the lawn chair and watched disinterestedly as the governor turned and waved to the crowd. He brushed his black hair off his face and leaned back with both hands behind his head. He was thirty-four now, a Honolulu prosecutor for nearly ten years, and he'd never been much for politicians or the people who hung around them. This little shindig was the last place Dan wanted to be on a sunny day off.

Of course, if he'd known that an assassin was poised ready to strike, he wouldn't have been so bored with the whole scene. But there was no reason to be concerned. As Jim Slaton took the microphone in his hand, Dan felt confident that HPD had done its job. If any troublemakers showed up today, they were ready. A security boat had cleared the water of surfers. The bright orange rental boards that the tourists bobbled around on now stood upright in their racks in front of the Outrigger Hotel next door. A hundred yards out to sea a dozen navy Seals stood in twos kneedeep along the coral reef. As he began to speak, the miked voice of the governor bounced off the high-rise hotels half-circling the beach, so the Seals could hear his words almost as easily as the thirty thousand people crowding the shore.

The governor banged his fist against the koa dais. He was a big-chested man with beefy forearms and salt-and-pepper hair he kept oiled tight to his scalp. The insubstantial podium shook as he pounded it.

"Who said I'm not for Hawai'ian rights?" he shouted, gesturing toward the two thousand VIPs seated at white picket tables on the lawn in front of the Royal Hawai'ian Hotel, the coral-colored empress that had been for over a half a century the backdrop for any politician who wanted the notions of power and beauty mixed in his favor.

"But just because I'm sympathetic to sovereignty doesn't mean I want to turn the clock back a hundred years. Hawai'i today is not the Hawai'i of a hundred years ago. We all wish it were," Slaton pushed on. His deep tan emphasized his pale blue eyes and the sharp chisel of his chin. "But a hundred years ago there was no Waikīkī. There were none of these magnificent hotels. There were no shopping centers in Pearl City. . . ."

The sun, now a couple of hands above the horizon, burned fiery holes in the backlit clouds. Nearly every shade of pink God created was somewhere in the sky.

"Who said I'm not for the rights of Hawai'ians?" Slaton asked again. That was going to be his refrain that day, Dan could tell. Slaton was one of those repeat-everything-ten-times kind of speakers. But then something hollow always sounded better as an echo.

"Well, let's see," Dan said sarcastically under his breath. "Who said he's not for Hawai'ian rights? How about every local on this island?"

He was sitting among Slaton's so-called VIPs at the Royal Hawai'ian. He'd never liked Slaton, but his boss, Honolulu Prosecuting Attorney Brian Reed, sitting next to Dan, was Slaton's biggest supporter. And why shouldn't he be? Everyone knew that when Slaton was through, Reed was going to be the party's next candidate to run the state.

"I have a vision for Hawai'i," the governor went on, "that has Hawai'ians and Japanese and Filipinos and Caucasians all living together side-by-side in harmony."

"Yeah, side-by-side in twenty-story condos built by the big developers who put you in office," Dan said. He was leaning back in his chair, his long legs stretched into the grassy aisle between tables, his fingers weaved in his black hair. He was as broad-shouldered and dark-tanned as the governor but Dan had gotten that way by spending his early mornings paddling an outrigger canoe. Slaton had a ski tan from Aspen and his shoulders were broadened from too many fifteen-hundred-dollar-a-platers.

This time his boss heard Dan's crack. But Reed still didn't catch Dan's sarcasm.

"He's in rare form, isn't he?" the bulky PA said, winking at Dan.

Reed wore the bright smile of the supplicant listening to his guru chant on. He had on a blue blazer over his dark blue aloha shirt. That was the only concession Reed would ever make to aloha. While everyone else had a Hawai'ian flag pin in their shirt collar, Reed had a NEBRASKA pennant hung on the wall behind the desk in his office and he flew back to see the Huskers play OU every year.

"Oh, yeah, he's rare all right," Dan said, shaking his head.

Though the day had all the trappings of a social occasion, Dan knew it wasn't. Reed was running on the Slaton ticket to hold the office of prosecuting attorney, to which the governor had made sure he was appointed when the previous PA's heart gave out. This fund-raiser was a perfect time to get the money he needed for that campaign.

"Takes guts to take a stand like this before an election," Reed said.

Dan raised his eyebrows. No matter what kind of face Reed put on it, he knew his boss realized exactly what this speech was all about. The Hawai'ian sovereignty movement had been attacking the governor's pro-development stance for years, and their growing popularity in the last several months had put a serious dent in his reelection plans.

"The Hawai'i of today," the governor went on, "has to be for all Hawai'ians. For the Filipina maid," he shouted, pointing down the beach at the hotels that hogged every foot of frontage, squeezing the Royal Hawai'ian into a squat stance. "For the Chinese banker, and the Samoan carpenter and the Japanese stockbroker. Hawai'i is for the Caucasian dentist and the Vietnamese store owner and the . . ."

Dan elbowed Reed. "Yeah, I wondered how he was going to be for sovereignty and still have the big landowners in his pocket. Yeah, that's it. Hawai'i is for everyone. Especially the handful of families that own the whole damn place."

Reed threw him a half-grin. His Irish face had turned patchy in the tropical sun. Here it was red, there white and crusty, here a yellow tinge of raised skin that precursed cancer.

"He's clever, isn't he?" Reed nodded with an approving shake of the head. Slaton was Reed's ticket to the top. He was riding his star and he saw Hawai'ian rights as the governor did, as a thorny storm of trouble to be watched like a hurricane building out beyond the periphery that could turn at any moment and destroy everything.

Dan drained his mai tai and motioned to the waiter for a refill. If he had to listen to this swill, it was better with a little buzz to ease the pain.

While Slaton droned on, a white stretch limousine pulled through the porte cochere into the arched driveway of the Royal. The lone passenger had her head partway out the open window, inspecting the insignia of the flying dragon above the porticos. Opposite the lobby, in the coconut grove planted by Queen Liliuokalani herself, a little Filipino groundsman was scraping leaves with a small green rake into a dustpan made from a ten-gallon can cut diagonally and fixed to a cut-down broomstick. The girl had never been to the Royal before. She'd walked by it on the beach once or twice but she'd never been taken to dinner there or slept in one of the old, elegant rooms.

The porter in a coral shirt and pants trotted out to get her door. She slid off the seat and stood up, and his eyes went immediately to the long stretch of black-stockinged legs beneath her black leather miniskirt. He wasn't used to someone this young, this beautiful, wearing a skirt that covered not much more than her rounded *okole*, checking into the Royal. He never saw this much leg unless it was on the beach out back.

The way she was packaged made his eyes bulge. She had on an expensive cream silk blouse and her breasts were full and, as far as he could see, suspended by nothing more than the friction of her nipples on silk. The heels were four inches, black and stiletto, and her hair was to her waist, full and black as only a woman with Polynesian blood can have. But he could tell by the roundness of the eyes and the heart-shaped chin that she was a *hapa. Hapa-haole.* Half Caucasian, half local.

The concierge checked her once and didn't bother with the lei, the aloha kiss, or the check-in. He knew who the girl was. One of the governor's "companions." The governor's wife would be coming too but, thank God, not until after the *lū'au* started and certainly not in the same room. Of course, that was his job, to make sure he knew who was who and which room was which. That would be something, he thought, the governor's wife and the governor's latest high-class call girl in the same room.

He had to admit it, though, the governor knew how to pick them. Young, with legs a mile long, and always *hapa-haole.* All that dark local skin surrounding those Caucasian blue eyes of a *haole* must have been what rang his libidinous bell.

The bell captain gave a tender toot on a bosun's whistle and a bellboy came running. The concierge handed the young boy a key. There was no inquiring about her bags. She would have nothing more than the straw bag that hung from her elbow.

The bellboy led her to the back of the hotel along the coral carpet trimmed in royal green, past the beveled glass and onyx marble, past shops with five-hundred-dollar handbags. "Undertaker boutiques" was what she called them, filled with black, featureless frocks, garishly orchided muumuus, and old-lady one-piece bathing suits.

The bellboy turned the corner, and standing in front of the bathers' elevator were two HPD. The lift, which was off limits that day even to hotel guests, was being used by the police to take the governor's VIPs up to the first three floors. He handed one of the cops the room key, bowed slightly, and turned back to the lobby. In the wall mirror across the hall, she could see the bellboy sneaking a look at her for the first time, raising his eyebrows heavenward in admiration. Their eyes met in the mirror and she gave him a smile.

"Purse," one of the cops ordered, and she handed it to him. His silver name tag said KANESHIRO.

He started rummaging through her purse and pulled out a plastic snap box in which she carried her contraceptive foam applicator. He showed it to a *haole* cop with a clipboard, who sneered when he saw it.

"I think we're going to have to search her," he said to Kaneshiro, who had begun to run a hand-held metal detector up her sides.

Her eyes leveled on the cop, who gave her back a dirty grin.

"Back here," he said, and motioned her to a door. When he opened it, she saw it was a janitor's closet with rags and brooms and the smell of disinfectant.

As soon as she stepped in, he closed the door and reached for her breasts. He began to move his palms around them, looking for nothing but his jollies.

"I wouldn't go too far with this, Thompson," she said, reading his name tag. "If I'm all wet when the governor gets there, I'm going to blame it on you."

Thompson's hands stopped for a moment then glided down between her thighs.

"Hey, you never know. Maybe you've got a concealed weapon up there."

"You through?" she asked.

"Yeah, you're clean."

When she came out, Kaneshiro eyed her to see how she'd taken it. *"Haoles* don't know shit about foreplay, do they?" she said to him.

Kaneshiro grunted a smart-ass snicker and adjusted his belt suggestively. Then he thumbed her to go inside the elevator. He reached in behind her and pulled the hold button. The doors closed and they went up to the third floor together.

When the door opened, there were suddenly so many cops in front of her that she hesitated for a second. Kaneshiro took her elbow and pushed and she got off. He handed the clipboard to a plainclothes city cop, who took the clipboard, scratched something on it, and handed it back to Kaneshiro.

A tall, young *haole* in a double-breasted silver suit with an expensive tailor's cut hustled toward her from down the hall. His blond hair was sprayed in place and the top pate bounced as he ran.

"I'm Greg Mathers. The governor's personal assistant. Come right this way," he said and took her gently by the arm and led her back down the hall. "How was the drive over here?"

"Fine," she said with an amused smile.

It was just like her roommate Cindy had told her it would be. The HPD would give her a hard time as usual. But once she got past them and into the hands of the governor's men, it would be like walking into the Ritz.

"They treat you like a little queen," Cindy had laughed. She was giving her this date as a favor.

"He's going to like you, Steph," she had told her. "And if the governor likes you, you got it made."

Cindy was hoping that Slaton would like Stephanie a lot because she didn't want to have to see him anymore, didn't want the beatings anymore. "Hitters," the girls called his type. Slaton was a hitter. It apparently excited him to give pain, to humiliate a beautiful young girl with blue eyes set in a Polynesian face. Like a lot of hitters, this one got more "enthusiastic" the longer they dated. First, it was a spanking for fun that made her cheeks glow a little. Then he tied her, then handcuffs, then one night he slapped her across the face as their sex began. It grew quickly more violent after that. So now she frequently bled during their sex—from the lips or her rear or maybe where he bit her neck or nipple.

Cindy knew he'd start off easy with Stephanie. She'd be all right for a while, probably. Nothing physical for a week or two. It would be several months before he crossed the line past cruelty into brutality. By then she'd have made a name for herself and she could quit him too. When the word got around to the businessmen that she was Slaton's mistress, especially the Japanese businessmen to whom prestige is more erotic than sex, she'd be set for life. In no time, with her looks, some billionaire would be keeping her in some big place at Black Point and she'd have to sleep with him maybe once or twice a year. The rest of the time she could work on her tan in Maui.

The governor's aide let her into the room, holding the door open for her.

"I'm sure you'll be comfortable here," he said. There was no hint of snideness in the remark. "The governor will be up in about an hour." He looked at his watch as he said it.

"Thank you," she said and smiled.

He nodded and shut the door. He had treated her like royalty, just like Cindy said. Except he had kept the key. If she wanted to come and go, she'd have to see him first. Just like a royal pet.

A short blond woman with a pert cut and a gray suit wound her way through the lobby of the Royal and down onto the beachfront lawn. When she spotted the table where Dan and Reed were sitting, she walked over and sat between them. Dan leaned over and kissed her, but her lips were stiff and unresponsive. He knew she was still upset with him from the quarrel they'd had the night before. It was the same argument they'd been having for months. Dan wanted a family. Cathy wanted to wait. Dan would ask how long and she never had an answer.

"I see you made it," he said.

"Yeah, I had to finish my opening for the Gorney case," she answered as if she were talking to just another lawyer at the office instead of the man she'd been engaged to for the past two years.

"How's it going?" she said more to Reed than Dan.

"You're missing a master at work," Reed said. "He's killing them."

Cathy's smile was as wide as Reed's. The entire office was filled with eager young attorneys hoping to ride Reed's elevator to the top. Slaton was that elevator.

Dan watched the two of them drooling over Slaton and shook his head in disgust.

Slaton continued to run through the litany of the dozens of races, nationalities, tribes, and lobby groups that populated the state. "The black army lieutenant, the German hotel manager . . ."

"Jesus! Here comes the part about the great melting pot," Dan groaned.

Cathy elbowed Dan in the ribs. "Come on, Dan," she said, looking around nervously. "Somebody'll hear you."

Dan didn't mind that she sided with Reed. They both knew who was running this town. "Signing her checks" was the way she liked to put it. He didn't mind that their politics didn't agree. It was their future lives together he wasn't sure about anymore.

"For better or worse our jobs depend on him," she said. The remark had a bite to it he was sure was left over from the night before.

"Maybe your job and Reed's," he said, nodding over to his boss.

She turned quickly to him with a smirk. Her legs were crossed and the long stretch of her thigh rose up the slit of her silk skirt. He only had to see that flash of leg to reconcile their differences. That and the fact that she threw herself into lovemaking with the same kind of obsessive furor that she applied to her career. In fact, it still excited Dan to watch her work in court. The short staccato questions with which she ripped away at a defendant, that shoulders-back, high-headed way she attacked, the fury with which she'd scream in her closing.

Despite all their differences it had been easy for them to work out a compromise in bed. Except last night and a lot of nights lately they'd never made it as far as the bedroom. So their lovemaking could no longer smooth out the hard edges of their differences.

Sergeant Joe Kalama of HPD walked up to the table just as Cathy was about to say something nasty. He and Dan had been close friends most of their lives. They had grown up paddling canoes together as kids.

Kalama leaned down so only Dan could hear when he whispered.

"It's Paul," was all he said, and Dan knew what he meant. His brother was drunk again. From the way Kalama had nodded with his chin over his shoulder, Paul was probably in the Royal's Mai Tai Bar right behind them.

Dan followed Kalama up the beach to the hotel. They went into the open-air bar and Dan heard a familiar voice behind a crowd of people.

"He's a phony," Dan heard, recognizing his brother's voice. The rest of the bar was silent. The usual hum of small talk and the clink of glass was stilled. Everyone there was a Slaton supporter, of

course. They'd paid a grand apiece to listen to his rambling plati-
tudes and schmooze at the *lū'au* afterwards with a bunch of other
powermongers in town.

"He just approved the Grand Kahana out in Haleiwa," his brother's voice accused. "It's sitting on the biggest Hawai'ian burial
ground this side of Honokahua."

Dan pushed his way through the crowd. It wasn't hard to get
through the stunned drinkers.

"Oh, come on, man," someone had yelled. "Jim Slaton got us out
of one of the biggest economic slumps since the Great Depression.
Waikīkī was a ghost town. Now look at it."

"Hear! Hear!" someone else actually murmured, as if this
were the House of Lords and not Waikīkī, where the memory of
Duke Kahanamoku still drew more nods of respect from the locals
than JFK.

Dan spotted Paul leaning over someone's shoulder at the end of
the bar.

"Ah, you're all in the bastard's pocket," Paul yelled and stood up
banging his drink on the teak bar. The liquor slopped over onto
his shirt but he didn't notice.

Dan reached his brother just as he was about to go after the
"Hear, hear" phony.

"Hey, bra," Dan said. "What's the deal?"

"There's no deal, Danny," he said to his younger brother.
"That's the problem. These hypocrites already made their deals
with Slaton. And the Hawai'ians ain't part of it."

"Oh, come on," a woman's voice piped in.

"Come on yourself, bitch," Paul yelled.

"Get him out of here!" a couple of suddenly brave gray-hairs
spoke up.

Even though Dan agreed with Paul, he knew his brother was
making this scene because of more than his disgust for Slaton. It
was more than just the booze taking control. These "incidents"
were becoming more and more frequent lately, and more and
more violent. They always seemed to end in a brawl with Paul in
jail or in a hospital with a beat-up face. It seemed like Dan was bail-
ing him out or picking him up at some emergency room every
other week.

Of course Dan knew why it was happening. Six months had passed since Paul had lost his wife and eventually his son in a metal-fusing crash out in the Wahiawa cane fields. His eight-year-old son Chris was in a coma from his injuries and had lived several months before Paul had finally agreed with the doctors to take him off life supports. Whenever Paul drank too much all he wanted to talk about was how he'd killed his own son.

"You didn't kill him," Dan kept assuring him.

"Sure I did," Paul would answer, his long, tanned arms slung over a chairback. "It doesn't matter if I'm to blame morally or anything. I had to load a gun and stick it to my son's head and pull the trigger. Just because it was for the better, it didn't make it any easier."

Instead of mouthing more empty pop psychology, Dan fell silent. The only thing he could do was try to keep his brother out of trouble.

Nowadays, Paul didn't seem to care about anything, least of all his health. Before the accident Paul owned and operated one of the most successful charter boat businesses in the Pacific with five boats booked months in advance. But since his family's death he had lost all but one of his vessels to the bank. He was left with the *Loa*, a boat he chartered now only when he ran low on booze money.

"Come on, let's get you home," Dan said, reaching under his brother's arm. Kalama had appeared on the other side of Paul and together they eased him out of the place.

They held him up as he stumbled down the plush carpeting of the Royal's walkways and came through the back garden straight into the shopping arcade behind the hotel. At this time of day when the tourists were looking for a place to have dinner, Kalakaua Avenue was busy with taxis. Dan waved once and a cabbie pulled to the curb. They poured Paul into the buffed black Cadillac.

"See you at Outrigger Beach tomorrow morning, all right?" Dan said to his brother. Kalama had gotten the old paddling team together again and they were practicing for the state senior championships later in the month over on Maui.

"Yeah, yeah," Paul mumbled and fell on his side on the backseat.

Dan gave the cabbie an address and a twenty, and he drove off.

"Thanks, Joe," Dan said to the big Hawai'ian.

Kalama shrugged. He had the kind of face on which expressions were easy to read. When Kalama smiled, it made Dan feel for the moment that things were going to be all right.

"Gotta get back. Da bruddas are restless," Kalama said and raised his eyebrows heavenward. The 'Ohana Society was scheduled to stage a sovereignty demonstration at any moment. It was going to be a long day for HPD.

When Dan got back to his table, Reed and Cathy were sitting side by side still wrapped up in Slaton's speech. Reed's hand rested on the back of Cathy's chair, her blond hair brushing his arm. Suddenly, there was a shout from down the beach and Dan looked over to see a group of Hawai'ians marching toward the governor. At the front was Peter Maikai.

Maikai, a tall, gray-haired Hawai'ian with the gut of a sumo, walked a pace or two in front of his people intoning a war chant. A dozen bare-chested Hawai'ians behind him blew conch shells, letting out a powerful, resonating *ooooo-uuuuuh!* that shook the highrise glass and drowned the amplified baying of the governor.

"Oh, crap," Reed said under his breath to Dan, "there's that *moke* troublemaker again."

Dan felt a sting when Reed cut into Maikai. The old man had taken in Dan and his brother when their parents had died. Even though Dan hadn't spoken to Maikai since the day the Hawai'ian had thrown Dan off his ranch over eighteen years ago, Dan still felt a deep loyalty to his adopted father.

Maikai was dressed in a loin cloth with palm bands around his wrists and ankles.

"Jesus," Reed said, "it looks like one of those damn Polynesian revues at the Hilton."

Cathy laughed. "Careful," she said. "That *moke*, as you call him, has a hundred thousand votes in his pocket."

"I know," Reed said. "Why do you think he pisses me off so much? He's just the kind of promise-them-anything jerk-off these natives eat up."

"Bringing Hawai'i together," Slaton was screaming, his mouth pressed close to the microphone, "certainly does not mean destroying . . ."

The conches blew again. The reverberating howl that echoed against the massive hotels was louder than any gunshot blast.

"Oh, my God," someone said behind Dan. Dan looked over his shoulder and saw Michael Maikai standing just a few feet from his table. Michael seemed a little breathless and had a frantic, frustrated look on his face. Peter Maikai's son was a tall, dark-faced Hawai'ian with a Harvard education and the best corporate client list of any lawyer in the state. Dan and Michael had lived together as kids on the Maikai ranch, but Dan was having trouble recognizing his foster brother since he'd dressed himself up in that Ivy League mentality. This was a Hawai'ian boy who never wore rubber slippers anymore.

"Oh, Jesus!" Michael said and shook his head, nodding toward his father, who had begun an old war chant as he waved a warrior's club in the air over his head. "Why does he have to embarrass me like this?"

In contrast to his imposing physique, Michael now had the worried look that his father put on a lot of people's faces these days. Michael's dismay puzzled Dan. He had assumed Michael would back his father. One thing Dan had learned when he lived on the Maikai ranch was that Peter Maikai was a man you didn't want to cross.

"Aren't you for giving back the Hawai'ians their land?" Dan said with a raise of his brows. He was like a lot of people who lived in the Islands. He knew the Hawai'ians were right to want back land promised to them by Congress for decades. But he didn't know exactly what they wanted or how they were going to go about getting it. That was why Maikai had become such a nuisance to Slaton. He had been the first one to unite the Hawai'ians, and it was scaring the hell out of those in power, most of whom were sitting on the Royal Hawai'ian lawn surrounding Dan.

"Jesus, Dan!" Michael groaned. "This isn't like the old days when we were growing up on the ranch, raising taro, singing songs with Uncle Charlie. The Japanese own this damn place now. If they have another recession, Hawai'i's in trouble. These people don't seem to get that. If they aren't careful, the Japanese will give it back in the same shape we left Nagasaki. Think what it would be like here if suddenly all these hotels were empty."

Dan tried to imagine the hundreds of self-contained ghost towns that would line Hawai'ian beaches if for whatever reason the tourists just didn't come anymore.

"Ah, relax," Reed said and finger-dusted some oyster cracker crumbs off his shirt. "It's a few *kanaka*s blowing off some conch shells."

But Dan knew it was much more than that. The sovereignty movement had spread to every island and a large segment of the locals were behind it. They were mad, they were vocal, and the sentiment to return the lands that the white man had stolen in a palace coup d'état just one hundred years before had turned into a mob on Waikīkī Beach. They were marching on the governor with a resolve that didn't look like a few restraining ropes and an outnumbered HPD were going to be able to contain unless they pulled out their batons. That was the one nightmare Slaton wanted to avoid at all costs. He knew with an old politician's instincts that this was the kind of incident, caught on video, that could hound him right out of office.

"Don't worry, Slaton can handle it," Cathy said and patted Michael gently on the arm. She'd picked up a little political posturing in the two years she'd been a deputy PA, and Dan knew from whom.

"'No," Michael said. "I better go down there. There's a bunch of paddlers with them. You know how it can get when they've had a half a case of brew."

Dan nodded his head. He'd paddled outrigger canoes himself since he was a kid and he knew exactly what Michael meant. Paddlers were the closest thing to Hawai'ian warriors left in the islands. They'd kept their ties with *'āina*, the land, and *moana*, the sea. They paddled not scientifically, but by their hearts, and they knew all the old myths and customs better than any other group in Hawai'i. Every day around sunset they would paddle out and make their paddles dance to the rhythms of their hearts and the sea. After their workout, they'd paddle back in, then drink beer all night, which is what they'd been doing all that afternoon at Duke's, the bar at the Outrigger. When they saw Maikai, they streamed out onto the beach to join him. Suddenly a politically inspired protest had its own royal guard surrounding their chief, their *ali'i*, bare-chested believers not in any political philosophy but in Hawai'ian brotherhood.

Security had already begun to tighten around Maikai. HPD and the hotel staff in windbreakers were moving through the crowd to reinforce the picket fence of cops in front of the podium. They all knew who Maikai was, of course. He'd been in the local papers for years and had even made the national news every now and then. Only last month he had had his picture in *Newsweek*—Maikai, Uncle Charlie Yates, and a few of the more radical leaders of the sovereignty movement. The picture was shot on Kaho'olawe, the island that the navy had given back to the Hawai'ian people. It was covered with ancient Hawai'ian burial sites considered holy places by the natives, and the navy had been defiling the sacred grounds for decades with sixteen-inch shells.

The governor looked down at the commotion in front of him. He'd been expecting some kind of demonstration. But he had to be careful. If he had the Hawai'ians thrown off the beach, he'd be reinforcing the charge they'd been hurling at him for years—that the *haoles* didn't give a damn about what the Hawai'ians wanted.

The governor smiled down at Maikai, pretending to enjoy these Hawai'ians in their colorful native garb.

"What we need is jobs and the only way to get jobs is to build a better, stronger economy."

The Hawai'ians knew what that meant. More hotels, more tourists, more money in the pockets of people who didn't give a damn what really happened to Hawai'i, as long as they got rich while it happened.

Peter Maikai pushed forward toward the locked arms of a line of deputies. The Hawai'ians weren't here to talk about the issues. They'd been talking for a hundred years.

"These lands are sacred to the Hawai'ian people," Maikai shouted. "And no *haole* is going to come in here and steal them away from us again." His voice fell heavily on the last word, conjuring up the missionary families who'd first swindled away their land. Those early families still owned a large proportion of Hawai'i: half of O'ahu, half of Kaua'i, most of the Big Island and Maui, and every inch of Lāna'i. And they ran their possessions like a corporate entity. Profit and loss, policy and procedure were the only things Maikai had ever heard from them. They had more power than Maikai, and the idea of doing the right thing at the sacrifice of profit was a laughable notion. To many Hawai'ians the only question that remained was, Who was going to fire the first shot?

"If it was up to you," Slaton said, waving a disdainful hand toward Maikai's group, "all locals would be back to living in grass shacks."

"That's better than these concrete *mea*," Maikai said, sweeping his hand at the hotels lining the beach. "You sold the Hawai'ian people out. Sold the land to the Japanese, to Canadians, to anyone who would line your greedy pockets with money."

Maikai pushed closer to Slaton, waving the war club before him. Except for the anger in the Hawai'ian's eyes, the club could have been nothing more than one of those long pepper shakers and Maikai merely an obeisant waiter about to season the governor's salad to taste. When he reached the yellow rope that separated the crowd from the dais, he stepped over it and kept coming at the governor. He stopped a few feet short of the podium and began to chant something, but Slaton managed to act as if he weren't there.

"Yes. Hawai'i truly is for all Hawai'ians. But we can't go back to Captain Cook," Slaton said, swinging his hand around to include the whole crowd up and down the beach. "Hawai'i is God's gift to the whole world now."

At that, Maikai threw down the club in front of him so it stuck, handle down, into the sand. "We don't need no damn mainland *haoles* to tell us what we should do with our land. The *haoles* were the ones who stole it from us and now they want to pretend that it never happened, that they deserve the land as much as we do. You stole the land from the Hawai'ian people and the Hawai'ian people want it back!"

Then Maikai pulled a short sword out of a palm-leaf scabbard and pointed it at the governor. "We want you off our backs. We want the lands of our ancestors returned to us."

It was the sword that caught Slaton's attention. As usual, he tried to talk his way out of a tight spot. "What do you call Kaho'olawe?"

"Kaho'olawe is nothing. Worthless to us now except to put the souls of our ancestors to rest. That's why the *haole* gave us the land back. He didn't want it anymore."

By this time, Maikai was surrounded by a dozen men in business suits with the familiar bulge in the side of their coats and the burned noses from standing in the hot sun too long. They began to shoulder the Hawai'ian back behind the barrier.

"Give us our land, *haole,* that you stole!" Maikai continued to shout as he was edged back. "That's all we want. We don't want a bunch of *da kine* double talk."

Maikai was pushing against the line of security, waving his sword. Two uniformed HPD made the mistake of grabbing Maikai by the arms. Angered, Maikai's followers surged forward and broke the line of security and pushed the uniformed men nearly against the platform where the governor stood.

The cops were shouting orders and pushing the protesters away from the podium. Suddenly a Hawai'ian hand pushed the face of a cop, and three more cops came to his aid. Eight or ten protesters fell on the police and they all went down, and the line of security protecting the governor was broken. Slaton was on his own.

Maikai broke loose and moved toward the governor, waving his sword. The governor edged back as Maikai came at him.

"I can't let you do it!" the Hawai'ian was shouting. "I can't let you do it! You're killing the Hawai'ian people!"

Joe Kalama broke through the crowd and tackled Maikai from the side before he could get to Slaton. They went down at the foot of the podium. Four or five other cops shoved through the scuffling mobs and picked up Maikai by the arms and began hustling him up the beach toward the Outrigger. Kalama was leading the way. He had ordered an HPD van to pull up to the hotel's service entrance near the Dumpsters. His plan was to put Maikai in the van and get him out of there as quickly as he could.

When they got near the top of the beach, a huge Hawai'ian came from behind the sea wall next to the Outrigger and blocked Kalama and the other policemen who had their hands on Maikai.

"Who the hell is that big *kanaka* Kalama's talking to?" Reed asked. He was standing on his folding chair, craning to see what was going to happen next.

"Uncle Charlie Yates," Dan answered.

"The holy man?" Cathy asked.

"Kahuna."

"Whatever," Reed said. "I thought he never came out of the jungle. What's the deal?"

"He's a relative of Maikai," Dan said.

"Hey, so big deal. All these *mokes* are related, aren't they?" Reed sneered and blew some air out of his lips in disgust.

Kalama stepped up to where Uncle Charlie was standing, his legs spread wide, his arms folded across his chest.

"Uncle Charlie," Kalama said to the old man and pointed at Maikai, "he breakin' da law, *Kahuna*. It's against da law."

"Against whose law?" Uncle Charlie said. "The law of the *ali'i*, the law of *'Āina*, the law of the Hawai'ian, the law of your mother Maili Kalikolehua or your father Joseph Kahikina?"

Joe felt surrounded not by the crowd that had pressed near to them as soon as they saw the *kahuna*, but by his Hawai'ian heritage. His mother was Hawai'ian, his father, his grandparents. And a man like Uncle Charlie Yates was believed to hear those ancestors, to speak to them, whenever the spirits moved.

There wasn't a man in the islands who didn't respect the power of Uncle Charlie. Men like Slaton dismissed him as a crackpot, but they knew he was as dangerous as Maikai, maybe more so. The Hawai'ian people were a superstitious tribe, that is, if believing the land and the sea were gods or that the spirit of a revered ancestor lived in a favorite shark is superstition. And nobody embodied those superstitions more than Uncle Charlie Yates.

"Uncle Charlie," Kalama said, "we takin' him away for his own safety."

"Good, Joe Kahikina Kalama," he said, speaking the policeman's full Hawai'ian name. "I take him for you, then."

Kalama had orders to get rid of Maikai, to take him to Ala Moana Park and let him go. Slaton wanted to make sure there were no martyrs on the ten o'clock news that night. If Uncle Charlie was going to get rid of him for Kalama that was even better. The last thing Kalama wanted was to be the cop who arrested Maikai or Charlie. He was Hawai'ian. His neighbors were Hawai'ian. He played rugby on Sunday afternoon with the brothers at Kapi'olani Park. He'd be one of those *da kine paoke'e* — a traitor.

Kalama stepped back and the *kahuna* took Maikai by the arm as if he were a wounded man coming back from the battleground.

* * *

The governor, still a little unnerved, made a few final comments about his respect for the rights of all Hawai'ians as they led Peter Maikai off the beach. Then he ended his speech and descended the podium into the crowd.

"I don't know what that boy is worried about," he told someone. "Take that project on the Hāna Highway. It's going to be a show-piece for the whole Pacific Rim. First-class all the way. We're going to put in a tram. Biggest in the world. Right from the beach to the top of Haleakalā. Hell, you'll be able to see the sunrise and be down on the beach in twenty minutes. It's perfect. No more two-hour drive to the top. Hell, if you don't get sick from the winding road, the damn altitude'll make you puke. This is perfect. We'll straighten out Hāna Highway so they can make the whole trip in an hour. And we won't get rid of one waterfall. In fact, our plans call for the addition of a couple after we divert Makapipi Stream."

Slaton moved slowly toward the lobby of the Royal, working the crowd, shaking hands. When he finally made it to the back where Reed was standing, they greeted each other with a macho vise-grip handshake and a pounding of each other's backs.

"Would you like that meeting now?" Reed asked. "We've got a room ready."

"Nah, not now, Brian. I've got a little personal business to attend to," he said and winked.

As the governor was led away by an aide to go up to his room, Reed smiled and leaned over to Dan. "He's got a meeting, all right. He's going to make a conference call with some high-priced pussy."

Cathy stepped between them. "I'll see you two at the *lū'au* later," she said. "I want to get in an hour or two of work before it starts."

Dan watched her as she strutted toward the hotel lobby. The tight skirt was cut just a little high for a deputy prosecuting attor-ney, but when the crowd parted for her he saw how lovely those legs were, and how easily they could distract a man. She looked back when she got to the raised concrete porch of the old hotel, and both Reed and Dan nodded at her.

"Yeah," Reed said, eyeing Cathy as she weaved her way through the crowd. "I've got to take off for a while myself. Hold down the fort until I get back, would you, Dan?"

Dan nodded and suddenly he was alone, wishing he were just about anywhere but with this crowd of big-dealers waiting around for their leader to get his rocks off and join them for some *kālua* pig.

Stephanie could see the governor working his way through the crowd from her vantage point behind the lānai curtain. The low sun was shining through the curtains, silhouetting her tall, full figure, the broad shoulders from surfing, the heavy Polynesian thighs, and the pinched waist of a *haole*. She didn't care much about his political agenda. They had their own agenda set right after he was through pumping hands, through whispering in ears. He would come through the door and, as Cindy kept telling her, she would know just by his first little gesture, by the sly smile or the anger in his face, what little game they would play that afternoon. Whatever it was to be, he wanted her dressed in black: a black necklace, a black French-cut bra, black silk stockings tied with a garter, black panties, and a white, long-sleeved silk blouse that led down to her lapis bracelet. That was it, though. There was to be no skirt. That was laid conspiratorially across the chair in the corner. If he beckoned her with a nod, she would pick up his drink—scotch, no ice, no water—and hand it to him as she knelt in front of him. He would sip the drink while she unzipped him, delicately pulled him out, and began the slow, ritualized worship he demanded.

CHAPTER
TWO

It was a short walk for Slaton from the beach to his suite. He walked down the arched walkway that led to the service entry. All along the way HPD had men positioned for his safety. As he approached a sergeant in an aloha shirt, the plainclothes cop pulled back the door to the kitchen and nodded. "Governor."

Slaton didn't answer. He gave a smirk to acknowledge the cop and went through the door and started to weave his way through the maze of stainless-steel tables. Around him were cops and cooks—a black-and-white peppering of uniforms. It was the most direct, least dangerous way to get to his room. All the help had been screened thoroughly. Most were long-time employees with families and homes but no politics. Nowadays, of course, that didn't meant that much. The Hawai'ian sovereignty movement had stirred up a nest of real trouble for the governor. The Hawai'ians wanted the land and the money they'd been promised by Congress and never got. That was a hundred years ago. And now he was stuck with it. Every damn potato slicer in this kitchen probably had some *moke* blood, some folks that came over on the *Kon-Tiki* or whatever they called it. The *Hokulea*. Yeah, that was it. Sailed from Tahiti in a grass boat. That wasn't his damn fault, though. This was 1995. Half the damn island was owned by Japanese. What the hell did they want? Did they want him to tear down the hotels and plant taro? Yeah, that would work. The big boys, the ones who put him in office, would go for that.

He tipped his head to the French chef who'd catered a few of the state bashes for him and came out of the swinging door and into the long corridor that led to the service elevator. He was glad to be out of the kitchen. He hated the kitchens. He knew it was better than the lobby, but all he could think about whenever he saw all those big pots hanging from above and the white stove hats and the slaw being hacked up by those machete-sized knives was RFK. Bobby lying on the floor of that hotel kitchen in L.A.

There were two uniformed HPDs at the elevator and several behind him, but he still didn't feel secure. He never did nowadays. There were just too damn many kooks like that nutcase on the beach.

"Good afternoon, sir," a tall cop said. Slaton could see below his open collar the tattoo circling his neck, the blue band of entwined leaves that proclaimed his *ali'i*, or royal, ancestry. Another descendant of King Kamehameha the Great, the Hawai'ian chief who unified all the islands one slaughterhouse of a day in Iao Valley, where they still chanted about how the Iao Stream ran red with blood and turned Kahului Bay a dark crimson.

The big Hawai'ian cop got on the elevator with the governor and they rode to the third floor, and when the door opened two more cops were stationed in front of the guest bank of elevators.

"Good afternoon, Governor," they said in unison.

"Afternoon," he mumbled back and walked down the long corridor to the last room, stuck the key in the floor-to-ceiling double door of the Queen Liliuokalani Suite, and walked in.

She was standing silhouetted by the late afternoon light radiating through the lānai curtains. The silver hue of the sunset filled the room. It lit her white silk blouse so it glowed like the silver tea setting on the dining table. Her black stockings shimmered as if sequined and the long flow of her dark hair shadowed her lovely face so he could see only the strong cheekbones. The whole scene lifted him. He felt the burden of his office slowly draining away. He always felt that way when he saw Cindy. When she'd come to him and place her full, warm lips against his chest and he'd crush his hands in that gush of hair, that rainbow of green eyes and black hair and full red lips. At times that was all he wanted: forget the governorship, forget the power, forget the wife. He'd just like to spend all day playing with his dark, young beauty.

"Come over here," he said.

Cindy had prepared her for how it would be. She knew what he wanted now. How they would play the afternoon out. She told her it might get a little rough. Nothing she couldn't handle. He'd lost it a few times with Cindy, but she had always been able to lead him into something else or make him come quickly. He'd lose his head of steam and a minute or two later, he'd be lying half asleep in her arms.

Stephanie walked slowly across the room, unbuttoning her blouse as she came toward him. When she came out of the harsh backlight of the lānai, he realized for the first time it wasn't Cindy.

"Hey, who are you? Where the hell is Cindy?"

"Cindy doesn't feel well. She sent me," Stephanie said with her most intoxicating smile.

"Oh, she did, huh? Who the hell does she think she's screwing with?"

She took another tentative step toward him in the shadowed room, and as she suddenly stepped into the shaft of light from a side window, he could see how beautiful she was. And how young.

"Jesus," he said, a little breathless. "You're a knockout, aren't you?"

"Cindy thought you'd like me."

"Yeah," he said, a hard smile edging his face. "Come over here."

She put her arms at her side and let the blouse drop down to the floor. Her four-inch heels clicked loudly against the marble. She could see his eyes narrowing with a sexual anger, looking her up and down, taking in the black garter and black silk hose and the black bush of hair. She stood in front of him with her arms to her side and a pleading, helpless look she'd rehearsed with Cindy.

He put his hands gently on her shoulders, then reached the right one between her breasts and slowly clenched the fabric between the cups and ripped off the bra so that it yanked her off balance and into him. He grabbed her by her hair and yanked her head back so she looked up at him.

"Are you going to do what I want tonight?" he shouted.

She felt a sharp, full, electrifying jolt of fear that made her stomach tighten so violently she thought she would vomit. It was his eyes. The brutality in them terrified her. She stepped back from him and tried to cover her breasts by turning to the side.

"How about a drink first?" She smiled and placed her long, red-nailed fingertips to his cheeks.

He smiled, then slapped her so hard across the face that her heels went out from underneath her and she fell heavily on the marble.

"Hey, I don't have to take that," she said angrily. "Even from you!" She knew immediately when she said it that she had made a mistake.

"Yes, you do, you fucking bitch," he seethed at her and picked her up by the hair, and slapped her again across the face. Then he pulled her face up close to his and all she could see was the anger in his eyes.

"Shut your mouth, bitch, or I'll slap it shut."

He shoved her down onto the hard marble. "Here," he said and pulled himself out and he was already hard.

He yanked her head back by her hair again and pushed the curls out of her face so he could watch her and she could look at him. A terrible smile spread his lips tight to his face. "That's it," he said. "That's it."

Tears ran down her face as she tried to please him. The more hungrily she devoured him, the less angry were his eyes. All she wanted to do was get out of there alive. But how the hell was she going to do it? She didn't have the knife she always had with her on other dates. The HPD had gone through her purse, felt her up. So she had no weapon. Besides, you can't pull a knife on the governor. You had to take what he gave you and like it. Cindy had warned her he could get rough sometimes but it was just an act. If she played her part, she'd end up like Cindy with a red BMW and the expensive jewelry Cindy was always flashing.

But still, in spite of what Cindy had told her, she was scared. She wasn't sure he hadn't just flipped out. All he had to do was get out of control just a little more and he might really hurt her, send her to the hospital. Or maybe even the morgue.

He pulled her up by the hair again.

"Please," she whimpered, but he wasn't listening.

He crushed his lips to hers and bit down on her lips until she could taste salt. When he pulled back, there was blood on his teeth and she knew it was hers.

That panicked her and she broke loose from behind him and ran for the door.

"Help!" she was screaming. "Somebody help me!"

She made it to the door and tried to open it but it was double-bolted and chained. By the time she unlatched everything and began to pull the door open, his big hand came down on the door and slammed it shut.

"Help!" she screamed one last time before he slapped her to the marble.

Dan Chin, the young cop in the hallway closest to Slaton's suite, heard the girl's screams. "Jesus," he said. "What the hell?" And he began to run for the governor's room.

Sergeant Nakamura, a slow-footed veteran, had to hustle to catch Chin by the sleeve before he got to the room. Nakamura had been assigned to Slaton before, posted outside the door when Slaton had one of his whores in the room with him.

"Slow down there, Hopalong," Nakamura said and tugged at the belt of his drooping pants that he'd loosened after the big plate of *lau lau* he'd had for lunch. "Our leader likes to get rough with 'em. Nothing to worry about. He's just having a little fun."

Chin had worked his first full year at HPD patrolling Manoa Valley, where the UH campus was located. When he heard he was going to guard the governor, he had called his mother so she could brag about it to Mrs. Ng next door.

"That doesn't sound like anyone's having fun to me," he said. "It sounds like someone's in trouble."

Nakamura gave a lippy smirk. "Ah, she's probably playacting for him. You know these high-priced bitches. They're all would-be actresses."

"Maybe we better just give a little knock," Chin said. "What if it's more than that? We're supposed to be guarding the governor. It's our ass if something happens."

"I don't think I'd disturb him." Nakamura shook his head. "You interrupt the governor when he's getting his rocks hauled, you could end up on the duty roster at Waianae Precinct."

Just then Stephanie broke for the door again. Slaton grabbed her and she screamed as he shoved her against the wall. The governor shouted something that Chin couldn't make out.

"That's it," the cop said. "I'm seeing if everything's okay in there."

Nakamura shrugged and stepped aside. "Don't ask me to visit you out in the cane fields."

Chin ran down the hall and knocked loudly at Slaton's door. "You all right in there, sir?" he shouted through the heavy koa doors.

The girl began to scream, "Get this maniac—" But Slaton clapped his hand over her mouth.

"Yes, yes," Slaton yelled at the door. "We're fine."

Chin hesitated a moment as he stared at the intricately carved wood of the door in front of him. "You're sure everything's all right, sir? If you need any help, that's what we're here—"

An explosive shout knocked Chin back from the door.

"Get the hell out of here!" Slaton bellowed. He had Stephanie pinned to the marble floor next to the door.

"Yes, sir," he heard Chin mumble, and the cop's footsteps receded quickly back down the hall to where Nakamura stood with a wide grin on his face.

"Don't ever try anything like that again, bitch!" Slaton said to her.

When she looked up into his eyes, he knew that she understood the position she was in. She was going to do what he told her to do, every last excruciating detail.

He pulled her by the hair into the bedroom.

"There's a red outfit in the closet. Go put it on," he ordered.

"All right," she said without hesitation.

She walked over to the closet and slid open the doors. One side of her face was numb and she could taste the blood in the back of her throat. Inside the closet was hanging a blood red silk sheath with spaghetti straps. She looked behind her at him. He was sitting in a tall wingback like a monarch. His back was to the curtain, so she couldn't see his face, only his massive shoulders filling the chair.

She pulled the dress from the hanger and it fell limply onto her arm. It felt as light as a tissue and the expensive silk ran like water in her hands. She put it over her head and it poured down her body and fit every round place, every soft curve, every ripple of ribs. It came down to just below her rear so the black garter straps showed below it where they clung to the black band of the stockings.

"Take off the stockings," he said nonchalantly, as if he'd asked her to fetch him a cup of coffee.

She began to walk to a chair.

"Do it standing up," he said, raising his voice. She stopped where she was and lifted one foot.

"Do it slowly."

She unhooked the first hook and reached back behind her leg for the second.

"Slower!" he shouted. As she unsnapped it, she felt one of her tears splash against the hand that held the garter. She reached slowly to the inside of her thigh and unsnapped the last hook. Then she slowly undid the three hooks on the other leg. She looked up at him and a sob came out of her lips unexpectedly. Her own fear scared her. She didn't want to set him off. He was in the chair watching her, sipping the scotch she'd poured for him earlier and set out on the table. There were several other full glasses that she had set about the suite because Cindy had told her he liked to drink while he played, wherever the game took him.

"Take them off," he demanded. She slowly rolled the stocking down her thigh, over her knee, and down her calf. Then she put her hand against the wall and slipped the stocking over her foot and did the same with the other stocking, switching hands against the wall for balance. When she was through she took the stockings and draped them across the bedpost at the head of the bed. If he felt in the mood, he'd use them to tie her hands to the bed later.

She watched him nod his head slowly in approval as he drank down the last of his scotch. She went to the table and poured it full for him. He slapped her across the buttocks again so it stung and took ahold of one of the garter straps and yanked the whole contraption down below her knees. Then he threw it out onto the lānai, where it fell at a man's feet.

The man looked down at the black nylon with eyes even colder than the governor's. He held the pig-boning knife in his hand while he watched through the curtain as Slaton ordered the girl around.

"Get on your hands and knees, you fucking bitch," Slaton said with a curled smile. "I'm going to fuck you like an animal the way you like it."

She didn't argue. All she wanted was to get this over with. Get him in her and tighten around him and work him hard so he couldn't help but come. Then maybe he wouldn't end up beating her to death. That's all she wanted now—to get out of this alive without getting hurt too badly.

The man watched as Slaton rammed into her and she cried out. "Shut up, bitch," he yelled and slapped her across the thigh.

"Oh, please, please don't."

"I'll do whatever I want with you, you fucking *moke* bitch." And he slapped her buttocks and slapped her again and then again. He grabbed her by the hips and drove into her and she was screaming from the pain and he was screaming too. "You fucking whore! You fucking whore!"

Then suddenly Slaton stopped and pulled out of her and stepped around the bed and pushed himself into her mouth again. She sucked him eagerly so he wouldn't hit her again. He groaned for a few minutes, then he pulled away from her.

Slaton reached up and took her face in one hand and looked at the mess of her mascara and the lipstick spread across her face.

"Go in the bathroom and doll up again, bitch. I want a lot of lipstick this time too. I love to watch those beautiful lips of yours at work."

He slapped her hard on the ass and nodded his head toward the other room.

"All right," she said as she walked across the room, through the living room of the huge suite, and into the bathroom. She shut the door and locked it and turned on the fan. Then she flushed the toilet so when she burst out crying he wouldn't hear her.

As soon as he heard the click of the door, the man slipped inside the curtain behind where Slaton sat in the wingback drinking his scotch, stroking himself in anticipation of the cruelty he had in store.

The knife cut across the governor's throat with a terrible ripping of bone and tendon and jugular. The golden scotch spit from his mouth and mixed with the first spurt from the artery. Reaching reflexively, the governor caught the knife before it cut all the way through his neck. Slaton's hand struggled with his attacker's for the knife.

Slaton had the knife by the blade and when the man yanked, it sliced off the governor's pinkie finger, the one with the huge ruby ring. It fell to the floor and the red stone clanged against the marble.

The governor pushed out of the chair onto the floor and felt a hammer blow to his back—hard and breathtaking. Slaton only realized it was a blade when it was being pulled out again. He turned over and gripped his attacker's arm as it plunged down again. This time they were facing each other and the blade caught the governor's shoulder. Slaton pulled him by the shirt with one hand on the knife and for the first time his attacker's face came into the light of the low slanting sun.

The man pulled back and broke free of the governor and drove the knife into Slaton's belly. The governor twisted away from his attacker with the long boning knife still in his stomach. Blood was running down Slaton's neck and from the squawk that came from his victim's mouth, the man knew he'd gotten the vocal cords. The red patch at Slaton's belly was spreading but the governor still had some strength left—the huge barrel chest, the meaty arms, the strong jaws clenched in pain and hatred.

Slaton pulled the knife from his own guts and came at his attacker.

The man backed into the living room and Slaton followed, his own blood dripping from the knife. The man looked around and picked up a heavy koa chair that sat beneath a mirror next to the door. He raised it above his head and ran across the room at Slaton. As Slaton slashed out with the knife, the man crashed it down on the governor's head. He knew by the way Slaton's body twitched that he was finally dead.

A glass broke behind him. Over his shoulder, he heard Stephanie gasp. He looked back and he could see the girl with her face all made up, the bright red lipstick on her full lips.

She backed out of the bathroom and ran for the front door. He pulled the knife from the governor's clenched hand, and went after her. When she got to the door, she tried to pull it open but Slaton had locked it again from the inside.

She was screaming as she pulled desperately at the door handle. Sergeant Nakamura looked over at Chin with a big, satisfied grin. "You wanna go save her again, Superman?"

"Screw you, Nakamura," was all Chin said as the girl screamed.

Stephanie turned and he grabbed her by the hair and in one quick yank cut her throat. She went down to her knees, the blood gurgling from her neck, the voiceless scream pouring from her, the black shards of death knifing into her vision until only a high-pitched wail remained like a radio trying to reach a station too distant to receive. When her face crashed against the marble she was almost dead, her life pumping out of the gash below her beautiful, agonized face.

CHAPTER
THREE

Dan flashed his ID toward the two cops at the elevator on the floor where the governor had been slain. Nakamura was sitting on a pulled-up chair along the corridor surrounded by three homicide detectives. Dan nodded to Lieutenant Iida, the chief of Homicide at HPD, who was standing next to them, grilling Chin. Iida nodded back to Dan and pointed down the hall to the knot of police standing outside the Liliuokalani Suite.

Joe Kalama was crouched just inside the door of the room, inspecting something on the floor, when Dan came in.

"Dan," Kalama said. "Reed's back in there." The Hawai'ian nodded, pointing over his shoulder to the bedroom.

Dan saw flashes from a camera snapping furiously from the room. Reed poked his head out the door. "Tell the coroner he can take him away now," he said to Kalama.

Reed motioned for Dan to come in. "Take a look at this mess, will you?" he said to Dan. "But I'm warning you, it's a butcher shop in there."

Dan stepped past Reed nonchalantly. He'd seen a couple of hundred murder scenes as a PA: pretty women with their faces beaten into ground meat, drug dealers with the tops of their skulls blown off, a maggot-ravaged corpse with one eye socket eaten away, the tongue swollen so huge it bulged out of the victim's mouth.

By the looks of things in the living room—the bloody prints on the walls, blood spattered on the furniture and pooled on the floor, a wide swath of crimson spread on the marble—a body had obviously been dragged into the back bedroom. Dan knew the size of the governor, too. A big man bleeds a lot more than a frail old lady. So there'd be a lot of blood all right. Blood he could handle by the buckets. But he never expected what he saw.

Slaton was strung by a rope to the poster bed, the rope wrapped around his neck so the deep gash at his neck gaped open like an exclamation. His stomach was ripped open from his crotch to his jugular and his guts, big handfuls of them, lay on the bed where he knelt. Both ears had been hacked off and his eyes cut out. On the floor next to the bed was his heart, smashed into mush as if someone had taken a mallet to it.

As soon as he took one look at this slaughterhouse, Dan had to run out onto the lānai to get some air. Cathy was out there already, and he nudged her aside as he vomited into a potted palm. Someone had already used the planter before him. When he looked up at Cathy and saw the sickly pallor around her ears and neck, he knew it was her he'd shared the pot with.

"I've never . . ." she mumbled at Dan, holding on to the rail unsteadily as if they were on a ship in thirty-foot swells. Then she put her hand on Dan's arm and he drew her to him. "I'm sorry," she muttered, and they both knew how incongruous the whole situation was. The horrifying scene in that bedroom had shocked them both. He gave her hand a small squeeze and she stood up a little straighter from the courage he was offering.

They stood out on the balcony that way for a minute or two.

"We better go inside," Dan said to her and took her arm.

"All right."

Reed was talking with Kalama when they stepped back in. Cathy went directly back into the front room without bothering to take another look at the gore. "I'm going to see what Slaton's assistant has to say," she said on the way out.

"Sure," Reed said, with a little grin.

Reed was fingering the big diamond pinkie he wore. He always seemed to be playing with it. If he wasn't twisting it around his finger, he'd take it off and shake it in his hand like a crap shooter hoping to roll a seven.

"I'd say somebody had a big fat hard-on for Slaton to go to this much trouble," Reed said to Dan.

A wave of nausea hit Dan again and he didn't answer. The stench from the slit-open bowels mixed with the salt air.

Dan turned his eyes from the eviscerated body strung over the bed and noticed for the first time a foot sticking out from the far side. The nails were painted red. The wide smear of blood that trailed from the front door led right to the blood-soaked foot. It was then that Dan realized it wasn't the governor's blood that was splashed all over the living room—it was probably this poor woman's.

"Jesus," he said to Reed as he walked around the bed. "Who's that?"

"Some escort service bimbo Slaton was hosing. Wrong place. Wrong time," he said and shrugged.

Dan got just close enough to look around the bed so he could see the girl's body. She was young, very young, in a short red dress pulled up to her waist. Her throat was ripped open and her eyes were staring dead at the ceiling. Despite the blood that was smeared over most of her body, Dan could see only the neck wound.

"Is the cut on the neck what killed her?" he asked Kalama, who had come into the room and was kneeling down next to her.

"Looks that way. That's the only knife wound. No signs of strangulation or cranial trauma. I'd say the neck wound killed her, all right. Looks like we got somebody who was mighty pissed at Slaton and she just got in the way."

Dan motioned to Reed. "Can we go in the other room? I've seen enough of this."

Reed turned and walked out the door into the living room area and went over to the koa dining table that sat in its own alcove. It was the only place that wasn't stained with blood.

"Lab boys dusted here already," he said. He pointed Dan into one of the heavy oak chairs surrounding the table and waved at Cathy, who was standing by the front door. Reed pulled out a chair for her and it made a loud screech on the marble floor.

"I know this looks like some nut went wild in there, but I think what we have here is an assassination. The girl gets it because she's in the way. That make sense to you?" Reed asked, looking to both of them.

Dan and Cathy were his two best prosecutors. They had excellent instincts for criminal law, and he'd often consult with them over which way they read a case.

"What else?" Cathy said. Her face was still a pale color and her hair had gone limp from sweat. "A politician of the governor's stature always has a shopping list of enemies. In Slaton's case that included just about every natural born Hawai'ian left in the state."

"That's what I was thinking," Reed said. He had a pencil out and he had pulled the pinkie ring off and slid it down the pencil like a ringer in horseshoes.

"Have you got somebody in mind?" Cathy asked.

"I'm thinking Peter Maikai," Reed said.

"I'll admit there's probably not a Polynesian in the South Pacific who isn't celebrating right now," Dan answered. "But I don't think Maikai's your man."

"Why not?" Reed said.

"For one thing," Dan said, "he's a seventy-year-old man with a bad heart. How's he going to pull himself three stories up a rope and then overpower a two-hundred-and-thirty-pound man the size of Slaton?"

Reed smirked. "All he'd have to do is surprise him with one of those Hawai'ian war clubs he was flailing around the beach this afternoon. One whack could bring down a two-hundred-pound pig. It could sure as hell take out a governor with his pants down humping some young babe."

"So what are you saying?" Dan said, a little irritated. "He waits till they're both ready to get it off and tries to do them both, but the girl makes a run for it?"

Reed was nodding his head.

"You can't be buying this too?" Dan said, looking at Cathy.

"Maikai did do everything but stab him on the beach today," she said. "And I think he might have tried that too if Kalama hadn't tackled him. I'd say Peter Maikai's certainly worth a strong look."

"All right," Dan said, "Let's forget he's got a heart condition and he's got two healthy people he has to overpower. How the hell did he pull himself up that rope with that heavy war club and an assortment of butcher knives? Don't tell me you think he could do that too? He'd have to haul himself up there hand-over-hand."

Reed's smile spread across his face. He took the ring and jammed it back on his finger. "I think you missed something, Dan."

He got up and motioned Dan out into the living-room lānai directly behind where they were sitting. "Step out here."

The lānai was at a right angle to the bedroom. The rope the killer had used was still tied to the railing of the balcony. From here Dan could see the overturned trash cans on the ground below that the killer had probably used to reach the rope. They were hidden from the beach and neighboring hotels and even the bedroom lānai by a stand of palm ferns.

From this angle Dan could pretty much make out the plan of attack. The Royal had a fancy bit of architecture that butted out from the corner where the killer would have been hidden from most views.

"What about it? I don't see any steps leading up there. He's still got to pull his own weight up."

Reed backhanded Dan's arm and pointed up above the bedroom lānai. Dan followed his boss's finger to the lānai above. There was another rope tied to the railing of the balcony:

"I guess you were too busy puking into the plants to notice anything above you."

Reed walked back into the dining room and sat at the table again while Cathy and Dan looked up.

"My grandmother could slide down that rope, croak the governor and his plaything, then slide down to the ground."

Dan was still out on the balcony and Reed was talking through the sheer sun curtains that ruffled in the trades.

"Okay," Dan said, "so maybe physically Maikai could have done it. That leaves about twenty more pieces to fit together before we even think of suspecting him. Like what's that slaughterhouse scene all about in there? That doesn't look like an assassination to me. It looks personal."

"I think I might be able to answer that," Joe Kalama said behind them.

Reed's face brightened. "What did you find?" he asked the cop.

"Well, I didn't find anything," Kalama said.

"Well, don't bother us then," Reed snapped loudly. His neck puffed up.

Kalama stared at Reed a moment.

"What is it, Joe?" Dan said.

"I'll have to show you what I mean. Can you come back into the bedroom?"

"Do we have to?" Cathy said reluctantly.

"Yeah, I need you to see some things."

All three shoved their chairs back, screeching painfully against the marble, and followed the sergeant back to where the governor hung.

Kalama tugged at his aloha shirt. His stomach bulged so the front of his shirt ballooned forward.

"There's something about this killing that's strange," Kalama said.

"Is that supposed to be news?" Reed said.

Kalama ignored the crack.

"See this rope around his neck," he said and reached up to touch it. "It's made of human hair."

"Yeah?" Reed asked. "Is that significant?"

"It's a Hawaiian strangling cord. In the old days, that's the way a Hawai'ian warrior would get rid of an enemy. A special good enemy."

"What are you saying?" Reed wanted to know.

"I'm saying this was done by someone who knew the old rituals of the Hawai'ian warrior."

Reed and Dan looked at each other a moment. "How about the rest of it? The gutting and the cutting off of his ears?"

"Actually, that was more a Samoan trait. But all of it was done by a Polynesian or someone who knew about Polynesian warrior rites." Kalama pointed at the corpse. "Without the ears the head is opened up so the centipede can lay its eggs in it. And they always take the heart."

"Jesus," Cathy moaned, her mouth and eyes open wide in disbelief.

"What about the girl? Was she killed in a ritualistic way?" Dan asked.

"Nah," the cop nodded. "I still think she was in the wrong place at the wrong time," Kalama said, repeating Reed's phrase. "He just killed her clean and left her."

Dan started to feel the nausea rising again. If Kalama was right, there was going to be a hell of a lot of bad feelings stirred up between *haoles* and locals. And that was something nobody wanted to deal with.

Kalama came up close and said in a low voice, "Maikai knew all about this stuff."

Reed was staring at Dan. When Dan looked over he had an I-told-you-so smirk on his face.

"Maikai's not the only one up on his Hawai'ian lore," Dan said. "The last twenty years they've been teaching the damn stuff in the grammar schools here."

Kalama pursed his lips as if in apology. "I'm just saying that I think a Hawai'ian could have done this."

"Or somebody who wanted it to look like a Hawai'ian did it," Dan argued. "I'm not so sure we want to jump to any conclusions is all I'm saying. We have a long way to go before we start naming suspects."

"Yeah, you're probably right," Reed conceded. "But I think every minute of Maikai's time since the incident at the rally better be accounted for."

Reed walked to the bedroom and said something to Kalama, then walked back to Cathy and Dan. "The next thing we have to do is figure out how we're going to handle the media. Look, it's been a long day and we've got a lot of work ahead of us. I'll see you both tomorrow."

The coroner's gurneys were wheeled through to the bedroom. Dan and Cathy stood on the lānai, watching speechless as they began to untie Slaton. Like everyone else, they were still in a state of shock.

Dan heard a thump and one of the lab boys say, "Be careful. It's the governor, not some homeless derelict."

"Let's get out of here," Dan said to Cathy, and took her by the hand.

CHAPTER
FOUR

Dan pulled up to Outrigger Beach and parked in the small lot across from the tennis courts. The sun was just showing in the sky behind Diamond Head. He had a couple of hours to spare before he had to be at the office. The governor had been dead only a few days, and Dan and every other person in the DA's office had been working almost continuously without a break. Slaton had been murdered with an obscene brutality, and Reed felt the pressure of the whole state and the entire country to catch the assassin.

At this hour, Waikīkī Beach was deserted, the big outrigger canoes laid out on the sand. The forty-five-foot-long hulls each rested on two old tires, their long bamboo arms set carefully on a padded wood block.

These old canoes were probably the only things on Waikīkī Beach that didn't have to be tied down. Everything else was stolen if left overnight. But the old outrigger canoes were the one sacred piece of property no local would touch. The canoe was the most visible symbol of the Hawai'ians' past, of the dying culture that the people who loved Hawai'i were struggling so desperately to preserve. The canoe was a sacred thing that tied all Hawai'ians to *'āina* and the sea.

Dan spotted Paul's bare feet resting on the hull of an overturned canoe and went over to him. He could see by the way his body was nuzzled down into the sand that his brother had probably slept there last night. It was anybody's guess how he'd ended up on the beach.

Dan kicked his brother's foot, and only Paul's eyelids moved in response. He looked at Dan once and closed his eyes again.

"You sleep here last night?"

"Mmm," he mumbled without moving.

"It isn't safe here at night, you know."

"They won't touch the canoes."

"That's not the point."

"Oh, shit!" Paul groaned. Dan knew what his brother was thinking. Little brother telling big brother he had to straighten up. Maybe he didn't want to straighten up. Maybe after his wife and his only child were killed, maybe he just didn't give a shit anymore. And maybe his friends and his relatives all trying to get him back to the living weren't doing anything but driving him deeper into despair. That's what he was thinking, all right. But Dan didn't care.

"How much did you drink last night?" Dan asked.

"Screw you, Danny boy."

"No, screw you, Paul. You've been drunk for months now. Melissa and Chris are dead. Let them rest in peace."

Paul groaned again and rolled over on his side away from the reproach of his brother.

"You drank yourself out of work. You drank yourself out of your home. I can't believe that goddamn hole you're living in at the Luahine. They murdered some old lady from Des Moines there the other night."

Dan knew that Paul was either going to start facing this thing and maybe start living again or he was going farther into his own private hell. By the looks of him, it was obvious he'd chosen the latter.

The ironic thing about it was that their roles were reversed now. Before, Paul had always been the one helping Dan. Paul had put him through college when Peter Maikai threw him off the ranch. Paul was the one who put him up when Dan separated from Darlene. Paul was also the one who told him not to marry Darlene, not to marry the first girl he slept with who looked like Lily, a long-haired local girl. Now here he was trying to help Paul. And not doing a very good job of it.

"Come on, we better get this workout in," Dan said and threw a paddle in the canoe.

"What's the hurry? Joe ain't even here yet."

"It's just the five of us today. Joe's too busy with the assassination investigation to get out."

Paul raised up on one elbow. "You guys know who did it yet?"

"No. But Kalama figures it's got to be a Hawai'ian who knew the ancient warrior rituals. The body was mutilated like a Hawai'ian warrior would have done."

Paul wiped sand idly from the canoe. "They looking at Maikai?"

"Yeah," Dan said in a curious tone. "How'd you know?"

"Hey, bra, it don't take Einstein to figure this one out. I saw on the news where Maikai made a big show on the beach that afternoon. Waving that war club of his at Slaton, telling everybody in earshot that the islands ain't big enough for both of them. Then later Slaton gets laid out like a beef tenderloin. . . ."

He threw the paddle into the hull and sat on the edge of the canoe. "One thing I know from personal experience. Cops don't think like Sherlock Holmes. They don't sniff around for the hidden pieces of some intricate puzzle. They see Maikai making threats, bingo! That's their boy. If it gets any more complicated than that, they give up."

Paul slowly pushed himself to his feet, groaning a little and rubbing his kidneys. He walked over to Dan's backpack and pulled out a red thermos, unscrewed the top, fished around in the sack again and found a chipped plastic mug. He poured the black, steaming liquid into it.

"Black?" Paul said, sounding annoyed. Then he laughed. "As if my taste buds could tell anymore."

He screwed the lid back on cockeyed and tossed it down so that escaping coffee stained the sand black. Dan reached over and uprighted it.

"I don't think Maikai had anything to do with it," Dan said. He reached for the knapsack and pulled out another mug.

"Why?"

"I just don't think he'd do it."

"Because he put us up for a while when we were kids?" Paul said and pushed his sun-bleached blond hair off his face with his forearm.

"Sure, that's part of it. We got to know him pretty well, don't you think?"

Paul laughed into his coffee. "Yeah, we got to know him well enough so when you knocked up his daughter, he threw you out on your ass."

Dan tossed what was left in his mug angrily into the sand. Paul knew his brother didn't like to talk about Lily. The way Lily had been ripped from his arms by Maikai. The way her father had forced her to abort their child. Dan had spent the last eighteen years trying to forget all about Lily Maikai and how much he'd loved her. How much he'd ached when he'd lost her.

"That was almost twenty years ago," Dan said.

"Yeah, so maybe you don't know him so good anymore. That many years can change a man a lot."

"You're telling me you think Maikai could have done it?"

"Not in a million years," Paul said, shaking his head. "You know I love the old *kanaka maoli*. But it doesn't matter what I think, does it? I just know how cops think. Maikai screams and yells that the governor's got to go and an hour later, he's gone for good. One plus one equals two. That's how a cop thinks. Notice I didn't say two plus two. That's higher math to a policeman. Of course, that's always been your problem, bra."

Dan looked over at his brother, who was rubbing the sleep and alcohol from his eyes, shoving his hair off his face, trying to get himself straight enough to get in the canoe and not fall out.

"Okay, so what's my problem?" Dan said with an annoyed tone. It irked him to be lectured by someone in that shape.

"Truth, justice, and the American way," Paul said.

"Yeah? You going to elaborate for me, big brother? Or do I guess what that hogwash means?"

"Reed's the PA. You're not. Everybody knows you're supposed to be the PA and you're not. Why is that?"

"Truth, justice, and the American way?"

Paul shrugged his shoulders at the obvious. "If I was Slaton, I wouldn't have picked you either. You've got too many scruples for the position. In case you haven't heard, Honolulu PA is a low-scruples job."

"Thanks for the vote of confidence."

"Why do you think Cathy's pissed at you too?"

"Jesus, who said she's pissed at me?" Dan said loudly.

"You're dumber than I thought."

Behind them a car door slammed. Michael Maikai got out of his Mercedes with still-wet trunks and trotted toward them followed by the Ahue twins, Kimo and Lenny, who made up the rest of their six-man crew.

Michael and Dan, who'd grown up together, still looked a lot alike. Michael was tall and built strongly in the shoulders and chest like Dan, but he hadn't acquired the rope of fat around the midsection that Dan had. His hair was thick and black like Dan's, too. In fact, when they were kids Dan was often mistaken for Michael's brother rather than Paul's.

"We better get hustling," Michael said. He picked up his paddle and tossed it in the boat. "Joe's not going to make it this morning."

"Yeah, I know. He called me," Dan said.

They picked up the canoe by the rails and trudged heavily down to the sea. When they slid the boat into the water, Dan straightened up and stretched his back before he started to paddle.

"Old at thirty-four. Jesus!"

"Quit complaining," Paul groaned back. "My head's pounding and I'm five years older than you."

Dan saw Michael smile. Even though Michael had protested when Kalama had called him to get the old crew together again, Dan knew he enjoyed these dawn workouts: the quiet of the ocean with just the sound of the paddles slicing through the water and the groans of the crew as they pulled. Michael was the Harvard Law School grad. In no time he was planning their workouts and the meets they had to enter to win the overall senior crown.

"Let's make it short and sweet today, boys," Michael said.

"Sounds good," Dan said and settled into the seat in front of Michael. He knew he had to be in Brian's office by eight, so short and sweet was all he had time for anyway.

They all began to paddle with short, quick digs toward the oncoming breakers. The swells on the south shore this time of year were no more than a foot so they took the first wave easily, then dug hard again to beat the next wave before it crested. A few more pulls and they were out beyond the surf line. Michael, the helmsman in back, dipped his paddle on the left side of the canoe and brought the nose parallel to shore. They would paddle slowly to Black Rock at the base of Diamond Head to get warm and in sync, then they'd start the workout.

Sure, Cathy was mad at him, Dan thought as he paddled. "Disappointed" was the word she'd used. Dan had refused to go along with the murder indictment of Kimo Mitchell, a Honolulu crime boss. Not because he wasn't sure Mitchell was guilty. He was plenty guilty. Responsible in all likelihood for the murder of at least eight people. The problem was, the governor was pushing hard for a big-time organized crime conviction, even though they didn't have the hard evidence to get Mitchell. The election had been a few months away at the time and it was the old story: Slaton wanted a flashy, tough-on-crime headline to boost his campaign. The governor had insisted, but Dan refused. When it came time to choose the new Honolulu PA, Slaton hand-picked Reed, a less experienced prosecutor, to run for the unopposed position. It meant that Slaton had all but appointed Reed over Dan. Cathy had told him for months what was going to happen if he didn't do what Slaton wanted. And, sure enough, it had happened.

Sure, she was pissed at him.

"Got any idea what Reed's thinking?" Michael asked from the back of the canoe.

A rain spout was hanging from a cloud over the ocean like a liquid stalactite. The curtain of opaque gray obscured the horizon behind it.

"About what?" Dan asked, knowing exactly what he was digging for. Michael wanted to know if Reed had enough to charge his father with the murder of Jim Slaton.

"About my client!" Michael said, meaning his father.

"Has he got a good lawyer?"

"Do you really think he needs one? There's no way he can be connected to the assassination," Michael said confidently, then added, "can he?"

Dan kept pulling slowly as they neared Diamond Head. When they got up close to the ridged cone, he felt the boat turning. Dan and Paul stopped paddling and let the boat turn a half-circle until they were facing north and Diamond Head was on their right.

"Well, does he need an attorney?" Michael asked again.

Dan shook his head nearly imperceptibly. There was a time when they wouldn't have had to play these games with each other. They had been as close as brothers until Michael went to the Mainland. When he got back after Harvard Law School and four years in a high-powered Manhattan corporate law firm, Michael had changed. Suddenly, Dan's old childhood friend qualified everything he said to him. He could never get a straight answer from Michael about anything. Dan turned his shoulders so he could look him in the face.

"Michael," he said firmly, "you know I can't discuss the case with you."

"Then you feel you've got something on him?"

"I didn't say that. All I can say is Reed and a lot of other people wouldn't mind putting your father away for a while where he can't do them any harm."

Dan knifed the paddle into the water with a loud "Ho!" feeling the strain of that first long pull.

They paddled for a while until they were in front of the painted rainbow on the side of the Hilton. When Michael gave the signal they began to dig hard for five hundred yards. They pulled up the paddles when they reached the marina, and the canoe glided ahead as they caught their breath.

They worked hard for another forty-five minutes, and Dan's mind began to drift as they dug through the swells. It had been months since he'd thought about Lily, about her long, full mane of black hair and the smell of pikake on her skin. She was smiling up at him from her bed, then he was in her and she was calling his name. Then he flashed to the scene where her father, Peter Maikai, had crashed his fist against Dan's face. He was yelling at him never to set foot on his property again. And never to try to see Lily if he wanted to live.

A brace of salt water woke Dan from his nightmare.

When Michael finally steered them around Kapi'olani Park and came past the Aquatic Center down the beach from the old Kaimana Beach Hotel, Dan saw the familiar figure of Joe Kalama standing on the shore waiting for them. He was wearing the same faded shirt and beige cotton pants he'd had on the day before and a look that said this was police business.

As Dan stepped out of the canoe, Joe picked up the front rail and helped them lift it onto the beach.

"Reed wants to see you in his office," he said.

"What time?"

"What time is it now?" Kalama asked.

Dan looked down at the black waterproof sport watch on his wrist. The stopwatch was still running so he clicked the function button to see what time it was. "About five after seven?"

"He said tell you fifteen minutes tops."

"Screw him."

Kalama grunted. "He's barking like a Moloka'i pig."

"So what's new?"

Kalama shrugged. Dan noticed a stain of coffee down the front of the cop's shirt.

"You get any sleep last night?"

Kalama shook his head. "Reed isn't going to let nobody sleep for a while."

CHAPTER
FIVE

The prosecuting attorney's office was across the street from Iolani Palace. Its grand façade had been ripped at by Hurricane Iniki back in '92, so the columns that fronted the place looked like toy soldiers undressed.

Dan didn't mind Reed calling him in early—this was the biggest case in the state's history—but he had planned to talk to Cathy that morning about their problems. With all the pressure they all were under from the Slaton case, he and Cathy were drifting farther and farther apart. They hadn't slept together for weeks. They hadn't talked except about work. He'd had to make an appointment to see her, for God's sake. That was what their relationship had been reduced to.

Dan took a side door near the Dumpsters, where a family of wild cats, mottled and green-eyed, lived. The long, asphalt-tiled hallway was empty at this time of the morning. He punched the button of the service elevator and went up to the tenth floor. He nodded to the receptionist out front and shouldered his way through the double doors of the prosecuting attorney's office. Reed's office was the last one down the hall. Dan knocked once and went in.

Reed was sitting in an old leather chair he'd moved into his office the day after he was appointed. He had his feet propped on a stack of file boxes at the side of his desk and he was sipping coffee from a big mug with 25 TO LIFE painted on it.

Cathy was sitting in a chair across from Reed, her high heels propped on the same box of files as Reed's. They were smiling when Dan came through the door. Both their faces went flat when they saw him.

"Dan. Good, you're here," Reed said.

"Good morning, Cathy," Dan said to her in a professional tone.

She slid her feet off the files. "Good morning," she repeated back. They had decided the day after they first slept together that they would never use the standard endearments at the office.

When Dan closed the door he noticed for the first time that Glen Iida and Joe Kalama were there too, sitting at the conference table in the corner behind the door. They weren't smiling, though. By the look of Iida, the swollen eyes, the rumpled clothes, it was obvious he'd been up all night working this case too. But then this wasn't some strangled hooker found floating in the Ala Wai Canal or a Flip gang-shooting in Kalihi. The governor had been assassinated. The media had been relentless. They wanted an arrest, or at the very least a suspect to chew on.

Reed didn't wait for any smart talk between the cops and Dan before he got to what he wanted.

"We're serving a warrant on Peter Maikai at his ranch on Maui tomorrow," Reed said. "I want you to go with Joe and Iida and make sure there's no procedural problems. We don't want any screwups on this."

Reed slipped his feet off the files and reached over and tossed a stack of papers at Dan. Dan picked them up and began to read.

"What's the hurry?" Dan asked without looking up. He was still thumbing through the paperwork. "What've you got that I don't know about?"

"Iida, give him a rundown," Reed ordered the Homicide lieutenant.

Dan could see Iida's chest rise and fall. The elderly detective didn't care for Reed's disrespectful manner. Iida had been in the 522d, the all-Japanese battalion that had been the most decorated in World War II. He had been next to Dan Inouye when the future senator from Hawai'i had lost his arm in battle.

Iida shuffled a stack of papers on the table in front of him and when he got to what he wanted, he evened the edges and put his finger on the page.

"First of all, Dan, Peter Maikai threatened the governor's life in front of thirty thousand people on the beach two hours before his body was found. Secondly," he went on, his finger tracking down the page as he detailed the points that would nail Maikai, "the suspect tried to gain access to the governor's room shortly after the incident on the beach but was physically restrained by two HPD officers and escorted back to the lobby."

"I thought you hustled Maikai out of there," Dan said to Kalama, who shrugged.

"Apparently he came back," Reed said matter-of-factly. Then he looked over at Iida. "Go on."

"Thirdly, the nature of the killings which have been identified as conforming to known Hawai'ian rituals of war, particularly the strangling cord made of human hair, again points to someone such as Peter Maikai who was intimately familiar with these rituals. And, fourth, the rope that led to Slaton's lānai was tied up on the rail outside Maikai's room."

Iida pushed the papers forward, sat back straight in his seat, and looked over at Reed again.

Dan kept staring at Iida then turned to Kalama, who raised his eyebrows.

"Yamanoha signed off on that?" Dan asked, referring to the judge who had authorized the warrant.

Reed shook his head.

"No hard physical evidence? No fingerprints? No murder weapon? No stained clothing? No eyewitnesses?"

"The guy made direct threats against him an hour before he was murdered and tried to sneak through security to get into his room. That's enough for a search warrant right there," Reed shouted back.

Dan stood up and tossed the warrant in front of Iida so that it knocked the Japanese's neatly stacked papers across the table.

"First of all, don't forget I was there. Maikai didn't make any direct threats. He never said one word about killing him. Or, in fact, doing him any harm at all."

"He said he was going to get rid of him while he waved a sword at him. That's not a threat?"

"Slaton was a politician," Dan said, turning to Reed. "Hell, half the state wanted to get rid of him. A couple people every night said it on the news. Any law student could get that thrown out. Besides, if it was such an obvious threat, why wasn't he arrested right on the spot?"

"You saw Slaton tell HPD to back off. He didn't want to make a scene with all those sovereignty fanatics around. They see one of their leaders get hauled off, Slaton was afraid they'd ruin his little party."

Dan gave a disgusted sigh. "That's a bunch of bull. And that part about trying to breach security at the hotel." Dan turned to Iida and poked his finger hard onto the table. "Did HPD keep a log of the comings and goings on the governor's floor that afternoon?"

Iida nodded his head proudly. "That's how I discovered Maikai was up there."

"Good work," Dan said. "So how many other would-be assassins tried to gain access to that floor?"

Iida's eyes narrowed to the thinnest of slits. "What do you mean?"

"You've got the log there?"

"Yes."

"Let's see it," Dan said sharply. Normally he liked Iida, who was conscientious and missed work about one day a decade.

Iida paged through the papers and slid out some paper-clipped sheets. Dan snatched them from him before Iida could offer them and began moving his head down the top page. "Eight, nine, ten, eleven," he counted. "Let's see, twelve, no thirteen, separate groups of so-called intruders were escorted off the floor while the governor was being murdered by the actual assassin."

This time Dan tossed the list in front of Reed, who hadn't said anything.

"And why even bother talking about the ritualistic angle?" Dan went on. "It doesn't even necessarily point to a Polynesian, which would narrow it down to a hundred, a hundred and fifty thousand suspects. Hell, there's probably a couple thousand *haoles* that know about that stuff too. My brother and I were raised on it."

"Okay, the ritualistic angle is weak, sure," Reed said. "But we're not basing the warrant on that. It's just supporting."

"It's supporting a bunch of other unsupported crap. And how about access? How the hell did he get in the room?"

"Come on, Dan, we already went over that. He slid down the ropes."

"Peter Maikai has a serious heart condition. According to his doctors he should be dead already. No way he's capable of climbing up or down a rope to kill a man who outweighed him by thirty pounds and was in great shape."

"He didn't look like a sick old man to me waving that sword," Reed said.

"Jesus," Dan said and threw his hands up. "Am I the only one here who sees how shaky this is?"

He looked at Iida, who stared back at him. His job wasn't to question his superiors. When Dan gave Kalama an inquisitive glance, the cop just shrugged. Outside these doors Kalama called Reed "Mr. Dickhead." In here, though, he had to go along with the PA.

"How about you, Cathy?" he asked.

"I think we have enough," she said firmly.

"You do?"

"Yes, I do, Dan," she said with a defiant rise of her chin. Dan knew what she was thinking when she gave him that look. It was just this kind of pointless standing for principle by Dan that always drove her nuts. If he wasn't so damn principled, he'd be the damn PA now and he really would be able to do some good. Why couldn't he just go along with the program like everybody else? Give and take until you get enough power, then you can tell them all to go to hell.

"And are you going to feel that way," Dan said, picking up the warrant, "when Michael Maikai gets whatever we do find suppressed in court because we tried to serve this piece of crap prematurely?"

Dan tossed the warrant back at Iida. "You don't have a damn thing. This office can't go along with this crap."

Reed cleared his throat a little. "I think what Iida's getting at here, Dan, is that Maikai's our prime suspect and we have a duty to at least follow up on what we do have."

"Come on, Dan," Kalama said, "there's got to be enough here for at least a warrant. Let's check his place out and see what we find."

Dan was silent for a second. He knew Kalama wasn't politically motivated like the others. If he thought they should have a look at Maikai's place, maybe Dan should listen.

"I agree with Kalama," Reed piped in. "Why don't you two get right on that so we have something to throw at the media."

"Wait a second," Dan said, holding up his hands to halt things. "Does that mean you want me to handle this case?"

Reed looked at him with a confused, pissed-off expression.

"The governor gets murdered. Who the hell do you think I'm going to give it to? You're my head attorney."

"I know how important this is to you and to all of us," he said, waving his hand around the room and then outside to encompass the entire population of Hawai'i. "But for as long as I can remember I looked upon Maikai as my father. I'd probably be the worst guy to put on this. You want somebody with some passion for this case. I know I wouldn't have my heart in it."

Reed looked impatiently at Dan. "You told me that was twenty years ago. Besides, didn't he boot your ass out when you were still in high school?"

Reed put down his coffee and walked over to Dan. "Do you know what this case'll do for your career? Your face will be on front pages all over the damn world. I'm handing you the prize of the century and you're telling me because the guy let you sleep under his roof for a few years, you're not going to want to be the one who nails his sorry ass. I don't get it."

"This career-move bullshit doesn't mean diddly to me; you know that, Brian. Especially if it's at the expense of Peter Maikai. When my parents were killed in that airplane crash on the Big Island, Maikai took me and my brother in. And we weren't even family. He was just my father's army buddy."

"Come on, Dan," Reed said. "We're not making all this up. If we have enough on Maikai, we're going to prosecute him. We're just doing our job. Nothing personal."

"Trust me on this," Dan said and rested his palms on Reed's desk. "I just can't do it."

"Well, who the hell is going to take this case if you don't? Who do we really have here with any high-profile felony experience?"

"Benson, for one," Dan said and held up one hand and grabbed its first finger with his other hand.

Reed shook his head. "Benson. That old fart has to leave the courtroom every fifteen minutes nowadays because his prostate is shot. Yeah, that'd be great. The whole world can hear him say, 'Excuse me, your honor, can we recess again so I can go take a leak?' "

"There's Devus."

"Gloria'd be okay but she's in the middle of that double homicide."

"Ikeda, then."

"Shit. Ikeda is useless these days. You know that. He's too busy hiring private dicks to follow his old lady around."

The two cops laughed at the reference to an assistant PA whose wife wasn't doing a very good job of keeping her affairs discreet.

"As far as I'm concerned, that leaves only two people with enough experience to handle this case: you and Cathy."

"Cathy's out," Dan said quickly. "She's got the same problem I have. No way she'd take a case that I had a personal conflict with."

Reed was silent for a moment. He walked back to his desk, swung around, and planted his hefty rear on the glass top. Behind him, the NEBRASKA pennant waved incongruously with the crossed bars of the Hawai'ian flag.

"I just want to know what the big hurry is all about," Dan said.

"What's the hurry?" Reed said loudly. "I'll tell you what the goddamn hurry is. Some maniac hacked the governor into little pieces a few days ago. Pulled his guts out with his hands and mutilated his face and genitals. His damn widow couldn't even view her husband's body because everyone was afraid she'd go wacky and they'd have to commit her." Reed was standing now and his voice had risen to a shout. "The people and the media from all over the country, all over the cocksucking world, in fact, have been waiting for us to tell them who killed the governor of fucking paradise! That's what all the hurry's about."

"You think they're on you now," Dan shouted back, leaning across the desk, his nose close to Reed's. "Wait'll Maikai's attorney gets all the key evidence thrown out because you let them pressure you into serving some bullshit warrant!" Dan was pointing out the window of Reed's office to the crowd of reporters that had staked out the front of the building.

"That's why I'm sending you out there with Iida and Kalama. To make sure nothing goes wrong."

Dan looked at Reed as if at a madman. "What are you talking

about? I can't get involved in this on an official basis. He brought me up, for chrissake!"

Reed stared at Dan awhile without speaking. Kalama shook his head in the corner. Then Reed calmed visibly and walked around his desk and took ahold of Dan's shoulder.

"Look, Dan, that's why I want you to go."

Dan stepped back and looked into the PA's face.

"I know you'll make sure Maikai gets a fair shake. And you're the best procedural man we have. I know you won't let anything slip by us. No little screwups that'll blow the case."

"If you've got a case."

"That's all we're trying to find out. If Maikai's innocent, fine, we'll back off. No harm done."

Reed was rubbing Dan's shoulder like a good dog's. Dan shook his head.

"Don't blow that smoke at me, Brian. This isn't for Maikai, or the people, or anybody else except you. The media wants a story. If they don't write about the suspect you've arrested, they're going to write about the suspect you *haven't* arrested. You want to keep them off your back, so you're giving them all you've got right now. I'll go out there for you but it's only because I want to make sure it's done right."

Reed reached over, pulled his jacket off the chairback, and went for the door. "That's all I wanted. In the meantime, I've got to keep those jackals off my back, so you can all do your jobs." He opened the door and looked back. "Now let's all get to work."

CHAPTER
SIX

Dan called to Kalama, who was crossing the street a block down from the courthouse. When Joe turned he trotted to catch up.

"Headed for the Gavel?" Dan asked, referring to the only decent bar within walking distance of the courthouse. After five, it was filled with lawyers, judges, clerks, bailiffs, and arresting officers trying to unwind after a day in court.

Joe backed through the heavy oak door with his shoulder and held it open for Dan. The dark, smoked-filled air enveloped them as they weaved through the tables. Except for a gaggle of reporters at the bar and a handful of HPD playing "hoops" over by the head, the place was empty. After eight, most of the attorneys usually went home or drifted back to their offices.

They ordered beer at the bar and took it to a high table in the back where they could catch a Wahine volleyball game on Channel Five. The University of Hawai'i women's team was always ranked in the top ten in the nation, and they always seemed to be on a local channel. Dan pushed back one of the heavy stools and leaned against the table.

Joe Kalama was as pure a Hawai'ian as you could find, except maybe for a couple of those direct descendants of King Kamehameha the Third with last names twenty letters long filled with vowels and apostrophes. Of course, all those *ali'i*-blooded *kanaka maoli* were tainted with some *haole* blood. A people who had almost no sexual strictures could not expect its blood to stay pure, especially when invading missionaries with their girdled emotions fell among them.

Kalama sat down next to Dan. The Hawai'ian's short legs didn't reach the metal footrest of the stool, still he looked eye-to-eye with Dan because his Polynesian build—heavy-haunched, heavy-bellied, neck and shoulders like a bear—lifted him.

"You going along with this Maikai warrant?" Dan asked.

Kalama took a long pull on his draft before he set it down loudly on the table. "I've got nothing to say about it, do I?"

"Why didn't you speak up when Reed was ramrodding it through?"

" 'Cause it ain't my goddamn place to tell Reed what to do. If I'm ordered to search his place, I'll search it."

Dan watched the TV as a girl nearly the height of the net slapped a ball down so hard into the court it bounced over the opponent's bench and into the stands.

"It isn't like you to back down when you think something's fishy."

"Fishy?" Kalama said and turned from the volleyball game to look at Dan. "What do you mean?"

"Come on. Reed's going after Maikai with both barrels and he's got almost nothing."

Joe set his beer down gently on the table and frowned at Dan.

"I can't be the one to make a fuss about this."

"Why not?"

"Because I'm Hawai'ian."

"That's exactly why I thought you'd be the one to back me. They're trying to use the sovereignty issue to show that Maikai would have a motive to kill Slaton. It's bullshit."

"Sure it's bullshit, but what am I going to do? I make a stink, he's just going to say I'm sticking up for Maikai because we're both *kanaka maoli.*"

The door to the men's room burst open and slammed against the wall behind them and Paul stumbled out, still fumbling with his zipper.

"Hey, if it ain't my old crew," he yelled and picked up a chair and slid it across the table from Dan and Joe. "Howzit, bras?"

"Good, man," Kalama lied.

"I wish the hell you guys would hurry up and arrest someone for croaking Slaton so these damn reporters will go back where they came from and I can drink in peace again."

"It looks like you're getting in plenty of drinking time," Dan said.

"Oh, crap," Paul said and looked at Joe. "My brother would make a great preacher, wouldn't he, Joe? Oral Carrier, we should call him, don't you think?"

Joe laughed and clapped Paul on the shoulder.

Dan slowly shook his head. Paul was drinking himself to death and Joe was acting like he was just a fraternity boy with a good liver out on a little beer bash.

"Tomorrow it'll be a seven months," Paul said.

"What's that?" Joe asked, confused.

Dan knew immediately what his brother meant.

"The accident was seven months ago tomorrow," Paul said and took a long drink.

The table fell silent. On the television the crowd cheered another Wahine point and the announcer frenetically described the smash on the replay.

"I guess that's why the doctor asked me to unplug him. I hear they give up after six months now. The insurance companies probably sent a doctor in to see if it was worth keeping Chris alive."

Paul was staring at something on the wall as he spoke.

"I doubt if that's what happened, Paul," Dan said and put his hand on his brother's shoulder.

Paul looked at Dan and sneered. Dan could see he was having trouble focusing on his face.

"Well, I don't doubt it for a second. Those bastards didn't give a damn about my kid. He was taking up bed space. That's all those bloodsuckers care about. How much revenue per bed. A kid hooked up to a machine ain't bringing in the bucks an open-heart patient would. Unplug him so we can keep those revenues up. That's what they were thinking."

Dan didn't say anything. Paul vacillated between blaming the doctors and blaming himself for letting the boy die, even though letting him go was surely the best, the most humane, thing to do. If

Paul wanted to rail on about doctors, it was better than putting the guilt on himself. The more Paul blamed himself, the more his alcohol consumption climbed.

Paul hung his head so his nose was inches from his half-empty glass. Teardrops started running into his glass and Dan rubbed his brother's shoulder. Kalama's face had fallen flat. It was always a shock to see how quickly Paul could go from backslapping horse-laughter to complete dejection where all he talked about was "blowing his useless brains out."

Paul raised his head and looked at his two closest friends. A pained grin broke across his face. "Ah, hell," he said and pointed at Dan and Joe's half-empty glasses. "You need another one?"

They both nodded and Paul kicked back his chair and headed for the bar.

Jerzy Epstein, a reporter from the *Honolulu Advertiser* who covered the legal scene, walked over to Dan and sat down on Paul's stool. Reporters often came into the Gavel to talk to the prosecutors and the defense attorneys about a case. Not so much to get a quote but to get an idea of when they should start to pay attention to a case. Everybody was paying attention to this case, however, and the crowd of media—reporters from every major newspaper in the country, all the big magazines like *Newsweek, Time,* and *People,* plus CNN and the networks—had created a logjam around the courthouse and the PA's office. Every morning it would be a fight for Dan to push his way in and out of the building. The Gavel was as yet undiscovered by the out-of-town press, but Dan was in no mood to talk to anyone, including Epstein. *Especially* Epstein.

"Got any suspects yet?" Epstein asked. He was a short, fat, curly-haired mess whom Dan had never seen in a clean shirt. Most of the time he wore faded T-shirts, usually celebrating a heavy metal rock concert back in the seventies.

Dan frowned and finished his beer. "Gimme a break here, would you, Jerzy? Reed gave you everything at the press conference today."

"That bluff job," Epstein said. He had on an old Aloha Week T-shirt with a faded bust of Kamehameha on the front. "Come on. You guys have something or you wouldn't be stonewalling everyone."

"We don't have crap. That's why you're not getting anything."

Epstein's old notebook was sticking out of his back pocket. He swirled his drink around in the glass a few times, thinking, then he took out the pad and slapped it idly on the table.

"Dan, I hate to push, but you owe me for the Crandall story. I held off on our ID of the dealers so you could arrest them without a struggle."

"So you want a freaking medal?"

"No, I just want you to treat the hometown press with a little courtesy. It's okay if you crap in the face of the Mainland guys. You'll never see them again. But we all have to work together here."

Paul came stumbling back to the table and placed the beers down in front of them. Then he pulled his stool out from under Epstein so the reporter fell on his rear on the floor, his drink cascading down on him.

"Jesus, what the hell?" Epstein said from the floor.

"Get the fuck out of here, Epstein, you maggot. They ain't got nothing for you. Can't you hear?"

"Ah, fuck off, Carrier. I'm doing my job."

"Well, go do it with the rest of your sewing circle," Paul said and sat down on his stool again.

Epstein got up and shouted at Dan, waving his empty drink at him.

"Okay, that means the rules are off. Anything goes now. Don't expect us to be there for you anymore. You better start coming up with some answers about who killed Slaton because the heat's on now."

"Fuck off, Epstein," Paul said.

"Yeah, beat it," Dan said and threw his hand at Jerzy. "When we get a suspect, you'll be the first to know."

The reporter stumbled back to his table and Paul turned back to Dan. "So who is your suspect? You still trying to nail Maikai?"

Joe's smile rose on his face, but he didn't answer.

"Oh, so it's Maikai, huh?" Paul said.

"It's nobody yet, wise ass," Dan shot back.

"Come on, don't give me that. The governor gets whiffed, you gotta be climbing up someone's ass." He looked Kalama over. "It is Maikai, isn't it?"

"Maybe we're looking at him," the cop said.

"Why?"

"Why?"

"Yeah, why?"

"Well," Joe said, "first of all, the scene he made at the rally. Second, we have two witnesses who overheard him say he was going to get Slaton just hours before he was killed. Then there's that damn rope hanging from his balcony."

"See," Paul said to Dan, "one plus one." Then he turned back to Kalama. "Sounds like a bunch of nothing to me."

"That's what I told them," Dan said. "Without something more concrete to connect him with the murder there's not enough for an arrest."

"That's what the search is for," Kalama said.

"What search?" Paul asked.

"The judge signed a warrant to search Maikai's place."

"Over on Maui?" Paul asked incredulously.

"That's where he lives," Kalama said.

Paul shook his head in disgust. "And you're going to let them?" he said to Dan.

"There's not a damn thing I can do about it," Dan said. He leaned back in his chair and let the overhead fan blow the sweat cool on his face.

"Well, I'll tell you what," Paul said. "There's something I can do about it."

"What do you mean by that?"

Paul didn't answer. He moved his fingers through his uncombed hair. "Michael know about this?" he asked.

"I don't know," Dan said.

"So you're just going to go barging in on the old man and roust him?"

Kalama slapped his fist against the table so the saltshaker leaped into the air.

"What the hell you trying to say? That we're persecuting Maikai? He's a suspect in a murder investigation. We've got a right to barge in if a judge says so. You don't give a suspect notice so he can have time to clean up."

Paul slammed his palm down next to the cop's.

"Well, you don't mind if I go along and watch, do you?" Paul asked. He was up on his feet, challenging Joe.

"Yeah, I do mind. This is police business. Don't stick your nose in."

Dan put his hand on Paul's shoulder. "Don't worry. I'm going along to make sure everything goes by the book."

"You hate his guts," Paul said.

"I don't hate his guts."

"Is that why you haven't spoken to him in almost twenty years?"

"I got over it."

Paul took Dan's hand by the wrist and pulled it off his shoulder.

"Sure you did, brother. That's why you've been sticking up for the old man while Reed is busy framing him."

"Hey, that's not fair, Paul," Dan said. "I'm the only one who's been defending the old man the whole time."

Paul looked at Kalama.

"He has," the Hawai'ian said.

"And how about you?" Paul said to Kalama. "What did you do, bra?"

"My job," the cop said angrily.

"Good. That's very good. Then I'll just be there to watch you do it."

"How are you going to do that?" Dan said. "The last plane to Maui left at eight-thirty."

"I got a boat, remember. If I leave now, I'll make it before daybreak."

Paul pushed back the stool and started to stumble toward the door. Dan went after his brother. He caught him by the bar and grabbed his arm, spinning him around.

"You aren't going anyplace in that tub, Paul. You're drunk."

"That's not your problem, is it?"

"Yes, it is my problem. That Moloka'i Channel is treacherous, especially at night in a tin can like the *Loa*. You'll kill yourself."

"Hey, I've paddled that channel in a fucking outrigger canoe, remember?" Paul said. By the way his eyes were focusing on Dan's ear, Dan knew his brother was in no condition to negotiate the open ocean alone.

"Yeah, with me and Joe at your side," Dan said.

Paul broke from Dan and pushed through the door of the bar, out onto Hotel Street. Dan trotted a couple of steps and walked with him.

"I can't let you do this, Paul."

"There's nothing you can do about it."

Paul turned around and faced his brother. His eyes locked on Dan's and, suddenly, it seemed as if he'd had nothing to drink all night.

"Look, Dan, you know Maikai. Well, maybe you used to know him. Maybe now you don't. I don't know. What I do know is I've been going to the Maikai place for years. And *I do* know him. He's liable to flip a coconut when he sees you birds raiding his ranch. You know how the Hawai'ians are about their lands, their precious *'āina.'* Shit, he's liable to pull out that machete of his and start charging. I just want to make sure nobody gets hurt. We owe him that much, don't we?" He hesitated a second and searched Dan's eyes for an answer. "Well, don't we?"

Dan didn't answer. Paul stepped off the curb and walked unsteadily across the street to a cab, near the lights of a mah-jongg parlor blinking next to a Korean bar. He opened the door of the cab, looked back at Dan, and stepped in, and the taxi drove off down the street in the direction of the marina where the *Loa* was tied up.

CHAPTER
SEVEN

Dan, Kalama and six others—an assortment of state police, HPD officers, homicide detectives, and lab technicians—flew to Maui the next morning. Kahului Airport had changed, of course, since Dan was a kid growing up on Maui. He remembered the old days when they drove to the airport to pick up friends of Maikai's who'd flown into Maui on single-engine six-seaters from Honolulu. The plane would taxi a few feet from the terminal and the pilot would hand each passenger his bag directly from the belly and they'd walk to where a weeping relative waited with an armload of pikake leis.

But you had to expect an airport in a place like Maui to change. Fortunately, the Hāna Highway hadn't. Sure, Paia was invaded by outdated hippies whose ideas of aloha was to snicker smugly at tourists. But past the wooden walkways of that one-block-long town, the highway turned quickly into a narrow jungle path, overrun by vines a hundred feet high and ferns that slapped at the HPD's windshields as they drove by.

Kalama drove while Dan navigated from the passenger's seat. Two HPD were crammed in the back of the tiny rental car they'd picked up at the airport. As Kalama negotiated the road, potted and unpaved in places, Dan rocked and jostled with the car. When they stopped in front of a one-lane bridge to let another car pass in the opposite direction, Dan held Kalama's arm a moment.

"Wait," he said. And suddenly the sound of the tradewinds rustling the leaves was so loud that it seemed at first a waterfall. Then Dan pointed through a stand of ohi'a and Kalama could see that there was a waterfall, the surface of the pool below spotted with huge yellow leaves.

Kalama drove on, accelerating on straightaways to make up time. He took a hairpin too fast and the back wheels of the Toyota slid against the wet clay embankment and bounced back onto the road.

"You still remember where the old place is?" he asked Dan.

"Oh, I think so."

"How long's it been?"

"Eighteen, nineteen years."

They rode in silence for the next ten miles. Kalama pressed to get there, braking at the turns then accelerating for the brief straightaways that lasted, at most, fifty yards. Then came another turn that sometimes took the car in the complete opposite direction, then back again heading south to Hāna. They drove on past the high-sculpted cliffs that resembled six-hundred-foot claws, then around another curve to the plunge of the turquoise sea and the white frost of waves breaking on the reef half a mile out.

There was something grating in Dan's stomach, a hard, cutting feeling like walking across new lava rock. Dan knew what the feeling was. It was Lily. He hadn't seen her since the day Maikai threw him out eighteen years before. All that time had gone by and the only thing he'd ever heard—mostly from Michael, who saw her once or twice a year until he'd taken over the legal business of the ranch last year—was that Lily despised him. Dan tried to think about Cathy as Kalama made his way around hairpin after hairpin. He kept bringing his mind back to Cathy in bed, those crystal eyes of hers that lit the bedroom at night. He forgot about the fact that their relationship was headed for a bridge he didn't think they'd ever be able to cross together. He was using Cathy to ward off the emotions he was feeling for Lily, feelings he'd tried to avoid for years. Long ago he had made up his mind to forget about Lily, forget about his guilt and get on with his life. But now he had to see her again and he was praying their meeting wouldn't be as hard on him as he dreaded it would be.

After an hour the road suddenly broke out into an open stretch of green, cultivated land that spread below them for a mile down to the ocean. Behind them were the hills that climbed gradually into the north face of Haleakalā Crater.

"See where the fields turn from gray green to the bright almost yellow green?" Dan said, pointing down below them.

"Yeah," Kalama said, nodding.

"That's where Maikai's place starts. The bright stuff is the taro."

"He still growing taro?"

"Nothing but. Gotta be Hawai'ian or Maikai thinks it's useless. Pineapple. That's a white man's crop," Dan said pointing at the gray-green fields owned by Maui Land and Pineapple Company that bordered Maikai's patches.

"How far to the gate?"

"Another mile at least. This is the biggest taro farm in the world right now."

The morning sun had begun to heat the black roof of the car as they drove past hill after hill of the broad-leafed plants.

"Dirkson still behind us?" Dan asked.

"Couple of curves back, I think," Kalama said, checking the rearview for the other car filled with detectives.

"Okay. There's a road up here that leads to the entrance. Pull over and we'll let them catch up before we go in."

Kalama slowed at the curve and then rolled the car up to a huge stone wall with an iron gate that blocked the road. Across the top in carved Hawai'ian koa was a sign:

KAPU!
MAIKAI RANCH
NO TRESPASSING
(Pig-Hunting by Permission Only)

Dan couldn't quite believe the size of this edifice in the middle of the jungle.

"What the hell is this?" Dan asked Kalama.

"I heard Michael put it up."

"Really?" Dan shook his head. Ever since his stint on Wall Street, Michael always seemed to have to have the biggest of everything.

Behind the main gate was a guardhouse manned by a uniformed security cop. He stepped out of the booth when the cop car pulled up and walked to the huge gate.

When Dirkson pulled in behind them, Dan opened the rusting door of the car. It creaked loudly as he stepped out. He shut the door and stuck his head back into the car. "I'll go announce us."

He reached inside and grabbed his briefcase from the floor, set it on top of the hood, and snapped it open. He pulled out some papers and snapped the briefcase shut again. Then he walked toward the guard, who was still standing at the gate staring curiously at the cars. He could tell by the four bulky men inside that this was not the usual carload of tourists who had made a wrong turn.

"Morning," Dan said to the guard, a smallish man.

"This is private property," said the man in a flat voice.

"My name is Dan Carrier. I'm from the prosecuting attorney's office. I have a warrant to search the Maikai ranch," he said and held the papers out in front of him so the guard could see them. He took them from Dan and looked them over for a minute, flipping the pages back and forth like someone who couldn't read, then handed them back.

"I'll have to call up to my boss to see if it's okay." He started back for the guardhouse.

"No," Dan shouted at him, "stay away from that phone. This is a search warrant issued by the Superior Court. If you don't comply with it immediately I'm fully authorized to tear this gate down and take you into custody for obstructing justice."

The guard's expression changed in an instant.

"Now open the gate and stay away from the phone."

The guard looked up at the guardhouse once, then back at Dan, and then at the car where Kalama had emerged. He started fumbling with his keys.

"All right, all right," he mumbled.

Dirkson pulled his car beside Kalama's and Dan called back to them. "Tell Terry to stay with this guy while we drive up to the main house, then hoof it up there on foot. It's only about a half a mile."

A bulky Hawai'ian man got out of Dirkson's car and walked toward Dan. He was wearing a T-shirt, O.P. shorts, and hiking boots. When he got up to the guard, he took him by the elbow and led him into the guardhouse.

The two police cars bumped along the dirt road through the canopy of banana trees. The road rose steadily to a plateau from where the sea came into view. Set before them was an old wooden house beneath two enormous banyan trees that took up a quarter of an acre apiece.

When Kalama drove closer, past the nearest banyan, Dan could see Lily standing on the old wooden lānai. She was almost exactly as she had been when he'd last seen her: tall and thin with broad swimmer's shoulders and blue black hair to her waist. Except that the last time he'd seen her she was pregnant with his child and Maikai was driving away with her to have the child aborted. "When we get back," Maikai had shouted angrily, "I don't want to see your *haole* ass around here no more."

For years after that all Dan knew about Lily was what he could find out from Michael—that Maikai had sent her to the Mainland to get her away from that "*haole* asshole." It was seven or eight more years before Dan first heard from Paul that Lily was back in Maui running the ranch.

But now that all seemed to Dan like something that had happened in another lifetime to another person. Dan was the most respected criminal prosecutor in the state, and Lily was one of the most powerful businesswomen in the Pacific. It was her shrewd marketing of taro that had turned the Maikai ranch from a struggling plot of poorly managed land into a multimillion-dollar phenomenon. Dan had seen her photo in places like the *Pacific Business News, Aloha* magazine and the business section of the local papers as those publications tracked the emergence of the crop that Lily Maikai had almost single-handedly tied to the growth of the Hawai'ian people's burgeoning pride.

Kalama swung the car around and parked parallel to the house. The dust from the red clay billowed toward Lily. She didn't move at all. Just her eyes followed Dan as he got out of the car. Dan gave a half-smile and a wave to her, but she didn't respond. Her arms remained folded tightly across her stomach, her eyes pinned on the intruder who had barged in uninvited.

Michael was running across the yard from behind the house when Dan turned around.

"What the hell is this?" Michael screamed.

"Michael, we have a warrant to search your father's house and the rest of the ranch."

"And this is how you serve it? Riding in here like a goddamn posse or something? Why didn't you tell me yesterday at the beach that you were coming? That's the least you could have done."

"It's a search warrant, Michael. There's no professional courtesy when it comes to this. Judge Yamanoha signed it and Reed sent me to make sure it's run fairly and by the book."

"I'm not talking about professional courtesy. Just a little common decency and respect for a friend."

Michael snatched the document from Dan's outstretched hand. He was shaking his head, making a show of his disgust.

"At least give me a minute to tell my father before you go charging in there."

"All right," Dan said and leaned back against the car. "But only a minute. Then I've got to start the search no matter how anybody feels about it." When he made the last remark, he looked up to see how Lily was taking all this, but she had vanished.

Michael slapped the warrant in his palm and hopped up the steps of the house. As Michael pulled open the screen door, Dan could see a swirl of Lily's white dress going up the staircase inside. At that moment Dan would have preferred to be almost anywhere else. Serving a warrant to arrest their father wasn't the way he wanted to return to the home they'd all once shared.

A moment later he heard Peter Maikai shouting and that was when he waved for Kalama and the rest of them to mount the stairs. When they reached the door, Peter Maikai was rushing down the staircase.

"Get the hell out of my house, you *haole* bastard," Maikai said. "I brought you up when you had nothing and this is how you repay me?"

Dan opened the screen door and stepped inside.

"Get out!" Maikai shouted.

Dan could see the war club dangling at the old man's side. Dan stepped forward and yelled to Michael, who was coming down the stairs behind his father.

"You better inform your father that this is official police business. If he interferes with this search, he will be arrested for obstructing justice, interfering with the service of a search warrant, and assault on an officer of the court."

Maikai stopped at the foot of the stairs and Michael put his hands on his father's shoulder. Dan motioned Kalama forward and the cop moved warily toward the old man.

"So you're taking the *haole*'s money now, huh, Joseph *Kahikina*?" Maikai said to Kalama. "Taking his orders like a good little *moke*?"

"Nothin' 'bout you, Uncle," the cop said, his eyes down. Although he wasn't related to Maikai, Kalama used the term *uncle* as a sign of respect. "We just try see if we can find who killed the governor."

"So you start here, huh?" Maikai accused, his eyes narrowing on the cowed policeman. Kalama was a Hawai'ian first, then a cop.

Kalama shrugged and sidestepped past Maikai. Two other cops followed him up the stairs.

"Come on, Father," Michael said. "We'll go outside while they snoop around."

Then Michael turned to Dan. "Make sure they don't bust the place up."

"Don't worry."

Michael nodded.

Lily came down the stairs, her eyes never touching Dan's. She walked past without a word and took her father around the shoulders, then she and her brother led him outside. Dan noticed for the first time how frail the old man really was. The club he held in his hand stretched his arm out as if he were holding a bowling ball. Dan was certain this old man could not have slid down that rope and then overpowered a man as big as Slaton even if he had surprised him. And to kill the girl too? It just didn't feel right to Dan no matter what Reed insisted.

"Let's get this damn thing over with as soon as possible," Dan shouted to Kalama, who was about to push through the door at the top of the stairs. It was the room that Paul and he had first shared when they had come to live with Maikai.

"The old man's room is the last one down that hall," Dan said to Kalama, pointing to a door at the far end of the balcony. "Try that one first. I'll start looking downstairs."

Dan looked out the screen door and saw Lily with her arm around her father, walking toward the stream that ran through the property. She was taller than her father, her white-sleeved arm held at a protecting angle. Michael was coming back up the steps.

"Dan," he said as soon as he'd opened the screen door, "this isn't your style. What kind of evidence do you have to support a search?"

"It's in the affidavit," Dan said and waved to the three cops who were still with him.

"Rich, you and . . . what's your name?" Dan asked, pointing at a uniformed state cop Dan had never met before.

"Howard Tacub, sir."

"Take Tacub and search the north side of the house. There's a long patio out back and a storage area behind that. Check it thoroughly."

The two cops nodded and disappeared through a door.

"Manning, you take the kitchen," Dan said to the remaining cop. "I'll look around in here."

When they were alone, Michael tapped the copy of the warrant he'd been given. "Yamanoha rubber-stamped this, I see."

Dan shrugged and began to go through a koa chest of drawers against the near wall. It was deep brown wood with ornate carvings of ancient warriors in full robes and headdresses. Each of them carried a war club like the one Maikai had waved at the governor. On top was a scattering of pictures, mostly of Lily when she was about the age when they had fallen in love. One of them showed Lily sitting on the poster bed in her room; the mosquito netting that he'd crawled under many nights was pinned open. The sun was coming in the window behind her and Dan could see the mammoth mango tree in bloom. That meant the picture had been taken in the spring, so they were probably making love to each other on that bed about the time that photo was snapped. Maybe his smell was still in the sheets as she sat there smiling at the photographer. Maybe she was still thinking about how wonderful it was when they were in each other's arms.

Dan put down the picture. He reminded himself how he had gotten over Lily long ago, how their lives had been separated, and how distant that time he had spent with her now seemed.

"I know this wasn't you behind this search, Dan," Michael said. "It had to be Reed. But what the hell are you doing here? You should have no part in this investigation. Was that Reed's idea too?"

"Look, Michael," Dan said, turning to his old friend. "Maybe it seems a little awkward, me being here. But there's no legal or ethical conflict involved, if that's what you mean. Besides, they don't throw cases out when a PA is sympathetic to the accused, only if he's got an ax."

"Who said you're sympathetic? You and my father are bitter enemies," Michael said. "At least, that's the way a jury will see it."

"I don't think I'd try to play that tune in court, Michael. It's ancient history."

"According to whom?"

"According to everyone. Maikai, me, Lily," he said and nodded out to where she stood with her father. "It's over. I'm here because I'm the head prosecuting attorney and I want justice done. My presence here is to ensure that your father gets a fair shake, not the opposite."

Michael's eyes narrowed and he walked up close to Dan. "That's bullshit and you know it. The prosecution is never on the defendant's side at any stage of an investigation. You're here to gather evidence against my father, not to see that his rights are safeguarded. And as to your feelings about the Maikais, it's strictly bad news as far as I'm concerned. I didn't know just how bitter you still were until I saw that look on your face when you served my father just now. You've been waiting a long time to stuff it up the old man's ass, haven't you? Reed might be the one pushing this, but you're enjoying the hell out of it, too."

Dan slammed the drawer on the chest and walked toward a nightstand by the TV. "Look, Michael, if you're trying to get me pissed off so I'll say something I shouldn't or do something I shouldn't, save your breath. I've been doing this for years. I can serve this warrant in my sleep and not violate one of your father's rights. So why don't you get us both a cup of Kona and then let me do my job?"

"You'd like that, wouldn't you?" Michael said, shaking his head. "Just sit here and have a cup of coffee together while you try to find something to convict my father."

Michael kicked aside a mango leaf the cops had dragged into

the house on their shoes. Michael's eyes followed a trail of red-clay footprints up the stairs. When the cops in Hawai'i broke down a door, they never bothered to leave their shoes on the porch, Hawai'ian-style, even though at home their old ladies would bash them with a bamboo switch if they dared to wear shoes in their own homes. Oddly, that was the one thing almost all Hawai'ians protested about when the police did a search of their homes. Not that they'd been roughed up, or that the cops had left the place in a shambles, or that some heirloom that had been in the family since the days of Lili'uokalani had been wrecked. But that when they broke down the door, the cops forgot to leave their shoes on the porch. It was the ultimate sign of disrespect.

"Bottom line here," Michael said, "is you shouldn't be here. It's not *'ohana.*"

"Bottom line is I am here legally and there's nothing you or I can do about it. You've got every right to be here as Maikai's attorney, but don't get in the way. And right now you're in the way," he said, pushed lightly on Michael's chest, and stepped around him.

"Oh, yeah, and by the way," Dan added, "I didn't know they were teaching *'ohana* at Harvard Law these days." It was one of Michael's sore spots and Dan knew it. Peter Maikai was constantly questioning his son's trustworthiness—his Hawai'ian loyalty—now that he'd been educated by the *haole.*

Joe Kalama came down the stairs carrying a plastic bag well out in front of him, as if he got too close to it, he would catch whatever was in it.

"We found a knife," he said to Dan.

"Let's see," Dan said and took the bag and looked through the cloudy plastic at the six-inch blade within. He recognized the knife immediately.

"We found it in a chest buried in the back of a closet in Maikai's room."

"I doubt this is the murder weapon," Dan said after he'd inspected it for a moment.

Kalama seemed mystified by the certainty in Dan's voice.

"It's a tribal knife given to all the Maikai sons when they achieved manhood," Dan explained. "Michael, Paul, and I all received one, carved and blessed by Uncle Charlie Yates. I've got one exactly like it at home."

"Well, maybe not exactly like it," Kalama said with an ironic tone. "This one has blood caked on the handle. And we found this with it."

Joe held up a Hawai'ian-print shirt like the one Maikai was wearing at the beach the day Slaton was murdered. It had several large brown stains that could have been blood.

"All right, Joe," Dan said. "Let's take it with us. We'll have the lab analyze both. I want you to make sure everything we take is meticulously itemized and then photographed in the location it was found. Got it?"

Kalama shook his head and started up the stairs again with the plastic bag and the stained shirt.

"And call Reed and tell him we've got something for the lab," Dan yelled after Kalama.

"What the hell are you up to?" Michael yelled at Dan. He was chest-to-chest with him now. "You know that knife's not going to lead to anything! That's the knife my father uses to clean wild pig."

"Don't get excited. The more we check things out in the lab that turn out negative, the better off your father is. If I go over everything that could be suspicious, it'll ensure that Reed won't want to send us back in to tear the place apart again."

"Don't try to sell me that bullshit. You're not here to protect anything except Reed's fat ass. Any little chance you can get to hang my father, you're going to take it," Michael spit at Dan. He turned and slammed his way through the screen door.

Dan watched Michael as he stomped down to the stream where Lily sat on the bank with her father under the banyan.

It was an hour later when the helicopter arrived. It hovered loudly over the house, then raised a storm of dust and leaves as it slowly lowered to the ground. Three lab techs and another HPD detective got off the helicopter as soon as it landed.

"Treacher, what the hell are you doing here?" Dan asked the detective as he came toward him. He was a tall, emaciated, ungainly tangle of limbs and horn-rimmed glasses who took the porch in one step.

"Orders from Reed," Treacher said, handing Dan a paper. "He wants the murder weapon flown out immediately and the whole place roped off while we search. He said to tear the place apart."

"What the hell for? We've got it covered. What the hell can you guys add?"

"Hey, don't get steamed at me," Treacher said. "Reed says you should call him anyway. Take it up with him. All I know is we've got to get it done in two hours. He's called a press conference for this afternoon to announce a break in the case and he wants everything we have."

"Oh, shit!" Dan groaned and slapped the paper Treacher had given him down on the side of the porch railing. "What does that maniac think he's up to? We don't have shit. All we found was a knife Maikai uses to clean pig."

Treacher shrugged and pushed by Dan. "Where's the knife?"

"Never mind about the goddamned knife. I'll take it back myself," Dan said.

"Reed says you're supposed to stay here."

"Screw Reed. Somebody's got to set him straight. Before he announces to the world that he's got the killer, we have to make sure we've got something besides a pig sticker here."

Dan turned and went down the steps toward the police chopper. But Lily stormed up to him before he got there.

"You never forget, do you?" she said.

"I don't know what you mean," Dan said.

She looked as lovely as he remembered, even if her bold green eyes vibrated with a hatred he'd never seen directed at him before.

"You've been waiting eighteen years to get your revenge. Now that he's old and weak, you figure he can't defend himself. You can do whatever you want."

"Lily . . ." he began to say, but she wouldn't let him.

"You want to destroy him, don't you?" she said, poking a long, unpainted fingernail at him. Dan noticed that she wore a gold ring on her right hand, nothing on her left. "Well, we're not going to let you, Dan. The Maikais don't walk out on their family like you did."

Dan was hoping to avoid this pain because that was all it was to him. Seeing Lily Maikai brought him nothing but pain now. But her last remark triggered his anger. He had a few axes himself he'd been harboring.

"I think you're forgetting your father threw me out of here."

Dan saw the anger in her eyes grow more intense. Lily wasn't a young, infatuated girl anymore. She was a grown woman now who had built a tiny fringe taro business into a multimillion-dollar concern. It was obvious that she'd stared down more than a few tough mongrels in her day. He realized she saw him now as nothing more than an ambitious PA trying to railroad her father on a politically motivated charge. The fact that, in her mind, he'd taken the first convenient opportunity to disappear as soon as he'd discovered he'd gotten her pregnant only added to her disdain.

"I know exactly where you're coming from, Dan," she said, and her hair flew off her shoulders as she shook her head at him. "Don't bother playing any games with me. Get your business done and get off our land."

Whatever he'd felt for her vanished with her last words. "Nothing would please me more," he said and turned toward the helicopter.

"You know," she said to him as he began to walk away. "It's not just the Maikais you're taking on. It's all the Hawai'ian people. And if you learned anything when you lived here, it was that once the Hawai'ian people decide to fight, they never back off."

Dan kept walking. He knew she was right about that. But he was hoping that someday they'd realize—Peter, Michael, Lily, and every other Hawai'ian—that he wasn't the enemy, even if he did reside in the enemy camp.

CHAPTER
EIGHT

Dan was in the front passenger seat of the helicopter with the incriminating parcel between his feet. As he looked down, he could see through the plastic bag the ornate handle of the knife that was so familiar to him. Buried somewhere in a box of old bric-a-brac from his youth, with an Eagle Scout patch from when he camped in Haleakalā and an old outrigger trophy and photos, curled and scratched, from his hitchhiking trip through the Northwest, was a knife identical to the one Reed hoped would put Peter Maikai behind bars for life.

The day Maikai had given Dan that knife was also the first time he had made love to Lily. He was sixteen, a man in the eyes of the Hawai'ian elders. Lily had walked with him to an old burial cave to cut the knife on a sacred rock. They could hear the roar of Waioli Stream, swollen by heavy rains, rushing through the gorge below. It was Lily who pointed out the rainbow arcing from Haleakalā to the sea. It was Lily who unbuttoned her blouse and let the hot sun warm her chest so that when he first reached for her breasts her nipples felt hot to his touch. It was Lily whose blanket they lay on and Lily who guided him gently into her. It was Lily who sighed in his ear, her breath hot against his cheek.

Once they spotted Koko Head from out in the Moloka'i Channel, it took only a few minutes to round Black Point and fly across

Waikīkī, its beaches peppered with a sea of black-haired Japanese, to the Iolani Palace downtown. Across from the Palace was the building that housed the PA's offices. On the top step, Brian Reed was at a podium crammed with a dozen or more microphones. KGMB, CNN, KHNL, and the local public TV station were all rolling and the newspaper photogs were snapping flash after flash. Beside Reed was the Lieutenant Governor Jayson Tanaka, and on Reed's right was Cathy in a dark blue linen suit tied tight to her neck. Under one arm she held a legal-sized manila envelope that was bursting with paperwork.

Dan turned to Treacher, who was in the back with another lab tech.

"What the hell is he doing?"

Treacher craned his long neck over the seat and looked down at the crowd of people below. "Press conference," he said.

"I know it's a goddamn press conference. But what the hell does he think he's doing?"

"What he does best," Treacher moaned. "Bullshit the media."

"About what, though? We don't have jack yet. Does he really think this pig sticker is some kind of case breaker?"

Reed looked up at the helicopter coming in over the trees. It fishtailed momentarily, looking for a clear spot, and finally hovered down onto the lawn of the Palace.

"Here they are now," Reed said with his head to the side so the TV cameramen would know not to roll yet. Then he addressed the crowd again for the record.

"My head prosecutor, Mr. Carrier, who you all know has been handling the investigation into this matter, has just now returned from Maui with physical evidence which we believe links a suspect to the assassination."

Jerzy Epstein interrupted. "Can you give us a name?"

"Not at this time. But I can tell you we expect to make an arrest as early as this evening. This is the kind of crime that traumatizes a whole state, that destroys the very fabric of a society, and we do not intend to let the guilty person go free for a second longer than we have to."

"What kind of physical evidence are we talking about?" another reporter asked.

"We hope to have all that in an hour or two."

"Do you have an eyewitness?"

"That's yet to be determined," Reed said.

Three more questions came at Reed, one on top of the other. He held up his hands and smiled. "Please, ladies and gentlemen, just give us a bit more time and I think we'll be able to answer everyone's questions," he said and dropped his hands. He looked at Cathy and she stepped up to the podium.

Dan trotted through the gate of the Palace grounds as Cathy took center stage in the biggest murder case in the country since RFK was shot in L.A. He looked up to see Reed put his arm around her.

"Ladies and gentlemen, I do have one more announcement. Ms. Cathy Darnold has been selected as head prosecutor for this case and from now on she will keep you informed. That's all we have for now. As soon as we make an arrest, we will call another conference."

"What the hell?" Dan said to himself. He and Cathy had been together the night before and she hadn't mentioned that Reed was assigning the case to her. All they talked about was that they were going to get married soon, and maybe have kids. They'd agreed that Cathy would have her career, but there were more important things in life than getting to the top of the heap. But as Dan watched her proudly stand beside Reed, it was obvious that a family was always going to be a secondary concern to her.

"Mr. Reed, before you go . . ." It was Epstein again. He was wearing a bright red shirt the way he always did at press conferences so he would stand out. "I understand that you are now your party's selection to succeed Mr. Slaton as governor. Can you confirm that?"

"Please, Mr. Epstein," Reed said, turning back to the microphones. "Let's put our governor to rest before we start talking about replacing him. Mr. Tanaka is running our state now and the only thing on my mind is to make certain that Jim Slaton's murderer is brought to a swift and sure justice.'"

He spun quickly, took Cathy by the arm, walked down the steps, and hurried back into the building. The crowd of media rushed after them, blocking off the entrance. Dan was right behind them, but it was impossible to get to them through the crowd. It was a good thing, because if he'd caught up to Reed he would have embarrassed both of them with CNN and KHNL and the rest still videoing for a national audience.

Dan hustled to the side of the building and went down the utility steps by the trash bins. Then he took a service elevator up to the PA's floor. The halls were dark and empty except for one security guard, who stood heavily against the wall by the water cooler, looking down at the press conference that was breaking up. The rest of the staff was either at the conference or out to lunch.

Reed had his arm on Cathy's shoulder and they were smiling triumphantly to each other when the elevator door opened. When they saw Dan, saw how angry he was, both their smiles fell flat. Cathy's eyes narrowed and Reed's hand dropped from her shoulder.

"What the hell do you two think you're up to?" Dan said.

Reed stopped in the elevator door a moment with his hand on the rubber safety stop. Cathy stepped forward, brushed past Dan, and headed for the office.

"Not out here, Dan," she said coldly.

He could tell by the set of her jaw, by the way her eyes assessed him, by the no-nonsense hairdo and the straight black pumps, that she meant business today, that she had calculated everything, that she had sat down calmly and rationally with Reed and decided in cold blood that she was going to take this case no matter what anybody, including Dan, thought about it. She opened the door to the office and walked in without looking back.

Reed let go of the door and a couple of assistants and two secretaries behind him shuffled off, holding the door one after another as they exited. The door nearly sank its teeth into the briefcase of the last one off.

Reed stepped up to Dan, who was still looking at the door Cathy had just disappeared behind. The PA put his hand on Dan's shoulder. Dan shrugged it away.

"We don't have shit yet," Dan said. "You know that. Much less a suspect."

"I don't know anything."

"Right."

Reed frowned. "Except I've got a hungry pack of wolves out there that need feeding."

"Yeah, but you can't tell them we've got a suspect unless we do. They find out you're lying and they'll make you look like a damn moron from here to Saudi Arabia."

"Who said we don't have a suspect?" Reed said. "Of course, we have a suspect."

Dan spun around and confronted Reed face-to-face.

"You're not talking about Maikai, I hope. Because we have absolutely nothing on him."

"We have a murder weapon."

"Good God, I don't believe this. We found a boning knife with hog's blood on it. That's all. If we arrest everyone at that rally who's got a knife for *kalua* pig, we'll have to arrest most of the local population."

Reed put his arm back around Dan's shoulder and Dan let it stay this time. They began to walk slowly toward the office again. The assistants and secretaries had gone ahead through the door and Dan and Reed were alone in the hallway. Standing there, Dan suddenly realized that Reed had set it up this way. He'd seen the helicopter land. He knew Dan would be spitting mad. When Reed was on the elevator, he'd probably told them all to get scarce and he'd handle Carrier.

"Dan, I know how close you are to the Maikai family. That's why I've taken you off the case," Reed said gently.

"I was never on the case. Remember?"

Reed just smiled patiently. "All right, you were never on the case. Whatever. I'm just saying you're too close to the family to be objective. I know that. If you were in my shoes, you'd see that knife only confirms what we've suspected all along—that Maikai killed Jim."

Dan broke away again from the ooze of ameliorating honey Reed was trying to softball him with.

"Well, before you sentence him to life, can we at least wait for the lab tests to come back?" Dan said.

"Oh, absolutely," Reed said as if it were some kind of concession to Dan's feelings. "I'll have Cathy wait to charge him until Dickenson comes back from the lab." He pulled up the sleeve on his jacket and looked at his watch. "I won't schedule another press conference before three. That's plenty of time."

"Are you out of your mind?" Dan shouted.

"No, you are," Reed shouted back. "If you can't see that a lot of shit points to Peter Maikai, you need a vacation. And you keep this up and I'm going to see that you get one."

"That's fine with me. Let me out of this nuthouse."

Reed rolled his eyes and sighed like he was dealing with a terrible two-year-old. He shouldered through the door and Dan came in behind him. Cathy was sitting on the edge of Reed's desk when they walked in.

"I'll tell you one thing, though," Dan said, pointing at Cathy. "You aren't taking this case."

Cathy stood and, turning her back to him, tossed a file on the desk. "That's not your decision to make," she said, facing the windows.

"The hell it isn't. We've been talking about setting a wedding date. I have a hell of a lot to say about it. In fact, it shouldn't even be a question."

Reed stepped between them and raised a hand to calm Cathy. Then he turned to Dan.

"Now, Dan," he said, "you know yourself that Cathy's the only one who can handle this case. Who's left? You can't take it. What choice do I have? Besides she's ready for a case like this."

Dan could see Cathy's eyes light up with the flattery.

"Why don't you take it, Brian?" Dan said. "You're still an attorney, aren't you?"

Reed's expression turned vicious. Dan had gone for the exposed nerve and had hit it. Dan had always gotten the tough cases in the past over Reed, and Reed resented it. Now that he was PA though, Reed had too much to risk to put himself under the scrutiny of a high-profile case like the murder of a governor. If he blew this case, he'd look like an incompetent in front of the whole world.

"I'm too busy keeping the dogs at bay. That's your job, Dan. You're the hotshot prosecutor. Except you're too chickenshit to go after this *moke*. This crap about Maikai and your parents is just a smoke screen. I don't get it. He threw your ass out because you were white. Why the hell are you sticking up for him?"

Dan looked quickly at Cathy. She was the only one from whom Reed could have gotten those personal details. She looked at him and shrugged, but there wasn't much of an apology in her eyes.

Then it came to Dan suddenly where the whole thing stood.

"You two cooked this whole thing up together, didn't you? That little show out front just now, hell, that was nothing but a campaign speech, wasn't it? That was the kickoff to your gubernatorial race. And what's that make you?" he said, turning to Cathy. "Are you his new press secretary?"

"Quit embarrassing yourself," Cathy said without emotion. "I thought you'd be the last one to let emotional things cloud your perspective. Peter Maikai is the prime suspect in the murder of the governor of Hawai'i. If you won't do your job and prosecute him, I will."

A cloud passed by, darkening the room, and though somehow her blond hair actually seemed more brilliant in the shadows, Cathy's green eyes went as gray as the sea before a storm.

"Believe me," Dan said, "the only people who are going to be embarrassed are you two when the blood on that knife comes back positive as the main course at Maikai's last *lū'au.*"

Dan turned and opened the door calmly and let it close behind him.

CHAPTER
NINE

Dan settled into a bar stool at the Gavel. It was still very early in the day, but he'd quickly tossed down two scotches and had his hands around a third when Epstein slid onto the stool next to him. Dan looked once at Epstein then went back to his drink.

"I'm not in a very good mood, Jerzy," was all he said while he looked up at the television that hung above the bar. *SportsCenter* was showing the highlights of the evening's hockey from the East Coast. Five hours ahead of Hawai'i in time zones, the Islander-Canuck game had just ended. The problem was that Dan, raised in Hawai'i, didn't give a damn about hockey.

"What do you think about Cathy prosecuting the case?"

Epstein had gone right for Dan's throat and they both knew it. It was obvious that he was still mad at the way he'd been treated the last time he was in here with Dan and Paul.

Dan slowly turned on the stool and set his glass on the bar.

"Jerzy, I'm getting a pretty good steam up here. I've only had three so far but I guess that's just your good fortune, huh?"

"Yeah?"

"Yeah, because if I'd had three more I'd tear your head off for asking that question."

"Kind of touchy about this case, aren't you? That because Maikai just about raised you?"

"Where'd you get that from?"

"Jesus, Carrier. I ain't deaf, dumb, and blind. I'm a reporter. I ask questions, people give me answers."

Dan slapped his glass down hard on the bar this time. But Epstein didn't flinch.

"I want to know where you got it from," Dan insisted. "Or you can kiss off any cooperation from me ever again. I'll freeze you out. You'll be useless to that rag you call a newspaper."

Epstein eyed Dan for a long time. He was wearing an old pair of cotton-topped flaps with HAWAI'I stitched in the material. He slid both feet to the ground as if to prepare for a quick getaway.

"Reed," he said.

"I thought so," Dan said. Then he slapped Epstein's shoulder. "Relax. You can't help it if you make a living fronting for barf bags like Brian."

"Can I quote you on that, Counselor?" Epstein said and smiled.

"Sure. I could use a vacation from this goddamn circus."

He tipped back his head and downed number four, nodded at the bartender, and in a minute number five was in front of him. He drank half of it in one gulp, ice and all. Epstein watched him do it and eased off. He was a reporter, but he wasn't sadistic. Dan was all right. He had helped Epstein plenty of times and never stiffed him when Epstein needed something and Dan could give it to him.

"It surprised me a little when Cathy was assigned this case."

Dan threw down the last of his drink. "Oh, I can beat that, Jerzy. I was surprised when she took it."

Dan slid off the stool and waved at the bartender. "Put it on Reed's tab, would you, Keoki?"

The bartender nodded and Dan patted Epstein's shoulder. "Off the record, Jerzy?"

Epstein nodded. "Sure."

"I think you better stick around. This case is going to get very interesting. I can just feel it. So far the governor has been murdered. His biggest detractor is about to be charged with the crime. And the PA who's charging him without a decent shred of evidence is next in line to take Slaton's place. And, as for me, the lovely little cherry on top of this piece of cake is that my fiancée is prosecuting."

Dan pushed the stool out of the way and it teetered like a drunk on one leg and then fell with a loud bang on the concrete floor. By then Dan was halfway out the door.

The late afternoon sun angled through the slanted roof of the Hotel Blaisdell across the street. By the golden tint already painted on the clouds in the south, it was going to be a good sunset, maybe a great one. Mount Pinatubo's eruption in the Philippines had added a spectacular hue to the sunsets in the last year, and the Honolulu skyline turned a deep pink almost nightly.

Dan slid behind the wheel of his pickup. He still surfed, and had never given up the rack and the rusted flatbed in back. He pulled out of the lot onto King Street and drove toward Waikīkī. He needed to talk to someone about Cathy. If he ran into her in this mood, he could kiss their relationship aloha. In fact, the way he felt now, betrayed, playing second fiddle to her ambition, he didn't know, frankly, if he gave a damn about her anymore. Except he'd see her, those eyes of hers, and he'd be all knotted up trying to figure out why.

He drove hard down McCully and swung onto the H-1 for no reason. He took the truck up to seventy and let her rip in the fast lane, the wind whipping dust and papers around the back.

It wasn't really fair to blame Cathy, though, was it? Reed was calling the shots. If he'd ordered her to take the case, she had to take it. She couldn't refuse. Not that she'd want to, of course, since any attorney would kill for a case like this. What the hell did she care if it made him look like an idiot?

He had to talk to someone and there was only one person close enough to him for that: Paul.

He turned off the freeway at the stadium, turned under the overpass, and got back on the freeway heading for Honolulu. He drove for twenty minutes until he got to Beretania then turned off and weaved through the late afternoon traffic past Ala Moana Center to the Luahine, the old fleabag across the street from the Ilikai Hotel. He found a parking place in the alley behind the building and pulled in next to the trash Dumpsters. Riveted to the brick wall next to the metal bins was a sign:

NO PARKING
VIOLATORS WILL BE TOWED AWAY
AT OWNER'S EXPENSE
(by order of the HPD)

Dan knew it didn't mean anything. HPD didn't bother with these alleys. They were too busy patrolling Kalakaua and Kuhio, the two main drags through Waikīkī that, since the influx of Japanese tourists, was a mayhem of double- and triple-parking.

Dan took the graffiti-filled elevator up to Paul's floor. The inside of it smelled like a New York cab. The hallway wasn't any better. The stand-up ashtrays were dented from drunks kicking them; the sand had long ago been emptied from them because the maids were tired of cleaning up the mess strewn across the floors every morning.

Dan knocked at Paul's door—the last one in the hall, almost directly above where his car was parked. He could see the bloodstain on the carpet from when two Japanese tourists, a husband and a wife on honeymoon who dressed in matching red aloha shirts, had been gutted, their cameras, their wallets, their jewelry, their lives, stripped from them.

Dan knocked a second time and then reached into his pocket and pulled out his key ring. Paul had given him a key "in case I croak." Dan let himself in with it.

It was dark in the room, even though the lānai shade was half open. The faucet was slowly dribbling water into its stainless-steel basin. Dan didn't bother to turn it off as he went by into the dark near the bed. The faucet always ran like that and no one had come to fix it and Paul didn't care. On the bed was a lump Dan figured was his brother sleeping it off again.

"Paul, hey, bra," he whispered, "it's Dan."

He poked the bundle. Then sat on the bed and grabbed with both hands and laughed out loud at the two pillows he'd mistaken for his brother.

He switched on the bedside lamp and took in the devastation around him. If Paul didn't ask for maid service, the management knocked off fifty bucks a week. Every possible level surface held an empty beer can or glass with the residue of some kind of liquor in it. In one, a bloated cigarette butt waded in some dark liquid. Half the queen-sized bed and all the chairs were piled with Paul's clothes. There were shirts and pants draped over the chairbacks.

Dan knew the bachelor's idea of grooming. He himself had had a few chairs hung with shirts he wanted to keep "ironed." That was before he met Cathy, of course. Now he hung his clothes in the closet: the shirts on one side, the pants on the other. He'd been civilized. There was no doubt about it. But now that Paul's wife was dead, his brother had lost all need for civilizing.

Dan looked at the red digital numbers of the clock radio on the table. It read 6:32. The sun had set, and a pink effusion settled into the room. He stepped to the window and looked down at his car roof and the wall of the parking garage across the narrow alleyway. In this dungeon not a breath of trades ever penetrated, so by midafternoon the place was like a bathroom after someone has taken a long, hot shower. He could have been in New York, Chicago, or Dallas on an early summer day when the temperature had not yet hit a hundred but the humidity was starting to build.

Dan switched on the ceiling fan above the bed and the old paddler creaked slowly into a wobbling, uneven motion, whipping finally with a loud slap at the air. He went to the half-height refrigerator and looked inside, but the light was burned out. He had to switch on the light in the bathroom across from it to see what was inside. He reached in and came out with an already opened beer. He drained it into the sink and rinsed out a glass from the table and dumped three ice cubes in it. He spotted a bottle of McGregor scotch sitting next to a carton of curdled milk. *The Toast of Scotland,* the label read. On the cap was the price: $3.99. He poured it into the glass until the ice cubes rose to the rim.

Dan threw the clothes from a chair onto the bed and sat down. Paul would be back soon. He had gotten in the habit lately of coming home early, so he could get some sleep for their morning workouts. He'd still be drunk but at least he'd be in bed early.

Dan sipped the scotch and winced at the metallic burn as it went down. He just needed to talk to someone. Paul, if he wasn't too drunk, would know what to tell him. Maybe that's why Dan had taken it so personally when Paul had gone downhill. He worried about his brother, sure, but he'd lost something else. When Maikai had thrown him out, he had moved into Paul's place and his brother had put him through school. But more than that even, they were best friends. When Lily had been taken from him, after Maikai had shipped her off to the Mainland to go to school and he was trying to get over her, Paul was always there to talk things through.

Dan finished the drink and filled it a second time. By then the last of the sunset had gone and he sat alone in his brother's dreary room and wondered how Paul had made it through this horrible year. Maybe Dan had been selfish the way he'd badgered Paul to stop drinking. If he really cared, maybe he'd do something positive, get him some real help instead of just pouring a lot of guilt on him.

Then he remembered. Paul probably wasn't coming back here. He had either sailed off to Maui as he'd threatened or he'd taken Dan's advice and, in all likelihood, he was still at the marina, sitting on his boat drinking, watching the sunset. He liked to sit on the deck with his feet on the bait tank with a case of beer and watch the sun dissolve into the Pacific.

Dan gulped down the rest of the drink and stumbled over the edge of the bed as he made his way to the door. He hadn't realized just how much he'd had to drink until he tried to stick the key in the ignition and it took three or four stabs. If he was caught driving in this condition, it would cost him his job, but he was suddenly desperate to find his brother. He pulled out of the alley and across Ala Moana to the Ilikai, then made a left and drove along the marina to the slip where Paul tied his boat. He got out and walked down the unsteady planks to the dock and finally saw that Paul's boat wasn't there. When he swung around, Dorie Gottschank was standing next to him. Dorie was the old salt who kept a drunken eye on the marina.

Dorie mumbled something. His teeth were gone and he never wore his dentures, so it was hard to understand him.

"What was that?" Dan asked.

"He ain't here," the old man said. He wore a chewed-up windbreaker with the sleeves cut off and the buttons long missing.

"I can see that. Where'd he go?"

Dorie spat on the planks between them and spread out the saliva with his deck shoes.

"Maui is what he said."

"Maui?" Dan said. "Then he left last night after all."

The old guy scratched his unshaven face; the gray stubble beneath his fingers sounded like sandpaper.

"Yep," he said and spat a big brown wad of juice into the water. "Grab that hose, would ya, Dan? It's hooked on the piling."

"Sure," Dan said and knocked it free with his foot. He tried to steer the old man back to Paul. "What do you mean? He never got back? Was he drunk when he left?"

"When isn't he?"

"Right." Dan sighed. Getting anything from Dorie but the day's fish count was impossible. The salt air rots more than wood planks. Dan was sure of that.

A wave of anxiety passed quickly over Dan. If Paul had gone to Maui, why hadn't he been at the Maikai ranch for the search this morning like he said he was going to be? Dan had thought at the time that maybe Paul had just come to his senses and hadn't bothered. Or he'd seen what a job it was going to be to sail to Maui and forgot about it halfway there. He could be anywhere now. Moloka'i, Lahaina, Lāna'i, even Kaho'olawe. In Paul's present state of mind, Dan didn't like the thought of his brother out in the middle of the Pacific alone.

Dan walked back to the car. He'd decided it was about time to confront Cathy. He drove directly to her condo in Manoa. As he pulled into the parking lot under the building, he saw lights on in her apartment. He knew she was home now because she was a stickler for turning off unnecessary lights. It was one of the things they squabbled about. She would follow behind him from bathroom to kitchen to bedroom, turning off lights. He knew she was right, of course. Like everything else from food to gasoline to electricity, everything was expensive in Hawai'i.

He knew what he was going to say to her. He'd been rehearsing it, shouting it at the windshield as he drove.

He let himself in with his key and threw his briefcase loudly on the kitchen counter so she'd know he was there. He could hear the computer keyboard stop clicking and the chair being pushed back.

"That you, Dan?" she asked from the second bedroom, the one she used for an office and guest room. He knew she was still angry at him because she always called him honey when they were alone. "That you, honey?" is what she usually asked.

She stuck her head out of the door. "Where've you been?" she said when she saw him turn to her. "Never mind. I can see you've been at the Gavel. And, of course, Paul was there too?"

"No, he wasn't," he said. "And by the way, I'm not drunk, if that's what you mean."

"Don't be so damn touchy, Dan. Why don't you just come out and say what you want to so we can get on with it. I took the case. You're pissed off because Peter Maikai looked after you when you were a kid. So what?"

"What do you mean, so what?" Dan shouted. He told himself he wasn't going to shout.

"You haven't seen him in fifteen, twenty years. Okay, if you have trouble with that, if you've got some kind of conflict, fine. But that's nothing to me."

Dan looked her up and down. She was wearing the same made-for-TV suit that she had on that afternoon at the press conference. Only she'd taken off the jacket and the heels. The matching earrings, gold with blue trim, were sitting on the dresser in the Lalique ring dish Dan had given her for her birthday.

"That's exactly the point, isn't it, Cathy? The whole thing's nothing to you. The fact that my feelings are involved, that's nothing to you. That we practically live together, that we're going to get married, that we want to have kids someday, that's nothing to you. The only thing that matters is that goddamn case."

He took a step toward her and rested his knuckles on the counter. "How long ago was it that you and Brian decided behind my back that you were going to take the case?"

She walked past him into the living room to the bar. As she went by she said, "What's the difference?" Then she added, "You want another drink?"

He shook his head and walked into the back bedroom to urinate. All those drinks had finally overloaded his bladder. The walls were swimming, the lights were overly bright as he stood at the toilet. Yeah, he had a pretty good buzz going, all right. When he went back into the living room, she was sitting on the couch armed with a half-drunk scotch.

"You know what really scares me about this?" he said. "You really can't see why I'm so upset."

"Frankly, I can't, Dan," she said and raked her fingers through her hair up the back of her neck. "I have no real conflict and I've been handed the opportunity to prosecute the killer of the governor. Christ, did you see who was at that press conference today? NBC, ABC, CBS, CNN, *The New York Times.* Court TV is negotiating right now to televise. And just because you lived at this guy's house for a few years you want me to give it up. I don't get it."

Dan sipped the scotch she'd poured him and set it on the end table next to the chair he liked.

"Whose idea was it for you to prosecute?"

She eyed him suspiciously. "What do you mean?"

"Did Reed suggest it to you?"

"I don't know. I guess."

"Or did you request the case? Did you go to Reed when I was in Maui and tell him you'd take the case? Maybe get down on your knees and beg for it?"

She looked silently into her drink. Her chin-length hair had fallen in front of her eyes.

"That's what I thought," he said. "You knew the way I felt, but you didn't care. It was a case of your career or me, and your career won once again, didn't it?"

She finally raised her eyes. He could see she wasn't going to back down.

"It's always black or white with you, Dan," she said. "That's your big problem. That's why Slaton picked Reed over you. It's black or white. A man's guilty, you go all the way with it even though a plea would put him behind bars. All right, so maybe it's not for as long, but he's in there."

She slammed down her drink and turned to the window. "Black or white," she said. "It's driving me nuts. If I don't agree with you, it's a problem. If I don't want kids now, it's because Cathy is obsessed with her career. It can't be anything else. Black or white."

Dan pushed himself up from the couch. "Maybe you're right,"

he said. "Maybe I just can't compromise all my beliefs as easily as you seem to be able to do."

"Jesus!" she said and got up.

Dan put his drink on the bar. "I think we need a little break."

"What do you mean?" she said.

"I'm going to spend a few nights at my place so we can think things over."

"Why, because I'm taking this case and you don't like it?"

"It's more than that, Cathy. You know that."

He grabbed the door handle, pulled it open, and began to walk out.

"Oh, before you go, Dan, there's something I should tell you. . . ."

He swung back around to her.

"The test came back from the blood sample on Maikai's knife," she said. "It's AB."

He stood with his hand on the doorknob as she walked toward him slowly. His knees felt a little shaky.

"Same as Slaton's?" he asked.

"Yes," she said, but there was no cruelty in the answer. It was all matter-of-fact, the way a clerk would read a guilty verdict in open court.

"He also said a few things," Cathy went on. "But Michael shut him up pretty quickly."

"Like what?" he asked.

"He admitted it was his knife. But claimed he hadn't touched it in years."

"What about the blood?"

She shook her head. "He said he didn't know where it came from."

Dan stepped out the door and she held it open.

"When are you going to arrest him?" he asked.

"Kalama's got him right now. They're holding him at Wailuku Substation. The winds are too heavy for the chopper to go up, so they're going to fly him over from Maui first thing tomorrow morning."

"How about the arraignment?"

"Soon as possible. Tomorrow probably."

Dan nodded. "Just be careful, Cathy. I know this case looks like a big fat career-maker to you. But I don't trust Reed. He's greedy. If he gets too greedy and screws this case up, I'll tell you right now he's not going to take the fall. All the blame's going to fall right in your lap."

"Don't worry about me," she said. "I can handle Reed."

He looked at her for a moment—the power dress and hairdo, the upthrust chin, ready to take on anything or anyone. Then he noticed her feet. Without the power heels, he thought, she looked suddenly like a little girl playing dress-up, unaware of a lot of things that were about to happen to her.

CHAPTER
TEN

Dan stood in the shower the next morning with the hot water cascading over the top of his head and into his face. The first sun had just broken through the early rain clouds that awaken the Manoa Valley each morning. He let the water pour across his face until it began to turn tepid then he grabbed the towel off the rack and started to dry off. His head was blurry from the alcohol and the early hour, but he wanted to get to the office before the rush of reporters who would gather outside waiting for the helicopter that would bring Peter Maikai in handcuffs to Honolulu to be arraigned for the murder of James M. Slaton, the governor of Hawai'i.

The drive into town was usually the best time in the morning for Dan. He savored the fresh, tropical mornings pungent with pikake and plumeria, with the salt air and the stark odor of the red dirt hillsides.

This morning was no different. In fact, his ballooning head craved the fresh air. It cleared the webs of spent alcohol dreams from his mind and gave him the feeling that everything was going to be all right. That was what Hawai'i always did for him. It made him feel lucky to be alive.

The parking lot of the building that housed the PA's office was still wet from the morning showers. He pulled the pickup into his usual spot and grabbed his briefcase off the floor. The halls of the building were dark and still at this hour. He had to switch on lights as he entered rooms. He went into the office kitchen and stirred himself a cup of instant coffee, dumped in a couple of teaspoons of nondairy creamer, and made his way back to his office.

As chief deputy PA one of Dan's responsibilities was the dispersal of cases to the other PAs. With Cathy now devoting all of her time to the Slaton case, Dan was obliged to distribute her workload to the other attorneys. By the time he had decided which of her cases was best suited to which attorney, it was nine a.m., his secretary had cranked up her computer, and the helicopter from Maui with Peter Maikai aboard was about to land in the lot next to the First District Court building.

Dan switched on the television on the table in the corner of his office. On Saturdays and Sundays when he was alone in his office preparing cases, he liked to watch the football games with the sound muted. Now, from the quiet of his office, he wanted to see the whole circus, with Reed as ringmaster, that was about to unfold below him.

The crowd of media had been assembling for an hour. It was one of Reed's tricks. He'd inform the media that a press conference was scheduled for at least an hour before he intended to go waltzing out there so "by the time I arrive," he liked to brag, "they're ready to tear each other apart to get the best shot."

They were ready, all right. What could be more dramatic than the prime suspect in the murder of the governor flying in through an early morning shower?

The helicopter thwacked above the building so that it sounded as if it were about to land on the roof. Dan saw its tail rotate around the trees circling the back lawn and come down slowly to a landing in the parking lot. The cameramen wedged closer. They pushed against the ring of the HPD Reed had positioned in a dramatic phalanx leading to the door of "777," which was what the First District Court was called because its address was 777 Punchbowl Street.

Dan looked at the TV as the camera zoomed into the cab of the chopper. Maikai was in the back, wedged between Kalama and Iida. When he slipped out of the helicopter his hands were cuffed together in front of him and the two cops each had ahold of one of the Hawai'ian's elbows.

Out the window Dan could see only the tops of their three heads as they made their way quickly between the hedges and kept coming toward the cameras. The TV caught a quick frontal shot of Maikai. He was dressed in a pair of old flaps, shorts that seemed massively large for him, and a tank top with a number on it. They had obviously caught him by surprise last night. This wasn't a man who had surrendered to authorities through the auspices of his lawyer. He'd been rousted, most likely from his sleep. Where the hell was Michael while all this was going on? Hadn't Reed at least given him the courtesy of surrendering his father into custody?

Then it struck him. That was not what Reed wanted at all. This was Reed's show. He wanted to bring Maikai in at nine a.m. for maximum exposure on the afternoon and evening news shows on the Mainland. Bring him in looking like a criminal, like a desperate man.

Well, he'd succeeded at that anyway. But there was something else. Dan was again struck by how drawn and frail the old Hawai'ian appeared. It was one thing to see him at his ranch when he was rested and secure. But here, after a night in jail, after a bumpy helicopter ride and a night of questioning and accusations, being torn from his family, being taken in a driving rain into this humiliation, Maikai looked different. He looked worn, so worn, in fact, that Dan thought he belonged in a hospital, not a jail.

The crowd of detectives surrounding Maikai pushed through the melee of cameras and reporters, their microphones and pads waving at the defendant as he was being escorted past them. The detectives pushed cameras out of the way as they shouldered a wedge through the crowd. As they rushed up the steps of the court building and then through the glass doors, the mob of media collapsed behind them to an ever-crescendoing snapping of cameras.

At the same time Reed and Cathy emerged from the side door and mounted a makeshift podium set up to one side. As Maikai disappeared down the darkened hallway, the media spotted the PA and his assistant and rushed toward them. The lightning pop of flash cameras and the boring heat of the kliegs drilled the faces of the two people who would carry the fight for the people against the man accused of killing their leader.

"Ladies and gentlemen," Reed began. "I have just a few statements to make."

Out of his window Dan could see Reed behind the microphones. But his voice was coming from the TV behind Dan. Reed was wearing a silver jacket over an aloha shirt. His hair was pumped up even higher than usual, the gray hidden behind the blond highlights he had professionally weaved into his hair. On his right shoulder Cathy stood grim-faced.

Reed looked down at a paper in his hand with some notes as if he were referring to them. He wasn't. He liked to go with the feeling of the crowd whenever he spoke.

"Today the Honolulu Police Department under my direction has placed Peter Kameaho'iho'i'ea Maikai under arrest for the murder of James M. Slaton, the late governor of the state of Hawai'i. Mr. Maikai was placed in custody last night at his ranch outside Hāna, Maui, by Lieutenant Glen Iida and Sergeant Joseph Kalama of HPD Homicide Division. We are planning to arraign the suspect sometime later today. Ms. Darnold," he said, placing his hand on Cathy's shoulder as she stepped forward, "as I stated before, will be handling the prosecution of the case. All of your questions should be directed to her."

Epstein was up front, shoulder-to-shoulder with all the network reporters. "What led you to arrest Mr. Maikai?" he quickly asked before anyone really knew Reed had opened up the floor to questions.

Cathy looked at Reed and he leaned over and said a word or two to her. Then she answered.

"A search warrant for Mr. Maikai's residence was obtained and signed by Judge Kaz Yamanoha. That warrant was executed yesterday and from evidence obtained during the search we felt we had enough to arrest Mr. Maikai, which we subsequently did."

Dan Rather, the CBS anchor, cleared his throat and the whole place froze, including Reed and Cathy, who looked down reverentially to the network anchorman as if their newborn was about to utter its first word.

"What evidence did you find?"

Reed put his hand on Cathy's sleeve before she could answer.

"Well, Mr. Rather," Reed said obsequiously, "I'm afraid we are just not able to reveal those facts at this time. But as soon as we can we will give you every detail at the first possible moment."

Epstein's mouth fell open at Reed's tone. If it was Epstein who'd asked the question, Reed would have probably blown him off with a perfunctory, "You know I can't answer that. Next question."

But since Rather could make Reed famous and that was something Reed wanted very badly, his answer came out almost as an apology. In fact, Epstein knew that if Reed could have found some way around it without blowing the case, he would have invited Rather out to Nick's Fishmarket for dinner and laid Maikai out on a platter for him.

"I'm afraid that's all we can give you now, ladies and gentlemen," Reed went on. "As soon as we know exactly when Mr. Maikai will be arraigned, you'll be notified. Thank you." And he took Cathy by the arm once again and they marched off the platform together and through the glass doors where Maikai had disappeared only moments before.

Dan went to the copier room to duplicate a motion. After ten minutes he heard Reed and Cathy's voices outside the door. They had taken a car the three blocks to PA headquarters, then had walked up the back way. Reed was lecturing her right outside the door where Dan stood with a fist full of papers, the machine whirring in front of him.

"There isn't going to be any deals for this guy. No offers. We've got this son of a bitch dead. We're going all the way with this one." Dan heard Reed snap off a laugh and there was silence for a moment.

"I'm going to make you a great big celebrity. All you've got to do is let me handle the media," he told her.

"I thought you said that I'd be fielding all the questions from now on."

Dan could detect disappointment in her voice.

"Ah, that was just a smoke screen. I want them to start thinking of you as being in charge. But," he said, and Dan could hear a rustle of clothing as if Reed had put his arm around her there in that lonely corner of the hallway, "those jackals can tear your hide off if you don't know what you're doing. Let me handle the media. You handle the case. Believe me, that'll keep us both up to our eyes in alligators. All right?"

There was silence during which Dan figured Cathy was nodding in agreement. She was so damn eager to climb the ladder she couldn't see that Reed was using her. The cameras would be focused on him whenever there were any around. He was going to position himself for maximum exposure. If they were able to nail up a victory in this case, he'd still be there taking all the applause, telling Rather, telling Jennings, telling Brokaw, telling CNN, *Time, 60 Minutes,* telling anyone who could forward his career what a brilliant PA he was. Cathy would still be a step behind him off his right shoulder and no one would even notice her. Unless, that is, the case went sour. Then Reed would disappear and Cathy would be alone in front of those microphones to answer all those embarrassing questions.

Dan walked back to his office and when he got there Cathy was just coming in the front door.

"Did you hear the press conference?" she asked Dan, looking at the television sitting on his table.

"I heard."

"What did you think?" she asked and sat on the edge of his desk.

"I think you better be careful," he said.

"We are being careful."

"Who's representing Maikai?"

"Michael Maikai," she said with an implied "of course."

"Where was he?"

"I don't know, frankly. He wasn't at the ranch when Kalama made the arrest. My guess is he's waiting for the arraignment. What's the difference? He can't accompany him during the booking anyway."

Dan sat down in his chair and swiveled around to the open window. The clouds were beginning to break up out over the ocean even though it was still raining hard there.

"Look, Dan, we've got a knife with blood residue that matches Slaton. Plus, the cut pattern and blade type is identical. It's hidden in a chest wrapped in a shirt with more blood on it. Couple that with his widely known hatred for Slaton and the rope hanging from his lānai, and I think we've got more than enough."

Dan swung slowly back around to her. "Oh, I don't doubt that. I just have some serious doubts whether he did it."

"Such as?" she said impatiently. She'd had enough of Dan's qualms about prosecuting Maikai.

"He's too old and too weak to take on a man of Slaton's physical strength."

"Oh, come on. Maikai could give you a run for your money. You know those paddlers. They've got incredible upper bodies. Even the old ones."

"That's true," Dan admitted. Maikai had continued to paddle into his sixties. "But Michael has told me for some time that his father has a serious heart condition that would preclude any severe strain."

"I heard that bluff, too," she snapped off. "I also saw our heart patient in action waving that club at Slaton at the beach five days ago. I'm not Christian Barnard, but his ticker seemed all right to me. Don't you think this is all just a bunch of defense-lawyer posturing? Michael's trying it out on us to see how it's going to fly."

Dan frowned. It was obvious she had her mind set. "All right, Cathy. I can see you're going ahead with this. But be careful. That's all I'm saying."

She slid off the desk. "Duly noted," she said and smiled. "Are you going to be at the arraignment?"

"Wouldn't miss it," he said as she went out the door. When the door was shut he said, "It should be a great photo op." And hurled his pen at the door.

CHAPTER
ELEVEN

A few hours later, Reed, Cathy, and Dan drove over to "777." The crowd of reporters parted for them as they made their way down the hall of the court building to Superior Court 2. Questions were being shouted at them, but Reed kept pushing Cathy forward. He'd told her just to brush them off with "no comment" and keep walking. Reed would handle them after the arraignment was over.

When Dan entered the courtroom, the first thing he saw was Michael bending over the rail talking to Lily, who was seated in the front row of the spectators' gallery. She was in a white sleeveless cotton dress and her black, full hair fell over her shoulders and down her back. Michael said something as Dan walked down the aisle and Lily looked over her shoulder at him. It wasn't the same look of contempt she had given him at the ranch, but a distant, disinterested one, as if Dan were a display she was considering at a store. She had obviously long ago gotten over him, had lost the sparkle that lit her eyes whenever they met.

Michael straightened as Dan approached and stepped in front of him as Dan swung back the gate and entered the attorney area.

"Dan?" he asked. "I wanted to know if you could do something about your office's request for no bail."

Dan stepped back slightly from Michael. Dan didn't understand why Michael was defending this case in the first place. It had been years since Michael had taken a murder case. He had long since settled into a private corporate practice and only handled a criminal case if one of his corporate clients found himself in a spot of trouble. In the last year he had cut back even on his corporate practice so he could help Lily run the Maikai ranch. That meant he was involved in Honolulu law circles even less than before. If Maikai wanted the best defense attorney to defend him in a homicide case, Michael was certainly not the man. But, of course, Dan also realized if Maikai was planning on trying this case in the streets, and by the size and noise of the demonstrations blocking Punchbowl Street, that was exactly what he was planning, then maybe Michael *was* the best attorney for the job. A Hawai'ian father and his Hawai'ian son being railroaded once again by the *haole* power structure. The Hawai'ian history books were filled with it. Like when the *haoles* who stole their land planted pineapple where there used to be taro and breadfruit, then brought in Japanese and Chinese laborers to tend Hawai'ian land. The Hawai'ian people had been driven off their own land and onto the welfare rolls just like the native Indians on the Mainland. Only in Hawai'i they hadn't even bothered to give them reservation lands, the lands that had been promised the Hawai'ian people by the United States Congress and that people like Peter Maikai had fought for their whole lives.

Dan glanced at Cathy and Reed, then back at Michael and lowered his voice.

"Michael, this is not my case. You must know that. I intentionally removed myself from it to avoid being forced to make just this kind of decision. The only one who can alter the motion for no bail is Reed. Ask him about it."

Michael shook his head sadly. "I thought I'd come to a friend first."

"I can't do anything for you, Michael," he said and began to turn, but Michael still had a firm hold on his arm.

"He's sick," Michael said.

"I know that too."

"No, you don't," Michael said, and there was a sadness in his voice that stopped Dan.

"How sick is he?"

"The doctor told me forty percent of his heart is dead. They don't think he's going to last long. He was okay on the ranch for a while. You know, maybe getting out for a rally here and there was all right. But you've got to know that a murder trial will kill him."

Dan looked at the clock then back at Michael. He didn't know what to say.

"I honestly don't know why they're so eager to press this thing," Michael said. "He's not a threat anymore."

"They have quite a lot of physical evidence."

Michael pulled him closer. "How do you know it wasn't planted?"

"I was there. Remember?"

Michael ignored him. "Talk to Reed for me, would you? He respects you."

Dan laughed a little louder than he'd wanted, but the noise of the crowded gallery muffled the sound. "He's got a very strange way of showing respect."

"Then talk to Cathy. You could make her see this is nothing more than a persecution."

"To tell you the truth, I don't think I can make either one of them see much of anything. This whole thing"—he waved his hand around the room at the commotion, the reporters, the crowd inside the court and out—"has blinded them both. I have absolutely no say in any of this. It's Reed and Cathy's show and they're not listening to me."

Dan broke loose and took a chair behind the prosecution table. He put his briefcase on the floor beside the chair and handed Cathy a file. She reached back to take it and smiled at him.

Ronson, the court bailiff, came through the side door of the court, the one that led to lockup. Following him were two jailers, then Maikai flanked by two more jailers.

Maikai was in a blue jail house jumpsuit and he was handcuffed in front and wore iron leg restraints that made him shuffle as he walked. His head was bowed and his long, gray hair fell down the sides of his face. When he lifted his head, Dan could see the sunken eyes, dark and tired. He looked as though he would collapse if the bailiffs let go of his arms.

Lily tried to get to her father, but Ronson stepped forward and restrained her from touching Maikai. Michael stood and led her back to her seat in the first row and she bent her head down and began to cry. It was the same way Dan had last seen her being driven away from the ranch by her father, her head down in the passenger seat, pregnant with their baby, weeping.

As soon as the jailers sat Maikai down next to Michael, Ronson went through the chamber door. A moment later Judge Garrett Shimada rushed into the courtroom. He was a short, half-Japanese, half-Portuguese local. He'd been a high school football star at Farrington, played at the UH and went to USC law school, then came home to Wai'anae to live in the same neighborhood he'd grown up in. Shimada had a quick laugh and an easy smile and he liked to joke with the attorneys during trials. But this was a day he was not looking forward to. Peter Maikai represented for many locals a sentiment that had been brewing for a hundred years. Every time Shimada drove through Waikīkī he remembered the days when he was a young boy who surfed the beaches that were crowded now with tourists, when no traffic clogged Dillingham Boulevard, when Kapio'lani Park was a playground of banyan and fields—not the home of the Kodak Hula Show.

Shimada climbed the steps of the judge's stand reluctantly and sat down in his chair, his face grim.

"Mr. Maikai, are you and your client ready to proceed?" he said to Michael without expression as if oblivious to the importance of this proceeding.

"My client is ready to be arraigned and if you would allow me, I will be requesting my client be allowed bail pending the conclusion of this matter."

"Fine, but one thing at a time," Shimada said and looked down at his case file. "This is case number F342768, *The People of the State of Hawai'i versus Peter Maikai.* He is being charged with two counts of seven-oh-seven dash seven-oh-one of the penal code, murder in the first degree. Is your client ready to enter a plea?"

"Yes, Your Honor," Michael said.

"Please rise, Mr. Maikai," the judge said. "Now, to the charge of two counts of first degree murder, how do you plead?"

Peter Maikai, standing next to his son, looked up at the judge and ignored the question.

"People like Governor Slaton," he began, "have gotten rich off of us for too long. It is time for all the people of *Hawai'i nei* to stand up for—" Maikai yelled as Michael grabbed his arm and tried to control him. Shimada cut him off.

"Mr. Maikai, I don't remember asking you about your political views. If you continue to spout them, I will be forced to make sure that every time you are in my courtroom you will sit behind that little glass booth," said Shimada as he pointed at a glass-enclosed room at the opposite end of the courtroom from the jury box. "You will not use my courtroom as your soapbox, do you understand, sir?"

Maikai didn't respond, and Michael said something to his father, then looked up at the judge. "He does, Your Honor. If it please the court, we are ready to proceed."

Shimada nodded and went on. "How do you plead, Mr. Maikai, to the two counts of murder?"

Maikai was looking down at the table. The judge patiently awaited his response. Maikai lifted his head and looked directly at Reed. "Not guilty," he said.

The judge looked from Cathy to Michael. "Have you agreed on a preliminary hearing date?"

"Yes, Your Honor," Cathy spoke up. "February fifth I believe would be a good day for both of us."

"Is that all right with you?" the judge asked Michael.

"Yes, that's fine, Your Honor. Now can I be heard on bail?"

"In due time, Counsel," Shimada said tersely. "Mr. Maikai, you are ordered to return on February fifth, 1995. Is that understood?"

"Yes," he said reluctantly.

"Now, Counsel, what do you have to say about bail?" Shimada asked.

Michael stepped behind his father. "Your Honor, we would request reasonable bail be placed on my client. He is seventy years old and has a very serious heart condition. The court is aware that my client is well known throughout the state. He was born and raised on Maui as were several generations before him. He is not a threat to flee the jurisdiction, and I feel that in this situation a reasonable bail is warranted."

"Yes, I am well aware of Mr. Maikai's reputation," the judge began, but then he was interrupted by Cathy.

"Your Honor, the state opposes that request, and I would like to be heard before you rule," she said. By the look on Shimada's face, he wasn't happy with her.

"Counsel," the judge growled, "I will be the one to decide if I want to hear from the People, not you."

The judge turned his attention from Cathy and looked at Michael. "Counselor, this is not an ordinary murder we are dealing with in this courtroom today. The governor of our state has been brutally murdered. This court must be absolutely certain that the accused stands trial for that crime. Therefore, I am denying your request for bail at this time. This case is adjourned until February fifth." And Shimada clicked the gavel lightly on the block and climbed down off the stand.

Michael Maikai rose as the judge left the courtroom, and he reached down and helped his father up by the arm. Ronson and another bailiff surrounded the defendant's table. They took the old man by the elbows and began leading him toward the side door to lockup. As they passed in front of Dan, who had walked over to talk to Cathy, Maikai reached over with his cuffed hands and took Dan's arm.

"I'm sorry, Dan," he said. "I'm sorry for everything." He began to weep and the jailers pressed in close to him and lifted him so his feet were barely brushing the floor.

"Wait," Dan said to them.

Joe Kalama, who stood behind Dan, stepped up. "Let him go a second," he said. "I'll take responsibility."

Ronson shrugged and nodded to the other jailer and they let go of the old man. Joe took Maikai by the arm and sat him down in the clerk's vacant chair. Dan sat next to him.

"What is it, Peter?" Dan asked as Lily walked up.

"I have to talk to you," Maikai said and turned and looked at Lily. Then back at Dan. "I have to talk to both of you. I need to explain."

"There will be plenty of time for that, Peter," Dan reassured him.

"Don't blame her for what happened in the past. It was all my fault."

He thought he knew what this was all about. Maikai was getting old and he wanted to set some things straight. But still it was a

shock to Dan. The last person he ever thought would ask his forgiveness was Peter Maikai.

"I don't blame her for anything," Dan said. "It's been a lot of
years. I've done a lot of growing up. Maybe what you did was the
best thing after all."

"I was wrong," he said emphatically. "I stole that baby from the
two of you because of my own fear. I didn't know what to . . ."
He broke off, sobbing, and Michael, who had finally fought his way
through the mob to where they were, pulled Dan away and put his
arm around Maikai.

"Father, look, this is not doing us any good." Then he turned angrily to Dan. "This is really a cheap trick, Carrier. You can see he's
not in his right mind. Whatever he's said to you, I'll get thrown out."

"Relax, Michael," Dan said. "He asked to speak to me, for chrissake. Besides, we weren't discussing the case. All right?"

He felt Maikai's hand on his sleeve again as Michael lifted his father to his feet. Maikai pulled Dan close and brought his mouth up
close to Dan's ear.

"Lily had the baby."

Maikai was pulled away then. The jailers led him to the door and
Lily followed. Dan was still standing at the clerk's desk with the
crowd buzzing around him, lost in those four words: "Lily had the
baby." Did he mean that Lily had *his* baby? Had she gone off to
have the baby and then raised it and simply never told him that he
had a child?

He turned to look for her but she had disappeared. He pushed
aside a few reporters and made it out to the hallway and spotted
her just going out the glass doors. He broke into a trot, weaving his
way through the crowded hall, and caught her before she reached
the parking lot.

When she turned, her face was pale, her eyes red from crying.

"Dan," she said. "I hope you're happy. You've finally destroyed
him. If he makes it through this, it'll be a miracle."

"This has nothing to do with me."

"I know. That's what you keep insisting. But it does, you know.
You're the chief deputy prosecuting attorney. You can't just hide
from your part in this the way you've tried to hide from other
responsibilities."

She stepped back from him, so the sun wasn't blinding her. "What is it you want?"

He had been so upset when Maikai told him about the baby that he had sprinted after her without thinking what he would say when he caught up to her. But now, in front of her, the feelings of the past that he thought were completely gone surged back.

"What is it?" she asked again. She still had those defiant eyes.

"He told me you had the baby. Did he mean our baby?"

She studied his face for a moment. "You didn't know?"

"Of course I didn't know."

"That's right, how could you? You left as soon as you found out I was pregnant."

"Is that what you think?" Dan asked.

"Oh, Dan," she said disgustedly and shook her head. What was the use of going over something that had happened eighteen years ago?

"Where's the child . . ." he began, then realized he didn't know if he'd had a son or a daughter. "Was it a girl or a boy?"

"A girl," Lily said. The anger in her voice had softened.

"Where is she?"

She lifted her head slowly. "You really don't know, do you?"

"No."

"My father made me give her up for adoption when she was born. I don't know where she is."

"Then why the hell did he even mention it to me? He must really hate me. What did I ever do to him besides fall in love with his daughter?"

He turned then and walked away.

"Dan," she called after him. "Dan."

He turned and she walked to him.

"He's been trying to find our daughter for months now. It's eating him up that he shunned his own flesh and blood."

A shower was starting to fall in the hills above the city, a gray curtain of rain obscuring Tantalus. In a few minutes it would be pouring where they stood now in a blazing hot afternoon sun. A few minutes after that the clouds would pass and steam would be rising off the pavement.

"He's sorry, Dan. About everything."

He watched the slow march of the rain showers down the mountain.

"I'm sorry too," he said, and left her in the parking lot with the sun about to disappear behind the approaching clouds.

He wanted to be by himself, so he drove slowly past Diamond Head and Koko Head to the cliffs above Hanauma Bay. From there he could watch the fish swimming in the clear waters beyond the reef.

He was the father of a seventeen-year-old girl, a girl he'd never known. When he got over his shock at the news, all he could think to do was get angry at Maikai for what he'd done to all three of them: to Lily, to Dan and to their daughter. All those years the old bastard had kept her from him. Why? Why would he do such a horrible thing? Maybe he hadn't acted honorably sleeping with Maikai's daughter under the old man's roof. Maybe he hadn't acted very wisely. But who does at seventeen? And then to send her off to have the baby and tell everyone she had had an abortion. It seemed so cruel, not just to Dan but to Lily and their daughter. It was as if the girl had been lost at sea and survived, yet her parents hadn't bothered to look for her because they all thought she was dead.

Dan sat on the lava wall above the marine sanctuary until the sun set, then he slowly walked back to his car. For years he had dreamed about Lily walking into his life again, dreamed of how she would put her arms around him and forgive him everything. Of course, that dream had faded a decade ago into an ache he no longer recognized.

CHAPTER
TWELVE

Dan rolled out of his bed at the Grand Mauian and heard the roaches scatter in the sink as he turned on the bedside lamp. There was nothing grand about the place. The digital clock flashed 5:48. The Outrigger State Championships were that morning and he had to be at the race site by six a.m. to get the rigging tied.

Dan and the rest of the crew had been training hard, looking forward to this race at Canoe Beach outside of Lahaina on Maui. But that was before the events of the last week. Before the man he'd once respected more than anyone else was arrested for the murder of the person many thought would be able to bring the state back to the economic prosperity it once enjoyed. And now the news from Lily that he had a daughter all these years. It had all begun to numb his enthusiasm. Besides that, he was pretty sure that the bad feelings that now existed between Michael and him wouldn't exactly enhance their chances of winning.

He didn't bother with a shower. He didn't have time. He'd flown over on the last flight from O'ahu, rented a car, and driven to the west side. When he got there he found the old dump of a hotel in Honokowai where a lot of the paddlers crashed. From there he could be at Canoe Beach in six and a half minutes tops.

He could have stayed at the Sheraton in Ka'anapali, of course. It was the hotel right next to Canoe Beach but the Grand Mauian was where the "team" had always stayed as kids mainly because it was the only place most paddlers could afford. Even though he could afford the Sheraton now, he still wanted to stay at the same place they'd always stayed, where the canoes were tied up in the parking lot, the outrigger standing next to them, riggings stashed in the trunks of the old cars. These rusted surfer heaps had been rotted by the beach air but still ran perfectly because the grease from the engine protected the motor, while the salt air ate away at every other part of the car, including the plastic seats and the dash.

It was raining loudly when he stepped out the door of his room. Paddlers were strolling back and forth from their cars to their rooms, unconcerned by the downpour, hauling out ice chests and rope and their favorite paddles. Dan put up the hood on his windbreaker and prepared to dash to his car, then pulled it down and walked in the same unhurried manner as the other paddlers. Back in Honolulu people would be scurrying for cover trying to avoid one of the glories of Hawai'i. The warm, refreshing rains confirmed the beauty of life here. The hustle of big-city America had overtaken Honolulu recently so that the people in O'ahu had to fly to Maui or the other neighbor islands to "mellow," to realize that this warm rain soaked only the senses.

By the time he had thrown his duffel bag in the back and gone back for his paddles, he was drenched. The water was dripping from his hair into his face, and his shorts and shirt and jacket looked as if someone had thrown him in a pool. But it made him feel good and awakened him as coffee could never do. Caffeine doesn't squish between the toes on your flaps or straighten the spine or splash open the eyes. Besides, he knew it would be dry at Canoe Beach even though it was only a mile or two down the coast. It always rained on the Napili end of West Maui as the clouds charged in from the north and dumped the moisture a half dozen times a day on Napili and Kahana and Kapalua. But five minutes away in Ka'anapali and Lahaina it almost never rained, and it was always at least ten degrees hotter. The streets of Lahaina in front of the T-shirt shops that overran the town baked like a griddle.

There was a bumper-to-bumper parade of canoe-laden cars and pickups on Honoapi'ilani Highway leading to Canoe Beach. Every vehicle had half-asleep paddlers with sandy feet and paddles sticking out the windows as they edged along the two-lane highway. The traffic bumped up on one another at the entrance to Ka'anapali. The oncoming lane was deserted until they reached the entrance to Canoe Beach, then that lane too was backed up for as far as Dan could see. A line of "paddle boats," as the paddlers called their cars, stretched toward Lahaina, where most of the other paddlers were staying, if they were staying in a hotel at all. A lot of them were camped on the beach and Dan could see their Colemans and campfires flaring in the morning half-light.

Dan had talked to Joe before he left Honolulu and Kalama had told him that Michael was going to pick up Joe at the airport on his way in from the ranch on the Hāna side. Dan was puzzled that Michael was blaming him for his father's arrest. Yet Michael's friendship with Joe remained intact and Kalama was the one who had arrested him! Sure, Joe was just following orders, but so was Dan, and Michael knew that.

Joe and Michael were supposed to be at Canoe Beach already because they had the canoe. They had to claim their spot early in the morning and get the canoe tied down. But Dan had still not heard a word from Paul, and he was worried about whether Paul would be there waiting. No one had seen him for days. As inebriated as he tried to keep himself, Paul had never missed a race, and this one, the state championships, was the biggest of the year. Paddling was the one piece of the past that didn't force Paul to think of his future as empty and alone. Out on the ocean fighting the swells with the rest of them, the past dissolved. The future was the next wave, the next pull, the next landmark they had to attain.

Dan assumed that Paul must have been hanging around Maui the last few days, probably visiting some of his old boatyard cronies. Or maybe he was camped out at his favorite spot on Kaho'olawe. It was against the law, of course, to step foot on the island even with the navy gone because there was unexploded "ordinance," as the government liked to call it, in the water and all along the shore and in the mountains. Nobody went there except for a few fishermen and some Hawai'ians who knew their way around—the activists like Uncle Charlie Yates who had camped out on the island while they were still bombing the place and, eventually, had won it back for the Hawai'ian people.

Dan pulled the car in on the far side of the lot. It was a good half-mile hoof down the sand from the racing canoes, but the old paddlers all headed for the spot because it was under the trees that fringed the south side of the cemetery directly behind Canoe Beach.

When Dan walked up, Joe was leaning over the canoe, one foot in the hull, one on the sand, lacing the rope around the outrigger booms known as *'iako*. Michael was washing something in the surf. The Ahue twins were down the beach cleaning equipment.

"Seen Paul?" Dan asked as he threw his duffel in the sand next to the canoe.

Joe didn't bother to look around. "Not yet," he said. "I thought he'd be with you."

"He never showed last night. I'm starting to really worry."

"It's early yet," Joe said and sat on the rail, dug his feet in the sand, and pulled hard on a rope tie. "Lash down the other *'iako*, would ya?"

"Yeah, sure," Dan said and grabbed some rope from Joe's bag.

Michael walked up from the surf and threw a washed seat down on a plastic cover he had staked in the sand.

"Where the hell is your brother?" He scowled at Dan.

Dan had had enough of Michael's attitude. It was Dan who should have been upset at Michael for not telling him all these years that Lily had given birth to his daughter.

"Don't get on my ass. I'm not any more responsible for him than you are for your sister."

"What the hell is that supposed to mean?" Michael yelled.

"It means why in the hell didn't you tell me I had a child?"

"Lily's got a big mouth," he said and turned away.

"Really?" Dan said. "Don't you think I deserved to know? What kind of a friend are you, anyway?"

"About as good as you, I suspect," Michael said.

"Get off it, Michael. I had nothing to do with the arrest of your father and you know it. And even if I did, what was I supposed to do? Because I'm your friend, you want me to ignore the fact that your father may have killed the governor?"

Michael took a step toward Dan and Dan did the same. Joe wedged between them before they could collide.

"Hey, bruddas," the Hawai'ian said. "Come on. You acting like kids. We stay workin' hard for the race. Don't screw up now."

The two old friends stared at each other for a moment over Kalama's shoulder. Dan was the first to walk away. He took a few steps, then turned around. "Fine," he said. "Let's get on with this."

He put his hand to his forehead and spied the beach toward the parking lot from where Paul would likely be coming, stumbling through the sand after a week-long binge, his head as big as a Moloka'i melon.

After a minute or so, he dropped to one knee and began to lash the last rigging.

"We better think about a replacement," Michael said to Dan. "We've got to be in the water in fourteen minutes. The conch blows in nineteen."

Dan sat down on the rail, swung his feet onto the sand, and spanked his hands together to get rid of some sand stuck to his fingers.

"Nobody's heard from him in how long?" Joe asked Dan after Michael went down to the water again to wash off some more equipment.

"Dorie saw him at the Ilikai Marina the night before we served the search warrant. He left in the *Loa,*" Dan said.

"He's been gone longer than that before without telling any-body where he was, ain't he?"

"Well, yeah, since Melissa died," Dan said. He stopped lashing and looked down the beach again. "He disappeared for two weeks once. He filled the boat up with booze and sailed over to Kaho'olawe and just sat on the beach and drank."

Kalama nodded his head confidently. "That's probably where he is right now."

"No, I don't think so. He hasn't missed one of our practices in months. So all of a sudden he misses the biggest race of the year?"

Michael threw the paddle into the canoe and stood up. His shirt was wet through from the exertion of lashing. "If he doesn't show soon, we better look for a substitute paddler," he said.

That was the first moment Dan let himself feel the acid rush of panic in his stomach. A drunk alone out in a small boat in the mid-dle of the Pacific. Anything could have happened.

"No," Dan said, feeling suddenly in his gut that Paul was in real trouble. "No," he said again. "There's not going to be any canoe race today. Something's happened to Paul and I'm not going to paddle around Maui when he could be out there right now needing my help."

Dan stood up straight and dropped the paddle he had in his hand. "I'm sorry, guys, but I just can't do this. Joe, I need you to call Gibbons in Missing Persons to get a search going for Paul. Coast Guard, HPD, the works."

"All right." Joe nodded.

"Thanks," Dan said and waved his hand over his shoulder as he stomped down the sand toward his car. He was hoping like hell that Joe was right about Paul. That he was just an unreliable drunk now, sleeping it off somewhere.

But he knew deep down that something was very wrong.

CHAPTER
THIRTEEN

The protesters had started gathering at the courthouse only an hour or so after Peter Maikai's arrest. The entire front steps of "777" as well as the lawn and sidewalk were covered with people, mostly in traditional Hawai'ian dress: barefooted in *malo*s, loincloths, in headdresses, in *wili* and *haku* lei, in long garlands of *ti* leaves.

The traffic, slowed to a standstill in front of the courthouse, was backed up past Pi'ikoi. HPD was trying to keep the cars and buses moving, but they weren't doing much good. The protesters took over the stage at the top of the steps and the tourists, thinking that this was another Kodak show, had begun to clog the sidewalks on the other side of the street past the old palace that symbolized the days when, not very long ago, Hawai'i was ruled by Hawai'ians.

The cameras were rolling, of course. It was the perfect setting. If they had hired a thousand actors to stage the event, they couldn't have done better. Protesters dressed up like a Polynesian cultural revue, dancing the ancient dances, chanting the ancient chants, holding signs that they wanted their leader released. They chanted that they wanted Hawai'i back, their " *'aina*," and the tourists to go home. The networks would take at least two minutes of this tape. Larry King would do a half an hour. *Nightline* would devote a whole show. They wanted the tourists to go home? How could Hawai'i exist without tourists? It seemed absurd to everyone but the Hawai'ians, who had thrived in these islands a thousand years before Captain Cook.

Peter Maikai's preliminary hearing was the first matter on the court's docket that morning. At the defense table Maikai was sitting next to his son Michael. Dan thought the old man looked as pale as the yellow leaves beneath a flame tree as he took a seat directly behind Cathy, who was ready at the prosecution table. Next to her was Joe Kalama, who, against his pained objections, was named the investigating officer on the case.

Lily Maikai sat tall in her usual seat behind the defense. Dan avoided looking at her, but he could feel her presence—the startling eyes, the strength of her bearing.

Dan had spent the entire weekend looking for his brother. As soon as the prelim was over he intended to go right back searching. He looked up from a report he was reading when Judge Shimada walked quickly through the chamber doors that the bailiff held open for him. Dan knew Shimada was smart enough to realize that no matter what happened with this trial it could be bad for him. He was planning to run for state Congress in a few years and he wasn't interested in being labeled as an enemy of the people.

The judge called the room to order. The attorneys and clerks did their verbal dance of names and numbers for the court steno to tap into record and then Shimada asked Cathy to call her first witness to the stand.

"Sergeant Joe Kalama," she said without looking around. She was in a forbidding dark gray suit and she'd worn the highest business pumps in her closet. Her hair was brushed back on the sides and ducktailed in the back.

Dan sat up in his chair. He always loved to watch her work. But now there was something else at play. This entire case was tangled up with their relationship, with their love, with their future. As she placed her pen on the table in front of her and stood, Dan felt his stomach drop—a feeling that could have been trepidation, or could have been like the excitement of watching a lioness stalking.

Joe walked up, took the oath, and sat facing the attorneys' table to the right of the judge. He stared at the floor, his beefy arms overflowing the rests, as he spelled his name for the clerk.

If the cop looked up, he could see in the back twenty or so Hawai'ians he knew including Marie Kaloa, a powerful Hawai'ian woman with royal blood who lived down the street from him. She was the *Kumuhula* who had taught his mother, his wife, and his two daughters the old dances. When she came to his house, she was called Auntie and treated like royalty because as the great-great-granddaughter of Queen Ka'ahumanu, King Kamehameha the Great's wife, that was what she was.

Cathy stood behind her chair and gripped the back with both hands like a pushcart.

"Sergeant Kalama," she began, "could you tell us where you were on the afternoon of January twenty-fifth, 1995?"

"The Royal Hawai'ian Hotel," he said softly.

Shimada had his head down, writing something. "Speak up, Sergeant," he said without looking up at Kalama.

"I was at the Royal Hawai'ian Hotel," Kalama repeated loud enough so Auntie in the back row could hear everything he said.

"And what was your assignment on that day?"

"I really didn't have an assignment, Counsel. I was off duty. I had gone there . . ." He stopped for a moment then went on. "Well, I was there to make sure there wasn't any trouble."

"Did you have reason to believe there might be some kind of trouble?" she pressed.

"The Department was told the 'Ohana Society was going to demonstrate at the governor's rally."

"I see," she said. She laid a notepad down on the table and walked toward Kalama. "Tell me, Sergeant, are you normally assigned to security at such events?"

"No," Kalama said, shaking his head. "I'm with Homicide."

"Then tell us, Sergeant, why on this occasion did you feel it was necessary to be at the Royal Hawai'ian?"

Joe Kalama drew a large breath and his eyes danced from Cathy to the back of the room, where the crowd of Hawai'ians, many of them relatives of his, listened closely to what he was going to say.

"Sergeant," Shimada prompted.

"I was at the Royal Hawai'ian because the leader of the 'Ohana Society at the time, Mr. Peter Maikai, is an acquaintance of mine and I felt if there was a problem I might be able to help keep things, you know, calm."

"And did you happen to see Mr. Peter Maikai that evening?" Cathy said as she pointed at the defendant.

"Yes."

"And where was he?"

"He was with a group of . . ." Kalama hesitated.

"A group of protesters?" Cathy prompted.

"I don't know if you could call them protesters."

"Oh? What would you call them?" she asked curtly. She wasn't sure to what Kalama was objecting. He was supposed to be on her side.

Joe looked toward the back of the courtroom and then at Dan, who was directly between the gallery of Hawai'ians and Kalama.

"I just don't know if I'd classify them as protesters," he said finally.

Cathy noticed Joe's nervous glance to his neighbors in the back of the room and moved over unobtrusively so Kalama's view to the rear of the courtroom was blocked.

"Detective Kalama, what did you observe this group doing during the governor's speech?"

"They were just standing on the beach, for the most part."

"Did they remain on the beach during the entire speech?"

"No. Toward the end they walked to where the governor was standing and started yelling at him."

Cathy took a step closer as she neared the testimony she was digging for.

"What kinds of things were they yelling?"

"They objected mostly to the governor's stand on pro-development and told him so."

"I see," she said and glanced down at her empty hands as if reading from notes. "And you said you know Peter Maikai?"

"Yes," Joe answered with a nod. "That's what I said."

Cathy turned again and looked to Dan as if to ask him what the hell Kalama's problem was. Why the short, terse answers? She was thinking about asking the judge for a recess to chew out Kalama's fat ass. Dan gave her back a short shrug and waved his head to go on. She turned again to Kalama, but her voice had an edge to it.

"All right. Peter Maikai was with the group of protesters on the beach?" She had put a sarcastic emphasis on "protesters."

"Yes, he was."

"Was he with them while they were advancing on Mr. Slaton?"

"Yes."

"Was he carrying anything at the time?"

"Yes."

Cathy paused for a second and stared at Kalama. Then she walked slowly over to where Dan was seated. Shimada drummed the bench with a pen and waited.

"What the hell is happening here?" she whispered to Dan.

Before Dan could answer, Shimada barked, "Counsel, are you finished with the witness?"

Cathy turned back to the judge. "Could I have a minute with co-counsel, Your Honor?"

"No more than that, Counsel," Shimada said impatiently.

"Cathy," Dan said softly, "this is a tough one for Joe. Half the people he grew up with are sitting back there listening to him betray one of his own blood."

"Come on. This doesn't have anything to do with whether Maikai is Hawai'ian and you know it."

"Maybe not. But you're not going to be able to convince them of that," he said and nodded over his shoulder. "Give Kalama a break on this one. Believe me, he's doing the best he can."

"He's acting like this is the first time he's ever testified."

"Just be patient. Kalama knows what he's up there for. He's just trying to save a little face by forcing you to drag the answers out of him. You're doing just fine. It's going to take a little longer, but you'll get what you came for."

"I better or I'm going to fry him," she said, and Dan knew she meant it. One word from Reed and Kalama could be walking a beat in Kalihi.

She walked back slowly to Kalama and spoke softly to him. "I believe you stated that Mr. Maikai was carrying something. Could you tell what it was?"

"A club."

"I see," Cathy said and she took another step toward Kalama. Shimada was watching her closely now.

"And while he was carrying this club, he and the others were coming toward the governor?"

"Yes," Kalama said.

"Were they saying anything?"

"They were yelling things. Trying to interrupt the governor's speech."

"And Mr. Maikai was leading the group?" Cathy asked.

"Yes, he was."

From the back of the room, a shout interrupted Kalama's answer.

"*He Kanaka pilau 'oe!* You're a traitor to the Hawai'ian people!" someone yelled. It was a deep, low, resounding big man's shout that shook the koa paneling of the room.

Shimada slammed down his gavel and eyed the spectators menacingly. "If I hear another outburst like that I will make sure whoever is causing it will spend a few days in the custody of my bailiffs." The judge turned back to Cathy.

"Proceed."

"You're worse than that traitor. *Aloha 'ino iā'oe!*

A massive Polynesian woman wearing sandals and a muumuu was suddenly standing in the aisle, shouting at Shimada. She had moved so quickly that the bailiff standing directly behind her hadn't noticed her move until she had blocked his view of the judge.

"You are—" she started to shout, but her shouts were muffled by the hand of the bailiff who had finally reached her. The bailiff put his arm around her chest up by her neck and put his other hand over her mouth.

"Take your hands off my auntie!" someone shouted. It was a man who overflowed two seats in the back row. When he stood and put his hand on the bailiff's arm, the cop felt surrounded by flesh and muscle. By that time half a dozen tan-uniformed bailiffs and three or four HPDs in black had run up to help. Four of them grabbed the man, who pushed two of them down with one effortless move of his arm. Two more HPD got behind him and all the officers pushed and pulled him out the back door of the courtroom.

The bailiff who was still wrapped around the woman looked up to the judge for instructions.

"Take her out," Shimada ordered.

Another jailer came back through the door after having helped subdue the man. The knot of his tie was facing his ear, his hair looked as if patches had been torn out, and dark sweat shadows ringed his neck and armpits. He grabbed the woman's other arm, and while she cursed in Hawai'ian at Shimada, the two bailiffs lifted her by her meaty elbows and carried her through the door, banging her head on the doorframe going out.

Suddenly, Shimada found himself in an unprotected courtroom that only a minute before was lined with police. Even though Kalama had stood, ready to jump to Shimada's defense, he wasn't going to be able to stop an angry group of fiercely loyal Hawai'ians.

Peter Maikai had stood and was facing the back, crying out to the woman as they hauled her away. Michael had his hand on his father's elbow, trying to pull him back down to his seat when three bailiffs rushed back through the door. They looked beaten up and their clothes were a mess: shirttails yanked out, collars this way and that.

They all ran directly at Maikai because the defendant is always the intense focus of any on-duty bailiff. If anything happens to the defendant, like for instance he gets away or assaults the judge, it's the bailiff's ass.

They leaped the gallery rail and took ahold of Maikai and spun him around to face the judge.

Michael had his mouth against his father's ear, talking furiously, with one eye on Shimada. Michael knew the judge had a reputation for tolerating just so much in his courtroom before he made everyone pay, including the attorneys.

Shimada was furious. He was a man who dealt every day with men who got their way by intimidating, beating, or killing other people. He could ring them in for twenty-five-to-life with a raise of his gavel without fear. But a moment ago he had suddenly found himself unprotected, and he didn't like the feeling.

"Mr. Maikai," the judge said, pushing his eyeglasses back on his nose. "If there are any further disturbances, I am going to hold you personally responsible."

He raised his voice and aimed the gavel toward the back of the gallery like a gun. "I can clear this room in a second if that's what it takes." Then he looked back to Maikai. "I will not condone any demonstration from you like the one I've just witnessed. Do you understand me?"

"I cannot control the anger of the Hawai'ian people," Maikai said. He was still standing, surrounded by bailiffs.

"Maybe," Shimada said coldly, coiled snakelike behind the bench, "but I can control what goes on in my courtroom. If anybody causes any kind of disturbance—I mean *anything*—I'm holding you responsible. You'll be handcuffed and shackled to your chair. Do you understand me?"

Maikai didn't answer. His gray hair, which had recently been cropped close to his head shown in the fluorescent light like an aura. Behind him the gallery was breathless, still, waiting to see if Maikai would back down.

"Mr. Maikai," the judge asked again. This time he didn't bother to shade the anger in his voice. "Do you understand?"

Before his client could answer, Michael stood and walked between him and the judge. He turned his back to Shimada and put his hand on his father and said, "Please." Maikai let the bailiffs ease him down into his chair.

"Your Honor," Michael said, turning back to Shimada. "First of all, I want to apologize for the disturbance. But, Your Honor, my client had nothing to do with that outburst and I think the court is being a little unfair."

Shimada shifted his gaze slowly to Michael as if he'd seen a roach crawling across his morning sweetbread.

"Counsel, right now I don't care what you think. If your client so much as twitches without my okay I'll make sure he isn't given a second opportunity."

Shimada's anger was scorching Michael, who took it without objection. He had wanted the judge's anger to shift to him and he'd gotten what he was after.

"Now sit down," Shimada ordered.

Shimada turned his head slowly to Cathy without taking his eyes off Michael. When a moment later his eyes shifted to the prosecution table, Shimada was back in control.

"Proceed, Counsel," he said to Cathy.

Dan watched Cathy as she took a step toward Kalama. He knew she could feel the power she held at that moment. She could strike and destroy the old man.

"Sergeant Kalama," she started slowly, "once Mr. Maikai and the rest of his group advanced on the governor, what happened next?"

"Mr. Maikai stepped over a rope separating the governor from the crowd and yelled at the governor."

Kalama was speaking loudly and clearly now. Dan could see that the brawl had angered his friend. He knew that Kalama respected Peter Maikai and what he stood for. But he was against violence. He had told Dan what Uncle Charlie had told him one day. Joe was drinking Primo with some buddies one afternoon after a softball game at Tenth Street Park in Palolo when Charlie appeared. Charlie liked a beer as much as any other Hawai'ian and had stopped to drink and talk story with them. The thing Kalama never forgot was what Charlie had said about the Hawai'ian Revolution: "We're going be the only revolutionaries who never fire one shot."

Even though the anger within the Hawai'ian people grew day by day, a Hawai'ian had never used a gun, had never shot anyone in the struggle. Kalama was proud of that. But Dan knew that something had changed for Joe after Maikai's arrest. He still loved Maikai, but he had been in that blood-drenched hotel room where the governor of Hawai'i was slit open from scrotum to jugular, his gizzards sprawled on the bed and his heart smashed by something like a club.

Cathy took another step toward Kalama. "Could you make out what Mr. Maikai was yelling at the governor?"

"Not really. I wasn't paying any attention to what they were yelling. I was worrying about the club he was carrying."

Dan knew Cathy didn't care what the defendant was yelling either. It was the club she was after.

"Why were you paying so much attention to the club?"

"I was afraid it could be used as a weapon," Kalama said.

"Was the club the only weapon you observed in Mr. Maikai's possession that afternoon?"

Without hesitation Kalama answered, "No. Later he also had what appeared to be a sword or large knife."

"I see. When did you first observe that?"

"As he got closer to the governor, he started swinging it in the governor's direction."

That was when Maikai leaped to his feet again. "I wasn't going to cut him," he yelled, and started toward Shimada, who leaned back from the advancing defendant.

A bailiff tackled the old man, and as they went down two other tan shirts fell on him. A pair of knees pinned Maikai to the floor.

"Shackle him to the chair," the judge yelled.

The aisle and walls of the court were lined with black uniforms now, and when the Hawai'ians in the last row tried to get to their fallen leader, the cops quickly surrounded them and shoved them out the door into the hall, where a regiment of HPD forced them out onto the square in front of the courthouse. They were chanting as they were pushed down the hallway, and when they poured out the door, a roar went up. A few minutes later they were singing *"Aloha 'Oe"*, the slow, pained dirge that Queen Lili'uokalani composed, in a depression she never recovered from after the overthrow of her monarchy, to mourn the passing of a great people and forgive those who had deposed her.

The judge gaveled the bench several times as if he were trying to hammer a reluctant nail. His hair flew about as he flailed. "Anyone who does not have a media pass is ordered to leave this courtroom." Michael stood up while the HPD were escorting the uncredentialed out of the courtroom row by row.

"Your Honor, my client's daughter and another member of the family," he said, pointing to Uncle Charlie, "request your permission to be allowed to stay during the pendency of these proceedings."

The judge looked at Lily and Charlie. He knew the *kahuna* was a fervent sovereigntist, but he also knew Uncle Charlie Yates was a man who preached nonviolence. If anyone could help prevent this uprising from turning into a bloodletting, it was this man.

"I have no problem with the two of them remaining," Shimada said. "I think they are aware of the guidelines I have set forth, and as long as they abide by them I will let them stay."

Shimada waited for the police and bailiffs to clear the gallery, then nodded once again to Cathy.

"Proceed."

Cathy, who had been leaning against the counsel table waiting for the police to take back control of the courtroom, stood, picked up a pad, and walked up to the sergeant again.

"Once you ran toward the governor and the defendant, what happened next?"

"I tackled the defendant," Kalama answered.

"Why did you tackle him?"

"Because I thought there was a possibility he might attack the governor with the sword."

"No!" Maikai shouted. Reflexively he tried to get up but his feet and hands were shackled to the chair, which two bailiffs were holding down.

"We want our land back by peaceful means," Maikai continued, "not violence!"

"That's it!" the judge shouted.

Suddenly Maikai's chest thrust forward and his eyes opened and he let out a loud groan that stopped everyone—the bailiffs, the attorneys, Shimada with his gavel raised above his head.

Maikai's mouth was open, but now nothing but a terrible wheezing gasp was coming out. His legs kicked back and his chest jerked and suddenly Maikai went to the floor with the chair on top of him as if it were a bailiff wrestling him to the ground.

Dan had stepped over the rail as soon as Maikai began to struggle.

"Get the cuffs off him, Donelly," he said to one of the bailiffs.

Donelly fumbled nervously with his key chain.

"Unlock the cuffs," Dan told him again.

The bailiff finally sorted out the key for the shackles and began working on the metal around Maikai's ankles.

"Get his hands first," Dan said.

Lily somehow had reached her father through the phalanx of police. She lifted his head so his face was no longer being forced into the hard floor.

Dan stood and looked around while Donelly worked on the cuffs.

"Did somebody call for the paramedics?"

"They're coming," Shimada said, and Dan knelt back down beside Maikai. When the shackles were finally off the old Hawai'ian's feet, Dan tossed the chair across the floor. It hit the empty jury-box wall and settled on its side.

Lily became aware for the first time of the maddening strobe of cameras flashing. When the courtroom broke apart in the confusion, newsmen streaming out the door to get to the phones had sent in their photogs and video crews, which had been banned from the courtroom, to see if they could sneak in a shot.

"The defendant in shackles had a goddamn heart attack right in the courtroom," a reporter shouted into a phone to his editor. "Jesus! You dream about this kind of shit."

Uncle Charlie eased between Dan and Lily, bent down and put his hand on Maikai's stomach, and began to rub it very slowly.

"Peter Kameaho'iho'i'ea," he said. "*Mai hopohopo Eola'ana ha kanaka maoli.*"

Maikai opened his eyes and looked at Charlie, and the agony drained from his face. Then his eyes closed and his chest stopped heaving.

Dan put his hand on Charlie's shoulder and pulled himself up. The paramedics were just coming through the door with gleaming metal suitcases in their hands. Dan waved at them, and they used the big cases to press through the crowd. When they got to Maikai, Lily and Dan and Charlie stepped back.

There was a color in Maikai's face Dan had only seen on corpses, a translucent hue that seemed unable to reflect light.

One of the paramedics, an elderly Filipino, began strapping things to Maikai's arms and chest. The other medic, a stocky white man with a neck that glowed red, pulled out a portable phone.

"We have an apparent heart attack here," he said into the phone and waited.

"Yes, the heart is arrested," he said, looking at his partner, who nodded his head to confirm that the patient's heart had stopped beating.

"All right," the medic said and hung up.

He looked at his partner. "Get the paddles," he said.

The Filipino pulled two silver discs from the case and placed them on Maikai's chest.

"Step back," he said to Dan.

"Clear."

And Maikai's body jumped off the floor. The Filipino put his hand on Maikai's chest and lowered his ear close to his mouth.

"We've got a pulse," he said to his partner with a wink.

Two more medics with a stretcher banged through the doors.

"Let's get him in the van."

They snapped open the gurney and Maikai was lifted onto it and a moment later they were heading for the door surrounded by cops. Lily started to follow, but a bailiff put his hand on her shoulder.

"I'm his daughter," she said.

When the bailiff's expression didn't change, she looked back at Dan.

"I need to go with him," she said. If there was any feeling for her left in him, any moment from the past that still meant something to him, she was appealing to that sentiment now.

Dan saw her green eyes shine with defiance, even as she pleaded for this favor. He nodded at the bailiff. "Let her go with him," he said.

The jailer dropped his hand and stepped back, and Lily ran by the side of the gurney as they pushed it out the door.

Everyone followed the gurney out into the hall and Shimada fled to his chambers. As quickly as a tornado strikes and is gone, Dan was standing alone in the empty courtroom with Michael Maikai.

"I guess you're happy now," Michael said.

"What do you mean by that?"

Michael slammed his briefcase shut. "I told you you were going to kill him," he said. "And now it looks like you may have."

CHAPTER
FOURTEEN

The nurse let the metal clipboard rattle against the steel bedstand as she dropped it on its hook. She was a small, squat, bull-necked grouch who had nine more hours to pull that night. She yanked open a metal credenza across from the bed. Lily could see in the drawer the soft touch of cotton balls in a glass jar and the hard plastic syringes with their stinging message at the ends.

Lily sat on the edge of her father's bed with his hand held between hers and waited for the nurse to knee the drawer closed. When she saw the needle in her hand, Lily quickly stood and laid down her father's hand. The nurse took his hand without love and turned it so the soft, veined underside of his arm showed. With the hypodermic at her side, she pulled his skin tight with her thumb, recognized something below the skin, and immediately pinned the spot.

Lily saw that her father hadn't even realized that he'd been pricked, that a vial of something golden, almost oily, had been injected into his arm. His weakness stunned her. She had never felt that Peter Maikai, the strongest man she'd ever known, a magnet to thousands of people, would ever die.

When she had taken over the management of the ranch, he had stood by her, taught her how to fight. And what a fight it was. A woman in a man's world. The big growers tried to shut her out when they realized that this little local crop was becoming more and more popular, that the demand for *poi* and the taro it came from would explode with the rise of Hawai'ian pride.

Her father had been at her side for every battle. When she saw now how close he was to death, it terrified her more than she thought possible. Her first thought was a selfish one: that he wouldn't be there for her anymore. Then she thought of how her father must be feeling and, strangely, that was when her fear dissolved, her stomach muscles relaxing for the first time since he'd collapsed in the courtroom. She knew that her father, Peter Kamaeho'iho'i'ea, did not fear death.

The nurse dropped her father's arm on the bed again, tossed the used syringe in a round disposal hole in the top of the credenza, and pushed her way out the door without a nod.

Lily sat back on the bed and held down the cotton on the puncture wound.

"Come closer, Lily," he said as if she were still his five-year-old, muddy as a cane ditch, dragging home from a day playing in the taro patches. He'd usually have a hose behind his back, the flow of water crimped off in his hand. She knew he was going to squirt her with the cold well water and she'd take off running for the hedge by the garage. He'd catch her well before she got there, of course, and she'd dance, screaming in the exhilarating splash of her father's attention.

Her father looked up toward her face. But by the way his eyes seemed to wander, Lily realized he wasn't even strong enough to really focus. He seemed to be looking somewhere at her lips, mesmerized, it seemed, the way she'd been mesmerized by her father her whole life.

Lily could see her father gathering himself before he spoke.

"Lily, I want to talk about some things before it's too late."

She was going to answer with a bluff about how they'd have plenty of time to talk when he got well, but she didn't. She knew there was no time for those games. She put her hand down close to her father's and said, "I'm here for you, Dad."

"Yes, you've always been there for me, Lily," he sighed and his abdomen seemed to sink all the way to the mattress.

After a moment he pulled her closer to him. "I need to talk to Dan and ask for his forgiveness."

It was the last thing she was expecting to come from his mouth. Once Peter Maikai marked a man bad, she'd never seen him change his mind. Forgiveness had always been as useless to him as guilt.

"Why?" was all she could think to say.

"Because what I did was wrong."

"We understand, Father," Lily said.

"No, you don't. I'm to blame for everything. I should never have sent Dan away. Or orphaned your daughter."

"Forget those things now. We'll find her soon and bring the whole family together again."

"What about Dan?" he insisted.

"When we find her"—she nodded and patted his hand in confirmation—"I'll make sure she sees him."

"Good," he said. "But I still need to talk to him. To both of you."

"He's supposed to be here soon," she said, knowing he was going to follow them to the hospital.

Maikai began to cough. His whole body from the feet to the crown of his head seemed to snap together as the spasms contracted his body.

She lifted his head and held the water glass to his lips and he wheezed down a few drops.

"Lily?" he tried to begin again, but he choked as he said her name.

She put her hands on his chest and eased him down to the pillow. "You rest for a while," she whispered. Her face was close enough to smell on his breath the chemicals that they were pumping into his arm. "And I'll go see if I can find Dan."

"Wait," he said. A sudden surge of energy gathered in him so that his eyes focused and he looked into her as only her father ever could. It always froze her helplessly when he did.

"Don't let them take the land," he said. "They'll mutilate it, Lily. They'll kill the wildness."

She knew he'd spent his life trying to protect that wildness, to nurture it, not just at his own ranch, but throughout all of Hawai'i.

"Don't worry," she said. "As long as I'm alive, I won't let them take it."

He shook his head slowly as if she didn't understand.

"Michael will give it to them, if you let him."

The idea surprised her. Michael? "No," she said. "He's a Maikai."

Perhaps the deepest sadness she had ever seen in her father's eyes overflowed his lids now.

"I don't trust my own son anymore," he said in a voice so low he sounded to Lily as if he was already speaking from beyond.

The words shivered her so that her shoulders actually shook from their coldness. By the look in her father's expiring eyes, she knew it was something he had always been certain he would never hear himself say.

Her impulse was to tell him he was wrong about Michael. But she knew her father would never make a statement of such weight if she could just smile the problem away.

"I will never let Michael sell it," she said. "No matter what."

"Promise me that, Lily," he said. "Promise me, Lily."

She stood with his hand still in hers and turned and knelt at his side. "I promise," she said into the ears of her dying father.

"I love you, Lily," he said as his suddenly lifeless eyes closed and his head turned to the pillow.

Dan made a U-turn at the top of the hill just before the visitor parking and parked on the street across from the emergency entrance to the hospital. He turned off the engine and rolled down the window and let the cool evening air blow against his flushed face.

From here he could see nearly all of the south shore of O'ahu. The Wai'anae Mountain Range falling away to Makaha, the wide, beautiful basin of Pearl, the jumbo jets descending in procession to the airport, the crowded lights of Honolulu silhouetting Diamond Head.

This whole matter with Maikai had disrupted his life and brought back feelings he'd pushed back into safe storage, packed away from his heart. But now there was a child. That meant that Lily and he would have to see each other. It meant that he would have to deal with his feelings for her while they worked out the details of what to do with their daughter, if and when she was found. Like an old divorced couple.

What the hell would he do with a child? Or was she a woman by now? And who knew what she had grown up to become? It could be wonderful to see his daughter, but it could also be a nightmare.

That, of course, would all have to be dealt with in due time. But for now he had to pay his respects to a dying Peter Maikai and then continue his search for Paul.

Dan opened the car door and stood with his arm on the top of the roof for a moment, breathing in the crisp air. Then he shut the door and trotted across the street and through the front lobby. He stepped onto the elevator and pressed the 6 and rode up. Michael was standing at the elevator waiting to get on when Dan stepped off.

"What are you doing here?" Michael growled at him.

"Come on, Michael. I know it's hard for you, but I'm worried about him too."

"Oh, you don't have to worry anymore. You've done your job. I told you this would kill him."

"What do you mean?"

"I mean he's dead. And you and Reed killed him." Michael stepped closer to him, and Dan was sure he was going to take a swing.

"Michael," a voice called from down the hall. "Michael, don't."

It was Lily.

Michael pushed past him onto the elevator and punched the button and the doors closed behind him. In a week, a month, a year, Michael would begin to realize that Dan wasn't responsible for all this. Maybe he even knew it now, but he had to vent his anger at someone.

Lily came toward him from the darkness at the end of the hall. She had a look of stunned resignation, as if she'd seen the worst someone could take and had come out the other side still in her right mind.

Without realizing it, Dan edged back from her. After what Michael had said to him, he wasn't eager to bear what Lily felt. She looked up at him with her swollen eyes and stared for a long moment.

"We have a lot to talk about," she said at last and took him by the hand, which surprised him. He could see the glazed, stunned look on her face that he'd seen on a lot of relatives who'd just lost a loved one.

They went down the elevator to the cafeteria. He bought them both a cup of coffee and they walked out the front door of the hospital. The moon, waned to a sliver, pierced the sky near Venus, a bright silver punctuation above it.

She turned to him and began to tell him what her father had said to her just before he died. She only managed a few sentences before she broke down, and suddenly they were in each other's arms crying. It frightened Dan when he began to weep with her. Was it Maikai he was grieving for, or was it Lily? Or was it the whole thing, those agonizing years of loss he never really got over?

They held each other for a long time before she began to tell him how her father had asked for Dan's forgiveness.

"I just wish you would have been able to talk to him yourself. I know it's hard for you to believe, but he really did love you. God, if only things could have been different."

"I don't blame him anymore. He was protecting his daughter. Maybe it was for the best," he said without really meaning it.

"No, Dan. He was sorry for what he'd done," she said. "I know now he made sure you thought that I'd had an abortion and never wanted to see you again. At the same time he was convincing me that you told him you were glad to get rid of me. I guess you've realized by now he sent me off to have the baby at my Auntie's on the Mainland. He had me give her up for adoption when she was born."

"Yes, I'd managed that much of it," Dan said.

They walked slowly down the hill from the hospital and crossed the vast lawn in front to a concrete area overlooking a reservoir. The almost moonless night made the water appear as if it were a pool of black ink. Then she brought up what had been aching in her for a long time.

"I wouldn't have minded if you'd called once or twice in the last eighteen years," she said. Her words had a bite to them, and he felt the old bitterness surface.

"I got thrown out, remember? All I knew was what Michael and Paul had relayed to me. They told me you never wanted to see me again."

"Of course I wanted to see you." She looked back over her shoulder. "I guess I was disappointed you didn't try a little harder."

"First of all, Paul tried to find out where you were taken. No one would tell him. I had no way of knowing where he had you hidden," Dan said. "Besides, why didn't you just write to me at Paul's? Or call? You had to figure I was there."

She didn't answer.

"By the way," he asked, "where did your father hide you?"

"Eureka, California," she said, still facing away from him.

"Eureka! What's in Eureka?"

"Auntie Pearl's sister."

Auntie Pearl was the nanny who had practically brought them up after Lily's mother died. Dan's face went tight with acknowledgment.

"Then what?" he asked.

"Then to Los Angeles to finish high school, then Stanford."

"Stanford," Dan said, shaking his head wryly.

She turned to him with a question on her face.

"Did you stay in contact with the child?" Dan asked.

She shook her head and found herself in front of a small cement toadstool and sat on it. Dan looked around in the dark and realized they'd walked into a child's playground with swings and climbing animals of wood and cement spread around the grassy area.

"Do you know her name?" Dan asked.

"Sharon Jenkins. But the adoption agency lost track of the adopting parents. They moved a lot so we had a hard time finding them. We couldn't locate them until recently."

"Until recently? So you found her, then?"

Lily shook her head again. She didn't look at him when she spoke and he could feel her sadness in the uncharacteristic slump of her shoulders. "No, she left home when she was fifteen and they haven't heard from her since. To tell you the truth, I don't think they really tried all that hard. The couple that adopted Sharon divorced two years later. The husband more or less abandoned them. Took off with some young woman, was the story the mother told. The mother married three more times by the time Sharon was a teenager."

Dan walked over to the fence, put his elbows on the top, and looked out over the dark ravine below.

"Sounds like she had a pretty good reason to want to get away from them."

"I guess," Lily said without turning to him. "But it's frightening to think what could have happened to her. A young girl alone on the streets. It's on the TV all the time."

Dan had seen enough in court to fill in the details. The garbage of society that preyed on these girls came through the system on a daily basis. There seemed to be an endless supply of them and an endless supply of destroyed lives to go with them.

She got up from the toy mushroom she was sitting on and began to walk again. He strolled with her along the fence that separated the barranca from the man-made lake below. To the west farther below them, the lights of a destroyer docked at Pearl Harbor illuminated the distance.

"You haven't had any luck finding her yet, have you?" Dan said without much hope.

"Not yet. My father tried for months. He contacted the adoption agency and then the parents. Then he put several private investigators on it. They never found anything. After a while it just hurt too much and he had Michael take over the search."

"What did Michael do?"

"What could he do? He hired two other detectives, with the same results," she said. "The only thing Father wanted at the end was to find his granddaughter and restore her to her rightful place in the family. He even changed the will so that if she was found she would inherit part of the ranch."

They walked a little farther, then down across the lawn again to the street. Finally he took her hand and stopped her.

"What changed him?" he asked her.

With her back to the harbor, her face was so dark he couldn't see her eyes.

"You mean about his granddaughter?"

His granddaughter! Until that moment Dan hadn't thought of her that way. His daughter was Maikai's flesh and blood too.

"About everything, I guess," he said. "His granddaughter, me, you. Why the change of heart?"

"I'm not sure except that the guilt about what he'd done to his own granddaughter, the way he'd turned his back on her, finally ate through all his bitterness. Remember my father had seen what the *haole* had done to the Hawai'ian."

"If that was so, then why did he take in Paul and me in the first place?"

She folded her arms across her chest as if she were cold and turned from him until the breeze was in her face.

"Your father saved his life. You didn't know that either, did you?"

Dan shook his head slowly. "I thought they were just old army buddies. Esprit de corps. That old macho crap and Maikai took it seriously."

"Your father dragged him out of a firefight and held off the North Koreans until the chopper showed up. Your father took several rounds during the wait and they both ended up in the hospital."

"So he felt obligated to do what he could for us?" Dan said.

"Yes, and because he was Hawai'ian he felt he owed your father an immeasurable debt. An immeasurable debt to a *haole.*"

"Except when I got you pregnant I'd canceled that debt."

"My father was Hawai'ian above everything else," she said. "His world was very simple. He lived for *'āina* and the family, both of which the *haole*s had done their best to destroy. That's the way he looked at it."

They began to walk back up the hill to the hospital in silence. When they got to where Dan's car was parked, he reached for her and they hugged.

"I'm so sorry," she said into his shoulder.

"So am I."

"Will you come to the funeral?" she asked when they separated.

"Of course. Will it be at the ranch?"

"Yes. He wanted to be buried beyond the bridge at Waioli Stream."

He let her walk back into the hospital by herself. Then he got in his car and drove back to the office. He wanted to find out if Paul had tried to contact him.

It was after seven when he arrived. He had begun walking up the steps to the PA's office when he saw both Cathy and Reed walking out the double glass doors, laughing. They saw Dan about the same time and immediately changed their expressions. Before they said anything, Cathy walked quickly up to Dan and placed her arms around his neck and held him.

Reed walked up and patted Dan's shoulder. "Sorry about Maikai," he said. "Cathy explained to me how close you really were with the old guy. I'm sorry it had to end this way."

Dan took Cathy's arms away and stepped back. "It hasn't ended, Brian," he said.

"What do you mean?" Cathy asked. "We heard that Maikai died."

"Yes, he's dead."

"Then that's the end of it," Reed said, a little baffled.

"The end of what?" Dan said.

Reed looked at Cathy as if to see if she knew what Dan meant. The chief prosecuting attorney of Honolulu was celebrating a big victory that Maikai's death clinched. He'd found Slaton's killer and justice was done. The only thing left to do now was accept the praise.

"The case is closed. I can't prosecute a dead man," Reed said with a little laugh.

"Right," Dan said. "But we still have to make sure he was responsible. We have a lot more work to do."

Reed waved him off with one hand. "Our job is done. Time to move on."

Dan stared at the two of them a moment and sighed. It was useless trying to convince Reed of anything right now. So why should he bother trying? "Actually," he said, "I came here to see if anyone has heard from my brother."

"I checked your messages, Dan, and I didn't see anything," Cathy said. "You mean you still haven't heard from him?"

"Not a word," Dan said. "He and Maikai were close. He needs to know what happened to him."

"Ah, don't panic," Reed said, waving his hand in dismissal of Dan's worries. "It's not like it's the first time he's pulled something like this."

Cathy saw the annoyance grow on Dan's face. She thought she'd better get Dan out of there before he said something to Reed he might not be able to take back.

"Let's go see if anyone at the Gavel's heard anything," she said and grabbed Dan by the arm. Then she added, "I think it's time we talk seriously about having a family."

"Really?" he said, a little dumbfounded.

"Yes, really." She smiled. "But just talk, all right? I'm not saying I've changed my mind."

Dan's shoulders dropped and he forgot Reed for a moment, which was what she was hoping.

"That's all I've ever wanted from you," he said. "To at least start thinking about it."

"I am," she said, and she knew he'd be content for a while with that.

As they walked away, she looked back over her shoulder at Reed. "See you tomorrow morning."

"Yeah, sure, sure, tomorrow," Reed said circumspectly, as if he were on the phone with his lover and he didn't want his wife, lying next to him, to catch on.

CHAPTER
FIFTEEN

It was a wet, wind-whipped day as Dan drove the Hāna Highway to Maikai's funeral. Instead of the clouds that continuously drifted through this area freshening the jungle with a soft sprinkle, dark black clouds of mourning crowded the sky and wedged against the slopes of Haleakalā, dumping violent downpours that drenched the area. Occasionally, it would begin to rain so hard it was difficult for Dan to make out the car in front of him, the trees and vines so wet that waterfalls sprung up among them, cascading down in silver sheets among the deep green of the jungle.

The highway was very crowded, and the two-hour drive took an extra hour. Cars packed with Hawai'ian families serpentined down the snaking curves in a long, slow procession. One of their most visible leaders had died a martyr at a time when the Hawai'ian people were becoming fully aware of how much they had already lost. Every Hawai'ian organization was to be represented at the funeral: the 'Ohana Society, the Royal Order of Kamehameha, the Ka'uiki Council. All the spiritual leaders were coming as well. All the *kahuna*s and many of the direct descendants of Kamehameha and Lili'uokalani and Queen Emma.

It was a sad, tear-filled day for the Hawai'ian people. When the procession of vehicles came to a full stop around the bottleneck of a tight curve, Dan could hear rising up the tall slopes of the hanging cliffs, the mournful chants coming from the cars.

Dan was still nearly a half a mile from the entrance to the Maikai ranch when the cars began to edge to the side of the narrow road and park. He pulled his rented Taurus to the side and turned off the engine. It wasn't going to do any good to squeeze closer. The road was nearly pinched closed by the cars lining both sides.

He had a parka in his backpack in the trunk of the car. He put it on, lifted the jacket hood over his head, and slung the pack over his shoulder. Then he began to walk toward the ranch. Soon the road began to crowd with people so that even on foot it was difficult to make much headway. He could only go as fast as the whole mass in front of him. There were families with kids skipping alongside and others held in back pouches. They carried great baskets of food and musical instruments—mostly guitars and *'ukulele* but also conch shells and gourds. Food and music. Wherever the Hawai'ians went, these were the two most important ingredients to any gathering. Whether it was Christmas or Auntie's birthday or a *kūpana*'s funeral, they would eat and drink all day long. They would play music and talk story until they were all exhausted, then they would go home.

The road turned upwards after a hundred yards. The long expanse of taro and pineapple lay below them, stretching down to the sea. Dan knew another way into the ranch along the footpaths on the beach, so he hopped down off the crammed road and plunged into the jungle. He soon found a trail he remembered from childhood. It was still well worn because it was the path the locals used to get to a favorite fishing spot. A couple hundred yards down the beach, Maikai had built a dock for the family boats: three dinghies and a small outboard.

Once Dan reached the dock he knew it would be a straight walk up to the home where he'd grown up. Besides, he wanted to go down to the dock anyway to see if Paul's boat was there or if anyone had seen it in the last week.

The path was very muddy in the heavy rain as he walked along the high banks that bordered the taro. He sloshed through deep puddles, and the dress shoes and slacks that he'd worn for the funeral were caked by a thick clay paste after a short distance. When he finally reached the ocean, his muddy shoes slipped on the jagged lava rocks that made up the beach in that area. After a while he had to pull his rubber flaps out of his pack. That was when he decided to change into shorts as well. The truth was most of the men were either dressed in long Polynesian wrap skirts, or they were in shorts, so Dan's long pants were out of place anyway. Only a dumb *haole* would wear long pants in this steaming jungle.

He stuffed his pants into the backpack with his shoes and began to pick his way along the rock until he made it to the dock. He still couldn't see the short pier that Maikai had built in a little inlet between a pair of high rocks because a jutting lava formation obscured the view of the dock until he was nearly on it. When he jumped down to the sand, he could see that Paul's boat wasn't there. Only Maikai's boat and an old dingy bobbing in the worked-up surf. He felt acid cutting through his guts. He was certain now that Paul wasn't just on a binge somewhere. Something was seriously wrong.

Dan could see an old man on the Maikai boat fixing wreaths and stringing flowers. He figured it had to be Francis Kane, a man who had worked for the Maikai family his whole life. He had helped Michael and Paul and Dan build their first outrigger and showed them the way the king's boatmen paddled the great royal canoe across the channel to Kaho'olawe, the island of the *ali'i*. While they paddled, Francis would tell them stories of his grandfather, who was supposed to have been the head paddler for Kamehameha's daughter, Queen Nahe'ena'ena.

The Hawai'ian language was made for storytelling, not for writing, and the Hawai'ians were practiced storytellers. They spent hours relating the great legends to their children with chants and songs thrown in. Francis would stand up in the prow of the canoe and, with his feet on the rails, would rock the canoe as he told about the great hurricane that ravaged the islands after the great Kamehameha died.

As Dan approached, he could see that Francis had been crying, probably for the last two days.

When Francis's eyes focused, he recognized Dan immediately. He stepped to the rail and hopped down into the water and embraced Dan.

As Francis began to weep in Dan's arms, Dan felt for the first time in years what it had been like to live on a secluded piece of land in Hawai'i among true Hawai'ians. The Hawai'ians were so much more open with their emotions than most people, and Dan had become accustomed to seeing them laugh throughout the day. At work in the taro patches, their woven hats stuffed low to their heads, they would be talking story, constantly giggling in their singsong manner, sometimes straightened into standing by the force of their own laughter.

As Francis sobbed in Dan's arms, Dan heard the first long moan of the conch shells and the men beginning the long, sad chant of mourning for their slain leader. For that was what Maikai had become, a martyred warrior, slain in a battle they had been fighting for over a hundred years.

Francis leaned back with his big hands still grasping Dan's shoulders.

"Why you never come see your Uncle Francis?"

"You know why," Dan said. Francis had been there the day Maikai had thrown him out.

"You still fighting with Maikai, then? He forgive you long time ago. He never tell you this?"

"Maikai never said a word to me until a few days ago."

He remembered Francis crying, with his wife, Luana, and some of the other workers as Dan walked down to the highway with a duffel stuffed with his possessions. Dan had walked most of the way to Paia, where he'd stayed at a friend's house for a couple of days. Then the friend drove him to the airport and he flew to O'ahu to live with Paul, who by that time was living in Honolulu working for a charter boat company.

Francis began to sob once more and drew Dan to him again.

"Maikai love you, Danny Kahanohano," he said, using Dan's Hawai'ian name bestowed on him by Uncle Charlie the day he was given the knife identical to the one that killed the governor, the knife the *haole* used to frame Maikai, a true *kanaka maoli*. At least that was the way the Hawai'ians saw it.

Dan took Francis by the shoulder and led him to a boulder near the dock, and they both sat down.

Before Dan left Honolulu he'd checked with HPD to see if they'd come up with anything on Paul. They had assured Dan that Paul was at the top of their hot sheet.

The moan of the conch shells blew out over their heads and the male voices in the throng of mourners answered, "*Aaaaa-uē Aaaaa-uē ua hala ē.*"

"Have you seen Paul, Francis?"

The Hawai'ian looked up slowly. "Paul always come visit."

"I mean have you seen him in the last couple of weeks, Francis?" Dan asked.

Francis looked out to sea and thought for a moment. "Yes," he said at last. "Come by last Monday, I think."

"Oh," Dan said. He knew for a fact that Paul was in Honolulu on Monday. That was the day they'd fought about whether he would take the boat to Maui. He couldn't have been here until Tuesday at the earliest. If, that is, Francis's failing memory was at all reliable.

"No, no, wait," Francis said, his dark eyes brightening. "What am I thinking? It was Tuesday because he bring present for Luana. He never forget her birthday. He make special trip he say for give her present."

Dan smiled. Then Paul had made it. That was a relief. But why wasn't he there when they were searching Maikai's house, as he had threatened?

"Now, you're sure you saw him Tuesday?"

"Sure. Luana's birthday," he said with certainty as if no husband had ever forgotten his wife's birthday.

"When did he leave?"

The Hawai'ian shook his head. "I don't know. I never see him again. We go Cousin Kimo's place for party."

Dan could imagine the scene as a couple of hundred locals—Filipino, Japanese, Samoan, Tongan, and Hawai'ian—all descended on Kimo's little shack above the beach outside Hāna, all with food and bottles of wine and beer and many with ukes and guitars and gourds, all singing and laughing.

Dan hugged Francis again and made his way up the hill through the terraces of taro to the highway and then through the gate of the Maikai ranch that only last week he had stormed, armed with a search warrant. Today the gates were staked open with bamboo poles and a flood of locals were trudging up the road to the house.

So Paul had made it after all. But how long had he stayed?

Whom had he talked to, besides Francis? Where was he when the search was going on? And why hadn't he warned Peter Maikai about the search? That was the reason he'd sailed the *Loa* to Maui in the first place. That meant he had to have left before the search. But where had he gone?

Dan followed the sound of the conch shells up to the house. In the field across from the house, the people had spread out blankets and *lauhala* and began singing when they felt like it, moaning when they felt like it, chanting now and then some unwritten chant that everyone seemed to know.

Walking among them dressed all in white, Lily was going from group to group hugging and kissing the men and women who wept on her shoulders.

The wind was blowing so hard that day the long fingers of the palm leaves rippled and snapped like tattered flags. The clouds had suddenly blown clear of Haleakalā, and Dan could see the greensward all the way to the top of the volcano's mouth.

After an hour or so, Uncle Charlie appeared out of nowhere, it seemed, and began walking toward the hills. And without a word the people got up and began to follow the *kahuna*. He wore a yellow-and-red headdress of *o'o* feathers and a drape of robed garlands that touched the ground behind him. A chorus of conches reverberated in the valleys behind them. Six tall Hawai'ian men, bare except for the simplest of skirts with *haku* lei crowning their heads, bore Maikai's litter piled high with maile up the mountain behind Uncle Charlie.

Dan knew where Uncle Charlie was leading the procession. He and Michael and Paul had played in those hills for years. The mourners would wind up Haleakalā on a foot-beaten path through a forest of umbrella-shaped papaya and overhanging vines that made it as dark as his old bedroom at dusk.

His old bedroom. It had been years since he'd thought of it. Lily, fifteen at the time, would pretend to walk down to the beach then circle back through the taro fields to his bedroom. It was in the rear of the house so it was blocked from the setting sun, the shadows of the volcano darkening their hideaway.

He remembered her hair, sea breeze and pikake, that covered their faces as they kissed. The full lips of her Polynesian mouth, the way her eyes, deep as an Indian's, shaped like a Malaysian's, begged him to release his spirit to her. The bedroom was the only place he had ever feared her. At such a young age she led him, surefooted as a *i'iwa* bird, to drink at the stream of her feelings.

He could see Uncle Charlie at the head of the throng stopping at the bridge. The *kahuna* turned to the mourners and raised a palm-branch scepter. The crowd milled to a halt, a few of the grief-stricken bumping those ahead of them, a few of the younger men still pushing for a better view. The old man turned, and his head-dress which soared two feet above his fully upstretched hands, spun with him. Then he began to walk across the rotted rope bridge that spanned the deep canyon. The Waioli Stream fell down from the clouds and cut its way through a two-hundred-foot drop.

Uncle Charlie pulled his way across the rickety bridge, hand-over-hand on the fraying rope handrails. Then two men took the litter from the others and stepped slowly and softly across. The only sound was the rush of the stream through the bamboo reeds, crashing against the brutally hard lava below.

In the mornings Lily used to meet him here when they were in love. Hiding in their cave, he would watch her scurry like a spindly-legged piper across that same bridge, her hair flying behind her. They would sometimes hike into the jungle above the ranch and look down at twenty-five miles of rugged coastline and a thousand miles of ocean more vast even than their young dreams. They had to do their dreaming in these secluded spots or hidden in his bedroom, her hand cupped playfully over his mouth as he moaned, "Ohhhh, Lily, I love you." Because they knew, even though it was never said, that her father, deep in his heart, didn't want a *haole* to touch his daughter.

When Maikai found out that Dan had touched her as deeply as a man can touch a woman, right up through to her heart, Maikai's hate and distrust of the *haoles* roared out of him and he struck Dan across the face with his fist. Dan was standing behind the house stripping a mango when Maikai hit him, and the blood spurted from his cut lip. Dan's adopted father screamed that he never wanted to see him again. That was the part that Dan had never told to anyone, especially Lily or Paul.

As soon as Maikai struck him, Dan, on his back from its force, looked up at Maikai and the anger drained from both of them for one everlasting moment. The shame they shared bound them: Maikai realizing that he hated someone he loved, Dan that he'd betrayed the man who had trusted and loved him.

When Maikai drove off with Lily the next day, telling Dan to get off his land, Dan felt that Maikai was right. Lily didn't deserve the mess he'd gotten her into. He was sleeping with his sister, for God's sake. Sure, there was no blood between them and they could be legally married, but it made little difference. Maikai was his father as surely as he was Lily's. The fact that Dan was *haole* only certified what Maikai already knew: the white man was no good for the Hawai'ian.

From that moment on, Maikai's Hawai'ian pride took on an almost violent fervor. Where before he was a strong, quiet supporter of the activists, suddenly he was their spokesman, their leader, the *Ali'i* they had all been looking for to unite them. In six months he had brought together all the factions, like Kamehameha the Great, into one Hawai'ian nation. It was a force of thousands that suddenly took aim at the elected officials of the state and asked them directly what the hell they were going to do about restoring the Hawai'ian people's dignity and their lands.

After the men had brought Maikai's body safely across the bridge, Uncle Charlie turned to the crowd across the ravine.

"Today we bury our brother, our father, Peter Kameaho'iho'i'ea Maikai, but we not burying Hawai'ian sovereignty with him. Hawai'ian activist is not just Peter Kameaho'iho'i'ea Maikai. Hawai'ian activist not one man. Hawai'ian activist is every Hawai'ian." And he swept his hand over the whole crowd, pointing out beyond them to encompass the other islands.

"Hawai'ian activist is the judge in the court, the baker making sweetbread. Hawai'ian activist the children in school, surfing, canoeing, chanting, learning all their ancestors' traditions. . . ."

While he stood listening to Uncle Charlie, Dan spotted Joe Kalama sitting in a group of locals. Dan recognized two of the fat, older women who sprawled on the ground next to Joe as Kalama's aunties. Dan had eaten *lomi* salmon at their house. The cop was bare to the waist, and sat side-squat on his heels. He could have been a Hawai'ian warrior listening to the king talking story about the great warriors of the past preparing his men for the battle before them.

"We place our brother into the loving hands of *Nā Akua,"* Uncle Charlie went on. "The Hawai'ian people can never be separated from our land because the Hawai'ian people and *Nā Kanaka maoli* are one and the same. The land, the people are the same."

Then two men who had been waiting on the far side of the bridge took the litter from the two carriers who had crossed the bridge with it. They were of the Alapa'inui family, who had been entrusted for centuries with the burial of the *Ali'i.* Only this family and this family alone knew in which secret caves they had placed the bodies of the dead royalty—the kings and queens, princes and princesses and the chiefs and their wives. There were hundreds of these royal caves, most no bigger than a sepulchre, pocketed away all over the lava hills, hidden by a ten-foot-thick drape of foliage that soon covered over the caves. Only these two would know where Maikai's body was placed so that no man could disturb his everlasting rest or steal any of his *mana,* his spirit, by taking his body or any part of it. Not even the family, Michael or Lily, would know. So that as the crowd waved mournfully to their departed chief as the bearers took him into the mountains, Michael and Lily, standing with the throng across the bridge, said good-bye to their father for the last time.

Then the crowd dissolved back down the hill, leaderless, Uncle Charlie disappearing in the jungle as suddenly as he had appeared to lead the procession. For the next six hours they ate and chanted and sang the old Hawai'ian songs. When they began to sing Lili'uokalani's *"Aloha Oe,"* the wind, as if on command, suddenly quieted, and the sad, plaintive song carried mournfully down the slopes to the ocean.

They lay on the meadow above the rippling taro patches, the air buzzing below with pineapple bugs. Dan sat with them, taking off his shirt and eating the *poi* and *kalua* pig and *lomi lomi* salmon and sticky rice from their woven baskets.

It was just before sunset when he walked around to the back of the house and stumbled upon Lily and Michael arguing.

"What are they doing here, then," Lily was saying, "if they're not trying to buy our land?" The way her hips were set and her eyes bored into Michael, Dan knew she was angry.

"We're just talking, Lily," Michael said. "It's all right with you if I talk to some of my friends?"

The mottled shade of the wind-blown mango danced shadows across her face.

"Those aren't friends. They're buzzards. You know what they do when they get ahold of a piece of land. They destroy it as soon as they possibly can."

"Come on, Lily," Michael said. Behind him the mango trees swayed with their heavy teardrop loads ready to fall at any moment. "They don't destroy it. They turn it into something everyone can use. Two hundred acres of this property is unusable the way it sits. You can't grow taro. It's too volcanic. The only thing you can do is build a place for folks to come and relax. Hizaga wants to build a very tasteful hideaway for the well-to-do. Private little bungalows—"

"Oh, so you've already decided how you're going to carve it up. My God, Michael, the men have not even returned yet with Father's empty litter."

"A lot of things died with our father the other day. You can't revive an ancient way of living." He pointed in the direction of the airport, where a string of jets floated one by one onto the runway. "It's the twenty-first century. We're not living in shacks on the beach anymore, so don't try to fool yourself that we are."

"You know I don't think that way, Michael, so don't try to use that on me. I'm talking about our father's expressed wishes not to sell the land."

"I never heard that. In fact, the last time I talked to him he was changing his feelings about the land. It was time to do something besides make *poi,* he told me."

"That's a lie and you know it," Lily said and turned from her brother. She knew then that Michael couldn't be trusted. As usual her father had been right. "He made me promise on his deathbed not to sell the land."

Michael shook his head and began to laugh to himself. "Of course, you would be the one he picked to burden with his deathbed wish. You were always a sucker for the old man's theatrics."

"What do you mean by that?" she said, the defiance back in her voice.

"Jesus, Lily, he's been running your life ever since you were a kid. That's what I never understood about you. If he took my kid away, I would have been mad as hell. You just loved him all the more."

"Maybe I thought he'd done the right thing."

"Bullshit, Lily," Michael said softly. "Then why didn't you ever get married?"

Before she could speak, he answered for her. "Oh, I know. Too busy with school, too busy running the ranch, too busy catering to the old man to ever have a life of your own."

She turned away from Michael.

"I'm not going to sell the land, Michael, no matter what you say."

"Lily, you think I don't already know that? That's what I told Hizaga."

"You did?"

"Sure, I did," he said. "I'm not a fool. I know I can't fight you." He patted her once on the shoulder and left her alone in the yard.

Lily turned as Dan came out of the shadow, pretending he'd just walked up.

"Dan," she said, still immersed in her conversation with Michael. "I'm glad you came. I wanted to talk to you about my father."

"I'm sorry, Lily."

"Don't be. None of this is your fault. None of it."

By the way she said it, Dan knew she meant not just Maikai's death in jail but about their past, about the baby, everything that happened between them.

She held out her arms and he stepped into them below the bedroom where they had conceived a child eighteen years before. It had been that long since they'd held one another. She felt exactly as he'd remembered her, a perfect fit in his arms, the lush hair in his face, the smell of salt air and plumeria. They held each other for a long time before she began to cry on his shoulder.

He held her with a slight rocking motion and then he kissed her cheek. He felt the warm wet of her tears on her skin and then the warmth of her lips as they kissed, sharing their grief and what they still felt for each other.

"Dan! Hey, Dan!" someone shouted behind him.

He broke from her kiss and spun around, almost expecting to be confronted by Peter Maikai again. But it was Joe. He was dressed now in long pants and a buttoned shirt, and now there was a look on his face not of grief, but of business. Police business.

"I just got a call from HPD in Honolulu. A fisherman spotted Paul's boat."

Lily's arms fell from around him as he stepped toward Joe. By the look on Kalama's face, Dan didn't know whether it was good news or bad.

"Where is it?"

"Off Kaho'olawe."

Dan smirked. Paul often went there to fish and a couple of times had camped out on the island illegally. It was the perfect place to get stinking drunk and hide away from the world.

"How about Paul?"

"Dan," he said and paused; his big hands were kneading something invisible in front of him. "The boat's been wrecked pretty bad."

There were treacherous rocks near the island. Paul had sailed those waters hundreds of times and he knew where the danger was, of course. But the last time Dan had seen Paul he was in no condition to spot trouble.

"How bad?" Dan asked.

"Sounds pretty bad."

"The boat's sunk?"

"I don't know," Kalama said. "They said they found it, was all."

"What about Paul?"

"I don't know that either."

"Well, who the hell does know?"

Joe put his hand on his friend's shoulder. "They're sending a chopper from Kahului to pick us up," he said, and as he did Dan could hear the distant thwacking of the helicopter. A moment later it came over the hill behind the house and hovered above the yard until the mourners had cleared an area large enough for it to set down.

Dan looked back at Lily and they smiled sadly at each other. Then Dan ran with Joe to the aircraft and they climbed into the backseats. As the chopper rose above the house, Dan realized for the first time how right Maikai had been about the strength of his movement, of the determination of the Hawai'ians to take back their land again. Before him was a sea of people spread out over the vast Maikai ranch. The throng stretched down the Hāna Highway, and the cars backed up now for miles had blocked both sides of the highway as far as he could see. They rose higher and he could see the bridge above Waioli Stream. Beyond the bridge, Peter Kameaho'iho'i'ea Maikai, the latest of their chiefs to die in battle, had been buried.

The helicopter swung around and headed toward the slopes of Haleakalā. Dan looked back and saw Lily still standing behind the house, alone again, watching him fly off.

CHAPTER
SIXTEEN

The helicopter swung south and followed the coastline over old Hāna, past Ōhe'o, and down the dry leeward slopes of the mountain. A few minutes later, they spotted Kaho'olawe and the tiny half-moon of Molokini swimming before it.

"According to the Coast Guard," Joe explained to Dan, "a fisherman spotted the wreckage and called them. That's when Iida got ahold of me."

The helicopter started crossing the eleven miles of water that separated East Maui from Kaho'olawe. They could see the round mound of Lāna'i, the rugged jutting mountains of Moloka'i, and off to the south the snow-dusted peaks of Mauna Kea and Mauna Loa on the Big Island.

Kalama hated to fly, especially in choppers. He had a tight grip on the restrainer hanging between the seats and a yellow cast to his face Dan recognized as pure fear. Joe's head was tilted all the way back against the headrest and his eyes were closed.

Neither of them could appreciate the splendor of the scene. Joe was holding tight to the backseat, Dan wondering what they were going to find on the other side of Kaho'olawe. Kalama wasn't telling him anything other than that they'd spotted his brother's boat. But had they found Paul?

As they neared the island, Dan could see the tourist dive boats bobbing in the protective shell of Molokini. Dozens of scuba divers hovered in the clear waters of the fish reserve.

Dan nudged Joe and pointed beyond the divers to a long, gray figure in the water, one end of which was shaped like a cudgel.

The cop looked sideways out the window without moving his head.

"Hammerhead," Dan said and shook his head with a wry smile. That was one of the things the resorts lining the beaches didn't advertise in their brochures.

Joe moved his eyes downward and raised his eyebrows.

"Sharks swim in the sea," he said, putting his head back against the rest. It was the expression the locals liked to use when a tourist asked if there were any sharks in these waters.

The helicopter's nose swung suddenly upward and they climbed over the 1,500-foot peak, Mao'ulanui, that topped Kaho'olawe, the craters from years of navy shelling showing in its pocked face.

When they came over the top and swooped down the back slope, Dan could see the protected bay of Kanapou. There were two small fishing boats huddled near a Coast Guard cutter. Beyond them, hung up on the reef, was what was left of the *Loa*.

As they approached the wreckage, the helicopter swung around and Dan saw that only the prow of the boat remained. The waves breaking on the reef were bashing apart what was left of it.

He motioned the pilot to get closer. As they descended, the wind from the chopper blades pushed what was left of the boat off the reef. The word *Loa* was plainly visible on the white hull.

"Jesus. There's nothing left of her," Dan said. "What in the hell happened?"

"Don't know," Joe answered. "All Iida told me was that they'd found the boat near Kaho'olawe."

"Do you want to land?" the pilot asked Dan and pointed at the beach below them.

Dan nodded once and the helicopter moved toward the shore. On rock-strewn Keoneuli Beach, they could see a handful of Coast Guard sailors spread out on the sand searching the debris of Paul's boat that had already washed ashore.

The helicopter settled down a few yards from the sailors and Joe and Dan jumped out. The wind was strong and blew the sand into

Dan's face as he made his way toward the officer who was walking to the chopper.

"Mr. Carrier?" the officer asked. He was a middle-aged man with a plump belly pushing against the tarnished buttons of his khaki shirt. He looked like he wanted to be anywhere but this bomb-infested beach on a Saturday evening. "I'm Dave Haskins."

Dan shook the lieutenant's hand and pointed at Kalama. "This is Sergeant Joe Kalama from HPD."

The two nodded and shook hands with one brief swipe.

"Did you find my brother?"

Haskins looked at Dan curiously. "That was your brother's boat?"

"Yes."

"I see. That's why they flew a PA over. I was wondering, on a simple boating accident." He said it mostly to himself then he added, looking at Dan, "No. We haven't found anything yet."

He nodded over his shoulder at the men kicking around in the sand, overturning the planks of wood and other debris from the *Loa*.

"We're flying in a crew to search up there, though." He waved toward the sloping hills behind them.

Dan didn't bother to ask what they expected to find at the thousand-foot level when the boat was lying destroyed at their feet.

"Have you got any idea what happened?" Dan asked. "This is a hell of a mess for just a boating accident."

"We're guessing a fuel line blew. That's the only thing besides a bomb that could do this."

"A bomb?" Kalama said, surprised. "Iida didn't say anything about a bomb."

"No, it wasn't a bomb as far as we know. The fisherman that saw it blow said he thought it went off like a bomb."

"Why'd he say that?" Joe asked. "There some kind of difference between a bomb going off and a fuel tank blowing?"

Haskins shrugged. In an hour, the full search team would be deployed and he'd be heading back to Pearl. There was a good game on the tube that evening and he was supposed to be relieved at seven, not poking around Kaho'olawe looking for a body that had been blown into shark bait.

"Where's the eyewitness?"

"We've got him right over here."

Haskins waved to one of his men. "I wanna see that witness."

The sailor walked over to a pile of lava rocks where an old man in shorts and flaps was sitting. His skin was almost the same dark brown as the worn-down lava. He was as thin as a famine victim, and when he pushed himself up he seemed to strain at the effort. When he got closer, Dan could see he was a mix of a lot of Oriental bloods, probably with some Portuguese thrown in.

"This is Makela Santos. He was the one who saw the accident."

The old man looked up at Dan before he spoke, and Dan recognized him.

"You dock your boat at the Ilikai sometimes, don't you?" he asked.

"Yes. Sometimes, if da feeshing good by da park," he said, and Dan knew he meant Ala Moana Park, where they practiced paddling most often. The fishermen would be trawling just beyond the breakers as they paddled out.

"You know my brother, Paul Carrier. That was the *Loa* you found."

"Da *Loa?* Sure, I know him. Sometime we go feeshing for mullet." He lowered his head. "Paul on da boat, den?"

"We think so. Did you see anybody?"

"Yeah," the old man said sadly. "Somebody on da bridge when da boat blow up."

"Was it Paul?" Dan asked quickly.

"I neva see."

"What do you mean, you never saw?" Dan asked impatiently. "I thought you saw someone on the bridge?"

"Sure. But neva see who. My eyes getting old."

"But you're sure you saw someone on the bridge?" Dan persisted.

"Don't know for sure."

"Damn it!" Dan said, throwing his arms in the air. "You just said you saw someone."

Joe stepped between Dan and the old man and gave Dan a look that said to give the old guy a break. Dan turned and walked a few paces down the beach.

"Dat's his brudda, see," Joe explained to the old man.

Makela nodded and looked over his shoulder at Dan.

"Just tell me what happened," Joe said. He had a notebook out, ready to take down what Makela said.

"Don't know. I been feeshing Moloka'i, den decide I going come Kaho'olawe for catch *opakapaka*. My friend say dey runnin' good here. So I come." His tobacco-colored hands pointed off to the leeward. "When I come 'round Lae oltālona I see his brother's boat. The sun very very bright today, so I cover up like this. . . ." He made a visor with his hands over his brow. "So I can see da boat and den it just blow up. Like dat. Big fireball. Plenty smoke, too."

"So let me get this straight, then," Kalama said. He was pointing the pen at the old man. "The boat hit the reef and exploded."

The old man shook his head. "No hit da reef. Blow 'em up out dere." He pointed to the middle of the bay. "What left float to da reef, get hung up on da rocks. Da current take 'em dere."

"So it was just sailing along when it blew?"

"Yeah, just blew. Like dat." He made the sound of an explosion and his hands flew up like he'd seen the pieces of Paul's boat do.

"Did you see Paul in the water after that? Swimming or on the shore?" Dan asked.

"I go over quick and look 'round. But nothing. Lotta *Manō* swimming 'round in no time, though, so gotta be something in da water, you know, for eat."

Dan winced at the thought of Paul in the water, maybe unconscious and bleeding and the sharks moving in.

"What kind of sharks did you see?" Kalama asked.

"Lotta hammer."

"Jesus," the cop sighed. He knew the hammerheads weren't shy about human flesh. A pack of hammers could devour a man in a matter of minutes and there'd be nothing left but his cap, if he was wearing one.

In the last few years hammerheads had been feeding on an increasing number of surfers and divers in these waters. It was another point of contention between the Hawai'ians and the *haole*. Sharks had for thousands of years been considered deities to the Hawai'ians, who believed that certain sharks carried the souls of ancestors. These sharks were fed and prayed to by the locals. All the sharks meant to the people who ran the hotels were one more pain in the ass driving business away.

"Thanks, Makela," Dan said. By the flushed look on his face, Kalama knew that Dan was also thinking about what the hammers could do. "You can go back to your boat now."

"I sorry about your brudda. He was good feesherman," the old man said sadly and walked back to the water. He climbed into a Coast Guard Zodiac and waited for someone to motor him back out to his boat.

"I wonder if Paul ever made it to Maui, then," Kalama said.

"He made it."

"Yeah, how do you know that?"

"You know Francis, the guy that takes care of the Maikai boats?"

"Yeah, I know him. He tell you Paul showed up?"

"Yes. He got there on Tuesday like he said he was going to."

"Then why didn't we see him at the search that day?"

"I don't know," Dan said. "Lily told me she never saw him at the ranch. I tried to talk to Michael, but he doesn't want to see my face."

"He still blaming you for Maikai's arrest?"

Dan shook his head.

"I'll talk to Michael about Paul. And you," Joe said.

"Don't worry. Sometimes you've got to blame someone for things you can't control. He'll come around."

"Whatever," Kalama said. "But can you trust that old bugga watching the boats? I hear he likes to smoke that *pakalolo* too."

"You can trust Francis," Dan said, looking off to the mountains. "Paul made it to Maui, all right. Why he decided not to come to the search like he said he was going to, or where he went after he arrived, or how he got over here," Dan said, looking around him at the wreckage of his brother's boat, "that's something I'm going to find out."

Kalama nodded his head and bent down and picked up a charred piece of the *Loa*.

"I'd also like to know what caused this explosion," Dan said.

"Like Haskins said, probably a fuel line. You know Paul, he was getting careless these days. You see that engine lately? It looked like he never did nothing except put a little gas in. If he was drinking and smoking . . ." Kalama let the thought sink in.

"Yeah, I know," Dan said and walked down to where the water ran up onto the rocky shoreline. Kalama was next to him.

"You don't think there's any way this could have been something other than an accident, do you, Joe?" Kalama had always been the one person besides his brother whom he could talk to about anything.

The cop shook his head slowly and put his hand on Dan's shoulder. He'd seen relatives trying to make sense of a senseless death many times before. It was always hardest for them to believe what was most obvious: that their loved one died for reasons God only knew. The same way Paul himself had been unable to accept the death of his family.

"That kind of thinking can only hurt you, bra," Joe said.

"God, I know that," Dan said. He was watching a piper chasing the receding laplets of water, then scurrying away from them when the water ran up the shore again.

"It just doesn't make sense to me, though. Jesus, I know Paul was my brother, Joe, and I'm probably letting grief get in the way of thinking clearly. But you know how it is when something doesn't feel right."

He looked at Kalama. The cop didn't put much faith in feelings when it came to investigation. He waited for the crime-scene unit and Forensics to do their job and for the witnesses to give their statements before he played any so-called hunches. And even then they were only hunches, which he knew amounted to less than zilch in a court of law.

Dan saw on Kalama's face what the cop was thinking.

"There's just some things that don't square, Joe. Where's he been the last week? And how did the boat just blow up? Paul was an expert seaman. He'd piloted the *Loa* for fifteen years without a hitch."

Kalama took a deep breath. He could see that Dan wasn't going to be happy until they talked it through. "So what are you saying, then?"

"Well," Dan said, picking up a piece of dull gray metal from the beach that was probably shrapnel from a navy shell, "if it wasn't an accident, then that leaves suicide or murder."

"Murder?" Kalama said, laughing it off with a scrunch of his face.

"First of all, I can't think of anyone who would want to kill Paul. But especially like this. This wouldn't have been some heat-of-the-moment killing. You know, okay, he's drinking and gets into a bar fight and someone pulls out a pistol and shoots him. Fine, that I can see. But if a guy's gonna blow up a boat, first of all, he's got to know what he's doing. Then he's got to do a little planning, bra. You don't get a little drunk and decide to plant a bomb on a boat because some guy insulted you. So that means Paul had a big-time enemy and, frankly, Dan, your brother didn't have many enemies that I knew of. Except maybe himself."

Dan didn't say anything. Joe could see he was still thinking.

"If someone wanted Paul dead," Joe went on, "a bullet would do just as good a job with a hell of a lot less trouble."

Joe put his arm around Dan and began to walk him down the beach away from where his brother's boat was strewn on the rocks.

"You know I'll make sure this is investigated thoroughly, but I don't think we're going to find anything like a bomb. You know Paul was hurtin' bad lately. He didn't care about himself and he sure didn't care about the *Loa*. He couldn't even take customers out for a dive anymore, it was such a mess. You know that. Think about it. He probably got drunk out here and he hit something and boom!" He said it softly to cushion the shock of Dan's brother's death. "Don't go doing this to yourself. Let me investigate. If I find anything, we'll get the son of a bitch that did it. But don't drive yourself crazy worrying about this whole thing. Paul probably hit something."

"You heard Makela, though. The *Loa* wasn't on the reef when it blew."

"Who says the old man knows what he's talking about, anyway? Haskins said it got hung up on the reef. But it doesn't matter, really. It coulda been anything."

Dan rubbed a mound flat in the sand with his foot and turned to the reef, where Paul's hull had drifted free.

"Yeah, I know you're right, Joe," he said. "You know a prosecutor, though. I'm just trying to make some sense of it."

"Some things you just can't make any sense of. You just gotta accept the grief and not let it tear you up, brudda."

Dan looked up at his friend and the big Hawai'ian was crying.

They'd just flown from the funeral of a friend and now another good friend was gone. Kalama had been the one to bring their old canoe team together again. He'd spent a lot of time trying to talk Paul back. And now it was all over.

"You're right, Joe. Just do me a favor, would you?"

Kalama didn't answer. He was looking out to sea, his cheeks wet with tears.

"Ask Michael what Paul was doing at the ranch and why he left before we got there?"

Joe looked at Dan and managed a smile. "No problem, bra. I'll find out what happened to Paul for you. That's a promise."

SEVENTEEN

Lily's flight from Maui was delayed, so she arrived at her appointment for the reading of her father's will an hour and a half late. David Collins, the attorney Michael had hired to probate his father's will, read it word for word while the two of them sat quietly.

Collins was a short, dark-skinned man with a full beard and touched-up black hair, and he perspired heavily even in his air-conditioned office, which he kept at arctic temperatures. When he was finished reading, he put the document down on the desk in front of him and looked to the two heirs for their questions.

"Well," Michael said, "no real surprises there."

Lily stared blankly at her brother. The refrigerated air was blowing directly on her shoulders. She had her hands on her elbows, hugging herself to keep warm. She turned to Collins, who she knew was an old crony of Michael's. "Are you sure that was my father's last will?"

"As you know, Miss Maikai, I didn't write this will," Collins began. "As far as I know, it is his final will. Do you have reason to believe there is a more recent document?"

"Of course it's his last will," Michael said firmly. "He kept it in his safe."

"That's not what he told me," Lily said.

"What do you mean? He never said anything to me."

"Well, he did to me, Michael. The day he died he told me that he left part of the ranch to my daughter. This will doesn't mention her at all. Father spent the last year and a half of his life trying to find his granddaughter. His intention was always to restore her to her rightful place in the family. You know that. You heard him say it on many occasions."

"Lily," he said and took her hand. "You know our father. He said a lot of things he didn't really mean. All this talk of *'āina*, for example. Did you know he had talked to Hizaga himself about selling the land?"

"That's a lie," Lily said. She had grabbed the armrest and turned to face Michael. "He told me on his deathbed not to sell the land to those vultures. Ever."

Michael put his other hand on his sister's shoulder.

"Another thing. Who wrote that will?" she said and waved disdainfully at the papers on Collins's desk.

"I did," Michael said.

"I thought so."

"Are you accusing me of something, Lily?" he said angrily and stood up.

"Oh, calm down, Michael," Lily said. "I'm not accusing you of anything. Not yet anyway. All I know is there's another will you don't know about."

"Another will? No. He would have told me," Michael said and nodded toward Collins. "Right, Dave?"

"It seems likely that since your father had handed over most of the legal concerns of the estate to Michael he would inform him of any changes to the will," Collins said.

"Believe me, Lily," Michael said, "there is no other will. Why would he leave part of the ranch to a person he wasn't even sure existed?"

"Well, why not?" Lily asked, a little baffled by the question. "He asked you to look for her, didn't he? You can't deny that."

"No. And I couldn't find her."

"Unless another will is brought to me," Collins interrupted, "or without more evidence that there is another will, we will have to conclude this will reflects your father's wishes."

"Good," Michael said. "Now that that's settled, get the probate started, Dave. But before we leave, would you assure my sister that the sale of the land can be handled through probate?"

"What sale?" Lily asked.

"Hizaga's offer, of course."

"Michael, this isn't the time or place to discuss Hizaga. I already told you how I feel."

"Dave, talk to her, would you?" he said as if Lily were not in the room, sitting right next to him. "Tell her that the best thing to do is take Hizaga's offer. If they don't build that park on our property, they'll just do it someplace else in Maui."

"That's not my function, Michael," Collins said. "That's for the two of you to work out."

"Well, all I can say is, it's too good an offer to turn down. What do you say, Lily?"

Lily eyed him ominously. It was as if he'd asked her to curse her father's name. "Michael, I am not going to agree to sell the land. Ever."

Michael stared back at her. "I think you'll come around after you've had some time to think."

"I wouldn't count on it," Lily said as she stood and walked to Collins's desk. She extended her hand. "I'm sorry you had to witness this. I apologize. If I can be of assistance or if you need me for anything, please contact me directly. Would you do that?"

"Of course," Collins said while Lily walked toward the door.

"Then I guess I'll have to force a sale, Lily," Michael said, and the comment hit her like a bullet. She turned to him.

"Michael, you can't be serious? What about the taro farm, the Maikai ranch?"

"That was the old man's dream, not mine. I have no intention of pounding *poi* the rest of my life, when Hizaga has offered to pay us both a fortune to unload that mud patch."

He put his hand on her shoulder again and she shrugged it off. "Lily, look, your share will come to something over twenty-five million dollars when it's all worked out, counting the upfront money and the paper we'll carry for a few years. But what it all gets down to is you'll be able to do pretty much whatever you want. I loved Dad, too, you know that. You know my law practice has suffered the last few years in order that I could help you take care of the damn place. But it's time for us to live our own lives. Father had his shot. He lived it the way he wanted. Now it's our turn. And I'll tell you, I'm not going to let some old hackneyed fairy tale about bringing back the old Hawai'i"—he pronounced the *w* as a *v* like a true *kanaka maoli*—"interfere with my life."

"But it's Father's land," she said.

"Not anymore, Lily." He walked to the door and pulled it open. Then he turned back to Collins. "Get probate started immediately."

Dan slid his boogie board down the deep slope of a solid seven-footer and then rode the cauldron of foam to the shore. For the last two days all he had thought about was what could have possibly happened to his brother. He wanted to settle the whole matter in his mind and an hour in the surf boogie-boarding usually helped. Dan found that the less tense he was, the better his mind worked. So he'd beat himself sore for an hour or so in some big waves out at Makapu'u—the arms and legs exhausted from kicking through tons of water, the shoulders and back aching from the pounding of waves and the occasional slam against the sandy bottom.

He placed the board on the sand and sat on top of it, looking out at the other boogie-boarders, all much younger than he, sliding down the waves, then rushing back out.

He wanted to believe that Paul's death was an accident but it still didn't sit right with him. If Paul had run into a reef and sunk the boat, Dan could accept that. But an explosion? Sure, Paul was depressed and he more than likely was drunk at the time. But an explosion like that old fisherman described had to be caused by more than simple carelessness. On the other hand, Kalama was right. No one had a reason to kill Paul, especially a premeditated killing like a bomb. At least no reason that Dan knew of.

And what about Lily and Cathy? He wasn't sure what to think about either one of them. To say the least, he was confused. He had wanted a family for some time, and now Cathy, he thought, wanted one too. At least she was talking about it again. Marriage. Kids.

Maybe all the doubts about Cathy were nothing more than his own rationalizations. Nothing had really changed lately, had it? Sure, Cathy had taken Maikai's prosecution against his objections, but he understood that now. Maybe it wasn't Cathy. Maybe the problem was Lily. Maybe Lily was the real reason he was questioning his future with Cathy.

He picked up the board in two feet of water, wedged it under his armpit, and trudged up the slope of the beach. He grabbed his towel without breaking stride and headed for his car.

When he got to his car he put the board down against the rear bumper and snapped open the trunk. He shook the board to get off some of the sand and worked the nose into the far corner so the skag would fit under the lip of the trunk. He put the towel around his rear to protect the seat, unlocked the door, and slid behind the wheel. Sitting next to him in the passenger seat was Uncle Charlie Yates.

Dan didn't see the *kahuna* so much as feel him. A huge presence next to him on the seat wearing pants that came to just below the knee and a shirt with a V-neck that looked handmade. There were symbols stitched along the bottom that Dan had never seen.

"Charlie, Jesus Christ! You scared the hell out of me," Dan said.

"Lily needs you," the *kahuna* said without moving his head to look at Dan.

The fear drained instantly from Dan and he could smell Charlie suddenly over the pungent brace of the ocean. Charlie always smelled of *kukui* oil that he spread on his upper arms, a tropical odor of raw green and spice. And whenever Dan noticed it, he was either standing in a *kukui* forest or Uncle Charlie was nearby.

Despite the smell, this massive man—six feet one or two and well over 350 pounds—could sneak up on you in a variety of ways.

"What do you mean, Lily needs me?" Dan asked, a little perturbed.

When he was young he was mesmerized by the way Charlie wove an intricate puzzle with that hauntingly low voice that could break into a chant in midsentence. Now, in his present state of mind, Dan was annoyed, impatient with the deep conundrums that Charlie used to communicate.

"Maikai save his land for the Hawai'ian people. Not the people who want her only for money."

"That's fine, Charlie, but I'm sure Maikai had a will and he put all that in there."

The Hawai'ian had not moved yet, not even a finger of one of his hands, which rested palms-down in his lap.

"No. It's not there," he said.

Dan wondered for a moment how Charlie knew what was in Maikai's will. But Charlie knew a lot of things Dan couldn't figure.

"You know, Charlie," Dan started out softly. "You never know what's in the mind of a dying man."

"I know what was in Maikai's heart."

"Well, yeah, I'm sure you did, but a legal document usually reads a little different than the human heart," he counseled. He dropped his keys in his lap and patted the old *kahuna's* shoulder. He probably wanted to live in those mountains above the Maikai ranch undisturbed until he died. If this land was developed, a golf course and some condos would probably get in the way of that dream.

"So what was in the will?" Dan asked.

"Whatever Michael want."

"Really? Tell you the truth, I'd have bet Maikai would leave most of it to Lily. She was the most like him."

"To Lily and your daughter."

Of course, that stopped Dan. Charlie had a dramatic knack that could knock a person off balance for days at a time.

"My daughter hasn't been found yet," Dan said.

Charlie turned his head slowly on his neck without moving his shoulders and looked at Dan with those dark Polynesian eyes.

"Michael take the land from your daughter."

"How? If the land was given to Lily in the will, he can't do a damn thing about it."

"Not the same will. The will not Maikai's will." And with a swiftness Dan thought impossible, the old man rolled out of the car and walked away down the beach and disappeared. It was a typical Uncle Charlie exit. He'd fed Dan with a lot of nonsense and vanished practically in midsentence, leaving Dan to figure out what the old crackpot was trying to tell him. Dan wasn't sure he'd ever understand the way of the Hawai'ian.

Dan drove home trying to sort it all out. What was Charlie saying? That the will was tampered with?

As soon as he walked into his apartment, Cathy charged him. She had a key to his place too, and she had waited angrily to grill him.

"All right, what's Lily Maikai up to?" she demanded.

"What do you mean?"

"I mean, why's she calling you? Are you two having an affair again?"

Dan threw his windbreaker on the chair and gave a weak laugh.

"Look, Cathy. Don't try to make anything out of this. We were kids. I haven't seen her in almost twenty years. She means nothing to me anymore," he lied.

Dan went into the bathroom, stripped off his trunks, reached into the shower, and turned the water on. Cathy was right behind him.

"And when were you going to tell me about your daughter?" She had the instincts of a good prosecutor. She knew exactly when to go for the throat.

"How did you find out about that?"

"What does that matter? Just answer the question."

"Oh, answer it yourself," he said.

"Okay, I will," she kept at him, pressing. "The answer is you weren't going to tell me, were you? That's what I hate about you. You're such a coward."

"Are we going to go into your analysis again of why Reed got the job and I didn't?" Dan snapped at her.

"Look, Dan, quit throwing that up in my face. You know you could have been the head PA. But you were too goddamn proud. You'd have to kiss a little ass. Well, welcome to the real world. It wouldn't have hurt you."

"Bullshit! It would have poisoned me the same way it's poisoning you."

Dan was screaming now and so was Cathy.

"What are you saying?"

"I'm saying I don't want you following Reed around like his little puppy."

She swung around on him and her eyes were furious. "Are you accusing me of—" she began, but Dan cut her off.

"Cathy," he said in a calmer voice suddenly. He knew he'd gone too far. And he didn't even know why. "I'm not accusing you of anything. It's just that instead of getting closer, we seem to be going in opposite directions. You know what I want for us," he said and paused. "I just want us to spend some time together, away from Reed and the office and everything else.

Just see how we really feel about each other. I think we just need some time."

"I'm not sure there's any time left for us, Dan," she said and handed a piece of paper to him. Then she turned and walked toward the door.

"Your girlfriend wants to see you at her place to talk about some goddamn will," she said from somewhere in the hallway.

It was as if she'd been watching when he'd kissed Lily that day at the ranch. A moment later he heard the door slam with a shivering finality.

CHAPTER
EIGHTEEN

Dan flew to Maui the next morning and drove straight to the Maikai ranch. The sun was in his eyes as Dan walked up the steep slope behind the house. Lily was standing on the other side of the rope-and-wood contraption that passed for a bridge. She was looking up to the mountains where her father had been carried a few days before to some secret resting place.

Dan called out her name but the winds were quick and loud, racing down the canyon walls and banging the branches of the trees together. He wrestled his way across the bridge and walked up almost to her shoulder. She turned when he crushed a clump of brittle grass underfoot.

"Oh, good, Dan, you've come," she said as if she had been waiting there for him. "I wasn't sure that you would."

"Of course I'd come."

Below, he could see the perfectly cut terraces filled with the waving neon-green leaves. He waited for her to tell him why she wanted to see him.

"It's Michael," she said at last. "The problem is he never really understood his father. He thinks Peter Maikai lived only in the days of the *ali'i*. But my father understood very clearly what it was going to take to bring Hawai'i and the Hawai'ians into the twenty-first century intact." She paused a moment to look up to Haleakalā

"This land was everything to my father. That's why we can't let Michael sell it."

The notion surprised Dan. He had always thought that Michael, deep down, wanted what his father wanted.

"He really wants to?" Dan asked without trying to hide his disbelief.

"As soon as he can."

Dan looked at her for a moment to see if she meant it. When he knew she was serious, he realized why she had wanted so urgently to see him. She wanted legal advice.

"He'd have to own it to sell it," he said after he thought it out. "What does the will say?"

"It says he can do whatever he wants, I think." She walked to the edge of the lava ledge they both stood on and pointed to the north. "I'm not exactly sure how he did it, but he's the majority owner of the ranch now."

"I see," Dan said and thought to himself, Then that's it. Lily could hang things up in court for a while but as soon as a judge understood the contents of the will, the process would move swiftly in Michael's favor. "Then if you want to do something about it," Dan said, "it's going to cost you a lot of money and it probably won't do you a bit of good."

She was a strongly built woman with firm, athletic legs. Her hips set her solidly over her feet when she stepped back from the cliff edge and turned to him again.

"What if that wasn't the real will?" she said.

"What do you mean?" Dan asked. He'd heard a lot of wishful thinking when it came to wills.

"We believe there was a second."

"Who's we?" Dan asked.

"Well, Uncle Charlie and I," she said and looked defensively into his eyes to see if there was a challenge there. When she saw Dan's eyes narrow, she said, "What's wrong with Charlie?"

"Hey, don't get me wrong, I love Charlie. Christ, I learned everything I know about Hawai'i from him. But we're talking about a court of law here. I assume you asked me here to get my legal opinion?"

Lily smiled and her shoulders fell at ease.

"I'm sorry, Dan," she said, and like that, she was crying. This sud-

den outburst was understandable. He figured the death of her father kept her off balance these days. She'd be all right, then mem-
ories of her father—his bare, garlanded feet on the litter, the soles
scrubbed clean by the preparers, rising up behind the litter bearers—would overwhelm her with grief.

"The last thing my father said to me before he died was, 'Don't
let Michael sell the land.' I can't forget that."

"What's the land worth?" Dan asked.

"I don't know, exactly. But Michael said Hizaga—"

"Hizaga?" Dan interrupted. "Those robber barons!"

The Hizagas had turned every lovely piece of land they bought
into a souped-up version of the Hawai'i that appeared in every air-
line ad. Las Vegas wreathed in plumeria.

"Michael said Hizaga offered him fifty million dollars. Michael
would fall for the sound of that."

Dan smiled wryly and shook his head in agreement. Besides
his top-of-the-line Mercedes, Michael drove a Testarossa and
leased a penthouse in Discovery Bay. He was a loud, aggressive
counselor for whomever paid him well, and he only spoke pidgin
now as a joke.

"I see two problems," Dan said. "First of all, I'm not sure Michael
would try to muscle you out like this."

"Why, because the two of you paddle together?" Lily said with a
derisive laugh.

"Come on, Lily. You should know better than that. My second
problem," he said, "is the will. From what you've told me and from
what Uncle Charlie hinted at, maybe the will was a phony." He
touched her for the first time that day, putting his fingertips lightly
to her back. "You know you've got to be very careful if you plan to
challenge it. Uncle Charlie is the only one you know who saw this
will, I take it."

"I really don't know."

"Then you have nobody to corroborate Charlie's story."

"It's not a story," she said, clearly angry.

"I didn't mean story. But you know Charlie, goddammit. He's a
kahuna and everybody knows it." He hadn't meant it to sound like
an accusation.

"Yes," she said, "and that means a position of great respect."

"Maybe to a Hawai'ian, but to everyone else it's like calling him a witch doctor. They're not going to hold court out in Iao Valley where Charlie rules the birds. You'll be going up before a judge," he said. "A judge who knows Michael."

She turned and went by him, toward the bridge. "So that means we just give up?" she said. "Don't you want our daughter to get what's rightfully hers?"

"Of course I do, Lily. But she might not even be alive. Who knows if we'll ever find her?"

She stopped at the foot of the bridge while he caught up to her.

"We don't have to give up," he said. "But right now Michael holds all the good cards. We'll need to find something else besides what Charlie knows. Do you know, for instance, exactly what this other will was supposed to say?"

"I believe it named our daughter Sharon as an owner of the ranch along with Michael and me."

"I don't get it," Dan said, clearly puzzled. He had his hand on the rope railing of the bridge and he could feel the wind swinging it in his hand. "It's so unusual. Maikai hadn't even found her yet and he had her in the will."

"That's what he wanted."

"I know, but the problem is a court doesn't like things that are unusual. They tend to lean toward something that they see every day of the year. A son and a daughter split the ranch. That they understand. But a granddaughter whom no one has seen in seventeen years getting a third of fifty million dollars? That's unusual. Uncle Charlie's unusual. We need something that will make sense to a judge."

They had begun to cross the bridge together, the long stretch of the rope swinging uneasily in their hands.

"Was your father able to find anything out about where Sharon might be?" he shouted to her. She was only a few feet ahead of him but the noise of the wind and the rushing water in the ravine below competed with his voice.

"Nothing yet," she shouted back over her shoulder. "Apparently, the private detective they put on it had traced her adoptive parents to Arizona. Tucson, I think it was. But the parents had lost track of her. The last thing I heard, they thought she was back here in Hawai'i."

"You got this all from your father?" Dan asked. "Did you ever talk to the PI yourself?"

She reached the other side of the bridge and hopped up onto the grassy knoll above it.

"Actually, it was mostly Michael who was in contact with the investigator. Father had turned everything over to him in the end. Everything except the taro business. I'd been running it for years anyway."

Dan caught up to her and they began the long walk down through the meadow to the Maikai house. Beyond them the bright afternoon sun sizzled on the ocean. The big breakers added a wide ruffle of fluffy white to the skirt of the shore.

"Look," Dan said, "why don't I go see this PI and we'll start from there? Maybe the investigator knows something about our daughter that we don't."

"There's only one problem," Lily said.

"What?"

"I don't know who the investigator is."

"Great!" Dan said with an exasperated look heavenward.

"But Uncle Charlie does," she said.

Dan smiled. "Is there anything Charlie doesn't know?"

"I haven't found it yet."

Dan and Lily laughed as they walked the last two hundred yards down the slope to the house. When they reached the front porch and climbed the steps, Uncle Charlie was sitting on the couch in the front room as if he'd been summoned. Dan had always thought of Charlie as a kind of servant who was so wise you would never dare ask him for anything. Yet he was always serving. Bringing great bunches of things to eat, or telling stories by the hour to the children. One time, Charlie may have even saved Dan's life, appearing out of nowhere with an herbal poultice after Dan had been bitten by a poisonous centipede.

Dan smiled when he saw the old *kahuna*. He'd never heard of Charlie ever boarding a plane, and yet the Hawai'ian traveled back and forth from O'ahu to Maui to the Big Island as if he had his own set of wings.

"Howzit, Uncle Charlie? I suppose you came to help Lily too?"

"I can only point you to trouble. I cannot pick up the club and follow you into battle. I am too old for that."

Charlie had a prodigious gut that pushed his shirt up in front of him. But his shoulders and arms were still powerful and the flesh had not yet begun to hang from the bones even though Charlie might have been as old as eighty now.

"So point away," Dan said. "Lily says you know the PI who Maikai and Michael hired to look for our daughter."

"Maybell."

And there it was. Dan had never had a shoot-the-breeze conversation with Uncle Charlie in his life. That was the thing about Hawai'ians he admired the most: economy of words. Even when they sat around at night and talked story, eating, drinking beer, they would go on for hours, but it was never aimless chatter. They talked in stories, and if you understood what the story meant, you knew what they were getting at. Uncle Charlie was always talking about *'āina,* but he never once said "ecology." He'd tell you about how the kings and chiefs watched over the land and you knew that to a true *kanaka maoli* the land and the people, Hawai'i and the Hawai'ians, were one and the same.

CHAPTER
NINETEEN

Dan called just about every private attorney he knew who was doing business on the island of Maui before he finally found a PI named Maybell located in Napili. Maybell's office was on the lower road past Alaeloa in an *'ohana* apartment behind the main house. The building was surrounded by a garden of orchid, hydrangea, and bird of paradise. The place looked more like a surf shop than an office. It had surfboards and sails and fins propped all about.

The front door was split, the top half swung back open, so Dan could look through the screen door into the place. The front room had a desk in it with a crack on one side and a couple of chairs like a waiting room. He could see the kitchen off to the left. The whole place was done up beach-style with wicker and plants and a lot of tracked-in sand on the floor.

He rattled the screen door a couple of times and a woman came out in a bikini bottom and a tank top. Her sun-bleached hair was pulled back with two combs and her knees had the large knobs that are usually caused by a lot of time on a surfboard.

She was surprised to see Dan standing at her door. "What can I do for you?" she said, seeming a little annoyed.

"I'm looking for a Mr. Maybell."

He could see a little smile form in one corner of her mouth.

"No Mr. Maybell here," she said and gave him a blank look.

Dan stepped back and looked around at the doorframe for a

name or a number he could go by. An old Japanese woman in the front house had pointed him back here.

"Isn't this 22B?"

"Sure is," she said and rolled a barbell with her foot back into a corner. By the muscles cut into her arms, Dan knew she did a lot more with those weights than roll them around the room with her painted toes.

"And Mr. Maybell isn't here?"

"Nope."

"That's funny because I was told he had an office here. He's supposed to be a private investigator."

She just shook her head, bored.

"Well, are there any private detectives around here?"

"Sure, you're looking at one," she said and sat back against the top of the desk with her feet crossed in front of her.

"Oh," Dan said. He could tell by the look in her face she'd expected him to be surprised. "Maybe you can help me, then?"

"I might," she said and stepped forward and unlatched the screen and held it open. "Come in."

"Hello, Dan Carrier," he said and offered his hand, which she shook with a grip tight enough to open a reluctant jar lid.

"May," she said and paused a full second before she said, "Bell." And she leaned sarcastically on the last name.

Dan frowned, then he let his mouth drop into a wry smile.

"I guess we're having a little fun today, is that it?" he said.

"Hey, it gets a little boring around here when the swell is flat," she said and waved out to the ocean through the front door. "A male chauvinist walks in, how can I resist?"

Dan put his notes on the desk and leaned over it. "I see. And how did you hop to my misogynistic tendencies so quickly?"

"You assumed only a man could be a PI. That's not a tendency. That's a full-blown bias."

She walked over to the desk and threw a magazine on the top. "Correct me if I'm wrong here," she said. "When someone told you my name was May Bell, you figured the slight pause between names you'd heard was a mistake. Your mind automatically saw May Bell as Mr. Maybell. Hey, you're the sick one. I'm just trying to identify who's infected with the disease."

Dan dropped his head. He had come here to find some information and he didn't even know what he was looking for. Michael had used this woman to find his daughter and told Maikai she'd come up with nothing. Dan was perfectly ready to chalk that up as true. The best PIs have the ability to get a stranger to open up to them for a minimum charge. This one drove clients away.

"I've come about my daughter," he said.

"Runaway?" she said quickly and sat down on the top of the desk. She had the kind of a body that would look wonderful in a short skirt: her legs taut and tan, the shoulders strong and high.

"What?" Dan said. "No. Well, she did run away, I guess. But that's not the point."

"That's typical, you know," May said and shook her head in disgust.

"What is?" Dan asked. She had him completely confused.

"The parents are always the last ones to see."

"Wait, wait," Dan said. He couldn't believe how quickly she had put him on the defensive. Suddenly, he knew that was exactly where she wanted him. Dan smiled. He had her number now. She controlled the game by always attacking. He stepped back and turned as if to go. Then he collapsed into a chair by the door as if he'd been shot.

"The water is the only thing I've ever really trusted," he sighed. And gazed out through the screen at the ocean, his shoulders limp, his hands slowly crumbling the piece of paper with May Bell's address on it. He tossed the paper ball on a long, lazy arc into a basket on the other side of the room and it rang with a hollow thump.

She walked over to Dan and knelt down in front of him. Now that she figured she had him beaten, whimpering like a puppy, her voice turned as soft as a school nurse's.

"How long has she been missing?" she asked.

"Well, quite a few years. We gave her up for adoption at birth," he said. "Her grandfather was the one who started looking for her, but he's dead now. I wanted to see what he found out."

She put her hand tenderly on his knee, the fingers long and unpainted.

"So your father . . ."

"Stepfather, actually," Dan said, his head still buried in his hands.

"Your stepfather hired another detective to look for your daughter?"

"No. He hired you, actually."

"Oh, okay. What's his name?" she asked.

He had her now. "Peter Maikai," he said, looking her in the eye.

As soon as she heard the name, she knew she'd been outplayed by Dan. She shoved his knee with her hand and stood up and went back to her desk.

"So I take it you're a reporter," she said. "I was wondering how long it would take you assholes to get around to me."

"What would the press want with you?"

She looked at him curiously. The games Dan played had her upside down. And she liked it.

"Because, bozo, I knew that as soon as a media type like you discovered I'd found an heir to a fortune left to her by the guy who assassinated the governor, you'd be all over me."

"You found her?"

"Of course I found her." She smiled when she saw his surprise.

"When?"

"No, no," she said wagging a finger at him. "That's all you're getting. The rest you pay for. I figure this is worth a movie of the week, at least. Beautiful young lady PI finds the secret past of the assassin." She blinked her eyes coquettishly. "I'm going to retire with one big score and buy a macadamia nut farm on the Big Island."

"I'm not the press or a TV producer," Dan said coldly. "I'm the girl's father."

"I don't care if you're the prosecuting attorney of Honolulu, it's *Dialing for Dollars* from here on out."

For Dan the game was over now. This private dick had found his daughter and he was going to find out what she knew if he had to bring in a whole crew—cops, detectives, warrants, the lot. Dan pulled his credential out of his back pocket and laid it on her desk.

"I'm not the prosecuting attorney of Honolulu. I'm the chief deputy prosecutor," he said, "and you're going to tell me everything I want to know or I'm going to throw your ass in jail for sixty days for interfering with an official investigation. Then I'm going to see what I can do about getting your PI's license revoked. Permanently."

She had her head bent down, looking at Dan's ID. Her long, blond hair was hanging down the sides of her face so he couldn't see her expression until she lifted her head. He knew by the look of defeat in her eyes that she was going to tell him everything.

"Look, if you think I've been hiding something about the assassination, you're wrong. I know enough about assassinations to know everybody smelt a conspiracy when Slaton was killed. But, believe me, there's nothing there," she pleaded. "The fact this guy hired me to find his daughter has nothing to do with the governor's death."

She was right, of course. But he wasn't going to let her know that he wasn't there to investigate the assassination. Not if he wanted to keep her nervous and talking.

"We'll decide that after we've investigated all the facts of the case," Dan said. By the sweeping look he gave her place, she thought he meant that they were going to tear her place apart, surfboards and all.

"Don't give me that," she said, her eyes narrowing. "A PA doesn't drive all the way out here unless he thinks there's something big going on."

She waved her hand at him, walked casually to the side window, and peeked out at the street, where Dan had parked his rented car.

"I hate to disappoint you, but all I did was find a girl the son asked me to look for."

"By 'the son,' do you mean Michael Maikai?"

She sensed his sudden interest. "Yeah," she said warily.

"So you never had contact with Peter Maikai?"

"Only his name on the checks."

"He never discussed any aspects of the case with you at all?"

"No, nothing," she said. She was sensing a way out. Maybe she wouldn't have to endure a mob of cops dinging up her boards. "The only contact I had with the old man was through the son. He handled everything."

"You never met with Peter Maikai?"

"Not once."

"He never gave you anything?" he was pounding away at her now.

"If I never met him, how could he give me anything?"

"Exactly," he said, knowing that he was finally on to something. "So when did you find the girl?"

She didn't hesitate this time.

"Right away, really. Took me less than a week and I had her."

"How long ago was that?"

"Several months," she said.

That meant Michael had known where his daughter was the whole time and he had kept it from his father. The greed that Maikai had feared in his son apparently wasn't just an old man's paranoid fantasy. Of course, if Michael had concealed her whereabouts that was one thing. But if he'd altered the will to his advantage or concealed a new one, that was quite another thing. That, in fact, was a crime.

Dan suddenly realized that everything Uncle Charlie had said he'd witnessed might, in fact, be true. The thing to do was to confront Michael with Lily on one side and his daughter on the other.

"All right, get me her address," Dan ordered, nodding his head toward her file cabinet.

She got up and pulled open a drawer and started leafing through it. She reached into a file and pulled out some papers, shuffling through them until she found one with red ink scribbles on it. She handed it to Dan.

"Is this it?" he asked and looked down at the paper. It read:

Sharon Jenkins
1818 Puumana St. #1230
Honolulu, 96815

Scribbled beneath the address were some directions on how to get there.

Dan slapped the paper once with his hand, put it in his pocket, and turned to leave.

"Thanks for your help, May."

"This is it, then?" she said, a smile starting to grow on her face. "You're not going to come back and rip the place apart?"

"Not unless you haven't told me everything."

"Now why would I do that?"

He closed the door behind him, then turned and looked back at her through the screen.

"Maybe so you'd have something to sell when *Prime Time* calls."

CHAPTER
TWENTY

1818 was an exclusive new high-rise condo overlooking the city of Honolulu from the steps of Tantalus. Luckily, Dan knew the cop at the front door who was moonlighting as a doorman.

"Hey, Doug," he said and shook hands with the Filipino. "Howzit?"

"No complaints," he said. "So what're you doing here, Counselor?"

"Got a friend," he said and pointed upstairs.

"Oh," the cop winked. A place like this was filled with women whose rent was being paid by someone else. He buzzed Dan past the metal barrier and Dan went to the elevator and punched 12.

A beautiful Asian girl answered the door at 1230. She was wearing a silk burgundy robe that barely covered her rear. Her black hair came down an inch or two past the bottom of the robe. It was that voluptuously thick Asian hair that flowed like liquid across her shoulders. She was running her hands through it when she answered the door.

Dan could see she'd just gotten out of bed. Her eyes were made up for the evening. Except that it was afternoon. She had only traces of lipstick in the tight corners of her lips. Dan recognized the undeniable look of high-priced sex.

The girl cracked open the door only as far as the chain would allow. "Oh, Jesus. I told the service not to send anyone up here."

"Who's anyone?" Dan said and smiled. But all he got back were blank, expressionless eyes dancing all over him.

"Look, I'm busy, sweetheart," she said, looking over her shoulder at the darkened bedroom behind her.

"I'm looking for Sharon Jenkins," he said casually and leaned nonchalantly against the doorframe. "Does she live here?"

"No, she doesn't," she said and quickly closed the door, the hard, white surface stopping a short eyelash from his nose. He could hear her high heels clicking across the marble of the entry and her saying, "Coming," in a voice filled with a lilting upper-class British accent and a breathy urgency.

He knocked again and this time when she opened it she nearly spit at him.

"I told you I'm busy, buster. There's no Shannon Jenkins here. If you don't go away, I'll buzz security."

Dan flipped open his ID and she didn't bother even to look at it.

"*Sharon* Jenkins," he said firmly, correcting her.

"Give me a break here, mister. I've already told you she's not here."

"I need you to answer some questions, then."

"I've answered all the questions I'm going to answer from you guys."

Dan didn't know what she was talking about, but obviously the cops had been questioning her about something. From the exclusive apartment, the silk robe, the sex in the middle of the afternoon, it was obvious that this girl was into a business that attracted cops, particularly vice cops.

Then it struck Dan, and when it did, it struck him hard. What was his daughter doing living in a place like this? She was seventeen and she was associated in some way with this kind of girl in this kind of an apartment? An apartment that as the second-ranking attorney in Hawai'i he couldn't begin to afford.

She looked over her shoulder nervously, then back at Dan. "Jesus, give me a break. Does it have to be right now?" she pleaded.

Dan shook his head. He could see a flake of white powder on the tip of her gorgeous, sculpted nostril and the nervous eyes dancing with paranoia.

"No. It doesn't have to be now."

"Thanks," she breathed and raised her eyes in relief dramatically.

"When?" he asked.

"When?" she said incredulously.

"Yeah, exactly. When will you be . . . done," he asked.

She looked around in amazement.

"This ain't Hotel Street, buddy. I don't do this by the hour. I'll call you when it's convenient," she said and began to shut the door.

Dan had his foot wedged in the frame. He pushed the door back so the chain was taut. One more push and it would snap off its mounting.

"I'll wait downstairs for half an hour, then I'm coming up to talk."

She shut the door without answering and he could hear her lilting voice again manipulating the next little one-act play, which, of course, was why she had risen to these heights so quickly. She could probably make a man believe just about anything. When it got to her level—the fifteen-hundred-dollar Anne Klein suits, the jag convertible, the hair flowing as if off a loom, the perfume in surprising places—the game was mostly mental.

Dan was standing in a recess of the hall on the far side of the elevator bank, from where he could see her door. He saw the guy come out of her apartment twenty minutes later. He was a tall, gray-domed businessman with a lot of gold on his hands and wrists.

She was still in the robe when she let Dan in. When she sat in front of him, she let him see everything. Her legs were very tight with a line of muscle in the calf. Her tan went right up the hip uninterrupted past her waist. He could see the heavy bulge of her breasts as they pushed open the robe, the tie wrapped loosely around the waist.

She looked up to him as he sat on the couch a few feet away and saw that he was looking at her. When she spoke to him, for the first time that lilt was in her voice, that little lift to her pitch that he found so obviously faked but still so appealing.

"Mr. Carrier," she said. "How can I help you?" And it was as if she'd cut the cigar and lit it for him and he could just sit back and inhale and she'd take care of everything from here on out.

"I'm sorry," he said. "I forgot to ask your name." He didn't know how to fake a Brit accent, but he said it as if he were pulling back her chair at a silver-strewn dining table.

"Cindy Lee," she said, giving him her stage name.

"Gee, that's beautiful."

"Thank you," she said, following the script. Normally about this time she'd ask him what his pleasure was that afternoon and the conversation would slide quickly into bed. But he took it another way.

"Like I said, I'm looking for a girl named Sharon Jenkins."

"Who I don't know. Yes?" Time was important to her and she wanted to skip quickly through the foreplay.

"I was told she lived here."

"Well, she doesn't. I had a roommate, but she died recently," and she pointed off with a long red fingernail at a picture of herself and Lily Maikai.

Dan was ten feet from the table, where the photo was set in a silver frame. He got up quickly and grabbed the photo, bringing it up close to his face. Lily was standing on the beach with this girl, their hair wind-blown and sandy, a couple of long-necked green bottles of beer hanging at their sides.

He stared at it for a long time before it dawned on him what he was looking at. If it was Lily, she had to be no more than seventeen or eighteen at the time, about the age when he'd last seen her. The only problem was the girl in the picture with Lily, the girl sitting across the room from him, would have been no more than five or six when Lily was that age. And Lily never had breasts that bulged from a bikini top like that, either.

"Who is she?" he asked the girl, although he was already sure he knew."

"My roommate."

"What do you mean, your roommate?"

"The one I told you that died."

He felt a terrible exhalation in himself and he sat down in a chair, still holding the picture.

His daughter was dead. He'd been told only a week before that he even had a daughter. And he'd spent hours every day imagining what she looked like, how she walked, what she'd done with her life. Of course, he could see all around him what she'd done with her life.

"Look, Cindy," he said. There was a pain in his chest that made it hard to get the words out. "I'm not just a PA. I'm her father."

"Stephanie's father?"

"Yes, I think so. Stephanie's father." He hesitated as he said the name. "I'm pretty sure Stephanie and Sharon Jenkins are the same person."

She didn't say anything for a moment, putting it together. Then her face went suddenly soft for the first time.

"I'm sorry," she said and her accent was a flat Southern California voice that he knew was probably bred in an upper-middle-class home on the West Side. Maybe Santa Monica, maybe Westwood. Once she dropped the Brit put-on, the lilt, he knew she meant what she said.

"She was a good girl," Cindy said. "She's probably the only real friend I ever had in this business."

Dan smiled at her and she reached across and touched his hand without a hint of sexual innuendo. It could have been the first time in years she had touched a man when it wasn't just business.

Then she suddenly withdrew her hand and sat back in her chair. She had covered herself completely with just the slightest adjustment of the robe.

"You don't know, do you?" she said.

"Know what?"

She stood and went over and poured a glass of something golden. "Would you like something?"

"No," he said anxiously. "I don't know what, Cindy?"

"You don't know what happened to your daughter, to Stephanie. I thought with all the cops that had come by to question me, that you being a PA and all, you'd know."

Dan didn't say anything. He just looked at her. He knew that what she was about to tell him wouldn't be pleasant.

"Wait a minute," she said, and her eyes grew suspicious again. "Stephanie said her parents were from Arizona. And they sure weren't any PAs. What kind of low-life trick is this, anyway?" She slammed the bottle down on the table. "I swear you fucking cops will try anything."

"The people in Arizona are her adoptive parents," he explained calmly.

"Oh," she said. "You're her real father?"

"Yes."

Cindy's eyes grew tender again. "I'm sorry. I didn't want Stephanie hurt anymore."

Dan nodded his head. "You said there was something I didn't know, Cindy."

She sat down and took a long swallow of her amber drink, then looked at Dan.

"She was murdered," she said softly.

"Jesus," he mumbled. He didn't want to know how far this nightmare was going to go. But, of course, that wasn't going to stop the inevitable.

"With the governor," she said as softly as she could because she knew it was a knife that was going to plunge deeply into Dan's heart.

All Dan could think about was Slaton, that sleazy old bastard, with a young, beautiful girl like Sharon.

"Are you certain it was my daughter?" he asked, but he knew by looking at the girl in the photo, who was the exact image of Lily at the same age, that it was his daughter and that she was dead.

"You're the one who said it was your daughter."

Dan's mind was searching for reasons to deny it. He was a PA. He wanted corroboration. And it was a way to fend off the pain that was eating like acid through his guts.

"Are there any of Sharon's things here?"

"Everything. I didn't touch a thing," she said defensively. "The cops told me right off not to touch anything until they said otherwise. So her room's still back there just the way she left it the day she was killed."

"Can I see?"

She looked at her watch. It was a slim, white-gold rectangle with diamonds circling the face. "It's the second door on the right. Go on back. I've got to make a phone call."

"Thank you," he said and went down the hallway and found the room. He could hear the lilt back in her voice as she explained her disappointment to someone on the phone.

The police had not ripped the place apart, probably because

they were still dealing with the governor's assassination. They were never sure who'd be following their tracks in an investigation like that. Some high-ranking fed comes in to check things out and something's not right and the captain could find himself out on the street patrolling Kalihi again. Some of the shoulders of Sharon's designer dresses had fallen off the ends of the hangers and the bed was obviously sat upon. But they'd put everything back in the drawers and shut them.

Except for the poster bed with a lace ruffle along the top, it wasn't a seventeen-year-old's bedroom. It was expensive and tasteful with a collection of expensive crystal next to a teak jewelry box and a John Ensign painting. There was a cherry antique Chinese writing desk in one corner and a large, angular chair in the other that could accommodate whatever the erotic imagination could conjure.

When he opened them, he could tell by the condition of the drawers that the detectives hadn't even bothered to look in them. They had seen what she was, knew Slaton's reputation with young local *hapa-haoles*, smirked a few times to each other, stuck their noses in some of the expensive lingerie, got her name, and left.

Dan found her real ID inside a locked diary. A key was strung on a bag of potpourri, and he tried a few locks until the diary snapped open. He didn't have the heart to read through it yet, but he'd found a driver's license with her picture under the back flap of the book, a little "secret compartment" that only pointed a good thief, or a good investigator, to where she hid her important things.

In the license photo her hair was long and full like Lily's and she had the same strong jaw and the same dark eyes. The lips were slightly thinner, though, like Dan's, and her grin, even in the dull gray of the overexposed DMV office, showed teeth like his. The name on the license read SHARON MARIE JENKINS. Her age was seventeen.

Another license in the name of Stephanie Johnson was in a billfold in the top of another dresser against the window. In this photo his daughter was made up for a night out and the birthdate indicated she was twenty-two. The way she held herself in the photo, she looked at least that old.

Dan pulled the license out of the wallet and underneath was a business card. It was Michael Maikai's.

Dan put the license and the diary in his pocket an instant before Cindy came into the room. She had a handful of pictures that she handed to Dan. They were all of Sharon with Cindy, or alone, mostly having fun, laughing, a glass of something in her hand. A party girl who seemed unaware that someday the party would end.

"Why don't you take these," Cindy said, handing them to him. "All I do is cry every time I look at them. I've got a couple I'll keep, if it's okay with you."

"That's fine, Cindy. Hell, you were probably her best friend anyway. You've got as much right as anyone."

Dan had left one of the drawers slightly ajar and Cindy went over and shut it. He noticed for the first time that she wasn't in the robe anymore. Somehow, in the few minutes that she was away, she had called a disappointed customer and put on a blue sleeveless silk dress and matching heels. Red lipstick colored her full lips.

"Could I ask you one more thing before I go?" Dan asked as she sat on the corner of Sharon's bed.

"You want to know why she needed those two driver's licenses you just put in your pocket?"

They exchanged knowing grins. "No, I understand that," Dan said. "I need to know if she saw an attorney recently."

"Hell, without attorneys and judges us poor working girls would probably be out of business," Cindy joked.

"I don't mean a client."

"Yeah, there was a guy. Good-looking local. About your age dressed in a thousand-dollar suit. Drove a big new Mercedes."

"That's probably him," Dan said.

"It was a couple weeks ago, I guess. He told Steph he'd been hired by her mother in Arizona to find her."

"Did she ever mention his name?"

"Probably, but I don't remember it. He took her out to lunch. I remember Steph thought it was a little strange, considering her mother couldn't afford to feed her when she was a kid. So how come she could afford Mr. Armani to wine and dine her?"

"What came of it?" Dan asked.

"Nothing that I know of." She walked to the closet and rehung some of the clothes. "Assholes," she muttered to herself.

"Can we talk again when I've got things sorted out a little better?" Dan asked her.

She nodded. "But could you do me a favor and call first? Give me a little time?"

She handed him a card that read simply *Cindy* in gold letters with her phone number printed in the bottom left corner.

CHAPTER
TWENTY-ONE

Dan rushed to catch a plane back to Maui. He had to tell Lily what he had just found. He leaned back all the way in his seat and looked out at the clouds drifting below him across the Pacific. Lahaina was off to the left with the magnificently eroded teeth of the West Maui mountains behind it.

He didn't know how he was going to break it to her. He could hardly believe it himself. It was enough that he had to tell her their daughter was dead. But to tell her that the whole world would think her father killed his granddaughter would destroy Lily. If only she had told him before that they had a daughter, he could have used the resources of the entire prosecuting attorney's office to find her.

Then he got angry all over again at Maikai. Didn't Dan have a right to know about his own child? And how about Lily? Didn't she have an obligation to tell him that he had a daughter? Of course, what good would it have done? He was only seventeen at the time. Barely capable of caring for himself, let alone for a mother and child. Lily wasn't to blame. He knew that. It was the circumstances at the time. Blaming Lily or Maikai or anybody else wouldn't bring back his daughter.

Before he'd left, he'd phoned Lily to tell her he had to see her right away and to meet his plane. She was at the airport when he landed. He kissed her cheek and took her hand and led her silently to the car. They drove out to Iao Valley. He wouldn't tell her why he had rushed over and she didn't push him. She knew that whatever Dan had found out probably wasn't good, though. She had sent him off to find their daughter and now he was back with the look of a funeralgoer.

They were sitting at a wooden bench in one of the pavilions at Kepaniwai Park when he told her. Behind her was the Buddhist temple painted red and gold with the steeply slanted roof designed to slough off evil spirits.

He turned and faced her and held both her hands between them.

"Our daughter's dead," he said.

Her chest heaved for several moments then she began to cry, little explosive sobs that she tried to hold back. He dreaded telling her the rest of it. Her father was dead. And now this.

When he left Cindy's apartment with Sharon's ID, he had gone immediately to Cathy's office. There he pulled the file and laid it out on the desk. The bloody photos of the murdered girl spilled out in front of him. That was what they'd always called her. "The murdered girl." He'd heard the name Stephanie Johnson once or twice and forgotten it, of course. She was unimportant to the assassination case. "A hooker in the wrong place at the wrong time," Reed had said, and nobody at Homicide or the PA's office had questioned that assessment. It was too similar to what they ran into every day to think anything else. A murdered hooker wouldn't cause a stir unless five or six of them were brutally murdered one after another and the media started running with the story.

"So you found her?" Lily said, and her deep eyes grew dark as a tomb.

"The PI had her address and I talked to her roommate," Dan said.

The pain of watching Lily as he told her became too much for him. He got up and walked over to a spreading banyan nearby and leaned against it. This was exactly the kind of hurt he had tried so hard to avoid ever since he'd lost his mother and father. He had always hoped he would never have to face this kind of pain again.

"Her roommate? Was she living with a man?" she asked.

By the way she said "man," Dan knew she suspected the roommate already.

"No, it was another girl. They worked together at an escort agency."

"I see," she said. And Dan knew that she did.

She walked over to him and he took her in his arms. The daughter she'd lost was a call girl. "How bad is this going to get, Dan?" she asked.

"Pretty bad, Lily," he said.

Just above them on the ridge, a monk began to toll a huge brass gong that hung in the garden before the temple. Its long, heavy, resounding *bong* echoed into the mountains rising around them. Lily stood and took his hand and began to lead him up the trail that went behind the temple and wound into the deep green of the valley above them. It was the first place he'd ever kissed her. As kids they had palled around for years at the ranch. Their touches had grown softer and more thrilling as they grew older. Maikai came here three or four times a year at least. The kids would run up into the mountains and play while he strolled among the graves and statues of long-past kings. Less than a hundred yards from here, thousands of Hawai'ian warriors had died in the bloodiest civil war the islands had ever seen. That was two hundred years ago, and the ghosts of so many dead haunted these places.

They walked up to a grassy promenade where they could see down the valley all the way to Kahului Harbor, where a Matson transport stacked with heavy metal containers was parked next to a white cruise ship displaying a happy little orchid on its stack.

When they sat down on the grass, she finally let go of his hand.

"How did she die?" she asked without looking at him.

"She was murdered, Lily."

"By who?" she asked without the slightest trace of shock.

"They don't know, Lily," he said.

"They?"

"The police."

"Oh, of course," she said and looked at him. She could tell by his face that there was more.

"Please, Dan, don't keep anything from me. Tell me everything.

Tell me . . ." Her voice began to break again and Dan reached for her. He held her hands in his.

"She's the girl who was found with Slaton."

He could feel all the resolve go from her and she began to cry again.

"You know what this means, don't you?" she said. "Everyone will think my father killed his own granddaughter to get at the governor."

He held her as she sobbed into his chest.

"I'm sure your father couldn't have killed anyone, Lily, but I'm not so sure about someone else close to the both of us."

"What do you mean?"

"All this time everyone thinks that Sharon was just simply at the wrong place at the wrong time."

"What else?" she said.

"Well, what if Slaton wasn't the target at all?"

She pulled back from Dan and looked at him curiously. What was he getting at? She wasn't at all sure she wanted to find out.

"What if Sharon was the real target?" he said. "And the governor's assassination was just a convenient camouflage for the real motive?"

"Dan, she was only seventeen. Why would anyone want to kill her?"

"There's something I haven't told you, Lily. Sharon's roommate said that our daughter had lunch with a lawyer just days before she was killed. The lawyer said he was hired by Sharon's adoptive mother to find her."

"Yes?" she said.

"That lawyer was Michael. I found his business card in Sharon's wallet."

"But Michael didn't know where she was," Lily said. There was almost a plea in her voice. "It couldn't have been him."

"He knew, Lily. The PI he hired found Sharon months ago and told Michael. For his own reasons he decided to keep it from you and your father."

"But why?" Lily asked.

"I can't answer that yet. But from what you and Uncle Charlie suspect about Michael and the will, we both know there's a lot of money at stake here. People have been known to do a lot of unspeakable things for fifty million dollars."

"I can't believe Michael could do such a thing."

"Neither can I," Dan said as he put his arm around her. They held each other for a while the way they used to when they were still just kids and the world had not yet fallen in on them.

Lily dropped Dan off at the airport. He was in a hurry to meet with Kalama, who he knew could help him sort things out. She wanted to go with him, but he told her it was best right now if he investigated this on his own. He'd call her regularly to keep her up to date. Then they kissed. There was a lingering note of passion in the kiss that he suspected would never go away.

Dan phoned Joe at several places before he finally traced him to the courthouse, where he was testifying at a murder trial. Dan knew the case well. The defense attorney was trying to convince the jury that his client killed her boyfriend because he was forcing her to become a drug addict. The attorney's major obstacle was that the prosecutors had found out she'd paid $48,000 in cash for a new Porsche the day she shot him through the back of the head with a Magnum.

"What's doing, bra?" Kalama asked. Dan could hear the low grumble behind the cop so he knew Joe was using the phone outside Superior Court 4, where all the attorneys and their clients discussed their chances.

"I need you to do me a favor," Dan said.

"Hey, da sun comin' up tomorrow." He meant, So what else is new?

Dan was standing in the parking lot of a convenience store in a windblown drizzle that was quickly soaking him. He was hunched in a Plexiglas halfbooth with a finger poked in one ear and the phone pressed tight to the other.

"Find out if someone else was in Maikai's hotel room with him that day," Dan said.

"All right."

"What are you doing now?" Dan asked.

"Right now?" Kalama said. It was the answer of a man who'd been in the military and the paramilitary of the police force for fifteen years. He knew how to avoid volunteering for anything.

"Yes, now," Dan pushed. Rain was running down the neck of his shirt.

"Well, I'm going to grab some mix plate at Palolo's. Then I got a couple witnesses I got to geev da kine to."

"I want you to check the file now," Dan said.

There was a pause. Dan could hear Kalama's heavy breath. "Right after lunch."

"Now. Then go by Palolo's and grab two plates and pick me up at the airport."

"Jesus, Dan. I'm supposed to knock off early today. *Pau hana* at two-thirty. Going feeshing with Reynolds in Makapu'u today."

Dan just waited while the rain grew heavier.

"What am I looking for again?" Joe finally asked, resigned to a day without fishing.

"Check who went up with Maikai to his room. Was anybody else with him? Anything."

"What time da plane coming?"

"Two-thirty-five. On Island Air," Dan said, pressing farther into the shelter of the Plexiglas as the rain turned torrential.

"So that's it, then? You need find out who in da room with Maikai?"

"Yeah."

"Then I go feeshing with Reynolds?"

"Maybe," Dan said. "See you at the airport."

"Wait," Kalama said. "What kine mix plate you like, bra?"

"Teri beef," he said and hung up.

Dan had been waiting outside the airport for almost an hour when he heard someone call his name. He turned and was surprised to see Lily running toward him. At the same time Joe pulled up in his unmarked unit. Without saying anything Dan opened the back door for her. Then he opened the front passenger door and got into the front seat next to Joe.

As Kalama pulled away from the curb, Dan turned to Lily. "I thought I left you back in Maui."

"You told me you suspected that Michael may have killed our daughter *and* the governor. You didn't actually expect me to just sit back and wait to see what you found out, did you?"

"Michael?" Joe said. He turned and looked at Dan. "What the hell is she talking about?"

Dan explained to Joe what he had found out about Sharon and how Michael had hidden her whereabouts from Maikai.

"Are you sure she was your daughter?" Joe said in disbelief.

"I'm sure. Besides the ID I found in her room, she's a double for Lily at that age."

"I have a hard time believing Michael would do it."

Dan noticed Lily nodding her head. Even though the evidence was piling up against Michael, she was still his sister. He was still Kalama's boyhood friend. There was a big part of Dan that didn't want to believe it either. Except the facts kept telling him that his sentimental feelings for Michael were wrong.

"Any more than you can believe that Peter Maikai would do it?" Dan asked Joe.

Kalama shrugged. "All right. Where do we go from here?"

"First of all, what did you find out?" Dan asked.

"Well, I can tell you Michael didn't take his father up to his room before the murders occurred, if that's what you were expecting."

"I don't know what I was expecting," Dan said. "So who was up there with Peter?

"Nobody," Joe said and punched the old Riviera through a red light. It was an HPD cruiser with the revolving blue light that the driver had to stick on the roof with the wire leading back into the car. "The security checklist has Peter Maikai going up alone."

"So no one was up there with him. Unless, of course, they found a way to sneak past security," Dan said and blew some air out his lips.

Lily leaned forward to see Kalama's reaction.

"Michael didn't have to sneak anywhere," Joe said. "He had his own room. Paid cash. Guess what name he registered under?"

Dan shrugged.

"Kaleokoa."

It was the name of their canoe.

"I took Michael's picture to the security officer on duty that day and he ID'd him. Michael's room was directly above his father's, which was directly above Slaton's."

They were driving on the long, sweeping overpass that swung on a lazy arc out of the airport onto the H-1.

"You think it was Michael who came down that rope?" Joe asked.

"Who in the hell knows?"

"Well, it looks like he had motive and opportunity. That's for sure. But, Dan," Joe said and he looked over at Dan, sad-eyed, "that's our brudda. I just can't believe it."

"Hell, I feel the same way, Joe.'"

Lily placed her hand over the top of Dan's and left it there.

"The problem is he may have killed our daughter and now he's trying to steal the ranch from Lily with that bogus will," Dan said.

Lily and Joe both looked at him. The traffic was moving along fast for this hour, and Joe was maneuvering between lanes as he stared at Dan.

"That's what I don't get," Kalama said and lightly tapped the wheel. "Why would he kill her if he planned on using that fake will?"

"I think I can explain that," Dan said. His eyes were glazed, staring straight through the windshield at the truth falling surely into place. "If the real will or a copy of it ever surfaced, Sharon would control her share. Michael didn't know what would happen then. If she were dead, however, then no matter what happened, her share would be split between Michael and Lily and he'd be in control again. Killing her was the only way he could be sure."

Lily and Joe shook their heads as they listened, trying not to believe what Dan was telling them.

"Once he found our daughter," Dan went on, "he waited for the right time, the right place, and the right circumstances. He knew his father would be leading that protest. That was the one predictable thing anybody did that day. I'll bet if we look into this further Michael was the one who arranged to have his father's room directly above Slaton's."

"Killing the governor, though, to hide the girl's murder?" Kalama said, shaking his head in doubt. "That's pretty risky."

"The ranch is worth fifty million dollars. Maybe more," Dan said.

"I heard someone say once it might be worth as much as seventy-five million to my father," Lily said.

"If he's in control, he can sell it and be instantly wealthy. If he's not, he doesn't get a thing except what he can make off the taro operation," Dan said.

They rode in silence for a while. Kalama weaved through the traffic at seventy-five miles an hour.

"I'm just not buying it, Dan. If Michael knew where Sharon was for months, I don't think he would risk killing Slaton to cover up that she was the real target."

"Come on, Joe. I'm not saying I'm positive that's the reason. But we have to start somewhere. Right now the only thing we have is that Michael's actions regarding Sharon's whereabouts and the possibility that he destroyed the will are both very suspect. And we all know he was at the Royal Hawai'ian that day and could have climbed down that rope a hell of a lot easier than his father."

Joe nodded his head. "And he could have easily planted the knife in his father's room," Joe added.

"Exactly," Dan said and looked out the window to see where they were.

"Get off here," Dan said, pointing to the Pi'ikoi off-ramp that was more like an alleyway than a major thoroughfare. A few feet after Joe pulled off, they came to a full stop sign on a residential street where little kids were wheeling around in little push cars. That was Hawai'i, a mix of the modern and the old, the gods of the *ali'i*s battling with the gods of money.

"One thing that don't fit, though," Joe said. "The will read fifty/fifty. Same/same. Right? So how he going sell without Lily giving her permission?"

Dan pointed to a phone booth at the side of the road. "Pull over, would you? I want to make a phone call."

"Just use this," Kalama said and grabbed the radio phone and offered it to Dan.

"I don't want anything going over the air until I make sure of a few things first."

Joe pulled around the corner from the booth and shoved the stick into Park.

"How about the fifty/fifty, though? How Michael going sell without Lily?" Joe asked again.

"I don't know exactly, but I've got a good idea. That's why I want to make this call," Dan said and opened the door to the cruiser.

*   *   *

After Dan got off the phone, he had Kalama drop them at Dan's car.

"Lily and I are going to talk to the attorney who's probating Maikai's will," Dan said as he got out of the car. "I'll call you when we get what we need. Then you and I are going to go see Reed."

"What for?"

"If I get the right answers from this guy, we're going to get Reed to reopen the Slaton murder case," Dan said. "We'll need full co-operation from the office if we're going to prove this."

Kalama was shaking his head.

"Reed ain't never going open this thing up again. He got his conviction neat and clean. An he didn't even have to go to court to get it. I heard him crowing about it the other day over at the Gavel. He figures this is what's going put him in 'Iolani Palace, you know that."

"Well, he's just going to have to postpone his coronation for a little while, isn't he?" Dan said.

"Don't count on none of that. If Reed admits he was wrong about Maikai, the Hawai'ian community will never forget. Peter Maikai will be a bigger martyr than he already is. I know one thing, if Reed reopens this case, and it turns out Maikai didn't do it, he ain't never going be governor of Hawai'i."

Dan nodded. Kalama was right, of course. But they'd have to force Reed's hand somehow. There was always Jerzy Epstein at the *Advertiser*. He'd love to drop a bomb like this on his old friend Reed.

Dan shut the door and leaned back in the window. "Do me a favor, bra," he said to Joe. "If you've got any pull with the gods, geev'em a little prayer for me. I'm hoping like hell I'm wrong about Michael."

"Yes, Dan," Lily said over his shoulder. "We all are."

CHAPTER TWENTY-TWO

Collins's secretary led them into his office and they waited twenty minutes before he joined them. He was in a blue, short-sleeved oxford button-down. His black hair was wet and slicked back, and his shirt was soaked down the back.

"Sorry, Ms. Maikai," he said. Then he recognized Dan, surprised to see him. "And Mr. Carrier? Why the honor?"

"I'm just here as a friend of the family."

"Fine," Collins said, straightening the back of his collar as he sat down in his chair. He pulled a handful of paper napkins from a bottom drawer and began to mop his forehead. "I got tied up down at the club in a tennis match. One of those damn tie-breakers that went on forever."

He slid the drawer shut with his foot and swung the chair around to face them. "Now, what can I do for you today?" he asked.

"I'd like to see my father's will, please," Lily said.

Collins folded his hands in front of him on the desk and screwed up the most earnest face he could muster. "I'm sorry. Lily, isn't it?"

"Yes."

"Despite what you may have seen in the movies a will is not made public until after the filing of a petition. The will is attached to the petition and only then does it become public," Collins explained patiently.

"What do you mean by petition?"

"It's a request of the court to probate. Until then all the documents are in my hands and they don't become public until that occurs."

Lily looked over at Dan a moment, but he was staring at Collins.

"But I'm not the public," she said. "I'm an heir."

"I'm afraid you're not officially an heir until the court says you are."

"But you already read it to Michael and myself just the other day," Lily said, clearly baffled.

"That was for his benefit, since he is the named executor."

He daubed again at the beads on his forehead. He'd made them wait, Dan thought, until his tennis match was over. And now Dan was pretty sure why. Collins was in control now and they were going to go by his clock, by his rules, in his office.

"When the petition is filed then the will can be examined by anyone."

Dan put his hand on Lily's under the desk so Collins couldn't see. He made eye contact with her for a moment to signal her that he wanted her to let him go after Collins now.

"Have you got a soft drink or something?" Dan asked.

"Sure," Collins said, pushed his chair back, and went over to a mini-refrigerator against the wall. He poured them both something clear and sweet with ice.

"So what you're saying is you won't show her the will or tell her what it specifically says?" Dan said.

"I'm afraid not."

"Can you answer a few questions, then?" Dan asked.

He didn't know much about probating a will except for what little he still remembered from law school. He wasn't sure how much of this was an intentional roadblock by Collins and how much of it was the truth. If Collins was trying to conceal something behind a wall of legalese, he'd simply refuse to use the way out that Dan was going to give him.

"You mean specifics about the contents of the will?" Collins asked.

"Yes," Dan said.

"No, I couldn't do that."

"How about if I demand to see the will?" Dan said, leaning forward for the first time.

"You mean as PA?"

Dan nodded his head. Collins's expression hadn't changed and he'd stopped sweating. Dan could tell this was a lawyer who enjoyed a good fight.

"Well, then you'd have to have a warrant, Mr. Carrier," he said. "But then you probably know that."

Dan sat silently. He could see that bullying Collins wasn't going to make him back down. But a well-placed threat might.

"I'm a little rusty on probate law. But isn't that confidentiality business at the discretion of the executor of the will?"

"Not really. At least not once it's turned over to me."

"But Michael Maikai is the executor, is he not?"

"Yes, he is," Collins said, and a faint attorney-client smile of benevolence straightened his lips.

"So the only ones right now who know word-for-word what's contained in the will are you and Michael?" Dan asked. He had both hands on Collins's desk now. He could feel Lily at his side watching him, and he felt a sudden school-boy pride. He was going to enjoy performing for her and it almost made him blush.

Collins pulled back the top drawer of his desk, fished out a paper clip, and began to bang together some papers on the top of his desk, as if he'd decided to get some work done while they chatted about unimportant matters.

"If you want to know something specifically about the will, you'd have to ask Michael."

Dan let the room settle a moment while Collins pushed the clip onto the papers, tossed the bunch in a pile on the corner of his desk, and looked up at Dan. "Was there anything else I can help you with?"

"How long have you known Michael Maikai?" Dan asked.

"Oh, let's see," Collins said. He was looking past them at the blank wall, remembering.

"You went to Harvard together, didn't you?" Dan prompted.

Collins looked back at Dan.

"Are you doing any business with Michael?" Dan persisted.

Collins's smile disappeared and his vision narrowed to just Dan's eyes. "What do you mean, *business?*"

"Besides probating the will. Are you involved in any other business transactions with Michael?"

"I've handled some of the Maikai ranch transactions. Gone to court, filed some papers on behalf of the corporation. That sort of thing."

"Did you and Michael buy some property together?"

"What's that got to do with this?" Collins asked sharply.

Dan shrugged. "Nothing, I guess."

Collins's snake eyes grew even thinner.

"How about the Hizaga deal to buy the ranch?" Dan asked as if he'd asked about the weather. "Don't you have a conflict of interest here?"

"I don't understand," Collins said.

"Do you understand the Rules of Professional Conduct concerning conflict of interest?" Dan asked.

Collins, feeling that he was being backed into a corner, started swinging. "I'm not going to listen to threats in my own office, Mr. Carrier. I don't care if you are a deputy prosecutor."

Dan rose when Collins did. "Look, Collins, we've been damn nice about this. I could have just busted down your door and shoved a warrant in your face."

"Then why didn't you?"

"Because I thought you'd be smart enough to take the easy road here."

"Come on—" Collins started to alibi, but Dan cut him off.

"You're negotiating the deal between Hizaga Development and Michael Maikai to develop the Maikai ranch. And you're also probating Peter Maikai's will. That means you're representing one of the heirs in a matter that directly concerns the outcome of the will. I won't even bring up the fact that Michael is the executor of the will and also your client."

Collins sat back down. Dan lowered himself back into his seat and watched Collins going over his options.

"On top of that, you and Michael are business partners in a Big Island company called Black Sand Development."

"How the hell—" Collins began, but he caught himself.

"Shall I keep going?" Dan asked. "That alone will get you into more trouble than you need."

Collins's eyes cleared and he looked at Dan again.

"Will you read it here?"

"No problem," Dan said.

"And . . . keep it between *us?*" Collins asked and circled his finger to include the three of them.

"We just want to look at the will. We're not after you."

Collins got up and walked into an adjoining room. "Get the Maikai files," he said to someone behind the door whom Dan couldn't see. He stood at the door and waited, and a minute later Dan heard some high heels clicking toward Collins.

"Thanks," Collins said and came back with a large manila envelope.

"Here it is," he said and put down the envelope in front of them. Dan let Lily pick it up and pull out the will. He leaned over her shoulder as she began to read. He put his hand on the page when she tried to turn it, then he said, "Okay," after a moment.

The document ran five pages, and when they were through, Dan pulled a piece of paper off Collins's notepad and wrote a few notes. When he was done, he stood.

"Thanks, I think we've seen enough," he said. "Are you ready, Lily?"

She stood up, a little surprised. "I guess so," she said.

"Good," he said, took her by the elbow, and led her out of the room without saying good-bye to Collins, who was behind the desk, his hair still wet.

They walked quickly down the hall to the elevator and went down to the lobby. He didn't say anything to her until they'd gotten into his car and pulled into the rush-hour traffic.

"Your brother's a very clever guy," Dan said.

He turned right at the red light and headed toward the mountains. The dropping sun was a searing orange in his rearview.

"What's he done?" she asked with a reluctant tone.

"Michael's taken over. I'm sure your father had no idea what he'd signed," he said and shook his head. "Of course, that won't mean a thing in a court of law. His heart may have been weak, but his mind wasn't. Nobody could refute that."

"But what's Michael done?" she asked again. This time impatiently.

"Well, by all appearances your father split the ranch fifty-fifty between you and Michael so that it would take both of your consents to sell the property. Or do anything else, for that matter," Dan explained. "At least that's what your father may have thought. Except that's not exactly what it says."

"Why? If I get half . . ."

"Well, because your father also instructed that, in regards to two percent of the estate, he wanted several trusts to be set up for an assortment of sovereignty groups of his choosing."

"And?" she said, her hands waving impatiently in front of him.

"That left forty-nine percent in your hands and forty-nine percent in Michael's, which still leaves both of you in control. Theoretically."

"What do you mean, 'theoretically'?" she said, her eyes narrowing.

"Because Michael was also named as trustor of those trusts, which means he really has control of fifty-one percent of the estate. Which means he can do anything he wants with it."

"And my father agreed to that?"

"Well, he signed the will. Although I'm certain he didn't know what the consequences of that move would be. It's hidden under a ton of verbiage. And the part where Michael is named trustor is buried five or six paragraphs down."

"You mean to say he can sell the ranch even if I oppose it?" she asked with a tone of disbelief.

"Absolutely," Dan said. "You'll get your share, of course."

"I don't care about the money. My father told me not to sell the land."

To the west the sea was golden behind her, and her honey-colored eyes were blazing.

"How can we stop him?" she asked in a cold, determined voice. In her lap one of her hands was bunched into a fist.

"It looks like your only hope is if we can find that other will."

"How about the PI's statement?"

"You mean that Michael didn't pass on the information he'd found out about our daughter?" Dan said and slowly shook his head. "That's not a crime."

"He concealed information."

"Yeah, but not in a criminal investigation. It's not a crime to keep a secret. He had no legal obligation to inform anyone that our daughter was alive and living in Honolulu. Especially without a will naming her as an heir."

Dan made another turn up into the hills.

206 / *Michael C. Eberhardt*

"The other will your father made out to supersede this one," Dan continued, "would have to be found before Michael could even be accused of anything. And you don't even know for sure now whether that will exists or not."

"I'm certain it exists," Lily said firmly.

"Why? Because Uncle Charlie said it does? I told you I can't use that."

"Not only Charlie. My father told me he'd taken care of Sharon in his will. And held my hand when he was dying and told me *not to sell.*" She had nearly shouted those final three words.

"That's not going to mean anything to a judge, unfortunately," Dan said softly. "We have to find that second will."

Lily started to cry as Dan turned the car into a narrow dirt road and bumped along for several hundred yards.

"Where are we going?" she asked.

"I think we need to talk before I take you back to the airport. I know of a little park where we can sit in private for a while."

He pulled into a long dirt drive with tall Norfolk pines lining either side. It led to a meadow of tall grass and wild bird of paradise.

He parked the car on the edge of the meadow and led her by the hand down to a small cove that overlooked the entire area. Below them to the south was Honolulu, to the north Pearl Harbor.

They sat and talked about everything, about all that had happened, about her father and her daughter and how it was when they were young and in love.

They watched the planes landing at the airport and held each other for a while as the sun went down. Her hair was full of the smell of pikake and he let it get to him. He pulled her closer to him and she looked up to him after a moment, and their eyes gave away their feelings. He lowered his lips to hers and her mouth spread open in a long, warm, thrill-seeking kiss.

They dropped slowly to their knees, still kissing, and his hand found her breast and she moaned with his touch and the remembrance of it. The many nights when she was alone, exiled to the Mainland, when she longed for him.

They fell back into the grass and his shirt was already off. She caressed his chest as he unbuttoned her blouse and placed his warm tongue on her nipple. She opened her eyes and the palms swayed in her vision, the grass soft and pungent all around her.

His hand was under her dress and she moaned again and called his name as he found the center of her longing.

"Oh, Lily, I love you," he whispered as they kissed.

He was naked now and her blouse was completely open and her dress pulled to her waist. He moved on top of her and suddenly the sun came out from behind a cloud and its fire was so bright in her eyes, she seemed all at once to come to her senses.

"No, Dan," she said.

But he wasn't listening.

"Dan, we can't." And he stopped.

"Lily," he pleaded breathlessly.

"We can't now," she whispered. "It's too complicated."

He didn't say anything.

"If we do this now, we could regret it," she said. "We'll never know why we did it and then it would be too late. We might have started something again that would hurt us both."

He rose to one elbow. He knew she was right. The whole thing was just too confusing. He didn't know what he truly felt about Lily. Was it simply their shared grief about their daughter? When the grief softened, they'd have another problem to deal with.

Or was it the past? Lily could be just a ghost from long ago that he had not yet reconciled with. In fact, that was the only good thing to come out of this. He might finally be able to put behind him all of those bitter feelings that had grown around his love for her. He'd had to form a hard shell in order just to survive, in order that it wouldn't eat at him. It had been a hard nut in his stomach for years, and he'd almost forgotten it was there, the ache calcified to a dead spot in his guts, until that day he saw her again on the porch of the Maikai ranch with the smell of plumeria flooding the air about him and the realization of just how beautiful she was.

He got dressed, then kissed her once more. Then he got up and helped her to her feet. "We better go," he said.

They walked back to the car and drove in silence for several miles.

"Collins didn't look all that worried," Lily said at last to take their minds off what had just happened.

"Why should he be? There's probably one will in existence now and they've got it."

"So you think Collins and Michael . . . ?" she said, trying to figure what Dan suspected.

"I'm certain Collins knows what's going on. He probably helped devise the scheme in the first place," Dan said. The streets were steaming after a light dampening.

"There's still Uncle Charlie," she said softly.

"I know, but it's still his word against Michael's. It's not nearly enough," he said. "One thing's for sure. If Maikai dictated a second will that was going to cut his son out of controlling the estate, he wouldn't have had Michael draw it up. And it's certain Maikai didn't write it himself, so he had to have had a lawyer do it."

He turned the car toward the sea and saw that the slopes of Diamond Head had gone completely dark.

"If he didn't trust Michael to draw up this new will, who would he go to?" he asked her.

"Well, probably Taylor Baldwin. He handled all my father's legal matters. Until Michael took over, that is," Lily said. "But he retired ten years ago, at least."

"He's still alive, isn't he?" Dan asked. Taylor had been an old man even when Dan was a kid. He would come to play mah-jongg with Maikai and two Chinese pineapple pickers, and he complained of creaking joints the whole time he sat on the porch of the ranch house and drank guava laced with rum.

"I think so."

"Then, he's not too old to make out a will. That's what a lawyer does when he retires instead of working at a hardware store. He handles wills and probates. Easy work, easy fees. Is he still over in Kahului?"

"No," she said. "He moved to Captain Cook."

"The Big Island?" Dan said. "When?"

"Gee. Years ago."

CHAPTER
TWENTY-THREE

The next morning Dan flew to Kona on the Big Island of Hawai'i to locate Baldwin, Maikai's old lawyer. From the airport it was a long, winding drive through groves of papaya and macadamia to Captain Cook. The afternoon sun assaulted the metal of the car and the scent of rotting fruit was heavy in the air as he wound through the jungle-fringed road.

When Dan got to Captain Cook, he drove back and forth, reading numbers on the mailboxes that stuck their heads out of the foliage every few hundred feet along the highway. It took nearly half an hour to find Baldwin's box. It was a handmade wooden replica of a barn with cattle horns sticking out of the top like on some eccentric Texan's Cadillac. Rawhide hinges held the little barn door in place.

Dan turned up the rutted dirt road and steered his way between potholes. It was the dry season, so the going, although bumpy, was navigable. The driveway went up a hundred yards through a canopy of green *ulu* trees before it suddenly broke into a meadow of grass beaten down by tires. Taylor Baldwin's place was a mobile home propped on wood blocks on a flat piece of property above the highway that had a wide view of the ocean. Next to the mobile home was a dirty pickup truck with a MAKAWAO RODEO DAYS sticker on the bumper. Behind the place was a burned-out wooden structure that looked like it had been a barn.

When Dan pulled up, a tall, sturdy old man wearing gym shorts and cowboy boots hurried out the screen door.

"The macadamia farm is down one more turn," he said. "There's a big sign on the left."

The old man was waving his hands to keep Dan in his car, but Dan got out anyway.

"Actually," Dan said, "I wanted to see you, Mr. Baldwin."

"That so? What for? We got plenty of vacuums, encyclopedias, supplemental health insurance, bottled water. You name it, we're set."

Dan laughed. "No," he said, raising his hands as if in surrender. "I'm not a salesman. I wanted to ask you a few questions. I'm a prosecuting attorney."

Baldwin inspected Dan, his bushy gray brows lowering as his face screwed up. "Not much crime around here."

"Actually, I'm trying to help a mutual friend of ours. Lily Maikai?"

"You fellas in the PA's office haven't been helping that family much these days. Besides, the only help a PA ever gives anyone is when he helps him find room and board at Halawa," the old man said, referring to the state prison.

"No," Dan smiled. "I'm off duty now. This is just family business Lily needed some advice on."

"Yeah, well, excuse me, but I never heard yet of a PA who was ever off duty," Baldwin said. Then he looked at Dan again curiously and stepped down off the porch. "Hey, you're Danny, ain't you? Danny Carrier."

"Yes," Dan said and grinned. "I didn't know if you'd remember me."

"Ah, hell yes. You and your brother were a pair. Salt and pepper, we used to call you. Your brother had that white hair and you were dark as lava."

Baldwin laughed about the past. Then suddenly he turned serious.

"Jesus," he said, "that poor family's had it rough as a cob lately, ain't they? First that mess about the governor and then the old man dies." Taylor was shaking his head. "How are Lily and Michael taking it, by the way?"

"As well as can be expected, I guess. They're both pretty tough."

"Yeah, I suppose so. Still, they had to be pretty upset when your office tried to hang Peter with the assassination and all. Looked like a railroad job to me, plain and simple."

Dan nodded. "I agree, but unfortunately it wasn't my call."

"Well, whoever made the call had his head up his ass. Ah, hell, don't get me started. I've been pissed ever since Peter was arrested."

Baldwin threw his hands up. "Don't get me started. Don't get me started," he kept mumbling. Then he gave Dan a pat on the shoulder. "So what did you come all the way out here for, Danny?"

"Actually, it's about my daughter," Dan said.

"So they found her?" Baldwin asked. From the old man's answer, Dan realized that Taylor knew something.

"Then you knew about her before?" Dan asked.

"Hell, yes." His eyes narrowed in on Dan again. "Peter was here a while back and he told me all about it. That was another fine mess. Whew!"

Baldwin turned and headed back up the stairs. "Come on in, son," he said. "I'm gonna brew some coffee. You want a cup?"

"No, thanks," Dan said, following Baldwin up the steps. The old man held the door for Dan and let it slap shut behind them.

"You sure you don't want a cup? It's Kona Royale. Grow it myself."

"Thanks anyway," he said and watched Taylor disappear into the kitchen.

Dan could hear the gas flame snap on over the stove as he sat down on the sofa in the front room. There was the clank of an old tin coffeepot on the metal burners and the refrigerator door opening and closing.

"Where did they find her?" Baldwin shouted as he stuck his head into the living room.

"In Honolulu."

"I'll bet that made the old man happy."

"He never knew."

The smile on Baldwin's face fell away. "You mean he died before he found out?"

"Unfortunately, yes."

"Ah, that's too damn bad. The old *kanaka* had his heart set on reuniting with her before he died."

"She died before he did," Dan said abruptly.

"That right?" Baldwin asked. "What the hell happened to her? She was just a kid." He was standing in the doorway, his shoulder resting against the jamb.

"She was the girl who was found murdered with Governor Slaton."

"Good God, son," Baldwin said, pawing the floor with his bare feet. He had taken off his boots and stood them up inside the kitchen door. "Maybe it ain't so bad that Peter died when he did. This would have eaten him up. He blamed himself for that whole mess with Lily and you."

Baldwin paused a moment looking out past Dan, to nothing in particular. "How's Lily taking this?"

"About the same as I am," Dan said. "It's a different kind of grief. I mean, neither one of us actually knew her. So it's more like shock than anything else. So much has happened, so quickly. The assassination. Maikai dying. Then our daughter . . ."

The sound of the kettle screaming drowned out Dan's words. Taylor lifted it off the burner and the kettle calmed down. A minute later he came into the living room with a cup the size of a wading pool and drank a big gulp as soon as he sat down in a huge recliner. By the expression of pain on his face, Dan knew the coffee was burning all the way down.

"Ahhhhh," Baldwin sighed with satisfaction. "If it ain't scaldin', it ain't no good."

He put the cup down on the table next to him. "Those idiots at your office don't think the old man killed his own granddaughter?"

"It looks that way," Dan said.

"Ah, hell, that's a bunch of bullshit," Baldwin said, pouring another scalding swallow down his throat. "Funny thing is, I fixed up a new will for him when he was over here. The old buzzard was lookin' for her then. I told him I knew a good investigator, so I gave him the name of a gal I knew in Maui."

"May Bell?" Dan asked.

"You know her?"

"I talked to her last week."

"Yeah?" Baldwin raised his eyebrows. "She's a doozy, ain't she? Bite your ass off, she gets the chance. Hell of PI, though."

Dan raised his eyebrows to match Baldwin's.

"May must not have found her or your daughter wouldn't have ended up with Slaton. Right?" the old man wanted to know.

"Yeah, she found her. Almost immediately, in fact."

Baldwin's eyes narrowed and his head drew back slowly. Something sure didn't make sense.

"I don't get it. Why the hell didn't Peter bring her home?"

"Because Michael was the one who actually hired May Bell. She had all of her dealings exclusively with him."

A knowing smirk formed on Baldwin's lips. "I see. And I suppose Michael never told the old man."

"That's the way it looks. But I understand that Maikai still included her in the will you drafted. Is that right?"

The old man gave Dan a sly grin. Dan could tell that Baldwin now knew exactly why Dan had flown from Honolulu and driven for an hour through the jungle to see him.

"Now come on, Danny, you know better than that," he said. "If I told you anything about the will I'd be breaking client-attorney confidentiality. Hey, I'm retired, I ain't senile."

"But, I'm certain that Michael is probating a will that he wrote for his father several years ago. A will that was drafted before the one you wrote."

"That little weasel," Baldwin said, shaking his head. "You know, when he first showed me that old will I should have told Maikai how his so-called loving son tricked it up to put himself in control of the whole shebang. But I figured Peter was changing it anyway, why spoil an old man's illusions?"

"I don't think Peter had many illusions left about Michael," Dan said.

"Yeah, probably not, because he had the good sense not to let Michael draw up the new one."

Dan scooted forward to the front of his seat and leaned over to Baldwin.

"Look, Taylor, I know what I'm asking is a breach of confidentiality. But can't you make an exception to help Lily? If that old will is approved, Michael gets control of the Maikai estate. He'll have the ranch sold off in a week to Hizaga."

"He dealin' with that rattler now?"

Dan nodded his head. "I heard Hizaga's already got plans drawn up to turn the Hāna coast into an amusement park."

Baldwin leaned forward in his chair, twisting the coffee cup in his hands.

"All right, suppose for the sake of argument that I ignore my ethical duties and verify your suspicions about what's in the new will. It won't mean a damn thing without the actual document, you know that, son. Any court will figure the old man didn't like the new will and destroyed it himself. Happens every day."

"I know that," Dan said. "But at least if you can verify for me what was in the will, it can confirm my suspicions that Michael had a motive to destroy it."

Baldwin shook his head slowly.

"I'm sorry, Dan. As much as I'd love to help you go after the little bastard with both barrels, I just can't. In my book a man lives or dies by his word. And I gave my word to each and every one of my clients for the last forty years that I wouldn't tell anyone anything they told me in confidence. If I break that promise, I don't deserve to be trusted ever again."

He picked up the cup again and took another long drink. "That's the way the old man wanted it and I have to respect his wishes or I ain't worth a damn as a lawyer *or* a man."

"I want to see that Maikai gets his wish, too," Dan said.

Baldwin, in the middle of a sip, lowered the cup just enough so his eyes peered over the rim of the cup at Dan.

"Sure you do, son," Baldwin said. "But you still can't see the will even if I'd let you. Because I don't have a copy. I had all my records in the stable back there." He pointed through the back of the house to where Dan had seen the pile of charred lumber as he drove in.

"The fire got it?" Dan asked.

"Everything."

"Jesus," Dan sighed. If Baldwin couldn't help him, maybe the witnesses to that will could. It was a long shot, but maybe Maikai gave them a copy. "You don't happen to remember who the witnesses were who signed the will, do you?"

"You don't know?" Baldwin said, surprised.

"No. The only one who seems to know anything about this will is Uncle Charlie Yates."

"That figures. He was Maikai's father confessor. Told him every damn thing."

"Do you remember who witnessed the new will?" Dan asked again.

Baldwin looked curiously at Dan for a moment. "It was your brother Paul and his wife."

Dan collapsed into the old chair at the kitchen table. "They're both dead," Dan said.

"No way," Baldwin said, in obvious shock. "Both Paul and Melissa? How in hell did it happen?"

Dan was shaking his head. "It's a long story. But both of them we're supposedly killed in accidents."

"Jesus, that's terrible, son."

Dan sat for a long time in silence with Baldwin, looking out through the screen door. The only two witnesses were dead and the lawyer who had made out the will had had his files torched.

"Tell me something," Dan finally asked the old lawyer. "Was the fire determined to be arson?"

"That's why I carry this around," Baldwin said and pulled out a shotgun from behind the curtain. It looked as old as he was. "The fire marshal said they set it under my bedroom window. If the wind hadn't been blowing *kona* that day, I would have been toast. Instead it raced on over to the barn and it went up like hog fat."

The image of Paul being blown apart on his boat flashed into Dan's mind. With Paul and his wife dead, the only one left who could testify that there even was a will was this old man. And Uncle Charlie.

"I'd keep that shotgun handy," Dan said. He pushed himself up from the old chair. "Thanks for your help, Mr. Baldwin."

"Hey, no problem, son," Baldwin said and walked Dan out the front door and down the porch to his car.

Dan could see Mauna Kea in the distance with a light dusting of snow on its summit. It was a strange place, the Big Island. You could stand in a lava cauldron bubbling at 2,000 degrees and look up and see a snow-covered mountain where skiers were shushing down its icy slopes, then turn around and see the surfers in Kealakekua Bay.

Baldwin put his hand gently on Dan's shoulder. "I'll tell you what, do what you can to find the will. If you can't, you and Lily come and see me. And bring the old *kahuna* too. I think, with his help, we can see to it that Michael will never gain control. I'm sorry, son. That's the best I can do for now."

"All right, thanks," Dan said. He understood the predicament the old man was in. "But could I ask you just one more thing?"

Baldwin stood, listening.

"Do you really think there's another copy of the will floating around?"

"All I can say is, I always have my clients sign a couple copies. I keep one and tell them to keep the other in a safe place. You know, in case of theft or fire." He pointed back to his burned-out barn. "I ain't all dumb, you know."

"No, I guess you're not," Dan said. "You know where Maikai put the other copy by any chance?"

Baldwin shook his head. "I don't even know where he kept the original. But I did tell him not to store it in the same place. Not even in the same building. If the place goes up, it'll probably get them both at the same time it's frying you. That's what I tell all my clients."

"Then maybe we've got a shot at finding it," Dan said hopefully.

"I wouldn't bet on it," the old cowboy said. "I forgot to mention that Maikai never listened to a word I ever said to him."

TWENTY-FOUR

The PA's office was unusually quiet for a Friday afternoon. Normally the secretaries would be planning their weekends, chattering between fits of typing as the deputy PAs and the clerks rushed to slip more paperwork into the system before the weekend.

Dan had called Kalama and told him to meet him at Reed's office. They went over on the phone what Dan had found out and how they would present what they knew about Michael to Reed.

"We've got to have his support if we're going to get Michael," Dan said to Joe.

By that time the detective had become reconciled to the strong possibility that Michael had done something wrong. What crime he may have committed, Joe wasn't exactly sure. But the idea that Michael murdered several people to gain control of a fortune was something Joe refused to believe. There had to be something they didn't see.

"Look, I don't know for sure about this either, Joe," Dan told him. "But are you happy with what happened to Paul or my daughter?"

Joe's end of the line remained silent.

"I don't want to pursue this any more than you do. I grew up with Michael, too. But let's find out. And without help from your office and mine, we'll never know. Michael's too smart to let us get close to his records unless we force him."

"What time are you talking about?" Joe finally said with a sigh.
"Four o'clock in Reed's office."

Dan arrived half an hour early at the PA's office and went to see
Cathy first. Reed was in there, sitting astride the desk. His ample
rear was dented by a pile of case files stacked on the desk that he'd
landed on top of. Cathy had her head back, laughing, and Reed
was laughing with her.

They didn't notice Dan until the door shut behind him and
Reed turned on the desk, the laughter still on his face.

"Hey, Dan, how are you?" he said and looked at his watch. "I
thought you said four o'clock?"

"I wanted to talk to Cathy for a few minutes before we meet."

Reed stood immediately and took a half-full cup of coffee from
her desk and started to leave. "Hey, no problem, Dan. See you two
a little later."

Dan could tell by Reed's obsequious tone that probably the entire
office knew that Cathy and Dan were having "personal problems."

Dan waited until the door snapped shut behind Reed, his soft-
soled shoes padding down the vinyl-tiled floor.

"Where've you been?" Cathy asked him before he had turned.

"Looking into a few things," he said.

Whenever they talked about themselves it always seemed to re-
volve around the law. He knew that was one of the problems they
were going to have to solve if they expected to go on. They had to
find some common ground besides sex and the law. And Dan
wasn't sure now what that was going to be.

"What things?" she asked. There was an annoyed edge to her
voice.

"Slaton's murder, of course," he said and held his hands up to
her softly. "Let's not go into that now, though, all right? That's
what the meeting is for. I just wanted to see you for a minute. See if
we could talk."

She took her hands off the desktop and leaned back in her
chair. It squeaked as it tilted back. It wasn't used to that position.
Cathy was always leaning forward over a stack of papers, her pen
twiddling whenever he walked in. Now she looked relaxed, her
hands folded in her lap.

"You're the one who stopped talking," she said without anger. "It's been business as usual around here."

"Yes," he said and resisted the impulse to turn her line back on her as he would in court. "Business as usual" was the crux of their problem. And, of course, some lingering feelings for Lily Maikai that could easily dissolve like cloud wisps on the slopes above the ranch. He wasn't prepared to throw away what he had with Cathy for something with Lily that could be nothing deeper than the kind of feelings an old song can dredge up.

"Look, I'm sorry. I guess I've been a little too sensitive about this whole thing," Dan apologized. "I thought you'd understand that my feelings about Maikai were difficult for me to just ignore."

"That's why I was upset," she said and stood suddenly. "I thought you'd give me a little more credit. Of course, you were upset. I knew that. We all did. Why do you think Reed didn't press you when you refused to take the case? He had to ask you, though. You're the chief deputy prosecutor of Honolulu. If he doesn't ask you to prosecute, it's like slapping you across the face."

Dan stepped over to the open window and leaned out. That was one of the advantages of this old building. Unlike a lot of the new buildings they were putting up in downtown Honolulu, it still had windows you could open. He could smell the damp odor of the ferns that grew up one side of the building.

"It was you I was upset with really for taking the case," he said. "But now that I've had some time with it, I understand why you did it."

"What could I do?" she said. She had her fists planted on the desk and she was leaning on them as she stood. "I'm a deputy prosecutor. Reed tells me to take a case, I've got to do it."

"I know that," he said, and turned and put his arm on her shoulder. She relaxed and stepped forward into his arms. They held each other, his arms around her shoulders, hers around his waist. He tried to kiss her lips, but she moved quickly to the side of his cheek. He wasn't going to just walk in there, tell her he'd been a jerk for two weeks, no matter how close he was to Maikai, and just kiss everything all right. She was going to make him work for his forgiveness; just a little, anyway.

"Let's go to Nautilus tonight for dinner," he said hopefully. He was feeling better already. Cathy was the only real thing left in his life now. They'd been together for over two years. Lily, no matter how strongly he felt about her now, could be just an old fantasy re-dredged. Cathy was real. They had something and maybe they would build a good life together once all this madness with the Maikais receded back into the past where it belonged.

"How about it?" he asked again. "Nautilus has always been our place."

"Tonight?" she asked.

"After we wrap up the meeting. It shouldn't take too long."

"Tonight's not good, Dan. I've got two murder prosecutions to prepare. Why don't we make it tomorrow?" she suggested.

"Tomorrow would be fine," he said and looked at his watch. "We better get in there. I want to get the ball rolling on Slaton's case again."

"What do you mean by that?"

He grabbed the briefcase he'd set down on the chair and opened the door. "I'll lay it all out in Reed's office."

Kalama was leaning against the wall playing with the water cooler when Dan spotted him. He was flipping the water off and on in intermittent arcs.

"Did you round up all the paperwork?" Dan called to him.

Kalama snapped the cooler handle one last time. "Yeah, I've got everything right here." And he showed Dan a brown accordion file.

"Good. Let's get in there."

Reed was on the phone, standing with his back to them, when Dan and Joe walked in. Cathy came in right behind them, fumbling with a file, busily scribbling notes in the margin. She didn't bother to say hello to anyone but instead walked straight to the chair at the side of Reed's desk, sat down, and kept writing.

Reed hung up and put his hands on the back of his chair.

"All right," he said to Dan. "You called the meeting. What's up?"

Dan was standing cross-legged, leaning against the metal cre-denza on the far side of the office.

"I want to reopen the Slaton murder investigation," he said sim-ply and firmly.

Reed's shoulders slumped dramatically and he let out an audible sigh.

"Goddammit," he said. "I know you've been going through a lot lately with your brother's death and all, but I don't want to hear any more of this. Maikai killed the governor. It's the easiest slam-dunk case in the history of this office. Those damn Hawai'ians have finally quieted down. And you want to reopen?"

Kalama didn't like the way this whole thing was starting. Reed had had it with Dan about this case. He could blow at any moment, and Kalama didn't want to be around for it. He shifted his eyes to Dan.

"Listen, Brian, I've come up with a lot of new evidence in the last few days," Dan said. "I think I'm on to something. There's a strong possibility that somebody else had a motive to kill the governor. And for some very different reasons than any of us ever suspected."

Reed spun the chair in his hands and sat down in it.

"Hey, the guy was assassinated. They've always got a million reasons. Oswald was a nutcase commie. The guy that took out King. Shit, he don't like Blacks. Sirhan? Hell, I don't even think Sirhan knows why he did Bobby K. The bottom line is always the same, though. They don't like the guy who's in power. This ain't an exam in quantum physics. It's politics."

Kalama was looking off to a corner pretending to check for geckos, trying his best not to get involved.

"The girl that was killed with the governor was my daughter," Dan said, hitting Reed with another bombshell. He knew if he was going to get Reed to reopen, it was going to take explosives. Maybe a lot of them.

"What?" Cathy screamed and dropped the file she was writing on.

"What the hell?" Reed said. They were both standing now with their mouths half-open and their eyes screwed up, which was exactly what Dan had wanted.

He didn't say anything. He let their minds chew over everything it meant. He was going to let them get it out of him.

"Your daughter? Who's the mother?" was the first thing Cathy wanted to know.

"Lily Maikai," Dan said.

Reed's head was shaking almost involuntarily now. What was going to happen next?

"You telling me that was Maikai's granddaughter in that hotel room?" Reed asked.

Dan nodded and the room went quiet. They had all been there to see the slaughterhouse someone had made of that hotel room, the marble floor slick from all the blood.

"And he butchered her too," Reed muttered. "Jesus! That diabolical son of a bitch."

"I'm sure Maikai didn't have anything to do with it," Dan said slowly.

Cathy walked over and put her arm around him. "I'm so sorry," she said, then whispered something in his ear. He squeezed her hand in response.

"Yeah, it's got to be rough," Reed said, but he didn't bother to get up. "God, take some time off. If that's what you need. Paid leave, of course."

Dan knew that Reed hadn't figured out yet what he had come there for.

"No," he told the PA. "I want to finish this case."

"It's finished," Reed said in a soft, conciliatory tone. "Just because your daughter was in the wrong place at the wrong time, that doesn't change anything. You must know that. The physical evidence still points to Maikai. Jesus, you can't investigate the death of your daughter. Take some time."

"There's some other things," Dan said without hesitation.

Cathy stepped out of Dan's arms and looked curiously at Dan as if he were a device of some sort that might or might not be a bomb.

Reed could tell that he wasn't going to be able to get rid of Dan that easily.

"What other things?" Reed asked in an annoyed tone.

"I believe that Michael Maikai has criminally destroyed his father's latest will. It appears that in that will, Peter Maikai named my daughter as an heir to part of his estate. And if that's true, Michael would have been prevented from controlling the ranch and selling it."

"What's it worth?" Reed asked.

"Anywhere from fifty to seventy-five million dollars."

"So why didn't he just sell his third? His take ain't crack seed."

Kalama handed the file to Dan then sat back and let Dan explain everything he knew about Peter Maikai's will.

"I still don't quite get it," Reed said when Dan was through. "Michael Maikai murders the governor of Hawai'i just to do away with your daughter," he said, his lips snarling into a smirk, "so he can sell the land against the wishes of his father. He doesn't wait to see if maybe, just maybe, after six months his sister will ease off her father's deathbed wishes, see all that money, and agree with him. Or, better yet, try to talk to his niece who, now no disrespect meant," he said, holding his palms up to Dan, "doesn't seem to be the kind of girl who'd be immune to a big payday. Let's don't mention the fact that Michael is a respected member of the legal community, an officer of the court, and you're accusing him of God only knows what." Reed slammed his hand down on the desk. "Oh, no, he butchers the governor and his own *niece* and tries to pin the whole goddamn massacre on his dying father. Now am I the only one in this room who thinks that this whole . . . *concoction* sounds just a little unlikely?"

Kalama still hadn't said a word.

"There's more," Dan went on, unflustered by Reed's sarcasm.

"Jesus, I hope there's more," Reed said, still on the offensive.

Dan related his conversations with Taylor Baldwin and May Bell. "Michael knew where my daughter was and never let his father know he'd found her."

"That's not exactly illegal, is it?" Reed said.

"It shows he didn't want her around."

"Maybe, but Peter Maikai didn't want Slaton around, either. Plus, if I recall correctly, the roommate said in her statement that your daughter was a last-minute replacement. Michael Maikai couldn't have known that that was his niece in the room with Slaton. So that blows the theory that he planned the whole damn thing. He couldn't have known. Am I right?"

Dan nodded his head. "Normally, I'd agreed with you, Brian, but—"

"But what? I mean is there any hard evidence to refute what we had against Maikai: the motive, the opportunity, the murder weapon wrapped in a bloody shirt in his closet? What have you got to refute any of that?"

Dan sat down in the chair in front of Reed's desk. Kalama stayed propped against the wall. Cathy had sunk back into her seat.

"Michael had a motive and the opportunity."

"Along with anyone else who didn't like the governor's politics who was at the rally. The only difference is it turned out that it was Peter Maikai's weapon that was used to kill Slaton."

"Yeah," Dan said. "It's the weapon that's always bothered me. Where were the fingerprints? Why would Maikai wipe the knife clean of prints and not the blood? And then just casually put it back in his room."

"No one said he was a genius."

"Bullshit! The weapon was wiped clean because someone else's fingerprints were on it. Then it was planted in Maikai's bedroom."

Reed shook his head again. "And you want me to believe that someone is Michael Maikai?"

"Who else? He lives in the damn house. He had access, motive. Everything."

Dan tried to calm himself. Then he went on. "Look, I need the resources of this office to help me investigate. I'm not saying I know for sure that Michael did it. But there's surely enough suspicion to warrant further investigation. Micahel's no idiot. He knows the law and how to get around most of what we throw at him. I can't do it myself and get the evidence I need."

Reed looked at Dan then at Cathy with a little smile, as if he couldn't quite believe what he was hearing.

"But that's the point, see," Reed said condescendingly. "That's the Catch-22 of law and you know it. You've got to have something first *before* you go fishing into somebody's private life. Unless you just want a judge to suspend Michael Maikai's constitutional rights on your say-so, so you can get to the bottom of this little fantasy you've cooked up."

"This is no fantasy, Brian. I know it seems like a long shot but everything points to Michael. And don't forget what happened to my brother and his wife."

"Come on, Dan, their deaths were both accidental and you know it," Reed said, sounding frustrated. "Besides, what do you mean, everything points to him? Before I walk into Yamanoha's chambers and ask for another search warrant, I've got to have something. Anything! So what have you got?"

"I've got everything I've told you," Dan said firmly.

Reed looked up at the ceiling as if praying for counsel. The fan above him had been spinning on that ceiling for at least ten years, and the wooden paddles were off balance and wobbled loudly. The noise it made was one of Reed's daily gripes, but he perspired too much in this climate to turn it off.

"Kalama, turn that damn thing to low, would you?" He pointed at a switch on the wall next to Joe.

Reed took a deep breath and his growing gut rose and fell with the effort.

"Dan," he said, trying to remain calm, "do you even know for sure if that was your daughter? I mean, is it documented? Can we prove it? Do you have copies of a birth certificate or adoption papers?'

"I plan on getting them," Dan said quickly.

"All right, that'll take some time. But let's say you do. We still have a big coincidence unless you've got a copy of this new will. Have you?"

Dan shook his head. "No."

"Can you get one?" Reed asked.

"I don't really know."

Reed leaned back in his seat. "Well, who's seen the will? How do you know it's even in existence?"

"The lawyer who drew it up verified it."

"He's got a copy?"

"It burned in a fire," Dan said.

Reed threw his eyes heavenward.

"How about witnesses to this phantom will?"

"My brother and his wife."

Reed got a look on his face as if he'd just bitten into a sour pineapple. "Your brother and his wife are both dead, aren't they? Do you know how far-fetched this all sounds?"

"That's just it. There are just too many coincidences," Dan insisted. "As a matter of fact, I think maybe Melissa's and now Paul's death could have something to do with the fact that they were the witnesses to the missing will."

Reed held his hand up to stop Dan. "Come on, Carrier. Please don't go any further. Now you want me to believe Michael killed your brother and his wife because they were witnesses to some damn will?"

Dan threw his hands out to Reed in frustration. "Damn it, Brian, I don't know what the hell to believe. Right now all I'm saying is that a will is missing and a copy of it burned up in a suspicious fire. Not only that, but the two witnesses to the signing of that will are dead. What the hell am I supposed to do? Just chalk it up as one big coincidence?"

Reed took another loud breath and looked at Cathy.

"Jesus! Maybe you can talk some sense into this guy?" he asked her.

Dan's eyes pivoted to her. Now he would find out whose side she was on. Not just in this matter, but in the greater scheme of office politics. Before this, they may have disagreed, but she had always followed Dan's lead, come to him to discuss the tough knots of a case she was trying to unravel, believed in him. The fact that they were lovers was something he couldn't count on much anymore.

"Dan," she said and reached over and touched his hand. "It's entirely possible that this Maikai woman set this whole thing up to gain some leverage in probate."

"What are you saying?" Dan asked, not quite following yet what she was getting at.

"It's obvious she wants to challenge the will. From what you explained the existing will gives Michael control of the whole ranch which, I might add, is not inconsistent with Hawai'ian patriarchal family customs. Doesn't the firstborn inherit the land usually?"

"Yes, but Maikai vehemently expressed his opposition to Michael controlling the estate. He knew he'd just turn around and sell it to the highest bidder."

Cathy still had her hand on his.

"And whom did he express this wish to? Besides your dead brother and sister-in-law."

"Uncle Charlie Yates."

"That witch doctor?" she said.

Dan let the comment slide. He'd thought the same thing himself.

"It was also the last thing he told his daughter before he died."

"The Maikai woman?"

"Her name is Lily."

Cathy released his hand and sat straight-backed in her chair.

"Sometimes you're so goddamn stupid about women, you know that?"

"Yeah," Dan said staring back at her. "I know that."

"All right, all right," Reed cut in, holding the palms out to his sides like a referee trying to keep two boxers in their corners. "Jesus! That's enough of that."

Dan got up from his chair and walked to the far window. Cathy went to the window on the other side of Reed's desk. The dropping sun flashing against the windows of the high-rise down the street blinded her for an instant.

Kalama stepped forward then and put the file down on the chair where Dan had presented his arguments.

"Brian, I think what Dan try say here," the cop started, using a little pidgin to ease into what he wanted to say. "Well, we need just a little bit help. We not going try drop any bombs. Maybe just sneak up on it quiet."

Reed slapped both his hands down on his desk and a box of paper clips flew across the room like a gaggle of tiny metal birds.

"Nobody's going to investigate anything about the Slaton murder. You're going to get your ass back to Homicide. And *you*," he shouted, pointing a chubby finger at Dan, "are going to start supervising the prosecutions of this damn office again. So I can get back—"

"Yeah, I know," Dan interrupted Reed's tirade. He was shouting too, now. "So you can get back to running for governor. That's what this whole thing's about anyway, isn't it? You're a big hero after you nailed Slaton's killer. But if Maikai turns out to be innocent, you're going to take the heat from every sovereignty group from here to Hilo. They'll turn on you and those political cowards that run the party will let them at you just to protect their own asses."

Cathy turned furiously from the window where she had pretended to be preoccupied by the view.

"That's not fair, Dan," she screamed. Her hair flew about her face the way it always did when she was upset. "Brian's been very understanding."

"Oh, shut up," Dan said and waved his hand in her face. "You think you're going to be his running mate, for chrissake."

She turned to Reed. "I can't talk to this jerk!"

She spat out the last word. Then she stomped by Dan to the door and went out.

"Well, how about it?" Dan said to Reed. "Are we going to get some cooperation?"

"You're going to get a leave of absence without pay. That's what you're going to get if I find out either one of you have spent two seconds pursuing this," Reed said, standing.

Then the PA hung his head a second and made another effort to calm down. "I know it's been tough ever since your brother died," he said. "I liked him too. He was a great guy. But it was an accident, plain and simple. You've got to put it behind you. Besides, maybe coming back to work, running the office, will do you some good."

Dan had calmed a little himself. He put both his fists on Reed's desk and leaned in close to the PA.

"Peter Maikai didn't kill Slaton," he said matter-of-factly.

"Goddamn it!" Reed yelled in his face. "It's over. The case is closed. I'm not reopening it and I don't want you to waste any of your time investigating any of your bullshit theories about somebody killing the governor to cover up the killing of some goddamn whore!"

"My daughter!" Dan shouted.

"Goddamn it, you don't even know if that's true. Some PI tells you your daughter was the one killed with the governor and you come up with this goddamn story. Give me a fucking break!"

"If you won't help, I'll investigate this thing on my own, then."

Dan reached for the file.

"You're not going to do a goddamn thing," Reed shouted. "If you do, I'll put you on administrative leave and you won't get within a hundred yards of this office while I'm still PA!"

Reed's jowls were a bright red now from the shouting. "And you," he said to Kalama, "I want your ass back over to Homicide. Or I'll make it my personal business to see that your ass is busted down to traffic. Have you got it?"

Kalama didn't answer because he figured the question didn't need an answer. But he was wrong.

"Have you got it?" Reed insisted.

"Yeah, yeah, I got it," the cop said. He was reaching for the door, trying to get out of there while he was still on Level Eight pay scale. He had a mortgage he couldn't support as a patrolman. He was reaching for Dan's arm, trying to pull him out of there too before it got any worse.

"Let's go, Dan," Kalama pleaded under his breath.

Dan took a step toward Reed instead.

"I'm not going to let my brother and my daughter be murdered and just go back to work so I can forget about it. This is all connected and I'm going to find out how." He turned and went toward the door that Kalama was holding open.

"Fine," Reed yelled at him, "but you're not doing it as a prosecuting attorney for this—"

The door banged shut and Dan could hear Reed still shouting. But he kept walking through the outer office, down the hall, and onto the elevator with Kalama pulling him by the elbow.

CHAPTER
TWENTY-FIVE

Dan woke the next morning with an ache all over his body. He tried some aspirin, but it didn't help. He was in his car driving up the hill behind Punchbowl to the graveyard where his daughter was buried, before he realized the ache he felt was grief. He'd been so absorbed trying to understand why his daughter and brother were killed that the sorrow of their deaths had not fully hit him. But suddenly, that morning, Dan was finally overwhelmed. He felt like he was drowning in pain and he had to be near his daughter to survive it.

He passed the beautiful Punchbowl Memorial, where acre upon acre of perfectly spaced white crosses covered the entire surface of the crater. Their symmetry seemed to lend a kind of logic to the death of so many.

Beyond was a Buddhist cemetery with its monuments and burning incense, rice bowls faithfully filled with white rice and boiled fish. Dozens of wild cats meowed ferociously whenever mourners dared to invade their feeding grounds.

Farther up the road, down a rutted lane pungent with fallen guava squashed into a pulpy liquor by tires, was a weedy public cemetery that meandered along a creek. There were no grand gates. There were no brochures with maps that marked each section of the graveyard with a comforting name like Wisteria Way or

Peaceful Lane. Dan just drove to where the graves were still fresh, their bulging mounds not yet settled.

Sharon's grave was the third one in the last row the grave diggers had started. Two other graves just down from his daughter's were already dug and covered with a tarp.

The plate at the top of her grave read STEPHANIE JOHNSON, the name she'd used at the escort service, the name Slaton knew her by as he'd whispered his warped desires into her young ears. Beneath her name was the date she'd died: JANUARY 25, 1995.

Surrounding the plate were two sprays of hand-strung flowers that he was certain Lily had laid there.

"We've got to get her out of here," he heard someone say behind him. He turned and Lily was coming toward him. She was in the shade of a pepper tree so her face was in shadow, but he recognized her anyway. Her shoulders were always perfectly still when she walked so that her head seemed always to be balanced on a cushion of grace. She was wearing a short sundress that came most of the way up the thigh. He could see beneath it a dark bikini. By the sand still on her rubber slippers, he knew she'd just come from a walk on the beach.

"I was just thinking the same thing," he said to her.

"I want to take her up into the meadow above the house."

"Not to the caves, I hope?"

"No," she said. "I think she needs me near her. And I know I need her."

She knelt and put another spray of flowers on the grave.

"I feel terrible," she said, still looking down at the grave, her fingers idly playing on the nameplate. "I keep coming back to the fact that it's my fault. I'm her mother. I should have fought for her. Michael was right about that."

"What do you mean?"

"He said I should have fought my father when he took her from me. He's right," she said.

Dan knelt beside her and a sudden kick of trades ruffled the flowers.

"It's easy for Michael to blame you for what you didn't do. But I remember what it was like back then. Peter Maikai was a very powerful man. He had to be to rally all those diverse groups of people behind him. Hawai'ians need a leader they fear. They always have, starting way before King Kamehameha turned Iao Valley into a graveyard," he said. "We were just kids then. Younger than Sharon."

She took his hand and they knelt silently before their daughter's grave for almost ten minutes. He'd always thought that perhaps the most important thing he'd learned from Hawai'ians was that silence was a precious thing that only the land can give. In the modern world with its buzzing copy machines, incessant infomercials, whacking helicopters, wailing sirens, that peace almost never came. That was why he had come to love canoeing so much. Out on the ocean all the buzzing and whacking and wailing was silenced.

Dan let the sound of the leaves flapping on a nearby palm talk to him for a few minutes. When Lily finally rose he walked with her to the street where her car was parked behind his.

"I think I've got the nerve now to go pack up Paul's stuff," Dan finally said. "I've been putting it off for a couple of weeks now."

Yesterday the landlord had called Dan to remind him that Paul's rent was past due and would he please come and move his brother's things out.

"Do you want some help?" she asked.

"That would be great, actually. I know I've got to throw some things out but I hate to make those decisions. Who knows what was really important to him?"

"That doesn't matter now," Lily said. "It only matters what's really important to you."

"Of course I know all that, but when you start going through a loved one's possessions, everything seems so important. I've already lost Paul, I want to hang on to everything I can of him. You know what I mean?"

She put her arm through his and opened his car door. "We'll do it together."

"Thanks," he said and got into his car, feeling a little less of the grief, as if he were at a dentist and the first wave of Novocain had begun to work on the abscess. He knew he had a long way to go to root out the grief, but at least the sound of her voice numbed the pain a little.

* * *

Lily started in Paul's tiny kitchen, where she determined that the collection of junky pots and pans, cracked plastic plates, and mismatched glasses could be safely dumped without any loss. Dan salvaged only an old coffee mug from New Zealand that Dan knew was Paul's favorite.

They talked it over and decided that all of the dress clothes—a blue blazer and some slacks and aloha shirts—would go to the Salvation Army and the rest of it would join the pots and pans.

The whole place was packed up in a couple of hours, thanks to Lily. Then they went downstairs to clean out Paul's old Toyota. It was an uncared-for get-around-town car. Most of the hinges were bubbling with rust, and the black vinyl seats were slit open, the breaches exposing the yellow foam cushion inside.

The family car, a five-year-old paid-off Volvo, had been demolished in the crash, and Paul had simply taken the insurance money and lived on it for the past several months.

Dan pulled the Toyota next to the Dumpster and got out. There were more clothes in the car, mostly sport odds and ends: baseball caps, running shorts, a clay-soaked sock that had scrubbed around on the floorboard on the passenger side for months.

Bending into the car, Dan threw everything over his head into a box with Lily standing by to pick up anything that missed its target. Anything they agreed was junk she tossed into the bin. Then he went to the trunk and cranked it open. The unoiled hinges creaked with disuse, and a stench of something dead and rotting pushed them both back.

Dan waved his hand in front of him and stuck his head into the cave of the trunk. He lifted a battered rain suit and underneath was a box of rotting pineapple. As he lifted the rubberized jacket, a swarm of black pineapple bugs flew past his head like bats from a cave.

"Jesus! Rotten pineapple!" he said.

"Whew! That's enough to get you high," she said. "Let's just drop the whole thing in the trash."

Dan stuck the upper half of his body inside again and lifted it out, holding his breath, his face turned to the side, and dropped the mess into the Dumpster.

Beneath the box of pineapples was a black accordion file that was sticky with fermented pineapple juice. Dan picked it up between his finger and thumb and dropped it on the sidewalk. Then he started pulling out tennis rackets, a scuba fin with one broken strap, handfuls of canoe lashings, and a ratty pair of gym shoes spattered with the yellow paint that Dan and Paul had used to paint Dan's apartment.

Dan tossed all of it in the box with the pineapples.

"Have you got an old rag there?" he asked Lily.

She reached into the pile of trash that was accumulating, fished out an old T-shirt, and handed it to him.

"How about this?" she said.

Dan took it from her and wiped most of the pineapple mess off the accordion file. He undid the elastic tie holding it shut and pulled back the flap. Inside was a worn-out manila envelope. It had been opened and closed so often that the metal clasps had both snapped off and the reinforced hole was ripped open. Written across the front in Paul's messy scrawl were two words that made Dan stop.

"What is it?" Lily asked, seeing the expression of horrified certainty on Dan's face.

He showed her the front of the envelope. She squinted to make out what it said.

"Sla . . . ton . . . cov . . ." Then it came together at once for her. Not just the words, but what they meant.

"Slaton cover-up?" she asked.

He rested the manila envelope on the hood of the car and pulled out the contents. Dan recognized immediately the files and the photos he held in his hands. Written again across the first page was the portentous phrase, *Slaton Cover-up*.

The first file in the stack was an HPD traffic collision report. On it were listed the parties involved in the accident. Party number one was Martina Patricia Gann. Next to her name was her age, twenty-two, and her description.

Party number two was Melissa Susan Carrier. Paul's wife.

This was the traffic report of the accident that had killed Paul's family.

There were also four photos of the accident scene with shattered windshields, car doors pried open by the Jaws of Life, and metal forged by the collision into obscene configurations. It had taken the fire rescue crew two hours to cut Melissa, already dead, out of the car. Her blood had dyed the front seat and dash.

Dan had seen this report and the photos before, so he thumbed quickly through them. Underneath this first bunch, however, was a supplemental report dated two weeks after the accident that he had never seen.

"What are they?" Lily asked as she looked at the crumpled wrecks of the two cars.

"They're photos of the accident scene where Paul's wife was killed. These are the accident reports," he said, showing her the stack of papers underneath.

"I don't get it, Dan," she said. "What does all this have to do with Slaton's murder?"

"I don't know," he said as he shoved the files back into the envelope. "But it looks like Paul did."

The next morning Dan was in the back of a two-man kayak paddling down the Ala Wai Canal. He could see the sweat running down Kalama's neck and shoulders into a yellow tank top he was wearing. They had made a pact to paddle twice a week to try to stay in shape, since Paul's death had broken up the canoe team.

Dan waited until they were through before he showed Kalama the files and the photos he'd discovered in the trunk of Paul's car.

"I've seen these," he told Dan, holding the rope of the kayak so it wouldn't drift off. "Paul made a stink around the station about them at the time of the accident."

"What was done about it?"

"Nothing, really. A lot of times when somebody is killed in an accident a family member wants someone to pay. But the department concluded it was nothing more than an accidental death. Besides, as you know, the driver of the other car died too. What are we supposed to do? Charge the corpse with vehicular manslaughter?"

"How about this supplemental report, though?" Dan asked.

"What about it?"

"Did you read it?"

"I don't know. That was months ago. I guess I did. Reports on fatal accidents don't make for very interesting reading."

"This supplemental report is very interesting, though," Dan said.

"Yeah? Why?"

"Because the IO states that he thought the driver of the other car wasn't the driver."

"Bra," Joe said. "You're going have to be a little more specific."

They pulled the kayak up onto the bank of the canal and Joe took the chain and pulled it through the eyehook on the boat. Then he padlocked it to the boat rack.

Dan picked up his dive bag and pulled out a copy of the supplemental file again.

"Look at this," he said, pointing to what the investigating officer had written. "Here it is. Party one. That's the girl, Marti Gann. Remember, she supposedly drove the car. It states she had no trauma to the chest."

"Well, so maybe it wasn't a total head-on collision," Kalama said. "If the car spun at impact, she could have been thrown sideways."

"Yeah, but if you look at this photo"—Dan pulled a glossy photograph from the bottom of the stack and showed it to the cop— "there's some damage to the steering wheel. I'd like to know what caused that?"

Kalama shrugged his shoulders disinterestedly. He wasn't a cop who went for building a case on evidence that could be explained a lot of different ways.

"Not only that," Dan went on, "but the girl had severe cuts and trauma to the head and face caused by glass. That means she was the one that hit the windshield on the passenger side. Here," he said and pointed to the shattered glass that pushed outward in the sickening shape of a human skull.

"That's what I just said." Kalama pointed at the report. "The IO says there was human hair embedded in the glass matching the deceased's."

"Right!"

"Yeah, right. So what are you getting at?"

"This." Dan pointed to the bottom of the page and read the last paragraph of the report. " 'All of the above is consistent with Party One being the passenger in a front-end collision.' " Dan was banging his finger on the word *passenger.* " 'Conclusion: Party One was the *passenger* in the car.' "

"It says that?" Joe asked. He slapped the sand from his feet and stood up and looked at the report again. "What the hell happened to the follow-up investigation the IO recommended here?"

"I don't know," Dan said, sliding the file and photos back into the envelope. "But we're going to find out."

"We? Oh, no," Joe said and began to backstep away from Dan. He had the towel draped around his neck. "Look, I can't be digging into this. It's my goddamn job if Reed finds out I've been anywhere near the Slaton case."

"So he doesn't find out."

Joe threw his towel down on his things disgustedly. "Yeah, sure, he doesn't find out. As soon as I go anywhere near those files he'll have me riding bike patrol in Waikīkī."

"You're not going to be investigating Slaton. This is a vehicular manslaughter."

"Hey, even Reed ain't that dumb. As soon as he finds out I'm looking into the death of Paul's wife, he'll nail me. You ain't foolin' anybody. He knows you suspect her and Paul's deaths had something to do with Slaton. Man," he groaned, "I got a mortgage I can't afford on what I make as it is. Lani had to take that secretary job over in Ward Center. Times are tough. I can't jeopardize my home for this," he pleaded.

They picked up the kayak together and slid it onto the rack next to three others. Then they walked silently to Dan's car and drove back to the Yum Yum Tree restaurant, where Joe had his van parked. They met there on the mornings they worked out, then drove over to the Ala Wai and paddled for an hour and a half. Then they'd drive back to the Yum Yum. By that time the restaurant had opened, and they'd grab a quick breakfast before Joe went to work.

Dan looked at Joe over the top of his coffee cup.

"I don't want you to jeopardize your job, bra. You know that. I just need to see the coroner's report that the IO based this supplemental on. And also I need to know where the IO is now. I have to talk to him."

Kalama was staring hard at the menu, pretending he was studying the full-color photos of the eggs drowned in hollandaise and the pile of macadamia-nut pancakes soaked in coconut syrup. When he finally lowered the menu, Dan was still staring at him.

"Brudda," he said, slipping into pidgin again, "you try break my *okole* on dis one."

Dan's grim expression slowly spread into a smile. Kalama was going to help him, of course.

"I get in big trouble, I going come see you for my house payment," Joe said.

"Thanks," Dan said. "We've got to find out who was driving that car and what it had to do with Slaton's death."

"I don't like when you say 'we,' " Joe moaned.

CHAPTER
TWENTY-SIX

Joe called Dan to tell him that Jerry Netter, the officer who investigated the accident, had been transferred to Narcotics soon after he started his investigation. Dan tried to get ahold of Netter for two days. He left several messages, but they were never returned. So Dan drove over to the King Street precinct where the Narco unit was housed and tried to catch Netter in his office.

Narco was a long row of portable classrooms that had been planted behind the main precinct. Dan parked across the street and went up the wooden steps that had been attached to the entrance. He pulled open the door with NARCOTICS stenciled on the front. They were constructing a new wing for the drug unit, but until it was completed they were housed in these discarded classrooms. Since most of the undercovers were dressed like kids in school with long hair, black high-tops, and earrings, these old classrooms lent an ironic air to the work being done inside.

Dan spotted an old friend named Gehrig who was on a rival canoe team.

"Gehrig, how are you?" Dan said from across the room.

"Hey, Carrier," he yelled back. "Man, I'm sorry about Paul," he said when Dan got close.

"Thanks," Dan said. "Look, Gehrig, do you know where I can find Jerry Netter?"

"Netter? He's probably in his office if he ain't on some weed stakeout."

Gehrig stood up from the desk and yelled down the long narrow room. "Turk!"

A black man in cornrows and a reggae tunic looked up. "Yeah?"

"Netter back there?"

"Yeah. Just went in his office," he yelled. Nobody else was paying them any attention.

"Thanks," Dan said to Gehrig.

He walked down the long row of desks and file cabinets. On his left were offices. In the first two an undercover was sitting behind a metal desk trying to squeeze a little information out of some snitch.

When Dan reached Turk, the black man nodded to an office two doors down.

"Thanks," Dan said. He knocked once on the door and opened it. The office was empty. Dan swung the door all the way open and stepped in. There was a cigarette still burning in the ashtray on the desk. A door led out the back of the office. Dan stuck his head out the door and saw the green flash of a shirt as it disappeared around the corner.

Dan trotted toward the end of the building. "Netter!" he yelled. "Netter, I want to talk to you."

When he got to the corner, Netter had disappeared. Dan heard a car start up in the parking lot and Netter's green shirt flashed by again behind the wheel of an unmarked white Pinto. It had a coke-spoon decal in the back window and a sound blaster that thumped rap at full tilt as Netter turned up the street.

Dan didn't bother to yell. Netter wasn't going to turn around even if he did hear him. He was trying to avoid Dan, and Dan was going to find out why.

Dan slammed the door and went back through the office. Gehrig was just coming into the room.

"You find him?"

"Oh, yeah, I found him, but he didn't feel up to an interview right now so he ran out the back door."

"Don't get sensitive, Carrier. It's only a rumor around here that we think the PA's office screws up all our busts."

"Well, maybe that's because more of the coke goes up your collective noses than it does into evidence."

Gehrig sniffed a few times and rubbed his nose. "Vicious rumor, man. Nothing but slander."

Gehrig and Dan laughed together. Dan always liked to visit Narco. Sure, they looked like a bunch of low-lifes over here but he never failed to get a good laugh whenever he was with these guys.

"You got any idea where I can catch up to Netter?" Dan asked and jerked his thumb in the direction the detective had run off.

Gehrig slumped his shoulders. It rubbed him wrong to cause trouble for another cop. He looked at Dan a minute.

"What's Buzzard done wrong now?" Gehrig asked, using Netter's undercover name. Every Narco detective had a street handle like the convicts they chased.

"This doesn't even have to do with a narcotics bust. I wanted to see him about a case when he was working the Pearl precinct."

"Oh," Gehrig said and relaxed a tick. "Wilson might know. I think they're on the same surveillance deal." Gehrig shouted across the room at the black detective. "Turk, where's that garden you and Netter are sitting on?"

"Out past Cooke ranch," Wilson said without lifting his head.

"Where past Cooke ranch exactly?" Dan asked him.

Wilson finally looked up. "We aren't ready for you guys yet."

"Jesus, you boys are paranoid," Dan said digustedly. "Lighten up, Turk. I need to talk to Netter about a vehicular manslaughter he investigated. It has nothing to do with Narco."

Wilson eyed him. "I'm going out there in five minutes. You can ride along."

The cane field where some enterprising dope grower had planted his garden lay in the hills above the Bonsai Pipeline. Wilson drove Dan in an old Volkswagen van that had probably been confiscated in a recent drug raid. The dope growers liked to use these old heaps to transport their harvest. It probably had enough resin caked to the inside walls to get the entire Narco unit high.

Wilson turned off Kalaniana'ole, the two-lane, potholed highway that edged its way along the north shore of the island. The dirt road he chose went past an old beach shack built beneath a stand of ohi'a trees and surrounded by wheelless cars up on wood blocks.

The road took an upward turn past the house. The cane was high and lush around them, so it was impossible to see anything but the view of the jagged mountains above.

"We're up on that ridge," Wilson said, pointing to a rock out-cropping that was the only thing in the area not completely covered in green.

"You know the drill," Wilson said. "We wait around for the boys to trim their trees."

The dope they grew in Hawai'i was mostly sinsemilla. It was a seedless harvest of marijuana that had to be nipped religiously throughout the budding period of the plant so that the resins of cannabis, the stuff that does the actual mind-altering, wouldn't be used up making seeds.

Wilson said the patch was a half an acre. Six hundred plants, bushy and in full bud, hidden in the cane. A crop like that was worth over a million dollars. It was just a matter of time before someone showed up at this green bank to make a withdrawal.

"The field's scheduled to be torched next week," Wilson said.

A cane field is burned to the ground before the cane is harvested, so if the dope growers were going to harvest this crop, it would have to be soon.

Wilson pulled the van into a blind of cane, and there was Netter's white Pinto with the dope decal in the window.

"We gotta walk. You in shape?" Wilson said with a half-grin.

"I forgot to bring my cane," Dan shot back.

Whenever an HPD cop razzed a Narco detective about his division, the drug dick usually jumped on the cop about his ever-expanding belly. That was the good thing about working Narcotics. The dicks in drugs were in shape. Of course, HPD officers joked that it was because they were too busy snorting to eat.

Netter was sitting in a folding aluminum beach chair smoking a freshly rolled joint when Wilson and Dan walked into his camouflaged den.

"Jesus Christ, Turk!" Netter said and tried to hide the joint behind his back. "What the hell is he doing here?"

"He's the fucking PA, Buzzard."

"The PA? Oh, Christ, man. What the hell is it now?"

"It's nothing," Dan said.

He watched Netter drop the joint inconspicuously to the ground and put his heel casually on top of it.

Dan looked at Netter's foot then into his eyes. Netter grinned sheepishly.

"Just checking to see if it was the real deal," Netter alibied weakly.

Dan ignored him and stuck out his hand. "My name is Dan Carrier."

"*Dan* Carrier?" Netter said. "Oh, shit, I'm sorry, man. I thought you were somebody else."

"Like who?" Dan asked.

"There's some nut by the name of Carrier harassing the hell out of me about some accident that happened months ago. Goddamn, I'm sorry. As soon as I heard the name Carrier, I ran out the back door."

"That nut was my brother, Paul Carrier," Dan said.

"Shit!" Netter said. There were so many ways he could get his ass hung out on this one. He knew a prosecutor didn't trek into some rat-infested cane field for exercise.

"I'd like to know where my brother got the report on the accident where his wife was killed."

"Is that what this is all about?" Netter said, looking at Turk for help. "You from IA or something?"

"Internal Affairs?" Dan said. "No, like Turk said, I'm the PA."

"Well, then what? All I did was give your brother some info to get him off my back. I figured he'd get it anyway. You know, Freedom of Information and all that."

Dan shook his head. "Calm down, Netter. I've got no interest in nailing you. I'm just here to find out who shut down the investigation. And why."

Netter shook his head. "I don't know why. As far as the who, it came from somebody upstairs. I didn't ask. It was a screwball case anyway. I was glad to be out of it."

"What do you mean screwball?"

"Well, you know, the circumstances weren't clear-cut," Netter explained. "Maybe there was someone else in the car. Maybe there were drugs. Maybe, maybe, maybe. Then your brother. What's his name?"

"Paul."

"Yeah, he's buggin' the hell out of me. You know, not that that's so unusual. Lotta times you know how it is, the family wants answers. Can't blame them for that. Except I didn't have any answers. I had a lot of questions. But no answers."

"So you were glad to get out of it?"

"Sure I was. I got two kids. This ain't my whole life. Don't get me wrong. I like being a cop. Pays the bills. Sometimes I even get to see the bad guys put away. You know, it's okay. But man, I don't need some grieving nutcase hanging all over me. You know, no offense. I know it's your brother and all but, man, he wouldn't let up."

"He had a nine-year-old boy in the accident who spent six months in a coma before he died," Dan told him.

"That right? I forgot there was a kid hurt, too. Shit, I'm sorry. God, that's bad. My boy's eight now. Man, that's rough." He was looking at his hands, shaking his head. "What do you want to know?"

"I want to ask you a few questions about your supplemental report," Dan said as he showed the file to Netter. "You said you thought the girl was the passenger in the car. Why?"

"Well," Netter said as he pulled out the photo and pointed at the front windshield. "Look how the glass is buckled out here. That wasn't any glancing blow. The girl's head and face hit it full force. The coroner picked glass out of her face for an hour just to get a decent photo of her. You know, for ID. If she was the driver, she would have suffered chest injuries. Look at the wheel."

He sorted through the photos again and pulled out a shot of the interior of the demolished car.

"See the steering wheel? Somebody's chest crushed it like that. That much force has got to do damage to a human body and the girl still had cans like a Playmate's." Netter whistled at the thought of the girl's breasts. "You see the coroner's shot of her on the table? Perfect chest."

"Yeah," Dan said and inspected the photograph again. "I thought the same thing myself about the steering wheel when I saw it."

"Personally, I thought it was pretty obvious what had happened. Somebody skipped the scene. From the looks of the car, he was probably drunk and maybe even coked up a little. I'm just the IO. I'm not the chief or the PA or nothing. What I put in the Supplemental is just my conclusion. But I thought the bit about the cigarettes would clinch it, frankly."

"You mean the fact that there were two different brands found inside?" Dan asked. "There could have been someone in the car earlier who just left them in there."

"Like you said, we found two different brands. The girl had a pack of Slims in her purse. And the other brand . . . let's see . . ." The IO took the report from Dan and fingered his way down the page. "Yeah, here it is. A Sherman. We found a Sherman on the floorboard in the back that had burned a hole in the rug."

"So maybe she had one or two in her purse and she decided to try another brand. Change of pace."

"Nah, she had a pack of Slims in her purse. She wasn't smoking the Sherman. I'd bet on it," Netter said. "I know you guys gotta prove beyond a reasonable doubt and all that. But I ain't buyin' it. Girl smashes in the passenger-side windshield. The steering wheel is bent inward and there's two different brands of cigarettes in the car when we show up. Don't try to tell me the girl was the only one in that car that night. I ain't buyin' it. Are you buyin' it?"

"No," Dan said. "I'm not."

"Well, there you are then."

Netter suddenly looked very worried. "When I got transferred out, I just forgot all about this case," he explained. "You know, somebody else was gonna handle it. It just wasn't my headache anymore. When your brother came to me, I thought he'd go away if I gave him copies of the files I had on it. But I thought things were being handled, you know, by *some*body."

"I think you're right," Dan said. "Somebody did handle things. First they got rid of you and then they buried the investigation."

Netter looked at Dan like he was on fire. "Oh, man, you better slow down here. That's some dangerous stuff you're coming up with there. It's probably just a paperwork screwup. Soon as I got transferred, the report probably got filed and nobody was anxious to take on any more work, so it got ignored. You know how it is."

Dan nodded. "Tell me," he said, "what was your next move? Before you got transferred, that is."

"You mean as far as this case goes?"

"Yes, what was your next move?"

"Well, the obvious, really. I was going to check the hospitals to see who was treated that night or the next day for any injuries that would match what happened to that steering wheel. Chest injury, head, neck, ribs. Anything like that. If I found anybody was treated, I was going to go have a little talk with them. Then I was going to try to match their blood to what we found in the car."

"The problem is," Dan said, "the car's long gone with all the blood on it. And from what I can see here, no samples were taken."

"Wait a minute," Netter said and reached for the report. "Yeah, here it is." He showed the report to Dan. "Did you check the mirror?"

"What about it?" Dan asked. He had seen that a small mirror was found in the backseat with the girl's purse.

"It was a coke mirror. It had residue on it."

"So she was high? Big deal. You'd almost expect drugs or alcohol."

"The mirror also had blood on it."

"Blood?"

"Yeah. I was going to have it typed before I left," Netter said.

"But why the mirror?" Dan asked. "Why not the rest of the car?"

"I would have typed the blood in the car too, but like you said, the wreck is history by now. The blood on the mirror is probably all you have left."

"So you never tested the mirror?"

"I never got a chance to order it. I got transferred first. That's the first thing I'd do if I was you. Then I'd go check the hospitals to see if anybody was treated that night for any kind of injury. If you find someone and the blood matches, then you've got your driver."

TWENTY-SEVEN

Dan walked up the back steps to the court building. Once inside, he took the stairs down to the coroner's office. The upstairs had been painted recently—the courts and judges' chambers and prosecutors' offices. But downstairs in the dungeon that no one ever visited, the paint was peeling from the walls. It had rolled down from the ceilings and hung on flaps from the upper reaches of the rooms.

The coroner's office took up one wing of the downstairs that it shared with the janitor supply room, employee lockers, and Security, where cigarette smoke billowed unabated in this posted "no smoking" building.

He turned the handle of the half-glass door of Forensics, walked past the partitioned outer offices and through to the lab area. Sitting with his feet up on a lab table, eating a *malasada*, was Chu. His back was to Dan and he turned in his chair when he heard footsteps. His eyes peered over the nipples of a corpse he'd been working on. The woman, with the first gray in her hair that nearly matched her skin now, was cut open from the throat to below the belly button and her rib cage was pulled open. The stench from her opened bowels mixed with the pungent odors of the reagents, the corrosive acids, and the mildewed walls.

Chu took another bite of the Portuguese sweet doughnut and it oozed jelly from both ends. The pathologist caught one long, escaping dollop with his big fingers and sucked it into his mouth with a satisfied "hummmm."

"Chu, howzit?" Dan said from across the lab. He was weaving his way across the large room filled with rolling metal gurneys, some with corpses beneath the pale green sheets, some bare, cold, reflecting the intrusive spotlights above that lit the room unevenly.

Chu shook his head as Dan zigzagged through the tables.

"You familiar with the expression 'persona non grata,' amigo," Chu said.

The pathologist stood and his head nearly banged the overhead lamp he was under. He was the tallest person Dan had ever personally known. He stood at six ten or six eleven. No one was exactly sure because Chu said he didn't know and no one could get him to stand next to a tapemeasure. They had once tried to hold a fake "Guess How Tall Chu Is?" contest for a phony charity and he still wouldn't do it. Chu was not that easily fooled.

Chu had a massive skull filled to the brim with gray matter. His shoulders spread out so astoundingly wide that he literally had to duck and turn to enter a room, the same way movers get a table through a door. The farther down one looked, the smaller Chu got, however. From his average-width hips, to skinny thighs, to sticklike calves and, finally, at the bottom, shoes shaped like yardsticks that slapped like a ruler when Chu walked.

Chu, extending his arm, reached halfway across the room and yanked down a half-sheet memo from Reed that was thumbtacked to a corkboard.

"Do you want the whole quote here, Carrier? Or should I give you the condensed version?"

Dan stopped before he got uncomfortably near the cut-open corpse and talked across the space to Chu. The pathologist could feast on a gooey doughnut while gaping at a disgorged female, but Dan never liked the idea of getting that blasé about death. He wanted to look at those crime photos of mutilated victims and feel the outrage a jury felt at the violation of a human body.

"Why don't you give me the short form," Dan said, not that interested in Reed's pronouncements. He could guess what it said anyway.

"Well, in a nutshell, Reed says no one in the department is supposed to do any work for you without his prior consent."

"That fat ass," Dan said, shaking his head in disgust.

Chu lowered his lids and mashed his mouth up in a disgusted smirk. Reed was not Chu's favorite person, either.

"So tell me what's come between you two lovebirds?" Chu asked.

"Slaton."

"I suppose you're not entirely happy with the outcome of our leader's investigation."

"What investigation?" Dan snapped.

"Exactly."

Unlike the PA's office recently, Pathology seemed to be the one department that really cared about solving a crime. Every single one of the young deputy PAs upstairs were working their way up some imaginary ladder. Most of them would end up in a corporate job in a couple of years, or they'd move on to Los Angeles or Dallas or Denver, where they could make a name for themselves. They all considered this a dues-paying gig. Half the time Dan spotted them in the law library downtown, they were trolling through the law magazines for job opportunities.

"How's Supernet going?" Dan asked, referring to the computer network Chu had started as a hobby. It had begun as a network for pathologists who wanted to share ideas and had quickly turned into a forensics clearinghouse. The latest techniques that would normally take years to work their way through the creaking machinery of big-city pathology labs now took days.

Chu knew Dan hadn't come to see him to talk about "the corpse superhighway," as Supernet had been nicknamed.

"So you want me to ignore this direct order from *der Führer*, is that it?"

"This isn't about Slaton," Dan said. "It's about my brother."

"Paul? That was accidental, wasn't it?"

"I meant the auto accident that killed his wife and boy."

"Oh," Chu said. He had his enormous hands behind him and one came forward and nearly touched Dan as he dismissed the past. "As I recall we never did any work on that accident."

"I know that," Dan said.

He wasn't surprised that Chu remembered an event from months ago. He remembered everything except the score when they played tennis and he was behind.

"Chu, I really need your help," Dan pleaded. "Can you do this for me?"

"No need to beg," Chu said with a wave. "I'll take any chance I can get to sodomize your esteemed leader, you know that. Now what do you need?"

Dan reached into his briefcase and took out the evidence bag Joe had smuggled him. It contained what was left of the accident. The car had been towed away and by now was probably a square block of metal. All the dead girl's personal effects—the purse, the jacket, the hairband, and earrings—were returned months before to her parents in Fullerton, California. What was left was the mirror with caked-on blood and the suspicious white residue, and the cigarettes found in the car that were left in evidence because they were suspected drug paraphernalia. The department didn't return coke spoons and roaches to their legal owner. If everyone dies in an accident and the case is closed, the evidence bag stays in custody at least the required twelve months. But, in practice, it usually took two or three years before the "expireds" were tossed out by a clerk.

"Chu, I need you to check this mirror for blood type. I'm trying to prove there was another person in the car with the dead girl. The original report indicated she was the driver. But I think she was just along for the ride. The IO thought so, too."

"Well, if the IO concurred," Chu asked, "why didn't they run these tests before?"

"He was transferred out and most of his report apparently got lost in the dead-file burial ground."

Chu sniffed at the incompetence swimming all around him like viruses in a petri dish. He reached across two tables and Dan handed him the evidence bag.

"Can I have the results today?" Dan asked a little sheepishly.

"I suppose I shouldn't be offended that you think I have nothing else to do like the rest of the indolent baggage around here," he said, then pointed at the woman on the gurney. "This lady awaits."

"She doesn't look like she'll walk out on you if she doesn't get any service."

"I suppose not, but at this very moment the bacteria floating invisibly by you are heading straight for her. You can almost hear the clinking of their tiny silverware being laid out for the feast."

"God, Chu," Dan said. "Do I have to beg, you sadistic little Maoist?"

"Absolutely. Plus, you owe me Sunday brunch at the Ihilani for this."

Dan smiled. Chu frightened the management of any restaurant serving a buffet when he swooped in with his eight-foot wingspan, juggling three plates piled with food.

"Just do this for me and you can bring a friend," Dan said and turned to leave. "Just make sure it's a *live* one."

CHAPTER
TWENTY-EIGHT

After his discussion with the Narco cop, Netter, Dan believed that if he could find a doctor who had treated someone in the other car the night Paul's family was killed, he would be well on his way to solving the other murders.

There were three hospitals on the west side of O'ahu within reasonable distance of the accident scene where a seriously injured person could go in an emergency. There was Tripler Medical Center, the massive pink outcropping of buildings in the hills above the airport, St. Francis–West Hospital in Ewa Beach, and Wahiawa General Hospital.

Dan went to all three hospitals that day and at each one it was the same story. He would go to their records department, flash his ID, and they'd show him the patients admitted the night of the crash. No arguments, but no results either. After that he would request to talk to the doctor working ER the evening of the accident. At Tripler and Wahiawa General, the doctor he wanted to see was at the hospital when Dan arrived. He took them down to their cafeterias for cups of coffee, but neither doctor could add anything useful. The doctor at St. Francis who was working ER the night of the accident was at home when Dan inquired. He talked to the doctor on the phone and made arrangements to interview him the next day, but Dan knew it was futile. None of the three doctors said they knew anything about the accident or recalled treating any patient that night for anything that could have been caused by such a violent collision. Dan was sure that they weren't trying to hide anything from him, either.

Dan had hit a dead end. There had been no patients treated that night or the next with any injuries that could have been caused by a close encounter with a steering wheel. If someone were driving that car besides the dead girl, and they were injured, then their injuries went untreated or they saw a private doctor.

Dan got in his car and sat behind the wheel for a while. He'd just talked to the ER doctor from Wahiawa General and he had no idea where to go next. He pulled the car out of the lot and drove onto Kameha'meha Highway. The velvet green Ko'olaus rose jaggedly to his left. The place where the accident had happened was on the road that connected the back way out of Wahiawa. Dan had never been to the accident scene, so he took the turn. He was just driving now, with no signs to follow, no leads.

The intersection where the fatal accident had occurred was a few miles down the road, and Dan drove past without realizing it. He pulled over onto the gravel shoulder half a mile past. The cane fields rose ten feet above him on both sides of the road. A mongoose stuck his snout out from the bush across the road and, seeing Dan's car, darted back in. Dan waited for a cane truck to go by, then he made a U-turn and drove back to the crash site.

Although he had never been there before, he recognized it immediately from the photos. A cane-road caution light blinked yellow fifty yards to the south. The bullet-riddled yield sign that the driver of the killer car had obviously missed was just up from the corner.

There was a wide half-moon of cane that had been permanently cleared on all four corners to help drivers see the oncoming traffic. Not that there was any danger, really. It was a very lonely back road in the country. The accident that had killed Paul's family was the only one the older locals who used this road could ever remember.

Dan pulled his car across the double-double yellow onto the gravel shoulder, where Paul's Volvo had come to rest with his dying wife and son inside. The airbag had exploded with the tremendous impact and the motor had been shoved into his wife's lap. No one knew how long Melissa had suffered before she finally died. But by the looks of the gouges on her legs, it appeared that she had struggled for some time before she bled to death.

Dan wasn't looking for anything, really. Maybe a perverse inspiration. Maybe Melissa's ghost would whisper something to him. He didn't know. He kicked at the gravel while he walked around inspecting the ground. Every accident scene he'd ever investigated, even months later, had always had some piece of the accident still scattered about: a shard of red taillight, some scrap of torn clothing, or maybe an earring. There was always something left behind after the ambulance and the tow truck had hauled away the remains of what was once a family and a family car.

Dan stumbled around with his eyes to the ground, and after a while found himself at the edge of the cane. Behind the fields a rainbow circled from horizon to horizon, six vibrant bands so clear, so distinctly separate, it looked as if there was a black line edged between each color.

Something winked in the mud a few feet into the cane. Probably an old beer can. Except it didn't reflect like dull aluminum. He picked his way down the embankment to the muddy irrigation ditch that bordered the field. It was clogged with broken beer bottles and cane leaf. Dan hopped over it, but the bank where he landed was soggy and his foot slid down into the muck.

"Shit!"

Dan pulled out his foot and it was caked with an overboot of mud. He kicked his foot to shake the mud free and it fell in big clumps from his shoes.

When he looked up again, he'd lost sight of the shiny object that had made him curious enough to jump into a drainage ditch. The sun was at a different angle from this side, and whatever he had seen failed to catch the light the same way.

Cane all looked the same once you lost your bearings. Dan could attest to that, all right. He'd gotten lost in a cane field once as a kid. The experience had scared him so much that afterwards Dan had shivered for two days as if he'd been caught in a blizzard. It had been more frightening to him than a closet full of boogeymen.

The cane, a dozen feet high all around him, blocked all sense of direction. He had to beat his way through half a mile of thick, tough, rat-infested, sharp-as-razor cane before he stumbled luckily onto the deserted cane road where Maikai had finally found him.

Dan beat around in the fringes of the field awhile, swearing the whole time. Then he gave up. He was just about ready to jump back to the other bank when he saw the tiny twinkle again. He reached down and picked at the metal, then pulled a ring of keys from the muck.

Dan bent down in the ditch and swooshed the keys around in the murky water until most of the caked mud was washed off. He filed through the keys, trying to rub the mud clear so he could read anything, any markings. There was no name, just a plain gold bar like at the gift shops around Fort Knox. Dan weighed it in his palm with an up-and-down movement. If it wasn't gold, someone had painted a piece of lead to fake the heaviness of the precious metal.

There were nine keys, several that could have been office keys, one obviously for a house, and two were large gray keys with black leather head grips. Across the top of the keys was printed MERCEDES.

These could have been anyone's keys, of course. But he was pretty sure some guy who owned a Mercedes hadn't just stopped here to take a leak and happened to drop his keys over the ditch into the second row of cane.

Dan was certain they had something to do with the accident. Paul's demolished car was a Volvo and the rental car was an American midsize, something with the name of an astrological sign. If he could trace these keys to a car, maybe he'd end up at the doorstep of a killer. And just maybe the person who drove the car that had killed Paul's wife was the person who'd slaughtered the governor and his daughter. Why else would Paul have marked the files from this accident with the words *Slaton Coverup?*

Dan got into the car again and this time turned left toward the H-1. His leisurely drive through Wahiawa would have to be postponed. He waited for a cane truck to lumber by, its filthy yellow cab belching black diesel smoke, and he pulled into the paved road, spinning gravel behind him. He had driven less than fifty yards before he slammed on the brakes. He pulled slowly over to the side of the road in front of a green highway sign with white reflector lettering. The sign read: WELLTON CLINIC.

If someone had been badly injured, perhaps thrown from the car, and that someone wanted to get medical attention, this was a likely place to do it. Perhaps the doctor would never even know that at least three other people lay dying in the wreckage.

Dan knew of Jerome Wellton, the doctor who ran this clinic. He'd been in the news and in the courts often the past few years for insurance fraud. He'd been cornered several times by overzealous investigative news teams, running behind him to his car, the video rolling. Dr. Wellton, a balding man in his fifties with a marathoner's build but the skin color of a shut-in, never looked at the camera or the interviewer as he mumbled, "No comment. No comment." Channel Two and Channel Nine had the same footage, and it had even made it as far as *Sixty Minutes.* Morley Safer was doing a segment on Medicare abuse, and the video of Wellton driving off in the latest Jaguar ragtop illustrated that the problem had spread as far as paradise.

Dan knew the case well because his office had filed charges against the doctor. The case had been specially assigned to Cathy. Because of the voluminous paperwork involved in the case, she had spent months preparing for the trial. A week or so before it was due to start, the case was settled. In the negotiated plea the doctor agreed to pay just over a hundred thousand dollars in restitution. For that the State would dismiss all charges against Wellton.

At the time Dan had argued that the agreement was far too lenient, but Reed had authorized it and that was that. Of course, it had taken a hell of an attorney to secure that kind of a plea bargain for his client. And Wellton had a good one. Michael Maikai.

Of course! Michael had been Wellton's attorney, Dan thought, as he sat in his car staring at the clinic road sign. Michael and Cathy had spent days—morning, noon, and late most evenings—trying to work out the restitution. Dan remembered it all too well. He was relieved when the case was finally settled. He had grown tired of waiting for Cathy to return from the office after her meetings with Michael. Most of those nights she'd fallen into bed too tired to eat or shower and certainly too tired to make love. In fact, if he had to name a time when their love had begun to sag under the strain, it would have been when she was hammering out the amount of restitution on the Wellton case with Michael Maikai.

Dan pulled forward on the highway fifty feet or so to a driveway and turned in where the arrow pointed. The long concrete approach was painted green and was bordered by palm trees. It swept grandly up over a hill and led another hundred feet to a turn-around drive. At the foot of the graceful oval curving of concrete was a white plantation house with green shutters painted the same color as the driveway. There were bird of paradise growing beneath the rail that surrounded the porch, a wide wooden deck with a swinging love seat in one corner. To the right of the front screen door was a small unobtrusive gold nameplate with WELLTON CLINIC engraved on it.

That was when Dan remembered that Wellton was running a fat farm here now. All the latest high-tech electronic fat-fibulating, low-fat-cuisine, *lomi-lomi* massage kind of place. They had a resident plastic surgeon, a hair couturiere, and a team of nail filers. It was a new line of work for the doctor. Six months before, this was a place where accident victims came because they knew Wellton would pad their bills for their insurance claims.

Dan opened the screen door and went in. A young Filipina woman in a stark white nurse's outfit and a white nurse's cap sat at the reception desk.

"May I help you?" she asked.

"I'd like to see the doctor."

"All right. Do you have an appointment?"

"No. I'd just like to ask the doctor a few questions."

"About a patient?" she asked and banged a few keys on her computer.

"No. It's not about a patient."

"Oh," she said and hit two more keys, then turned to Dan. "Then we'll have to make an appointment for you to see the doctor. He'll have to examine you before he can answer any of your questions."

"No. I need to talk to him now," Dan said and put his ID under her nose. "I'm Dan Carrier from the PA's office."

Her eyes glazed for a second as she looked at the ID. It had been a while since the cops had been around. She ahem'ed a few times before she got up.

"All right, sir. I'll see if the doctor is available," she said and disappeared through a door behind her.

Wellton rushed from the back rooms a few moments later and waved to Dan to follow him out the screen door. Dan didn't recognize him at first. He'd had a new head of hair stitched to his skull since the last time Dan had seen him on TV. It was a big, high, black pomp like Reagan wore when he ran the country.

When they got out to the lawn-colored driveway, he turned on Dan.

"What's this about, now?" he said impatiently. "This has all been taken care of, I thought."

Dan put up his hands. "Don't get excited. I'm not here about your past problems."

Wellton looked at him curiously. "I thought Emi said you were from the police?"

"I'm a PA."

The doctor shrugged. "What's the difference?"

Dan ignored the crack. He thought he might be on to something and he didn't want this quack to derail him. If someone was badly injured in an accident and that someone didn't want to wait around for the police to see how he'd turned a quiet little country road into a graveyard, there was a good chance he'd try to get to the nearest medical help on his own. If the driver of that death car saw the clinic's road sign, he could have staggered here to get that help.

"I want to know if you treated a patient sometime last year who may have been injured in an accident."

"You mean an auto accident?"

"Yes."

Wellton shook his head so vehemently Dan thought his rug was about to fly off his head.

"This is not an emergency room. There's never been an ambulance patient that was ever admitted here. So your answer is no."

"Look, let me be frank here," Dan said. His voice was nonthreatening, the way a man of the law would speak to a helpful citizen. "There was a very bad accident about six months ago at the intersection right down the road from here. Two cars collided late at night. A woman and her child were killed in one car and a woman in the second car was also killed."

"Yes, I remember reading about that in the papers. Very tragic."

"Did you treat anyone, probably a man, for any injuries from that accident?" Dan asked. "My guess is he didn't come here in an ambulance. He may have even walked here."

"That doesn't sound familiar," the doctor said. He was less hostile now that he knew Dan hadn't come to hassle him. "What were the injuries?"

"I'm not sure, exactly. But in all likelihood they were to the chest or ribs. There wasn't a lot of blood in the car so it's unlikely it would have involved much in the way of facial lacerations."

"Yes," the doctor nodded. "If the face were cut, there'd be a lot of blood. That's for sure. When was the accident exactly?"

"August seventh of last year."

"What day of the week was that?"

"Saturday night, late. Sunday morning, really," Dan said.

"I can tell you right now he couldn't have come here. I've never opened the office on Saturday or Sunday. This is a clinic. I close the door and go home at 4:30 every weekday," he said proudly.

"But you live out back, don't you?"

"Yes. But, like I said, the clinic is closed."

"Do you mind if we look at your books for around that time?" Dan asked. "Maybe he came in the next morning."

"Sunday?" Wellton snorted. "He'd have to catch me on the ninth hole then. I've got a standing tee time at Makaha on Sunday morning."

"Why don't we check it? You never know."

"Don't you think I'd remember?" The doctor shook his head and the hair stayed in place. "You cops are all the same, aren't you? You just can't resist digging into people's business. I told you I'm not open those days. I don't treat patients on Saturday night *or* Sunday morning. Besides, I don't believe your bullshit for one second. All you want to do is nose around and see what you can find. I know your type," Wellton said with a point of his chin. "I get accused one time of padding a bill, and before I know it, Mike Wallace is sitting in my reception room with a microphone."

"It was Morley Safer," Dan said matter-of-factly.

"What?"

"It was Morley Safer in your reception with the mike. How'd you slip out of that, by the way?"

"A little thing you'd never think of, I'm sure. I was innocent," Wellton said and punctuated his point with his index finger. "Not everybody's guilty like you cops always assume."

"So, fine. You're not guilty. So why can't I look at your books, then?"

He stood up close to Dan. "Because you haven't got a warrant, that's why."

Dan ordinarily would have backed off, but he was desperate. He wanted to know why the doctor was getting so huffy.

"I just might do that," Dan said.

On his way back to the pathology lab to see what Chu had found out, a call came through on Dan's car phone from Lily. She had a business meeting in Honolulu, which was over, and she'd called Dan to see if he could take her to the airport. While they waited for her flight, they could have lunch and talk for a while.

She was sitting on the steps outside Taro Enterprises when he drove up. As soon as she stepped into the car, he started apologizing.

"I can't make it for lunch."

"Why?" she asked.

"I have to get back to HPD. They're running some tests for me."

"That's fine," Lily said curtly.

He explained to her what he had found out since the two of them had discovered the file in Paul's trunk. She cooled down when she realized that Dan was on to something that could be important.

"So what do you make of it?" she asked.

"I don't know yet, but I'm pretty sure Paul found something out. And it sure is funny how your brother's name keeps popping up."

"It still could be just coincidence, Dan."

"Maybe," he said, not really believing it.

"It seems like such a lot to believe that the accident that killed your brother's family is somehow connected to our daughter's murder." Lily shook her head and watched a big yellow-and-white bus amble by. "What do we really have to tie it all together?"

Dan lifted his shoulders and let them drop in a confused sigh.

"Nothing concrete yet, other than that damn folder of my brother's with 'Slaton Coverup' written on it," Dan said, shaking his head in doubt. When they spread it out in the bright daylight like this, it was full of holes he could see right through.

"And just because Michael represented that doctor doesn't prove anything," she said.

"I guess not. But I have a feeling that these keys mean something," Dan said as he dropped them in her lap.

"What am I supposed to do with these?"

"Do they look familiar?" Dan asked.

Lily rubbed some of the dirt off the key that read MERCEDES.

"Well, Michael has a Mercedes that he keeps at the ranch, if that's what you mean."

"That's exactly what I mean."

She looked at him with a doubtful expression. "What do you want me to do?"

"See if that key fits his car."

She looked at the key a long time as Dan drove toward the airport.

"You've got to be wrong about this, Dan," she said softly without much conviction.

"I really hope so, Lily. I really do. But I have an idea that someone in that car that night lost those keys."

"Sure. Probably the girl who was killed."

"No. I called Kalama and he checked it out. She owned a Toyota," Dan said. "Lily, please, just do it, will you? What harm can it do if he's innocent?"

"All right," she finally agreed.

It was the last thing either of them said until he dropped her off at the airport.

CHAPTER
TWENTY-NINE

Joe met Dan outside Pathology to give him complete copies of the files of Slaton's murder and the vehicular manslaughter of Paul's family.

"Where's the supplemental report?" Dan asked as he flipped through the papers Joe had stuffed into a greasy paper sack. Kalama wanted to make it look like he was giving Dan another batch of Lani's homemade *malasadas*.

"That's everything. I checked Traffic, Homicide, your office, the works. I couldn't find it," Kalama said with a shrug.

"What do you make of that? A disappearing report?"

"It's not like it's never happened before," Joe tried to explain.

Kalama didn't want to even consider the possibility that someone in law enforcement had gotten rid of it. Being in the middle of something like that wouldn't be fun. A cop who drops dime on even the sleaziest fellow cop is like a case of bad breath. Nobody says anything, but their faces turn sour when the stinker's around. Joe could think of more pleasant ways to spend the next ten years.

Dan pushed the papers back in the bag. No use jumping on Kalama's back. He'd risked his pay scale just getting it for him.

"You eat any lunch yet?"

Kalama shook his head and put his paw on his bulging gut. "I had a doughnut around ten. How about you?"

"Coffee," Dan said and gave a sour look. "Let's go see what Chu came up with. Then I'll buy you lunch at Kaimana."

Kalama's face spread into a smile. It had been years since they'd eaten lunch together at the Kaimana Beach Hotel. There was a garden restaurant under two spreading banyan trees that sat right on the beach. A low rock wall separated the tables from the sand and the most beautiful young women in Hawai'i tanned in thong bikinis a few feet away. The trade winds would blow through the trees as the girls barefooted across the sand down to the ocean, sliding chest-first into the water without getting their hair wet. They would step out of the sea glistening with salt water and walk back to their straw beach mats. After daubing their faces with a dry towel, they'd turn with their bare round rears facing Dan and Kalama and sit gently down. Then they would reach into their great straw beach bags for a plastic squeeze bottle of baby oil and begin to rub it liberally up their brown arms, on their legs, up their inner thighs. Then they would form a comfortable spot by moving their *okoles* back and forth on the sand and, satisfied, they would lie back down, slick with oil, their breasts at attention covered by the skimpiest of veils.

The smile dropped from Kalama's face. He suddenly remembered that he had met his wife at Kaimana Beach. "Oh, brudda, Lani going fry my ass but good if she catch me there."

"Blame it on me," Dan said and slapped the big Hawai'ian on the shoulder.

Chu had his hands inside the chest of a corpse when Dan and Joe walked in. There were human organs laid out on the table next to the body and Chu was humming *"Nessun dorma."*

Dan and Joe both stopped across the room from Chu when they saw what the pathologist was doing.

"Mr. Carrier," Chu said, looking up. "Good news. The blood on the mirror was O positive. The girl's was B."

"Yes," Dan shouted. "That means there *was* somebody else in the car."

In his excitement Dan had nearly leaped the table to get to Chu. He pumped the pathologist's hand profusely until he realized there was a human heart sitting on the table in front of him. He backed off a few steps, but he was still smiling.

"Before you get too excited, there's an extra little wrinkle you might want to hear about," Chu said.

"Yeah?" Dan said, "What is it?"

"You know those cigarettes? The two different brands? I analyzed them for saliva."

"Yeah?" Dan said. "And?"

"B on the long white cigarette."

"So. That's the girl's type," Dan said.

"And *AB* on the Sherman."

Dan's mouth fell open and he sat back against the lab table. "Are you telling me that there were three people in the car at the time of that collision?"

"It looks that way."

"Jesus fucking Christ," Kalama swore. This case was becoming the headache of all headaches. "But there's one problem with that theory," Joe said.

"I know," Dan said waving him off. "I'm way ahead of you. The Sherman could have been left by someone else at just about any time."

"Exactly. A john of hers could have dropped it on the floor the day before, the week before. Anytime," Joe said. He was swinging his hands around at the uncertainty of this so-called evidence. "So that blows the cigarette theory."

"Not really. It was a Hertz rent-a-car from the Royal Hawai'ian," Dan said.

"So?" Chu said.

Joe understood immediately what Dan was getting at. "The Royal makes sure that agency religiously douches those cars out like the inside of a washtub before they send them back out."

"And guess what time the girl picked this rent-a-car up?" Dan went on.

Kalama shrugged his shoulders. "I give."

"According to the report, about an hour before the wreck. Plus, the accident happened forty minutes from the place she rented it. I'd say whoever was smoking that Sherman was definitely in the car when the accident happened," Dan said.

"You three old ladies through with your sewing circle yet?" some-one loudly interrupted from behind them.

Reed was standing in the door of the lab. He didn't look happy.

"Brian, I'm glad you're here," Dan said excitedly. "I was about to come and see you."

"About what?" Reed snarled.

"I found out that the accident that killed my brother's family was never fully investigated."

"I told you to leave that shit alone," Reed yelled and came at Dan waving his arms.

Kalama stepped back as if to get out of the line of fire, but he suspected his turn was next.

"The girl who died wasn't the driver," Dan said.

Reed stopped as if Dan had slapped him across the face. His eyes opened wide from the impact.

"Then who was?" he asked.

"We don't know yet, but we've identified three different blood types in the car."

"And you still think that somehow all this is connected to Slaton and your brother's murder?"

"And my daughter."

"And your daughter?" Reed said. His voice was filled with disgust and the steam was back in his face. "Goddammit, Dan. I told you to back off. Have you got any idea what I've been doing all afternoon?"

Dan shook his head.

"Thanks to your fucking grandstanding, I had to try to talk a very pissed-off doctor out of suing everybody in this goddamn state for harassment."

"You talking about Wellton? I didn't harass him. I thought he might be a witness, so I asked him a few questions. The accident happened just down the road from his place."

"What the hell's your problem, Carrier? Damn it, let HPD do their jobs," he shouted and slammed his palm down on the table in front of Dan.

Dan leaned across the table toward Reed. "HPD supposedly did their job and they screwed it up."

"Yeah, well, fine. I could give a shit on a six-month-old case in which all the witnesses are dead. What I care about is a litigious doctor with a big fat hard-on for the PA's office."

Reed bunched up his fist in front of Dan's face. "Leave Wellton alone. He already told you he doesn't know anything. He doesn't have a reason to lie. So get off his ass."

"Wellton's a damn liar. I'm certain he treated someone who was in that accident and I'm going to prove it. You should've seen the expression on his face when I showed him those keys."

"Yeah, what keys?" Reed asked.

"A set of keys that were found at the accident scene. They've gotta belong to the person who was really driving that car."

Reed shook his head and walked over to a chair, sat down, and leaned back.

"So now you've got some keys that you believe belong to the driver of the car?" he said.

"That's right," Dan said. He had folded his hands confidently across his chest. Both Chu and Kalama were content to let Dan hang himself if he was going to. It was his damn theory, anyway.

"How did you get ahold of these keys?" Reed asked.

"I found them myself when I was out there poking around," Dan said with a proud little smirk. "They were buried in mud at the edge of the cane field. In a violent collision like the one that night, you know yourself that stuff goes flying all over the place."

Reed didn't say anything for a moment. Apparently the lost keys had struck a note of truth with him. The PA had been to enough accidents to know that the impact and the confusion afterwards can turn a crash site into a regular lost and found. Months afterward victims of an accident still claimed they were missing purses, watches, or even wedding rings they thought were just about welded to their fingers. A set of keys in the edge of a cane field? It rang true.

"All right," Reed said at last with a conciliatory nod of his head. "Maybe you've got something here."

Dan took a deep breath. It was the first time he knew for sure that he was really on to something. If Reed was ready to listen, maybe now they'd have a chance to unlock this puzzle.

"Now, what about these three blood types?" Reed asked.

Dan explained that Chu had found the different blood types on the two cigarettes and the mirror.

"All right," Reed said. "What were the types?"

"O pos, AB, and B neg," Chu rattled off.

"So, there'd be a good chance if we can tie someone to those keys, we could nail his ass cold with the blood type? Is that it?" Reed asked.

Dan was nodding his head, trying to hide a grin. "I'd say it's only a question of time before we find the owner. Then with a DNA match, we'll have our killer."

Reed was looking out the window with a distracted, far-off look. He was putting together what it all meant. "I think you could be right, Dan," he said.

"So you'll put pressure on HPD to open the investigation into the possibility that someone else was driving?" Dan pressed.

"Yes, I will. Under two conditions."

Dan was listening.

"You're too close to this thing with your brother and sister-in-law and all, so I'll take it from here. I'll reopen immediately and I promise to get to the bottom of this case if you stay clear."

"And the second condition?" Dan asked warily.

"The Slaton case is closed. One bag of snakes is enough. Besides, I don't believe for a second that these two cases have anything to do with one another. No matter what your brother wrote on some file he had stuffed in his trunk."

Dan nodded reluctantly. But he knew if Reed ever did find out who was in that car that night, it would explode open the Slaton case no matter how hard Reed tried to keep a lid on it.

"I'll go along with that," Dan said. "I just want to find who killed my brother."

"Good," Reed said. "Now give me the results of that blood typing and the keys. I'll meet with Lieutenant Iida this afternoon before I leave and turn everything over to him."

Chu handed the PA the path report on the typing. Then Reed held out his hand to Dan.

"The keys," Reed said.

Dan threw his hands up apologetically and said, "I don't have them. I gave them to Lily Maikai."

"Lily Maikai!" Reed shouted. "What the hell is she doing with them?"

"She's going to her ranch to see if the keys fit Michael's Mercedes. She's on a plane back to Maui right now."

"Goddamn it, Carrier. According to you those keys are a very vital piece of evidence. And you just gave them to her? You're fucking up here, Carrier. Get those goddamn keys back before she loses them and I have to explain to the whole goddamn world that my chief deputy prosecuting attorney gave our strongest piece of evidence to the suspect's sister."

"All right," Dan said, and he and Kalama squeezed past Reed and left.

Dan and Kalama skipped the sea of bikinis at the Kaimana Beach Hotel and grabbed a quick plate lunch at Zippy's. Joe hadn't said a word since they'd left Chu among his body parts. He'd ordered a cup of coffee and some fries and sat back without talking. His eyes were up in the trees watching the mynahs that were farming the sidewalk outside the fast-food joint. Whenever a piece of somebody's lunch fell on the ground, a mynah would hop boldly over and snap it up.

Dan noticed a heavy look on Joe's face as he played with his wilted fries. He was worrying over something.

"What's the problem, bra?" Dan asked.

Kalama picked up the file next to Dan that he had given him and fished a paper out.

"Slaton smoked Shermans."

Dan's mouth stopped in midchew. "You're kidding," he said. "You're not suggesting that the governor . . . ?"

Joe shoved the paper across the table. "Guess what his blood type was?" he asked as a mynah snatched a piece of bread from a table nearby and flew off.

"AB?" Dan asked without looking at the file.

Joe nodded his head slowly.

"Then Slaton may have been driving that car," Dan said.

Joe kept nodding unhappily. An investigation like this could sink more than a few small outriggers like Kalama's. Murder. Cover-up. It scared the hell out of him, and he knew there was nothing he could do about it. Paul had been murdered, his family killed. He wasn't going to stand around and let that happen to a

brudda. But he was still worried about his own family, their brand-
new house in Aiea, everything.

"Jesus," Dan said, ignoring Joe. He said it loud enough so a few
people looked over from their *saimin.* "Slaton cover-up! Paul
didn't mean the cover-up of Slaton's murder. He meant that Slaton was trying to cover up his involvement in the accident."

Kalama sat silently, nodding his head in agreement. As soon as
he'd realized that was probably Slaton's cigarette in the car, he'd
quickly surmised the rest of it.

"Okay," Dan said. "Slaton was AB, the girl B. But who else was in
the car? And whose blood was on that damn mirror?"

Kalama remembered the keys.

"What kind of car did the governor drive?" Joe asked.

"Nah, I know what you're thinking," Dan said. "He had that re-
stored Caddie, remember?"

"That's right. How about his wife?"

"A Lexus."

Dan threw his half-eaten plate of food into the trash next to him.

"Who the hell else was in that car?" Dan asked.

"Maybe Lily going find out when she try open Michael's Mercedes," the cop said sadly.

CHAPTER
THIRTY

Hurricane Fred was moving due west just south of the Hawai'ian Islands and the entire state was on a hurricane watch. Storms like this growled in the Pacific all the time during hurricane season. When a storm was close enough, you could feel the wind, but you were safe unless the storm suddenly changed direction. That was what happened to Iwa and Iniki: they were just a couple of bullies blowharding to the south until they turned due north and wiped out Kaua'i and O'ahu.

After Dan and Joe had finished lunch, Joe received an urgent message that there had been a shooting at the Wellton Clinic and someone had been killed. Dan got in the cruiser with Joe and they both drove out to the doctor's place.

A crowd of HPD cruisers and unmarked cars clogged the oval driveway of Wellton Clinic. A brace of wind rattled the top of the palms as Dan and Joe drove in. By the time they got out of the car, the winds had ascended to ground level, gusting so forcefully that it was hard for Dan to open the door.

The coroner's van was parked on the lawn next to the porch. The side door was open and a lab tech was pulling equipment from the van. Dan knew the body was still inside, then. If they were ready for the body, the back door of the van would be swung open, waiting.

Jerzy Epstein appeared suddenly in front of Dan. He stood with his pad dangling in one hand. A pen in a little snap holder tied around his neck hung at his chest. His tight curly hair was ruffling in the stiff wind.

"Carrier, is it true Wellton got his head blown off in there?" Jerzy said without a hello.

"What did Iida tell you?" Dan said, hurrying to the porch to get out of the mounting storm.

"I'm just trying to confirm with you," Epstein lied.

"Confirm what?" Dan sniffed. "That they told you to get lost?"

They took the steps together and suddenly, with the wind blocked, they stopped shouting.

"I don't know anything yet, Jerzy. You probably know more than I do."

"I was just figuring this had something to do with that fraud case of his. Maybe a disgruntled patient he'd overbilled? You know a lot of his old patients put up a hell of a stink after that wrist-slapping you guys gave him."

Dan stopped before he got to the screen door and frowned at Jerzy.

"Look, you're a lot better in the speculation department than I am. That's not my job. So let me do my job. The sooner I do, the sooner you can do yours. That sound sensible?"

Epstein's eyes grew narrow and mean.

"That's another thing," he said as Dan opened the door. An HPD stepped in front of Epstein as Dan went past. "What are you doing here, anyway? Word I got is you're suspended. I can work on that story if you wanna freeze me on this one."

Dan turned and pushed back past the guard. Jerzy stepped away when he saw the look in Dan's eyes. Dan grabbed him by the shirt and pushed him backward down the steps. Epstein nearly fell as he hit the lawn-colored driveway that had been Wellton's pride.

"Hey, back off, Carrier. I got a right—"

"You don't have shit and you know it. I don't know how the hell you always end up at the these crime scenes before we do."

"Because we aren't on the public payroll. We actually have to work for a living. We hear a call, we don't finish our lunch first."

The heavy wind was blowing their words around like newspaper. They were shouting yet nobody else could hear a word they said.

"I'm warning you, Epstein," Dan said, his face up close to the reporter's. "Get off my back. I'm taking this case very personal. You understand?"

Something in Dan's eyes told Epstein this was not just their normal quarrel. He'd argued with Dan many times. But no matter how they fought, it was always just business. When it was over, they'd still have a beer at the Gavel. There weren't any hard feelings. That is, until the next case when Jerzy wanted something and Dan wouldn't give it to him.

"Tell you the truth, Carrier, I don't understand. This have anything to do with Paul?"

Dan was taken aback by Jerzy's guess.

"Why would you think that?" he said, trying to cover.

The last thing he wanted was for the papers to be on to what he suspected. Dan searched Jerzy's face for an answer. Did he know something?

"I don't know," Jerzy said. "Paul came to me a couple of times about the accident that killed his family. Wanted to know if I knew anything. The accident was right down the road, wasn't it?"

"Yeah," Dan said and calmed quickly for his own good. Jerzy was one of the best crime reporters he'd ever known. He was always asking what if, what if, what if? Putting together disparate pieces of this crime or that suspect and seeing if any of it fit.

Dan suddenly realized that Jerzy Epstein didn't know a thing. He was just digging.

"Nah, trust me on this," Dan said. "It doesn't mean a thing. I haven't been suspended. I was with Kalama when he got the call. As far as who got it in there, I'm not exactly sure myself. But, in any case, you gotta get that from HPD, you know that. Iida will let you know the particulars ASAP."

Epstein inspected Dan's face. He'd almost gotten under Carrier's skin far enough so he'd tell him something he wasn't supposed to. That was Epstein's greatest tool. He'd irritate the cops and prosecutors with his relentless badgering until he'd get them pissed off. Occasionally something he could use would come out with all the steam. And Jerzy would feel he'd done his job.

Dan went back up the stairs and through the screen door. The reception area was crowded with cops. Three or four homicide detectives were surrounding Emi, Wellton's nurse. Her long, black hair which was usually tied back behind her, was scattered around her shoulders. Her dark brown face had a red glow as if someone had been slapping her. Her eyes were swollen and her cheeks wet. With one hand she kept daubing her eyes with paper towels one of the detectives had given her. Then she'd wipe her nose with some toilet paper she had in the other.

One of the detectives would ask her what happened and she'd say two or three words then she'd start howling all over again.

Dan and Kalama pushed through the crowd and spotted Iida just inside the door leading from reception to the back of the place.

"He's in the back," Iida said and pointed behind him through a long corridor. Then he turned back to a lab assistant of Chu's who was showing him some paperwork.

Dan followed Kalama down the hall past a dozen examination rooms. All the doors were propped wide open and lab teams and detectives were in most of them, fishing around in drawers, checking windows, dusting surfaces with the gray powder that would reveal a stray print.

The hall came to a T and Kalama took the left turn when he saw flash bulbs going off at that end.

The photographer from the coroner's office was just coming out of the door when they reached Wellton's office. Oddly, they were all alone inside. All the other cops had had their look and gone to work searching for evidence or a cup of coffee.

It was a large room with a three-piece wicker living room set at one end surrounded by potted palms. A koa sculpture of the war god Kū sat on a pedestal of lava rock, and there were expensive pieces of Lalique crystal on the mahogany shelf holding the books in place. The whitewashed ceiling was vaulted and the wood beams matched the finish of the cane furniture.

The left side of the room was dominated by a huge, deep bourbon-colored desk. On top was a manila file with its contents spilled out. Wellton's head was resting facedown on the papers. It was as if the doctor were taking a little nap while he waited for his next patient. Except that his blood had soaked the papers a bright red and was dripping off the far side of the desk onto the white Berber carpet.

There was a spray of glitter on Wellton's back that Dan realized was glass. Larger shards were scattered on the desk, soaked with the blood still dribbling from the doctor's head. Behind Wellton was a window with sheer sun curtains flapping in the mounting wind.

Dan walked over and pulled back one side of the curtains and inspected the fist-sized hole that had been blown through the window.

Iida stuck his head through the doorway. "You want to talk to the nurse before we send her home? She's the one that found him."

"Sure," Dan said and nodded toward Wellton. "How long's he been dead?"

"They're guessing a little over an hour. The nurse figures she scared the killer off. She heard the back door slam," Iida said and pointed toward a small adjoining room filled with file cabinets. A door that was still slightly ajar led to the outside. "She called immediately and it took us thirty-five, forty to get here and we've been here for, let's see"—Iida looked at his watch—"another thirty-five, forty before you got here. So figure an hour and a half tops."

By the looks of Wellton, it had to be right. Blood was only beginning to blacken the base of his skull where the bullet had entered. The bullet had exited where his Adam's apple used to be and it still oozed the brighter red blood, so it looked as if someone had smashed a tomato on his neck.

"What did he get it with?" Kalama asked. "A Magnum?"

"Not that big," Iida said. "Thirty-eight's more like it. But from close range, and there's a lot of tearing from the glass, too. So it's a bigger mess than you'd expect."

Kalama looked at Wellton's face, which was shredded from the chin to the nose; his eye sockets were filled with blood as well. The spray of blood from the bullet led across the floor and splattered on the wall across the room.

"No shit," the cop said to himself.

Dan was looking through the window to the ground below. "How about shoe prints outside the window?"

"We're checking it."

Dan walked to the doorway that led into the anteroom off Wellton's office. File cabinets lined both walls. Most of the drawers had been opened and hastily shut again so they remained ajar several inches. The last cabinet in the row had all four drawers still partway open, with the bottom drawer pulled all the way out. Files were spread out on the ground on either side of the drawer.

"We're figuring robbery at this point," Iida said. "We're not sure what they got, though. The nurse said the doctor didn't keep a lot of cash around. It's not exactly a cash-and-carry business."

Iida's lined face worked its way into an embarrassed smile. That's as close as the Japanese lieutenant ever came to a joke unless he was mixing sake and beer at a karaoke bar. Then he'd get up and sing, "Oh, What a Beautiful Morning!" or "I Enjoy Being a Girl" like a giggly schoolgirl.

Dan grunted to acknowledge the old detective's wit.

"What did she see?"

"Nothing. She went down the road to get a mix plate for lunch."

Dan nodded.

"After lunch she was unlocking the front door when she heard a pounding coming from the back of the place. She hurried in and called for the doctor. She thinks she heard the door slam as she was running down the hall. But it could have been the wind banging around."

"Was he dead when she found him?"

Iida motioned with his chin toward Wellton's corpse. "Well, if he wasn't, he was in no mood to talk."

Dan looked at Wellton's gaping throat and smirked.

Kalama was picking up the files off the floor in the anteroom and stuck his head back out.

"Does the nurse have any idea what they were after?" he asked. "The cabinet that's been ransacked has a locking file," he said, examining the busted lock.

"Maybe that's where he kept the cash," Dan said.

"That's not what the nurse says," Iida answered.

"How about enemies?"

Iida shook his head.

"None according to her. She thinks Wellton's a saint. Everybody loved him, she says."

"Is that right," Dan said, shaking his head. "How does she explain the indictments for insurance fraud and the guilty pleas he bargained?"

"Nothing but a big mistake," Iida said flatly.

Dan raised his eyebrows. He was shuffling through the Rolodex on Wellton's desk. The vacant eyes of the doctor seemed to watch him as he inspected the listing of names.

"How about the files?" Dan asked Iida. "Does she know if they got off with any particular ones?"

"We went through that already. She says she's got no way of knowing if anything's missing. It would take weeks to reconstruct what's there and what's not," Iida said. "Well, let me know when you're through in here and I'll let you talk to her."

"Thanks, Glen," Dan said.

As soon as Iida was out the door, Dan went into the file room with Kalama.

"Let's see if we can find anything. Like a file for the driver of that car."

Kalama looked up at Dan, who was standing over him. "You expecting some kind of miracle?"

"It wouldn't hurt."

"I think you're reaching, but if he was keeping anything a secret, it probably would have been in that cabinet," Kalama said and pointed to the locking cabinet on the end. It had two security locks and the drawer was set in a stainless-steel frame. The bottom drawer had been completely busted off its hinges by something very heavy that had left big sledgehammer-sized dents in the side of the cabinet.

The inside of the cabinet had been ransacked. Files were strewn on top of the cabinet and on the floor beside it as if someone had taken a handful of files then dropped them to the ground one by one.

Dan flipped through the pile, looking for anything on Slaton or Michael. "Nothing here," Dan said after a few minutes.

Kalama picked up what was left of the files on the floor and stood. "You really think Wellton's murder is tied in with the accident?"

"My guess is it is," Dan said, placing the files on the top of the cabinet. "Let's go see what the nurse has to say."

They went back out to the reception area. The nurse was sitting in a chair, still mopping her face with a wad of paper towels.

Iida was standing by the desk. "Dan, I think you should listen to this."

Iida pressed the button on the office answering machine on Emi's desk. It whirred for a few seconds, then clicked and began to play back messages.

"These all came in during lunch when the nurse was out," Iida said.

Three quick call-me-back messages played. Then Michael Maikai's voice was on the machine.

"Dr. Wellton, this is Michael Maikai returning your call. I'm not in my office. But since you said it was an emergency, you can reach me at 282-4992."

Dan's face went pale. He reached over and pushed the replay button and listened carefully to the message again. Then he turned to Kalama.

"Joe," he said, "I need your car. Can you catch a ride into town with Iida?"

Kalama looked over at Iida, who nodded.

"Good," Dan said and headed for the door.

"But what's the rush?" Kalama asked.

"I want to see what Michael's up to."

"Why? He probably didn't have anything to do with this. Wellton was probably just calling his attorney after you grilled him this morning Besides, you don't leave messages on the answering machine of a man you're about to murder."

"I know that," Dan said. "But the number he left was Cathy's."

CHAPTER
THIRTY-ONE

$\mathbf{A}$ panicky, sick feeling passed over Dan when he heard Michael give Cathy's phone number on Wellton's machine. It was the one number he knew better than his own. Worry about Cathy's safety pushed him harder as he drove toward her condo.

Why was Michael at Cathy's place? In the last six months Cathy had prosecuted the cases against Michael's two most prominent clients, Dr. Jerome Wellton and Peter Maikai. It now looked as if those two cases may have been connected. Paul must have made the connection. His brother kept talking to him from the grave. Paul's words—*Slaton Coverup*—had eventually led Dan to Wellton. But Dan still didn't understand what it all meant.

He turned up the winding narrow road into Manoa Valley. Cathy's condo was partway up one of the valley walls, so he could see it from several miles away, the yellow stucco building sticking out of the green hills. Sometimes he could even make out her red BMW parked on the street below. But not today, with the clouds rolling over the back of the valley dumping water all the way down.

It was raining hard when he pulled into the driveway below the apartment, the wind from the approaching hurricane driving the drops sideways into his face as he got out of his car. He still didn't see her car anywhere, but the lānai door was ajar. Cathy was compulsive about locking the lānai. She'd prosecuted rape trial after rape trial in which the accused had gained entry from a lānai left open for air.

The urgency tightening his stomach had not eased. It gripped down harder as he ran up the stairs.

He used his key to let himself in, but the door banged to a halt after three or four inches. She'd put the chain on. That was like her.

"Cathy," he said, not yet screaming.

He heard something, he thought. This time he called her name more loudly. Then again.

"Cathy! Cathy!"

He closed the door and ran outside again to the lānai and called out. "Cathy!"

He was pacing below the lānai shouting her name.

Then he noticed what he thought was smoke coming from her bathroom window and a jolt of fright went through him. He looked again and knew by the way it dissolved a few feet above the window that it was steam. Steam coming from Cathy's bathroom. A sudden relief came over him. She was taking a shower.

He trotted to the side of the building and yelled up toward the bathroom window. Because the apartment house was built on a hillside, the window was ten feet higher off the ground than the lānai in front. The steam was rushing out and up the side of the stucco wall. He could hear the hiss of water coming from the shower.

"Cathy! Cathy! Are you up there?" he yelled, the wind and rain damping his words.

He waited with his hands still held to the sides of his mouth to focus his shout.

"Cathy!"

Then he thought he heard a crash of something like a bottle smashing, and the knot was back in his stomach. He took off running up the stairs to her door.

He unlocked the door again. "Cathy!" he was yelling as he tried to squeeze his face in the tiny sliver the chain allowed. He could hear music coming from the back rooms now. Something he didn't recognize. The kind of schmaltzy stuff that Cathy hated. He put one eye as far into the crack of the door as he could. All he could really see was the kitchen and a slice of the living room by the couch. The kitchen seemed unusually messy for Cathy, especially since he hadn't been around lately to cause his usual dishy mayhem.

Then he saw a wine bottle that had tipped over. Its crimson contents spilled out onto Cathy's new white carpet like Wellton's blood had spilled out onto his. Panic struck him again.

Dan stepped back and rammed his shoulder into the door and he heard the doorframe crack. He moved back to the far wall and ran at the door with all his weight behind his left shoulder and crack! The doorframe splintered and the lock fell away. He pushed back the door and kicked the fallen chain away from his foot.

Nothing else was knocked over in the living room or kitchen except that two cushions from the couch were flung across the floor.

He went quickly into the bedroom. "Cathy?" he said, not shouting, just searching. "Cathy?"

Her bedroom looked as if two wild cats had gone at it. The covers were torn off the bed, one pillow teetering on the edge, the others scattered around the room. Her perfumes and jewelry were in place on the bureau but next to the bed one of her favorite cream silk blouses was sprawled on the floor. A dark red stain shocked one breast. The other side was slashed open, the buttons torn off, the silk ripped apart. Her delicate black bra was still inside the destroyed blouse as if both had been removed with one terrible yank.

"Cathy!" he cried out, "Cathy!" as he ran into the master bath. The door was closed and the music was turned up loud enough to muffle any scream. He threw open the door and the heavy wave of hot steam wet his face, pushing him back.

Groping toward the shower, he slipped, and all at once Dan could see. The cloud of steam pouring from the windows lifted the room's fog a foot or two off the ground. He could see a blur of flesh behind the opaque doors of the shower. Then he heard her moan.

He jumped to his feet, ran to the shower door, and pulled it back.

"Cathy!" he cried, "Cathy!"

Michael was standing above Cathy. He had her hair pulled tightly back in one fist. In his other hand he held himself and Cathy was enjoying the pleasure he was offering her.

All three of them stared at one another, Dan looking, it seemed, into both their eyes at once. At the expressions of ecstasy turned to terror.

No one said anything for two or three seconds, except Cathy let out a gasp and took Michael from her mouth.

Then Dan's anger exploded. He grabbed Michael by the hair and pulled him out of the shower. Cathy came screaming out with him because Michael's hand was still entwined tightly in her hair. Most of the fog had escaped into the bedroom, and Michael tried to follow it, kicking and shouting and flailing his arms as Dan pummelled him with his fists. Cathy was screaming, confused by the riot of arms, legs, and fists. Michael got to his feet somehow, but the tile was still slick and he went down easily when Dan caught his ankle.

Michael's chin caught a stool and blood spurted from his lip. He rolled over and tried to kick free of Dan's grip.

Cathy was up now, pulling at Dan. "Don't do this, Dan," she was yelling. She saw what had come over Dan. It was a look she'd seen on quite a few convicted felons. I don't care what happens, that look said.

"Don't do this, Dan!" she screamed.

She pulled him but he pushed at her, and then he was after Michael, who had managed to get up again.

This time Michael made it to the bedroom before Dan could catch him. He clubbed Michael with his fist across the shoulders and Michael tripped across the side of the bed and fell to the carpet. Dan was on his friend, who was still dripping from his hair and face, his chest slippery as Dan straddled him. He slugged Michael somewhere around the nose and cheek. The punch didn't land very flush, and Michael rolled Dan off him. Blood was spread across his face.

Michael got up and grabbed a granite statue of Venus that Dan had given Cathy. It was as long as a club and just as heavy.

Cathy ran into the bedroom yelling, "No! Michael!" and tackled Dan to the ground.

"Put that away!" she screamed.

"When he cools off," Michael yelled. "When he cools off, I'll put it down."

"Dan," she said, on top of him. "This isn't the way, Dan," she said. "Not like this."

"Shut up," he yelled and pushed her off. He eyed Michael, who still held the statue cocked at his ear, ready to strike.

"You know what this asshole is, don't you?" Dan said to her. "He's a killer."

"Get off my goddamn back, you fucking maniac," Michael yelled. "You're just like your brother. You get something in your head, you won't let it go."

"You mean like who killed his family," Dan shouted back.

Michael dropped the statue to his chest. "I've heard what you think," he said. "Cathy told me all those nutcase theories you've got about how I've murdered half of Honolulu."

Dan wanted to charge Michael again. The thought of the statue coming down on his head didn't bother him. He was looking for a way to get at Michael.

"Dan," Cathy said, seeing what was in Dan's face. "Goddammit. This won't help."

"It'll help me," he said. "I'd like to strangle both of you."

Dan turned to her. "I don't get it. You know there's a good chance he killed the governor and my daughter. You were there. You saw what a savage he is. He killed them both for greed too. Not out of anger or anything. Just plain old cold-blooded greed."

As if the air had been let out of her, she sank to the bed. "He didn't kill them," she said softly.

"That's your pussy talking, sweetheart. I think he did. And I'm going to prove it."

She stood up again and this time she screamed. "He didn't kill them!"

"Why, because you like the way he fucks?"

That tore at her and she dropped her arms from around her waist and stepped toward him. If she had a knife, she would have lunged at him. Instead she cut him open with her words.

"No, you big ass," she screamed. "Because he was with me the whole time someone else was killing the governor. That's why."

It was a long, jagged shard of broken trust that she drove through his heart. He gasped and almost went down to his knees from the pain. He was a fool. He'd even seen her name on the security checklist at the Royal but hadn't bothered even to look when she was up there. She was the last person he would suspect.

He trusted her.

Dan slowly straightened up. He gave her an ironic smile and shook his head slowly.

"Thanks for fucking my girl, old buddy," he said to Michael as he slammed the apartment door behind him.

CHAPTER
THIRTY-TWO

It was a slow, numb ride back to Dan's apartment.

His fiancée and his old friend had been sleeping together for months. He shook his head in disgust. He should have known. He should have seen something. That day at the Royal, the day Slaton and his daughter were murdered, Cathy was down the hall in Michael's room betraying him. He could imagine them in the luxurious sheets of the Royal. . . .

He pulled up in front of his apartment in a daze. The wind held the door of his car closed until he leaned his shoulder against it and pushed. Then the wind caught the door and blew it all the way open, straining the hinges. He grabbed the door and shut it firmly as the car was buffeted by another big gust.

He barely noticed the heap of clothes huddled in the shadowy corner next to his apartment door when he walked up. He didn't realize it was a woman until she lifted her face off her knees and looked up at him.

"Mr. Carrier," she cried. "Help me!"

He looked closely at her as she rose from where she was sitting and suddenly he realized it was Cindy, his daughter's roommate.

She looked as if she'd been beaten up. Her eyes were swollen and her cheeks puffy. Her hair was weaved sloppily down her back, and there was no lipstick or shadow or blush. Without the makeup, Cindy looked about fourteen.

"He's going to kill me," she said.

"What?" Dan said, trying to clear his head of the shock that Michael had just given him. He was still imagining Michael and Cathy in bed, and Cindy was talking about murder.

She had stood by grabbing his leg and hoisting herself up. Now she was very close to him and the terrified look in her eyes was enough to awaken him.

"Come in," he said.

She looked around nervously as he unlocked the door, and ran ahead of him into the room as soon as he swung the door open. She snapped on the TV and sat down on the coffee table in front of it and flipped the stations until she found what she was after.

"There," she said and pointed at the screen. "He killed him."

"Who killed who?" Dan asked and stepped around the set so he could see the screen.

Iida was being interviewed by a young newswoman at KHNL.

"We have no suspects at this time," the lieutenant said. "All I can tell you is Dr. Wellton was murdered with a high-caliber gun sometime around twelve-thirty this afternoon. We don't have a motive at this time."

Dan looked at Cindy and she began to cry. He walked to her and she grabbed him around the waist and he patted her head. She cried in bursts that exploded from her mouth as if someone were stabbing her.

After a while he raised her face with the tips of his fingers under her chin. "Cindy, who killed who?" he asked again.

"I was in the car that night," she said as if she hadn't heard his question.

"What night?"

"The night he killed that family?" Cindy sobbed. "I'm sorry," she said over and over. "I'm sorry. I was just so afraid that they'd kill me too."

"You were with Slaton that night, weren't you?"

"Yes," she mumbled and raised her head and looked at him. Dan understood the danger she was in. There were four people in the car that night. And now only Cindy and the killer were alive.

"You were in the backseat with the governor, weren't you?"

"Yes."

"Then who was in the front with your friend Marti? Who was driving?"

She stood and her eyes were so filled with hate, he thought if she had a knife she would have plunged it into his heart.

"Your boss," she screamed. "Brian Reed!"

Dan shook his head as he pushed his fingers through his hair.

"That son of a bitch!" he said, and she fell into his arms again and began to sob.

"He killed that doctor," she cried. "I'm the only one left who knows what happened. He's going to kill me, Mr. Carrier. He's going to kill me."

Then, as if the fear were chasing the words from her, she sat down and began to tell him everything.

They had been partying for hours after a fund-raiser at the Royal Hawai'ian. Reed and Slaton and Marti and her. The girls had been snorting cocaine. Reed and Slaton had been drinking champagne, lots of it. First Cindy went into the bedroom with Slaton and then Marti joined them. Then Brian came in and the men took turns with both girls.

Around eleven, they decided to drive out to Reed's beach house in Waimea so they could get really wild. But the governor didn't want to risk getting spotted in his or Reed's car. So he had Marti go down and rent a car from the Royal. She drove it around to the dark side of the hotel, and Slaton and Cindy got into the back with a couple of grams of cocaine and two bottles of Crystal. Reed pushed Marti over and got into the driver's seat next to her.

They threw the first bottle of champagne out the window into the bushes of the H-1 freeway a few miles down the road. Cindy kept filling the coke spoon and ladling it up her and Marti's noses. Reed and Slaton kept passing the champagne bottle back and forth as Reed drove.

Reed took a back road past Wahiawa at Slaton's insistence. The road was empty and Reed cut his half of the road from the middle. They all laughed when he nearly lost the back wheels in a ditch. But he pulled it out, fishtailing once. Then he was back on the accelerator, pushing it, rolling down an empty back road through the cane fields.

A Volvo turned onto the road ahead and its headlights swung level with Reed's eyes, blinding him just as he passed the sign for Wellton's Clinic. Reed swerved, but he was already on the Volvo as Marti started to scream.

Cindy's head flew forward against the front seat and the impact knocked her out for a few seconds. There was blood dripping into her face when her head cleared, a warm, wet, foreign taste that burned her lips. She didn't realize it was Slaton's blood until she lifted his head and saw that his face was a cascading sheet of blood. He was holding his forehead and moaning, his mind still uncertain where he was or what had happened.

She pushed Slaton back against the seat and she saw that there was a deep wound on the top of his head. She took off her thin, white cotton jacket and put it over his scalp. Then she took his hand and pressed it in place on the jacket.

After that she turned to the front seat.

"You okay, Marti?" she asked.

Marti was slumped over in the front. Cindy looked up and saw that the windshield was completely shattered.

"Marti?" she said and reached over and pulled her friend back by the shoulders. Marti's head dangled as if her neck had no bone in it. Cindy lifted the girl's head and it swiveled unrestrained on her shoulders. When Cindy turned Marti's face around she gasped. Her face was crushed, the nose and lips exploded open and flattened, the cheeks torn apart with glass shards imbedded in them.

She was dead.

Cindy reached over for Reed, but he wasn't there. The driver's door was slung open.

"Jesus, what the hell happened?"

It was Slaton in the back, coming to.

"We crashed into another car," Cindy said. "Marti's dead and Mr. Reed's gone."

"What do you mean, gone?"

"He's just gone."

Slaton kept shaking his head to clear it.

"What about the other car?" he asked.

"I don't know," she said.

Cindy looked out of the window and she could see for the first time where they were. When she had first looked up she'd thought she was in a fog like on the Mainland, a thick soup that clung to the ground. But there was no fog in Hawai'i. What she had thought was fog was really the billowing dust from the collision—the spinning and rolling of more than a ton of metal in this dusty crossroads. Now that the dust was beginning to settle she could see the wreck of Melissa's Volvo.

"Go see how the people in the other car are doing," Slaton said. "And I'll look for Brian."

"Are you all right?" she asked.

He was wiping the blood from his eyes with the white cotton jacket.

"Yeah, it's just a lot of blood. I'll be all right. How about you?"

"I'm fine, I think."

"Good."

Slaton tried to open his door but it was stuck. After he made a few shoulder butts, Cindy tried hers but it had been fused shut by the impact.

"We'll have to go out the front," she said.

They crawled into the driver's seat, where Brian had been only a minute before. Cindy looked at Marti again, and the blood was still running from her nose and mouth.

"Jesus!" Slaton said when he saw Marti.

A wave of nausea rose in her stomach as she approached the other car. It was fear more than a weakness for blood. She didn't want to see what she knew she was probably going to find in that car. It was a lot worse off than their car. The front end was gone, folded back into the cab of the car. The roof was nearly flattened and there wasn't an unbroken window in the entire car. The back window had popped out completely and lay on the gravel shoulder next to the car, ready, it seemed, to be installed as soon as the mechanic showed.

Cindy heard Melissa before she saw her.

"Ohhhhh, please," she moaned.

She was begging for her life, probably to God, in a voice so pathetic it froze Cindy a few feet from the car. Then she saw Melissa for the first time through the windshield when she lifted her agonized face.

A mother, a housewife, Cindy thought. She had a simple short haircut and she was wearing a white T-shirt whose shoulders were splotched red now.

Cindy ran to her window. "Are you okay?"

The woman looked over slowly, then down. The steering wheel had her belly wedged tightly against the seat and it looked as though it had cut through both her legs. There was blood pooling in her lap.

Cindy looked down toward the woman's feet. All she could see was metal. The engine was shoved into the place where the bottom half of the woman's legs should have been.

"What's your name?" Cindy asked, trying to comfort the woman.

"My son . . ." she said.

Cindy looked into the backseat and, sure enough, there was a small boy, seven or eight probably, in a baseball uniform. His feet were pointed up at the ceiling and his face was mashed against the floorboard. His head was bent at an impossible angle like Marti's.

Cindy tried to get to him, but all the doors were welded shut and there wasn't enough space left between the roof and the windows to crawl through. She'd have to leave him where he was and hope he would be all right. But she was pretty sure he was dead already.

The woman at least was still alive.

"My son," she said again when Cindy got back to her window.

"He's fine," Cindy lied. "What's your name?"

"Melissa Susan Carrier," she said as if filling out insurance forms.

"Just hang on, Melissa. The ambulance is on its way."

Cindy ran back to where she'd left Slaton.

"Mr. Slaton?" she yelled.

Except for Melissa's moans, the only sound now was the rustling of cane leaf.

"Mr. Slaton," she called into the darkness.

There was nothing for a minute, then, "Cindy," she heard someone grunt in the dark.

"Cindy. Over here."

Cindy stumbled toward the sound of the voice.

"Watch out, there's a ditch there," somebody warned.

She stopped and she could see right below her someone crunching around in the cane. She could barely see the slope of the ditch, but she ran down it anyway. Her momentum carried her up the other side. She crawled the last few feet to where Slaton was holding Reed in a sitting position in the cane.

"I think he's going to be all right. He's just groggy."

Cindy nodded and bent down to Reed.

"Let's get him out of this cane," Slaton said.

Cindy grasped Reed's arm and helped him up. He was dazed and shivering even though it was still eighty degrees outside. They stumbled and all three of them went down in the stagnant muddy water of the ditch. Reed let out a pained groan.

"Oh, God! My chest."

"Hang on, Brian. We just need to get you up this little bank here," Slaton told him.

"You'll be fine," Cindy soothed.

They lifted him up to the car and sat him down by the front wheel.

"How are they in there?" Slaton asked Cindy, nodding toward Melissa's car.

"They're both dying. We've got to get an ambulance soon or they're not going to make it."

The governor's response shocked her.

"First we need to get the hell out of here."

It was at that moment that she knew how deeply she would always be involved in this.

"The woman in the front seat is dying. There's blood coming out of her from all over."

"Does she know how many of us there are?"

It was the coldest thing she'd ever heard a person say.

"Let's just leave everything as it is," Reed said with a pained expression. "There's a clinic just up the road from here. There's a doctor there I know can treat us. If we're lucky, he'll be there."

"What about the woman and boy, though?"

Slaton reached down to pick up Reed. "When we get a chance, we'll call an ambulance."

"All right."

"Get your purse and anything else you can see that can identify any of us," Slaton said.

She crawled back in the car and grabbed her purse.

"Hurry!" he yelled, and she crawled back out.

"Here's your wallet," she said and handed it to him.

"Jesus!" he said and stuffed it in his back pocket. He tapped Reed's pocket for his wallet and, finding it, said, "Let's go."

"All right," Cindy said and reached down and helped Reed to his feet.

No cars passed them as they walked in the middle of the paved road. When they reached the sign, Slaton led them in the dark up the oval driveway of the clinic.

Then they both helped Reed up the front steps of the house.

"Stay here with him," he said to Cindy. "I'll go find that doctor."

She heard his footsteps crunch off in the dark. After a while she could hear his voice. Then a porch light snapped on at a building in the back and Slaton was lit below it.

A few minutes later, Slaton and a tall, balding man rushed forward in the dark.

"All right," Wellton said, bending down over Reed, "let's get him into the clinic."

Wellton unlocked the door, snapped on the lights inside, and held open the screen door.

"Bring him through to the back."

They laid Reed on one of the paper-sheeted examining tables and Wellton went to work on him. He had been a good doctor before greed corrupted him.

"I used to work on a trauma team," he said without looking up. He was asking Reed to take deep breaths and was tapping and feeling his way around the PA's body.

"He's all right, I think. A slight concussion and two or three cracked ribs. He's going to be very sore for a few weeks, though," Wellton said and looked up at Slaton's head.

He took Cindy's jacket, which was dyed completely red with blood, and examined Slaton's head.

"That'll need some stitches. Sit over here," he ordered the governor.

Wellton washed Slaton up, then stuck a needle in his scalp.

"Novocain," he said, and a few minutes later he began to stitch the governor's head with what looked to Cindy like her grandmother's carpet needle and thick black thread.

She plopped down on a little swivel stool by the door and swung around and put her face in her hands.

"We've got to call an ambulance," she said.

"As soon as we're gone, the doctor will call, won't you?" Slaton said to Wellton.

"Yes, of course."

"We're going to take the doctor's car out to the beach house and he'll cover for us. Isn't that right, Doctor? Unless, of course," he said, looking at Cindy, "you want to go back there and wait for the police to ask you a lot of very uncomfortable questions."

Cindy thought about all the drugs that were somewhere in that car. She had managed to retrieve her purse, but what about the rest of it? No, she wouldn't like to be there when the cops showed up.

Wellton kept stitching. It was obvious to Cindy that Slaton and Reed had made a deal with him. It had something to do with some kind of trouble the doctor was in because when they were leaving, Wellton took Reed by the sleeve.

"Then you'll fix it?" Wellton said. "There won't be any jail time?"

"You won't even see a cell," Reed answered.

"And the fine?"

"You'll be able to afford it," Reed said.

Wellton nodded.

"Pick the car up in Waimea in a couple of days," Slaton said, and Wellton nodded again.

There was still no one on the road when they drove back to the corner and turned. Melissa was still in her car, unconscious by now, her blood still draining from her. Her son in the back dipping more deeply into a sleep from which he would never awaken.

"And they just left them there to die?" Dan said with an anger that made him shudder.

Cindy nodded her head nearly imperceptibly.

"I didn't want to. I begged them to call, but there was just too much at stake, they said. I was afraid, Mr. Carrier," she cried. "I knew they'd just kill me if I ever said anything."

Dan held her. She was a kid too, really not a lot older than his daughter had been.

"He killed Slaton and Stephanie and now the doctor," she said sobbing. "He's going to kill me too."

"You mean Brian Reed?"

She nodded her head as it rested on his chest.

"He killed Slaton?" Dan asked her.

Cindy shook her head. "I was supposed to be there the night that Stephanie and the governor were murdered. But Stephanie took my place at the last moment. Even Mr. Slaton didn't know she was taking my place. Don't you see? Reed didn't know that. He thought I would be there. He was going to get rid of Mr. Slaton and me at the same time."

"Reed must have known that Paul was on to him," Dan said, "so he wanted to kill Slaton and you to get rid of the only witnesses to the accident?"

"Yes. Don't you see? Now that he's killed the doctor, I'm the only one left who knows. He tried to kill me once but got poor Stephanie instead. Help me, Mr. Carrier. I'm the only one who knew he was driving that's still alive."

A panicky feeling came over Dan when he remembered those keys.

"Those keys I found had to be Reed's," he mumbled.

Cindy looked at him curiously.

"What keys?"

He didn't answer. He realized with growing terror what he had done. All Dan could think about was what he had told Reed earlier at the lab: "I gave Lily the keys and she is on a plane right now to see if they fit Michael's Mercedes." Dan now realized that he'd handed Lily the only piece of physical evidence that could connect Reed to the accident and, thanks to Dan, Reed knew it. With those keys, Reed knew he would hang. His political ambitions would be through. That comfortable little throne of Slaton's that he figured to ascend would be gone. Everything, including his freedom, would be gone. Dan was sure that Reed would do anything, kill anyone, to get those keys back. And it was up to Dan to find Reed and stop him.

CHAPTER
THIRTY-THREE

Dan dialed Reed's office to find out where he was. His secretary said that he'd canceled his afternoon appointments and left. He hadn't told her where he was going.

Dan called the airport next. None of the airlines were flying to Maui because the wind had picked up past fifty knots. Even the big commercials trying to land at windswept Kahului Airport were being tossed about like butterflies. When one of them bent its nose gear while landing, all incoming flights were canceled until further notice. Dan found out that the last plane had landed around four o'clock, however. Still plenty of time for Reed to have already caught a flight from O'ahu, to have already rented a car, to already be on his way to kill Lily.

Dan hung up and dialed Wellton's clinic to see if he could find Kalama. But he'd gone back to the office already, and that was where Dan finally located him.

"Yeah?" Joe answered. He figured it was McInerny updating him.

"Joe?"

"Dan?" he asked. "What is it?"

"I know who killed Wellton," he said.

"Okay," Kalama said and sat back on the desk.

"And Slaton and my daughter," Dan added.

"Paul too?" Kalama said with a hint of sarcasm.

"I think so," Dan said hesitantly. "You with me on this?"

"I'm sorry," Kalama said, impatiently, "I don't believe Michael killed three or four people for fifty million or fifty billion. I just don't believe it. He'd have to confess it to my face and I'd still have trouble with it. No. I don't buy it. I don't care—"

"Reed," Dan interrupted him.

"Reed?"

"Reed was driving the car that killed Paul's family."

"He was? Where did you get that from?"

"Cindy Lee, my daughter's roommate, is sitting right here. She was in the backseat with Slaton."

"So that *was* Slaton's saliva on the Sherman?" Joe said.

"That's right," Dan said. "And I think Reed's flown to Maui to cover his ass."

Kalama's voice got suddenly solemn. "You think he's going after the keys?"

"The last plane landed around four. He had plenty of time to catch it."

"If he did, he's leaving a pretty obvious trail."

"He doesn't know we have Cindy. Besides, I know what he's thinking. If he doesn't get the keys, he's going to hang. So he's willing to risk it."

"He'll have to kill her," Kalama agreed.

"That won't bother him. They can only execute you once," Dan said. "I'm sure that's the way he's thinking. He's desperate. He has to kill her as soon as he gets the keys from her."

"He'd be stupid if he didn't," Kalama said, and the phone went silent for a moment. They both knew what the other was thinking.

"And Reed's not stupid," Kalama said for both of them.

"He is if he thinks I'm going to just let him kill her," Dan said, feeling terror for Lily.

"The problem is none of the local or state cops from Kahului can get there. The Hāna road outside of Kahului closed twenty minutes ago."

"That means it was probably still open when Reed got there," Dan said. He felt his stomach sink. "Then you better get me a chopper so I can fly directly to the ranch."

"They won't let a chopper up now. The hurricane's just sitting between the Big Island and Maui. Winds are already at one-sixty-five around the eye. All it has to do is turn one degree this way and start charging up that channel and it'll wipe out Maui."

"How about a small plane?"

"That's what I'm trying to say, Dan. All small craft and helicopters have been grounded."

"Nobody'll fly me?" Dan asked. "How about that Tongan pilot, Faaula? He'll do anything."

"It doesn't matter," Joe said. "It's not Faaula's call. The Chief can't even send him up. It's a set procedure. The department won't let helicopters go up in anything stronger than fifty knots. It's way past that out there now."

Dan slapped the coffee table next to Cindy. She was lying half on it now like a three-year-old who sleeps wherever she falls.

"Look Dan, with all the help at the ranch, do you really think Reed will try anything?"

"If the storm has hit Maui as bad as you say, I'm sure all the ranch hands are taking care of their own places. Lily is more than likely there alone."

"You're probably right."

"I know I'm right, damn it! I have to get over there, Joe," he screamed.

"All right, Dan, calm down. The only thing I can think of is to call Michael at his office and see if he's still around."

"He's around," Dan said in a tone of voice that made Kalama hesitate.

"Look, he has his two-seater at the airport. I don't know if they'll let him take off. But there's not much they can do once you're on the runway."

"Michael and I aren't exactly on friendly terms right now," Dan said.

"Well, you'll have to get friendly real quick. He's your only choice."

"I guess," Dan said, thinking about that afternoon. If Cathy hadn't been there to slow Dan down a little, he probably would have tried to kill Michael.

"If he knows Reed's going to try to kill his sister," Kalama said, "and, you know, you explain how you know now that Reed was the killer. Maybe say you're sorry—"

"Sorry?" Dan shouted. "Bullshit. That asshole is sleeping with Cathy."

"What?" Kalama mumbled in shock.

"That's right. I caught my old buddy Michael screwing my fiancée," Dan said and filled Kalama in quickly on what had happened, how suddenly Dan's own fiancée was Michael's airtight alibi.

"No shit," Kalama said. "Well, at least you know he didn't kill anyone. You know he loves Lily. He always has. Probably just as much as you do."

Dan knew Joe was right about Michael. After a minute he said, "Okay, keep trying to get ahold of Kahului Substation and I'll call him."

He dialed Cathy's condo, and Cathy answered after she heard Dan's voice on the answering machine begging Michael to pick up.

"Dan," she said. She was into her reasonable voice, the one she used at sidebar to cajole a judge. "Why don't we all cool off a few days? Then we'll be a little less emotional and we can work this out without anyone getting hurt."

"Reed's going to try to kill Lily," Dan said to shut her up.

"Come on, Dan. First you accuse Michael of murder. Now Reed?" she said. He could hear her take a deep breath on the other end. "Dan, ever since Paul died you've—"

Dan cut her off. "Reed was driving the car that killed Melissa and Chris," he said. Then he briefly explained what Cindy had told him. When he got to the part about the keys, Michael interrupted.

"You sent Lily to check to see if the keys fit my car?" He was on the couch next to Cathy, listening on her portable.

"Yeah," Dan said. "I was wrong about that. But I'm not wrong about Reed. He has to kill her, Michael. They're his damn keys."

There was silence again. Cathy and Michael were looking at each other, both with phones to their ears.

"Look, Michael," Dan said softly, "are you going to help me save your sister or aren't you? We've got a lifetime to hate each other, but Lily needs our help now. Reed should have landed in Maui by four-thirty. He could be at the ranch two or three hours after that. We have to get there first."

"He would have a hell of a time making that drive with the wind and high surf pounding the coast road," Michael said.

"Is Lily's life worth taking that chance?"

Michael's end went silent for a moment. "And you're sure about Reed?" he finally asked.

"I'm sure," Dan said. "That bastard killed Slaton and my daughter and maybe even Paul. He won't hesitate to kill Lily."

Michael didn't say anything.

"Come on, Michael. I'm sure Reed's on his way. We have to get moving!"

"Meet me at the airport," he finally said. "Gate H, Diamond Head side. I can be there in twenty minutes."

"Thanks," Dan said and hung up. He turned and pulled Cindy up by the shoulders. She was hugging her arms together as if it were forty degrees out. "Cindy, don't worry. I'm going to stop Reed. You'll be safe here. But, Cindy, I need you to do something for me."

She looked up at him, fighting her fear.

"Try to get hold of a Sergeant Kalama. He should be at the station. Tell him what I'm up to. Tell him to get someone over to the Maikai ranch as soon as possible. Storm or no storm." He was still holding her up by her shoulders. "Can you do that for me, Cindy? Call Kalama."

Cindy slowly nodded her head.

"Good," he said and brought her over to the couch where the phone was and handed her Kalama's number. Dan grabbed a parka from the closet as he went for the door. When he looked back at Cindy, she was still sobbing but she had already begun to dial Kalama's number.

Michael showed up at the gate to the runway just as Dan did. He didn't acknowledge Dan. He just punched a keypad, the gate cranked open, and he drove through. Dan slipped through behind him and they sped to the hangar where Michael kept his one-prop coffee grinder. Dan didn't like to go up in it even in good weather.

Michael pulled beside the hangar and jumped out. He still hadn't made eye contact with Dan, who pulled in beside him. Dan got out and followed Michael to the small, dapper little plane with the brown pinstriping that Michael was so proud of.

Michael knocked the concrete block loose from the wheels and opened the cockpit door. He threw a small duffel in the back and climbed in by stepping on the stirrup and then pulling himself directly into the seat.

He put the key in the ignition as Dan was settling down next to him. The prop kicked over and after Michael checked a few gauges, they started taxiing.

"Aren't you going to radio the tower?" Dan wanted to know.

"What's the point? They don't want anything to take off."

They pulled out into a heavy rain and Michael taxied to the south runway and stopped. Then he picked up the microphone and snapped the "voice" button.

"Tower, this is Hawai'i light, nine, seven, four, seven, one, N. Taking off on runway five, nine, L. Bound for Hāna."

"Nine, seven, four, seven, one, N. I wouldn't advise—" the tower crackled, but Michael reached down and snapped off the radio.

The takeoff was smooth, but as soon as they were airborne the plane began to bounce and weave. Dan strapped himself in as tight as he could pull the belt and wrapped his arm around the restraining bar next to him.

They fought the wind for forty minutes before they reached Moloka'i. Michael was riding the wind like it was a big north-shore swell. Down one side, up the other, his teeth gritting as he fought the stick. Dan was too scared even to throw up.

"If it's like this the whole way, I'm not sure we're going to have enough gas," Michael said and tapped the gauge.

"You didn't check the gas?"

"We were half full. Half that will usually get you there. But we're heading into eight-mile-an-hour headwinds."

They reached the coast of Kaho'olawe twenty minutes after that.

"This is taking longer than I thought," Dan said. "Reed has to be there by now. Where in the hell is Maui?"

"It's out there," Michael said, pointing into the gray in front of them.

Michael turned south to head around the back side of Haleakalā. On a good day, he'd take the route over the crater. But it was too dangerous for that now. They'd have to go the long way around the volcano.

Thirty minutes later Hāna Airport was below them. Michael flew low over it for an inspection, then banked up and came around. The runway was clear but for a scattering of palm leaves blowing across it.

He approached low over the taro fields and just before he was going to touch the wet tarmac, a gust picked up the Cessna and threw it down again. The front wheel buckled and the right wing touched. The plane spun and there was a loud twisting of metal and the sound like a mechanic dropping his full tool box on a concrete floor.

Dan was hanging upside down in the cockpit when the plane finally came to a halt.

"You all right?" he heard Michael say. He was somewhere beneath him.

"Yeah, I think so."

"When you release the belt you're going to land on your head, so be careful," Michael said and climbed straight past Dan out Dan's door, which was on top now.

Dan pushed the button, the belt snapped, and he caught himself with his free hand. His ankle banged painfully on something metal below.

"Shit," he said and grabbed the doorway and pulled himself out.

Michael was down on one knee, surveying the wreck.

"She's had it," he said to Dan as he walked over to him. "The wind will pick her up and break her to pieces and there's not a thing I can do about it."

"Yeah," Dan said. He didn't give a damn about Michael's airplane. He was thinking about Lily. The two of them ran to the tower and jumped into an old clunker that Michael used to get back and forth from the ranch.

They weaved through debris blocking the roads and turned onto the Hāna Highway that serpentines along the rugged coastline. The highway often closed even in minor storms. The slopes of Haleakalā above would turn into a torrent of newly sprung waterfalls. Bushes and limbs and mud would clog the streams and they would overflow the old wooden bridges connecting the highway. If one bridge went out, the whole highway would close because there were no diversions, no way to detour around the smaller bridges. It was the only road.

Then the waves would pound the coast. If the swells grew to sixteen, eighteen feet, the waves would break sometimes directly on the road. Then it became a game of guts, a game of, Do you think you can make it past before another set of waves sends tons of fast-moving water crashing onto the road? A road on which you may have gotten stuck, your engine dying because you miscalculated just how deep the water on the road was.

Two miles out of town, Michael pulled the car up to a ROAD CLOSED barrier winking orange. The Maikai ranch was another fifteen miles down the road.

There was no one guarding the entrance to the Maikai ranch when Reed pulled up to the gate. The old Filipino who usually sat in the guardhouse had gone home to evacuate his wife and eleven kids to the church basement in Hāna. He'd left the gate swung open as Lily had told him to do in case of emergency.

Reed drove slowly to within fifty feet of the house and pulled behind a storage shed. He took a gun from the glove compartment and placed it in his coat pocket. When he got out of the car he surveyed the grounds to make sure no one was outside.

He crept along the outskirts of the yard hiding behind the bushes and stopped near the porch where he could see into the house. Lily was in the kitchen preparing for the storm. Reed stood outside the house, waiting. He wanted to be sure she was alone before he went in and killed her.

THIRTY-FOUR

Michael abruptly stopped the car on a rise overlooking Maka-pipi Stream. They had plowed through several swollen streams and the old Buick had powered through them, huge rooster tails splashing up on their sides as he sped through the rushing water.

Michael stuck his head out the window to survey the raging stream below. The way the banks sloped quickly into the jungle and the beach widened abruptly at the mouth of the stream, it was impossible to tell how deep the water had risen. On the other side, Dan could see that the rising sea had crossed the road. Foam now roiled where the highway used to be.

"We could hike upstream to the rock overpass and then walk along the slopes to the ranch," Michael suggested to Dan.

"How much farther is it to go that way?"

"Mile, mile and a half maybe."

"We can't spare the time. We have to try to drive as far as we can. Every minute counts. Reed has to be there by now."

"All right, but if the car gets swept off the road we'll be under tons of water, so roll the windows down. That's the only way we'll be able to get out."

They cranked the handles, and the rain and wind hit them with such force that it was almost impossible for either of them to see where they were headed.

"I'll tell you another thing," Michael said. "We better get our asses into that basement at the house before this damn thing really hits. If it does turn this way and we're still out here, it'll be our asses."

Michael let off the brake and started the big rusted heap down the slope to where the water had topped the bridge. It was a raised road where the stream flowed through a concrete half-circle below. The flood had clogged the inlet with debris and the water was rushing over the top. With the rain pelting their faces it was impossible to see how high the water was going to come up on the car.

Michael eased into the stream and then pushed down the accelerator and they began to ford steadily across. The water was almost to the bottom of the doors.

Dan had one arm wrapped over the seat back, his seat belt unbuckled, his other hand on the door handle.

Michael kept the motor revving high to prevent it from stalling. Suddenly, the car dropped a couple of feet and the water level rose and rushed into the rusty old bucket.

"The road's gone," Michael yelled.

"Christ, keep going. We're almost across!"

Michael pushed down on the accelerator until he was nearly standing from the pressure. The car moved slowly forward again. Then, suddenly, it started turning sideways, slipping into the powerful current of the stream.

"We're going over!" Michael shouted.

But the motor was still running, and they were still churning forward even though they were almost completely sideways. Then the back wheels caught something solid, the car righted, and they spun back onto the road, up and out of the stream.

The floorboard of the car was six inches deep in muddy water but at least they were on higher ground.

"That was very close," Michael said, "very close."

Dan shook his head as he wiped the muddy water from his face. They came to the top of the rise looking down on the river behind them. It was only a short drive now to the ranch. If Reed was slowed enough by the road conditions, maybe they'd get to Lily in time. Then they could all ride out the storm in the basement that Maikai had built before any of them were born.

Just as they reached the turnoff to the ranch, an old banyan tree crashed in front of them. Michael pulled up before the fallen tree, which completely blocked the road. Its branches had been stripped bare and the trunk had been sheared off at the roots by the force of one violent gust.

"We'll have to hike from here," Michael said as the two of them got out.

Dan walked around to Michael, and they climbed over the tree and began running down the road. Large chunks of pavement had been washed away, and debris continuously rolled by them: coconuts and lava rock and fleeing animals, mostly.

"How much farther?" Dan asked. He was next to Michael, both of them jumping over anything in their way. They were in a panic to get to Lily. If she'd been dead for hours, that was one thing, but if she'd been dead only minutes, it would haunt them every day of their lives.

Reed entered the house through the front door and walked quietly into the kitchen, where Lily was bent over the sink filling some gallon water containers. On the table behind her were flashlights and batteries and canned goods.

"Hello, Miss Maikai," Reed said.

"Jesus!" she screamed, startled by the intruder. It took her a second to realize who Reed was. He had his parka up around his ears and he was soaked through.

"Mr. Reed? What are you doing here? Is Dan all right?"

"Yes, he's fine," he said. "I came up here to get the keys he gave you."

"The keys?"

"To Michael's car," he said. Reed had walked across the room until he was only a stride from her. His pistol was tucked into the back belt of his pants so the parka hid it from view.

"Oh," she said, "you didn't have to rush over here. They don't fit Michael's car anyway." She looked at him curiously for a second. "How'd you get through?" Lily asked. "I thought the roads were closed." She was starting to get a little nervous. Why would Brian Reed drive through a treacherous, closed-out ocean road to retrieve some keys he could send anyone for?

Reed watched her closely as she calculated.

"I need the keys," he said in a frightening, low voice that made her shiver.

"Where's Dan?" she asked. "I'd like to talk to him first."

Reed drew the gun from his belt with one hand and grabbed her by the shoulder with the other, shoving the cold steel of the barrel against her throat. He didn't have time to satisfy her curiosity. He had to get the keys and then kill her outside somewhere. He wanted to make it look like she'd been killed in the storm.

"Just get the keys, bitch!" he yelled. "I'm not going to say it again."

Reed saw Lily's eyes shift over his shoulder and he felt someone behind him.

"Put the gun down," a deep voice said.

Reed turned quickly, but a powerful hand grabbed Reed's hand. The gun fell to the ground. Reed looked up and found himself face-to-face with Uncle Charlie holding Peter Maikai's old war club cocked above his head.

"Thank God, Charlie. I didn't know what to do," Lily said and reached down for the gun. As she reached for the revolver, Reed kicked her in the face and she fell back, half unconscious.

Reed dived for the gun as the *kahuna* took a swipe with the club and caught him on the back of the shoulders. The powerful blow knocked Reed halfway across the room. He landed under the old wooden kitchen table in the corner where the gun had been kicked. Reed grabbed for the gun as Charlie took another swipe at him. Charlie's blow landed on the top of the table, and the whole thing collapsed on Reed's head.

He lifted the club again and Reed fired into the *kahuna's* chest once, *bang!*, twice, *bang!* And Uncle Charlie fell back against the cabinet, where Lily was coming to.

Reed pointed the gun at Lily.

"Charlie!" she screamed, "Charlie!" And cradled his head in her lap.

"Get up, bitch!"

Lily tried to stand but slipped in the pool of blood that was flowing from Charlie's chest. As she fell, Reed picked her up by her collar with the gun cocked at her head.

"Get the fucking keys," he yelled, "or I'll beat them out of you!"

Her dress soaked in Uncle Charlie's blood, she led him upstairs. He pushed her onto the bed in her room. Lily got up on one elbow. "You killed my daughter and the governor, didn't you?" she guessed.

So she wanted to talk, Reed thought. He could spare a little time to find out what she knew. Find out, maybe, what Dan thought he had on him.

"You've been listening to your boyfriend too much," Reed said. "Why would I want to kill Slaton or his little whore?"

"Because you were driving. You're the one who was responsible for the accident," she screamed.

"The accident?" he said, still pumping her. "The accident was a blessing in disguise. Hell, the governor of Hawai'i was in that car that night. His career was over if anyone found out. I could get anything I wanted from him after that. It didn't matter who was driving. I had something on the governor and I took advantage of it. He was the one with everything to lose. I had everything to gain. That accident was the best break I ever had."

"What happened? Did you figure you got all the mileage you could out of it? Your career couldn't go any further, could it? Not with Slaton in your way," Lily screamed.

"Enough of this bullshit! Tell me where the keys are or I'm going to start having some fun with that cute little body of yours and then I'll beat it out of you." He banged her ear again with the gun so a long, high ring drilled through her skull. As she laid facedown on the bed, bleeding from one ear, he turned her over and grabbed her dress and her bra. "Are you sure this is the way you want it?" He looked her up and down the entire length of her body.

"It's under the desktop." She pointed toward a small student's desk with a fold-up top.

Reed let go of her and tried to lift the old wooden lid, but it was locked. He turned to her with the gun pointed at her head and cocked the trigger.

"Don't play fucking games with me. Where's the fucking key?"

"Over there," Lily said as she pointed to her dresser.

Reed snatched the tiny key and opened the desktop. Next to a half-filled box of mostly wrapperless crayons were the keys Reed had lost that night as he lay sprawled in the cane field.

He pointed the gun back at her. "All right," he said, "get up!"

"Now what?" she asked. She had never been this scared. Her mouth was so sticky her words came out parched.

"Now we get up like I told you," he said softly, then he screamed, "Or I slam this fucking gun against the side of your head again!"

She crawled off the bed, staying as far away from Reed as she could. She went out the door where he was pointing with the gun and he got behind her. He stuck the gun in her back, grabbed her collar, and force-marched her to the kitchen, where Uncle Charlie was lying, his blood spread across the floor now.

Reed pushed Lily from behind and she tripped over Charlie and fell to the floor on top of him.

"What are you going to do?" she asked as she cradled Charlie's bloody head in her hands.

"Shut up and grab his legs," he said and took Charlie by the shirt and started dragging him out the door with the gun still on Lily. The bullet holes in the old man would set off a trail of evidence that could lead back to Reed. But a hurricane can cover up a lot of evidence. If he could throw them both in one of those ravines their bodies would be dragged so far out to sea no one would ever find them. They'd just be a couple more people missing and presumed killed in the storm.

Lily and Reed pulled Charlie's body up the hill behind the house until Reed dropped him. He stood up and looked around and spotted the old wooden bridge that spanned the stream.

"Over there," Reed said. "That looks like a perfect place for an accident."

Michael was breathing hard as he and Dan ran for the ranch. But he was in good shape and he easily leaped a dam of foliage three feet high in the road. Dan, right behind him, took it like a hurdler.

"From here," Michael said when Dan was beside him again, "it's less than a half a mile to the house."

"If Reed made it through before they closed the road from Kahului side, he could have been there for a while," Dan said as they fought the rain driven, against their faces by the mounting winds.

The hurricane had just turned and was heading now for Maui. The exposed belly of the Hāna coast would take the biggest blow.

When they finally made it to the house, Dan crashed through the front door with Michael right behind him.

"Lily?" they both called out.

Dan went upstairs while Michael ran to the kitchen. Before Dan reached the top of the stairs he heard Michael scream out his name. He ran back down and found Michael on his knees, staring at the blood leading out the back door. The panic in Dan's stomach tightened.

"Lily?" Michael yelled. "Lily?"

"We're too late," Dan said, looking down at Michael.

"Maybe not," Michael said as he reached for his father's old club. "Uncle Charlie's here. He wouldn't let anything happen to her."

"Somebody's hurt bad," Dan said as he motioned toward the blood leading through the doorway.

Dan ran out the door with Michael behind him holding Charlie's club. They both stopped when they reached the top of the rise behind the house.

"There she is," Michael yelled as he saw Lily standing on the bridge with somebody lying next to her. They both raced to her calling out her name.

When Dan reached the bridge, he realized it was Uncle Charlie next to her. The wind was loud now, ripping the grass and shaking the trees.

"Watch out!" Lily yelled. "He's got a gun."

"Just keep on going," Dan heard a voice from behind him say. Dan and Michael turned and saw Reed walking toward them. Michael lifted the club, ready to swing it at Reed.

"Put it down, Maikai," he said, pointing the gun at him.

Michael dropped the club and Reed walked closer.

"I had a feeling you'd make it. It's really too bad, though. I'm going to miss my head prosecutor."

Dan took a quick step toward Reed and Reed cocked the gun.

"Cindy's with Kalama right now," Dan said with his hands out as if to offer help.

"I've already thought of that," Reed yelled above the noise of the wind and rain. "A hooker who's been busted so many times that she decides to implicate the head PA and the former governor in some ridiculous crime. Now who in the hell is going to believe any of that bullshit? There won't be any corroboration. Even Jerzy will see it my way. And he hates my guts."

Reed's smile broadened. "I've got the only reliable evidence that ties me to that accident," he said and patted the keys in his pants pocket. "Now why don't you both join them," Reed said and stretched out his hand graciously, pointing Dan and Michael to the bridge.

Dan hesitated and looked around, but there was no one who could help them.

"I'll shoot you right here and now," Reed said and blew off a round that disintegrated one of the rotten planks of the bridge near Lily.

"All right, but what's the point of killing us?" Dan asked, though it was obvious. He was looking for anything to stall Reed.

"I'm not going to kill you," he said. "The hurricane's going to kill you. Now get out there!" he shouted and pushed Dan in the back so he stumbled into Michael, who was now at the foot of the bridge.

Reed took a step closer and waved Dan and Michael toward Lily. When Dan crawled next to her he could see that Charlie was dead. His eyes were open, his pupils rolled upward.

"Push him off!" Reed yelled.

"Go to hell!" Dan shot back as he stood up and reached for Lily's hand.

Reed took another shot at the wood planks beneath their feet.

"You won't shoot us, Brian. How are you going to explain it?" Dan said as he took a step closer to Reed.

"I'll shoot if I have to, Carrier. I'm here to save you and Lily from Michael. You set it up for me," Reed laughed, and he shot again at the planks. "Now get back."

They all took several steps farther onto the bridge and then looked back at Reed. They weren't sure what he was up to until he took out a knife and began cutting through the rope that held up the railing.

"Brian, don't," Dan yelled and grabbed the opposite rail and lunged back at Reed.

Reed snapped off two more rounds; the wood exploded at Dan's feet.

Dan lurched back to Lily, who was holding on to Michael.

"Hang on," he said to them.

Reed cut through the rope and the last few stubborn strands ripped apart from the weight. The bridge leaned to the left, and Uncle Charlie's body rolled off and fell into the roaring water below.

As Dan and Michael hung on to the remaining rail and Lily hugged Dan's waist, Reed sawed through the rotted threads of the remaining rail. When it gave way the three of them found themselves gripping desperately to the wood planks of the bridge floor. From eye level, spread-eagled on the bridge, they watched Reed work at the first foothold with the heel of his heavy boot.

Every kick shook the flimsy rope contraption. The wooden stake it was tied to became weaker with every blow until the last of the rope slipped free. Now they were all hanging with their arms over the top of the bridge floor, their legs dangling a hundred feet above the raging current below.

Dan watched Reed kick at the last foothold.

Lily started to lose her grip.

"Grab on to me," Dan yelled to her. Raising himself so his elbow was on the wood plank, he grabbed Lily with his other hand. She held him around the neck as he slid closer to her.

Reed kicked furiously at the remaining foothold. Then he suddenly stopped and stood looking at something on the other side of the bridge. "No," Reed screamed then doubled over and collapsed to his knees. There was an agonized grimace on his face. He looked up again and pointed his gun across the ravine. But something hit Reed's face and the top of his head exploded as he pitched backward. He began to roll down the steep slope toward the gorge. His body hit a boulder at the edge and was catapulted into the air, his legs and arms flying about as he fell until he disappeared in the water below.

Hand-over-hand, the three of them made it back to where Reed had been trying to kick out the last stake. Dan helped Lily and then Michael up. Then he turned to see where the shot had come from. On the other side of the ravine, on a bluff in front of the papaya forest, Paul stood with a rifle, the scope still cocked near his chin.

The wind was howling through the forest, the rain falling almost horizontally. Even though Paul was only about thirty feet away, Dan had to shout as loud as he could for Paul to hear him.

"You were the one who killed Slaton, weren't you?" was the first thing Dan said.

Paul lowered the rifle. "They killed my family, Dan, and there wasn't anything anybody would do about it. Those bastards! They could cover up anything they wanted. They left them there to die. All they cared about was their own asses."

"But why did—" Dan began but Paul knew what he was going to ask.

"I didn't know it was your daughter. My God, Dan, you don't think I knew it was my own niece. I didn't know, Dan. I'm sorry. I'm so sorry."

"I could have helped you, Paul. Why didn't you let me help?"

"It was my problem, not yours. They would have killed you too to keep it quiet. They had too much to lose."

"At least let Michael and me help you now. It's all over," Dan yelled. The wind was still gusting, but the rain had subsided a little for the moment.

"I already went to Michael for help. Didn't I, Michael?"

Paul turned the rifle on Michael, then fired a round at a tree next to him.

"I went to him after I found out they thought Maikai did it. Tell Dan what you told me, Michael," Paul shouted. "Just disappear. That's what he told me. My attorney. My old buddy. We were like family. He told me he'd take care of everything. He gave me a hundred thousand dollars to disappear with. Tell him, Michael. Tell him, you greedy son of a bitch!"

Michael backed up. He had his eye on the rifle. "You know everything already," he said to Dan softly.

"Tell him," Paul kept shouting, "how you told me if they ever did find out I killed Slaton, it would be better all around if they thought I was dead. You told me it would ruin Dan's career if they found out his own brother killed the governor. My old friend Michael. He's the one who blew up the boat, you know, so I could make a clean start. At least that's what he told me. Go to the Mainland, he said. Change your identity. Start over."

Lily looked at Michael. "How could you do that to our father?"

Michael was silent. The wind was whipping his stylishly cut hair around his face.

"That's the real sad part, Lily," Paul went on, "your so-called brother got real creative and planted my knife in his father's room. Of course, when I read about that in the paper, I didn't understand. What good would it do me to frame the old man? I was already supposed to be dead. Why pin it on his own father?" Paul was pointing the rifle right at Michael.

"He's flipped," Michael said to Dan without moving his lips. "Talk to him, Dan. It's not going to do any good to shoot me."

Dan watched as Michael squirmed. "Maybe not," he said. "But I might enjoy it."

Dan turned back to Paul. "Put the rifle down, Paul," he shouted. "It's all over now."

"No, it's not," Paul said. The rifle was tight in his left fist. "I want to know why he framed his own father like that. That's the thing I don't understand."

Dan looked at Michael as he took another step away.

"I think I know why," Dan said to Paul. "He knew his father wouldn't last long behind bars. And he was right. Isn't that how it was supposed to go, Michael?" Dan said and took a menacing step toward Michael.

Michael stepped back and picked up the old war club, squaring off, prepared to take a swing at Dan if he came any closer.

"None of you can prove a goddamn thing and you know it," he yelled. "Paul's word isn't worth shit. Who's going to believe him? He killed the governor, for chrissake."

"Michael, what are you saying? Are you admitting that you framed our father for a few dollars?" Lily asked, trying not to believe what she had just heard.

"Come on, Lily, he was dying. We both knew he wasn't going to last much longer anyway. And I couldn't take a chance with you. If it was up to you, you would have told Hizaga to take a hike. Along with his fifty million. And for what? For this goddamn patch of *taro!*"

"I won't let you get away with it, Michael," Lily said, standing beside Dan.

"I'm afraid it's out of your hands, little sister," Michael said coldly. "According to the will, I'll dictate what's going to happen to this ranch. And there isn't a damn thing you or Dan or his lunatic brother can do about it. Nothing."

"I'm sure Taylor Baldwin will have something to say about that," Dan answered.

Michael smiled. "That old fart wouldn't last ten minutes on a witness stand. Besides, unless he has a copy of your phantom will it doesn't matter. You know that."

Dan knew Michael was right. Michael had a valid will and Dan had nothing but Paul's accusations. And it was going to be very difficult to use anything Paul had to say in a court of law.

A bullet exploded at Michael's feet. They turned and saw Paul with his rifle pointed directly at Michael. "No, Paul!" Dan shouted. "Not like this. We'll get him."

"Don't worry, Dan. I'm not going to kill that sack of shit. I just wanted all of you to see who and what he is. And now that you have, I think it's time for a little fun."

Paul rested the rifle on the ground.

"Lily," Paul shouted. "I think you should have the honors."

Lily stared at Paul, clearly puzzled.

"Michael, give your sister your father's club," Paul demanded.

Michael stepped back a few steps. He wasn't about to give up the only weapon he had on this side of the ravine.

Paul picked up the rifle and aimed it at Michael.

"I said give her the club!"

Lily reached out to her brother as he handed the club to her. The three-foot-long piece of carved wood was almost black from the rain.

"Good," Paul said. "Now, Lily, grab it by the top and twist. The head of King Kamehameha will unscrew."

Lily tried, but the slippery top wouldn't budge. Dan took hold of the club and grunted as he strained to loosen it. Finally, Dan twisted the club and it busted loose.

"Now, look inside," Paul shouted.

Dan turned it upside down and out came a typed document. It

was very dark, but Dan was able to make out what it said. " 'Last Will and Testament of Peter Kameaho'iho'i'ea Maikai, the third grandson of Prince Leleiohoka.' "

Lily stood next to Dan as he held it up. They scanned it quickly, trying to protect it from the swirling mist.

" 'The distribution of my estate shall be as follows: I give all of my estate in three equal shares. One to my son Michael. One to my daughter Lily and the remaining share to my granddaughter, Sharon Jenkins, the issue of my daughter Lily and my godson Daniel Carrier. And if my above named granddaughter cannot be found within one year of my death, or she fails to survive me, then I direct her share shall be divided equally between her natural parents Lillian Maikai and Daniel Carrier.' "

Dan rolled it up quickly and reached for Lily's hand.

"What does that mean?" Lily asked.

Dan held the document in front of Michael's face. "It means he can't sell the land without our consent."

"Yours and mine?" she asked.

"Exactly. Our daughter's share will be divided between you and me."

"This is bullshit!" Michael yelled. "You're not going to get away with this. Let me see that!" Michael reached his hand out to Dan.

"No way!" Dan said. "You're not getting a chance to destroy this one like you did the original."

"You know I won't give up without a fight," Michael said as he turned to walk away.

"Michael," Dan yelled. "I wouldn't contest this will if I were you. That is, unless you want to make public what Paul said you were up to. Isn't that right, Paul?" Dan yelled as he turned to where Paul had been standing. But his brother was gone.

"It looks like your brother's still dead." Michael smirked.

"Only for as long as he wants to be," Dan said. "He loves this land as much as we do, remember."

"Nah, he won't come back," Michael said with a cocky grin. "He'd be walking right into a murder conviction and you know it."

"I don't think any of us know what Paul would do. If you want to chance it, go ahead and fight us. See what happens. But I think you should consider yourself lucky. You'll still have a license to practice law, your share of the taro operation and, most of all, your damn freedom. But I'll tell you one thing, Michael, you're no longer welcome around here. Get your ass back to O'ahu and stay there!"

Michael turned to Lily. "Is that the way you feel too?"

"Yes, Michael, it is. As soon as this storm passes, I want you to go," Lily answered as she reached for Dan's hand.

Michael nodded. "If that's the way you want to play it." Then he turned to Dan. "What about Paul's bullshit about me planting the knife to frame my father?"

"There's not much I can do about it without Paul to back me, is there?" Dan said. "But don't ever try to press me."

Michael stared at Dan a moment, then marched ahead to the house.

The rain had begun again, more ferociously than before, so it stung as it whipped against their faces.

"We better get to the house before this thing hits full force," Dan said.

"You mean *our* house," Lily said as she kissed him on the cheek.

"Yes, our house."

"What about your job?" Lily asked. "With Reed gone wouldn't you be the one to take his place?"

"Maybe. But that's Cathy's dream, not mine. She can have it. This is my dream. This is what I have wanted ever since I can remember. To live here with you."

Dan turned and looked back across the bridge. He was looking for Paul. His brother had lost everything and now he would be forced to lose his identity. He would live the rest of his life under an assumed name in hiding, wanted for the murder of the governor of Hawai'i. Or maybe someday he'd be found or come out of hiding and Paul would face the charges against him with Dan at his side.

"Keep safe, brother," Dan said to himself as he pulled Lily close to him.

"No matter what has happened," Dan said as they looked across the ravaged taro patches to the beach being bashed by the mounting breakers, "we have to preserve this land for all Hawai'ians. That's all Peter Maikai ever wanted."